Quis Custodiet

Manna Francis

 For information, address Casperian Books, PO Box 161026, Sacramento, CA 95816-1026.

www.casperianbooks.com

Cover images by Orit "Shin" Heifets

ISBN-10: 1-934081-12-4
ISBN-13: 978-1-934081-12-9

Table of Contents

Quis Custodiet

Prologue

❖

Accents weren't by themselves an automatic reason for suspicion. However, there was a known correlation. An accent meant someone who had been brought up in a household where English wasn't the first language, probably immigrants or traditionalists. And, perhaps, along with a harmless attachment to an old language there might be a less harmless adherence to other old ideas: nationalism, unionization, freedom of speech.

Traditionalist, idealist, political criminal—these were points on a sliding scale.

As the secure connection was audio only, the slight accent to the man's voice was reassuring, even though it could be the result of computer manipulation. Member Three of Hellenic resistance cell beta-one-forty-seven didn't recognize his accent, but nevertheless it gave him a feeling of solidarity. A conviction that he and the stranger he had never even seen were comrades.

He sat in a darkened room with two others from his cell, listening to voices over the comm. Large gatherings were far too dangerous, and only for important decisions did they risk many simultaneous small meetings.

"Moving too soon jeopardizes everything," the stranger said.

"There'll never be a better time." The man who replied had a distinct Greek accent—the spokesman for the Attican resisters, and the only member of the network who spoke directly to the outsider. Him, Member Three knew well, or at least the voice he used over the comm. "We're in danger here every day, but while they think they control us, we have the freedom to act."

"Regretfully, sacrifices sometimes have to be made," the man said. "You are one organization, and we move when the bulk of our forces are ready. Later."

"Later will be too late. We can take the city and then the rest of the country will follow us, I know it."

"And then they will take it back." Touch of impatience in his voice. What *was* the accent? "A city, a district, even a country—these mean nothing. If you act alone, the Administration will concentrate its forces. You might hold out for a few days, you might survive on the run for a few weeks, but in the end you'll fail."

"We're not afraid to die," the Attican spokesman said.

"In the long run, to quote Keynes, we are all dead. However, we cannot afford to waste lives. Or opportunities. An open, armed revolt will cause the Administration to crack down across Europe. Sometimes it takes as much courage to wait as it does to attack."

"Wait. I must discuss this with the cell leaders."

The speaker muted. In the tiny, stuffy basement, Member One turned away and entered a discussion over the second link with the other group leaders. Her voice rang oddly in the room, translated smoothly and instantaneously into measured male tones. Member Three imagined this scene repeated across Greece. How many cells? How many people ready to fight if the word was given?

After a minute, he caught himself biting his nails and made himself stop. Gina hated the habit.

In one way, the command to wait made sense to Member Three. Primarily because it was what they had always done—met, planned, dreamed. But never, actually, done anything. Talking was safer. Not much safer, within the Administration, but still a hell of a lot less dangerous than taking to the streets. For the suppression of riots, the Service had an extensive array of what they described as nonlethal weapons. Some of them even were, because it was considered important to take a good haul of prisoners for questioning.

Glance at his watch. They'd been here for fifteen minutes—getting close to the mandated limit of twenty, a security restriction designed to keep prying monitoring systems from noticing their clandestine comms. One day, perhaps soon, no security precautions would be enough. And then…

The cell structure was scrupulously maintained within their resistance organization. That had proved its value, but it hadn't kept cell beta-one-forty-seven safe, or God only knew how many others. Any or all of them could be arrested at any time. The thought of I&I, of what waited for him in the underground cells there, brought an acid taste of fear.

Member Three, despite his subversive activities, didn't like to think of himself as a violent man. For I&I, however, he was willing to make an exception. Legal torturers, passively supported or at least tolerated by the majority of citizens who, sedated by Administration propaganda, bought into the myth that it was necessary. That was one thing their anonymous contact was clear about. When the Administration fell, I&I must be eradicated. He'd said that more than once.

All the resisters knew people who had entered the doors of I&I, and rather fewer who had emerged alive and free. Some, like Member Two, had more personal experience. Two was outside somewhere, watching the street, ready to raise the alarm. He didn't talk about his time in I&I hands, not while sober. And when drunk he'd say things that no one wanted to hear. I&I was a rallying symbol, as well as a terrible threat. It embodied all the reasons why the all-encompassing Administration had to be resisted. When I&I was no more, that would signal the return of freedom. Repeating that to himself helped get him through the moments of doubt, when he wondered why the hell he came to these meetings when nothing ever *happened.*

He understood Member One's impatience. The tension had become unbearable. Trapped, exposed, the drive to act, to end the suspense in one way or another, affected all of them. Member Three knew what the decision would be before Member One reactivated the speaker on the comm.

"Two months," the spokesman said. "That's all I can give you. Then we move. If we don't at least try, then everything we've done up to now will be in vain."

Silence. Then their contact said, "Naturally, I can only advise you. Two months, then. I will ensure that is taken into account as the wider plans develop."

They left the room separately. As he walked across campus in the warm spring sunshine, back to his office, Member Three—now plain Alexandros Vasdeki again—thought about the meeting.

Sacrifices sometimes have to be made.

We can't afford to waste lives.

For some reason, the contradiction nagged at him. Which, Alexandros wondered, meant the most to the man?

Chapter One

❖

Toreth thought it had been almost a perfect Sunday so far. A lie-in and a late breakfast in bed, followed by the massage he was owed from the previous weekend. No fuck yet, but the morning was building nicely towards it. All his basic needs satisfied by lunchtime, and then the rest of the day still to go.

He lay flat on his stomach, chin on his hands, eyes closed. Warrick lay half on top of him, pleasantly heavy, cock nuzzling against him, oily hands still working lazily on his arms and shoulders. Not a cuddle, obviously—just an intermediate stage between the massage and the imminent fuck.

Only one thing stopped it from being absolutely perfect—tomorrow Toreth had to catch a flight out of New London, headed for an I&I internal review in the Athens station Political Crimes section. It was scheduled to last up to a fortnight, could easily take three weeks, and wouldn't entirely surprise him if it took a month, if he actually found anything wrong. It wasn't in itself a bad thing. A few years ago he would have been fighting hard for the assignment. Regular office hours, a nice hotel, decent expenses preapproved, a chance to get away from the unseasonably soggy spring weather, and probably plenty of available fucks.

None of whom would be Warrick.

The idea bothered him. It bothered him that it bothered him. Maybe he could fly home for a weekend in the middle? No—without an excuse that would be unbearably pathetic. Maybe he could persuade Warrick to fly out to Athens.

"I'm going to miss this," Warrick said, now apparently numbering mind reading among his many talents.

Toreth opened his eyes and turned his head, resting his cheek on his hands. From there he could just see the cabinet, framed in wine-red velvet. "Bollocks. Friday—that's what you're going to miss."

A pause, then Warrick said, "I hadn't even thought about it."

"Liar."

"No, I'm not. The statement applied equally to every day." Warrick paused and kissed his shoulder. "Although I will admit that Friday is perhaps a little more equal than the others."

"I'll call you."

"Mm? That'll be nice."

"No, I mean I'll call on Friday. We can talk through it instead. Next best thing."

Toreth felt the shiver ripple through the body above him. "Oh, God. Yes. That would be..."

"Nice?"

"Very."

Taking advantage of the oil, Toreth slipped out from beneath him and reversed their positions, pinning Warrick to the bed, face down. He didn't put up much resistance.

"We could do it now, if you like." Beneath him, Warrick went absolutely still. "A few days early. It wouldn't matter." He ran his hand through Warrick's hair, tilting his head forwards, then bit hard, at the junction of neck and shoulder.

Warrick moaned. "I don't...I don't want to."

"Now, that is a lie."

"Yes, it is."

He took hold of Warrick's wrists and stretched his arms out, burying his face in Warrick's neck. God, he smelled fabulous. Fuckably fabulous, and if Toreth hadn't been hard already, this would have done it.

Moving higher, he brought his mouth up to Warrick's ear, kissing and licking between phrases. "It'll give me something to think about on the flight. You look so fucking good like that. Helpless. Begging for it. When I can do whatever I want... hurt you...take you however I want...fuck you...make you come when I want you to...touch you when you can't—"

"Please—oh, God." Warrick took a shuddering breath. "Pl—plastic duck."

Toreth let him go, and knelt up. "Sure?"

"No, not at all. But the rule is no more often than every six weeks, and besides—"

"You've got very important investors coming in tomorrow, so you don't want to be bruised to fuck. Sorry. I forgot."

Warrick laughed, shaky and breathless. "So did I, very nearly."

Tempting to try to change Warrick's mind—he sounded open to persuasion, which was unusual. However, for this one thing, the rules weren't just part of the game. Neither of them wanted to risk what had happened at the beginning of last year happening again.

It had been months since Warrick had begged for an early session. A good thing, because saying no to sex didn't come naturally to Toreth. But he had seen sufficient addictions—and created enough deliberately at work—to know that abandoning the restriction could lead to unpleasantness. So they had to stick to it, and Toreth had broken another rule by using the six-week limit to tease.

Which was okay, because some rules were better for being broken occasionally. Once was enough, though.

"Right," Toreth said. "Something else, then?"

"Oh, very definitely yes, something else."

"What?"

Warrick rolled onto his back and looked up at him. "Make me an offer."

Toreth considered. Something good, because it was the last time for a while. Also something not at all like the suspension fucks, because he didn't want Warrick fantasizing about furniture while they were fucking. Not that he had any evidence that Warrick ever did, but he didn't like to dwell on the possibility.

"Sixty-nine?"

"Mm." Warrick smiled, reaching for him. "Sold."

Slight taste of oil, but mostly salt and sweet, unmistakably Warrick. Toreth always started off with the resolution "perfect timing—we'll come together." He liked the challenge of coordination, but not as much as he liked the feel of Warrick's mouth, sucking him. It was easier with other men. But with Warrick, when he could feel him, smell him, taste him, it was somehow too much. Minutes would pass and he'd keep the intention clearly in mind. Then he'd forget, remind himself, forget, remember again, and then finally forget for the last time, far too busy feeling to think of anything.

Not coming together, but it didn't matter. Him first this time, arching back, letting go of Warrick, and it was so good . . . so *good.*

A minute or so's blissful haze, sliding dangerously towards sleep, before a gentle nudge against his lips reminded him of the job in hand. As it were.

It was no hardship. Toreth loved the slide of satin-smooth skin over his tongue. He played for a while, teasing, showing off his technique, keeping it going until he got what he wanted.

"Toreth . . . please. *Please.*"

His favorite word, delivered with the kind of feeling that deserved a reward. He tightened his mouth, letting Warrick press deeper.

Warrick gasped, his fingers digging hard into Toreth's hips, then all in one breath he said, "Christ yes that's it don't *stop,*" his voice rising as he came.

Rearrangement of bodies, and then a warm, contented silence.

Toreth listened to the rain against the window. It had been nothing special. That was the strange thing. Nothing special, just another Sunday fuck with Warrick, and it was still wonderful. Very occasionally, Toreth wondered why it was so different with Warrick. Or how. Any of those short, difficult question words, none of which he could answer. Then he would give up and not think about it again for a while.

Two weeks. At least two bloody weeks until he'd even get a *chance* to wonder again.

"I'm going to miss you," Warrick murmured into the pillow beside him.

Mind reading again. "You said before." Actually, he hadn't, quite. But Toreth felt too thoroughly satisfied to stop himself from adding, "Me too."

Chapter Two

Toreth strolled through the Int-Sec check-in point at the Athens airport, waving his ID over the scanner. 'Ports all over the Administration were much the same in Toreth's experience. There wasn't much about this airport that said "Greece." A statistically more Mediterranean cast to the faces and a less frenetic pace than the vast New London terminals, but nothing more than that.

Toreth should've been hard for the promised I&I escort to miss, being blond and dressed in black. No one in the crowd seemed to be looking for him, though. He stood in the arrivals area for fifteen minutes, wondering if Sara had got the details right. Silly idea—of course she had. Sara being Sara, it was a hundred times more probable that the fuckup was at this end.

Just as he'd decided to give it five more minutes and then find a taxi, he caught sight of an I&I uniform. A few seconds later, the man noticed him and raised his hand in greeting. Toreth studied him as he strode over—classic dark Mediterranean, wearing the uniform well. The prospects for the fortnight were picking up already.

The man offered his hand with an easy, apologetic smile. "I'm Senior Para Dimitri Karteris. You must be Senior Para Toreth."

"Nice to meet you."

Close up, he was older than Toreth had first guessed, giving the impression of youthful good looks slipping into a debauched middle age. Toreth began to appreciate Carnac's idea of picking an attractive liaison. Especially when here, as with Carnac's visit to I&I, it was in his host's interest to keep him happy.

"I arranged for your bags to go straight to the hotel," Karteris said as they walked to the exit. "We picked you out a comfortable one. So if it's okay by you, we'll go to the division."

The division head kept him waiting for three-quarters of an hour, which more than canceled out the positive benefits of meeting Karteris and driving through the warm, sunny city. Toreth had been at the New London I&I office at six that morning, finishing work on his active cases. Combined with the flight over, it left him impatient to start and annoyed to have yet more of his time wasted.

It turned out that the man wasn't even in his office. He finally appeared at nearly three o'clock, carrying a battered brown leather briefcase and obviously only just returning from lunch—or conceivably even arriving for the first time that day. Vassilakis looked younger than Toreth knew he was, fit, tanned, and unexpectedly highlighted blond. A man who didn't stress himself out over his job, or probably anything else.

"I was delayed, I'm afraid. Glad you got here safely. Come in, come in. Coffee's on its way."

When they were seated in the comfortably furnished office, Vassilakis asked, "Do you sail?"

Toreth blinked. "No."

"Pity. Ah well, I'm sure you'll find plenty to keep yourself busy."

Sheer perversity, and lingering irritation at the wait, put a touch of disapproval into Toreth's voice. "I'm here to do a job, not for a holiday, sir."

Vassilakis stared for a moment, then nodded quickly. "Of course. I meant—Ah! Coffee!"

While the coffee was served, Toreth inventoried the room more carefully. Vassilakis had the cleanest senior management desk Toreth had ever seen. Possibly the cleanest full stop. Subtracting the family photographs, a wooden model of a yacht and a bronze inkstand, the only thing left was the screen, currently switched off.

He focused on the inkstand. A group of dolphins carried between them a beautifully realistic boy, dead or unconscious. Waves curled around the base, the details so fluid that they virtually seemed to move. The patina suggested, in Toreth's limited experience, a genuine antique. Probably worth a fortune, and at the New London I&I Vassilakis would've been lucky if it stayed on his desk for a week.

"Sugar?" Vassilakis asked.

Toreth looked up. "No, thanks."

"Now." Vassilakis settled back in what was definitely not a standard issue chair. "How have you found the Athens division so far?"

"Quiet." Toreth expanded his hand screen. "Have you read the report?"

A flicker of distaste crossed Vassilakis's face. "I have. I cannot say that I agree with it, though. Particularly the conclusions. I strongly refute the idea that any of my sections are ineffective, Political Crimes especially." Strong protest or not, his voice never wavered from its relaxed drawl.

"Nevertheless, sir, there is a problem here that someone felt was worth setting up an external review for."

"Vassilakis, please. Or I shall be forced to address you by rank, Para-investigator."

"You don't think there is any cause for concern?"

Vassilakis waved his hand dismissively. "Forgive me, Toreth, but New London is a long way from Athens. They don't understand the situation here, or the culture. Athens—Greece as a whole—is a very different place to the busy north and west. Not rich, by Administration standards, but the poorer classes are relatively not so poor. Crime is lower, too, compared to other regions of Europe. Why would the citizens here want to rebel against the Administration?"

"Why do they ever? Idealists aren't logical, at least as far as I've ever been able to see."

"But resister activity here in Athens is—" He snapped his fingers. "We haven't had so much as a demonstration in two years. We haven't had a bombing, a shooting, any kind of serious incident, in four. It makes no sense for them to send you here."

"The point is that I have a social dynamics report saying that correlating resistance activity and informant reports to Political Crimes with final arrests and convictions leaves—" Toreth flicked to the introduction to the report. "A significant statistical anomaly."

"Statistics." Vassilakis sighed, then reached out and repositioned the yacht slightly to catch the sun. Miniature brass fittings, presumably perfectly scaled, glittered. "Well, as I'm sure you know, Toreth . . . "

"There are lies, damned lies, statistics, and directives from the top levels of I&I to look into all three of them before Internal Investigations starts taking an interest."

Vassilakis laughed. "Not quite as I remember the quotation."

"Do I have your cooperation, sir?" Toreth asked directly.

"Of course you do, man." The surprise seemed genuine enough. "As you said, you're hardly Internal Investigations. We have nothing to hide here, certainly not from our own."

As far as you know, Toreth thought. He wouldn't put money on Vassilakis knowing what went on anywhere in the building outside this office.

"Well, sir, I won't take up any more of your valuable time." He couldn't help the sarcasm, but the division head seemed quite unruffled.

"You've met Senior Para Karteris? Good. He'll make sure the rest of Political Crimes do everything they can to help. Anything you want, he can provide." Vassilakis poured himself another coffee. "Good luck, Para-investigator. And—" He smiled. "Enjoy your stay."

When he left the office, Karteris was waiting for him, chatting to the admin and looking about as energized as Vassilakis. He stood up quickly enough, though, when he caught sight of Toreth.

"How was the boss?"

"Relaxed," Toreth said.

Karteris grinned. "He usually is. He knows he's lucky to have such a quiet station. So, what now?"

"Tour of the place?" Toreth suggested.

"Sure. No problem."

Unlike I&I New London, the Athens office had very few open plan areas for the sections. Everything was laid out in corridors, with tiny offices and unexpected meeting rooms. Toreth put a map on easy recall on his hand screen, as there would be very little as embarrassing as needing to call Karteris for directions inside the building.

The security in the place appalled him. He'd been surprised to find the main doors standing open and unguarded when they first arrived, but he hadn't thought too much of it, assuming the approaches were under surveillance. However, the slackness seemed pervasive. They strolled through most of the building with a minimum of card access doors; most of those seemed to have the lock deactivated anyway, as they opened without a card. Only the entrance to the detention and interrogation levels had the kind of security he was used to.

Still, the building seemed to be rather older than the I&I headquarters in New London, so perhaps there were some excuses. Or maybe the rest of the staff were as confident as Vassilakis that resister activity was nonexistent.

Detention and interrogation themselves were reassuringly busy. Of course, that only pointed up the difference in performance between Political Crimes and other sections. He wondered if that had been the stimulus for the internal review; the original trigger was one thing the otherwise comprehensive report didn't mention.

Karteris seemed to know everyone they met, and introduced people readily. Toreth's presence produced a polite level of curiosity, but nothing more. Political Crimes was a different story. The staff were all there, and the warren of offices hummed with studious activity. However, the paras and investigators hung back, avoiding meeting his gaze, until Karteris sought them out. Not that it necessarily meant anything was wrong—Toreth would've reacted in much the same way to an external review at the General Criminal section.

The friendliest by far—which wasn't saying much—was a pasty-faced, slightly overweight young man called Manos Priftis, who turned out to be Karteris's junior. He was clearly under orders to be pleasant to the visitor, but he still departed with speed when dismissed.

The only person missing was the Political Crimes head of section.

"Oh, George," Karteris said when Toreth asked about his absence. "He'll be around later in the week, I expect. I did remind him you were coming, but he went up to the north for a long weekend, skiing. Mind you, he doesn't usually make it on Mondays, anyway. Or Fridays, sometimes. Tuesdays and Thursdays can be iffy if the snow's good."

Toreth blinked, wondering if he was taking the piss, and Karteris grinned. "He had a family promotion, somebody or other's nephew. Things run more smoothly when he isn't here. Saf—Safiye Yilmaz, his admin—handles everything important, anyway."

Once the idea sank in, Toreth could see the advantages of a regularly absent boss. If only Tillotson were someone's nephew. That led to the rather distracting thought that Tillotson must have parents. Parents who had, somehow, slipped through the genetic screens to produce him.

"Now," Karteris said when they'd met the last Political Crimes staff, "what about an office? There's one empty if you'd like it, but there's a spare desk in mine, might be friendlier. As you prefer, of course."

The offer surprised him. Toreth had been considering taking a leaf out of Carnac's book of tricks and asking to share, as much to see what Karteris's reaction would be as because he wanted to. The preemptive offer had ruined the tactic, but Toreth decided that sharing still made sense in terms of getting to know the section quickly.

As the office already had two desks, moving in was easy. They made a leisurely start, sorting out which cases Toreth would review. To Toreth's relief, Karteris admitted that the lack of more serious resister activity had rendered Political Crimes, if not negligent, then possibly less than diligent, and also seemed genuinely willing to consider ways to remedy the situation—"seemed" being the important word. After only a couple of hours in the man's company, Toreth recognized a kindred spirit and therefore set a large question mark beside anything Karteris told him.

When the section began to empty at the end of the day, Karteris stretched, making rather more of it than was necessary for the amount of work they'd done, and finished up with a smile that could've advertised toothpaste. "Want to go for a drink? I can show you round the bits of Athens tourists don't usually find."

Outside, the air wasn't hot, but it was warm and dry. They paused at the gates, looking at the city. The I&I building stood on a hill, and directly across from the main entrance the clear dome of the Acropolis dominated the scene, slightly distorting the shapes of the white buildings within it.

Karteris took him to a small bar not far from the I&I offices. No one gave a second glance at their uniforms, and Toreth saw others in I&I black dotted around.

He absorbed the atmosphere while Karteris negotiated the tab with the barman.

His kind of bar, he decided after a few minutes. The adjective he'd pick to describe many of the patrons was "available." A place to come for a relaxed evening's hunting, with a solid prospect for a fuck of some kind at the end of it. Perfect. He wondered if Karteris had been checking up on him.

They spent an hour chatting—social crap, not work—during which Karteris mentioned three times that he and his wife lived virtually separate lives. The offer wouldn't have been more obvious if he'd stripped naked and revealed a "fuck me now" tattoo on his arse.

They finished their drinks, and Karteris asked, "What do you want to do next? We can stay here, go someplace else. Find something to eat." Lift of a lazy eyebrow. "I can take you home and show you some Greek hospitality. I'm a reasonably good cook, amongst other things."

Toreth considered the proposal, and came to a surprising conclusion. "Actually, I'm shattered. Late night, early morning. I'll be a fucking zombie tomorrow if I don't get some sleep. How about one more drink and then I'll call it a day?"

"No problem." Karteris smiled. "Entertainment is all on expenses, so feel free. You can get me one, too."

As Toreth walked away, he heard Karteris call, "Hey!" When he looked around, though, the para was beckoning to someone on the opposite side of the room.

Toreth ordered drinks and looked at his fractured reflection in the engraved mirror behind the bar. Not too bad, but, God, he must be getting old if a decent night's sleep sounded so much more attractive than a fuck. It didn't matter—he had the rest of the assignment to catch up on one wasted evening. He certainly didn't intend to pass up chances for the whole fortnight. After a few days' abstinence he wouldn't be able to stop himself if he wanted to.

Toreth paused, drink halfway to his lips, and considered the idea. That was crap. He didn't *have* to fuck anyone at all while he was here. Then, between taking a mouthful of ouzo and remembering why he never drank the foul fucking stuff, it somehow turned into a resolution.

Partly it was just to see if he could. One thing he couldn't resist was a challenge, and as soon as he thought that he couldn't do it he knew he had to try.

Mostly it was the image of how incredibly pleased Warrick would be. After (Toreth gritted his teeth unconsciously) Girardin, they'd come to an unspoken agreement whereby Toreth did what he wanted but didn't flaunt it, and Warrick didn't ask questions if he didn't want to hear the answers. It worked fine, for Toreth anyway. For Warrick, too, he supposed. Still, Toreth knew that Warrick…well, didn't exactly hate that Toreth fucked around. Or maybe he did hate it. In any case Warrick certainly didn't like the idea, and sometimes Toreth knew full well it was at the root of a bad mood on Warrick's part.

So it would make a nice present, and Warrick would be happy which meant great sex, and it was easier than trying to think of something to take back for him, and anyway, why the hell not? He could do it, easy.

Toreth was about order a whiskey when it occurred to him that keeping his alcohol consumption in check would be a good idea. He caught a wry smile in the mirror. Not so confident in his resolution, after all. He changed it to a glass of grapefruit juice and was about to leave the ouzo on the bar when he had second thoughts and took it with him.

When he found Karteris, the senior was talking to a young man attractive enough to test Toreth's resolve right there.

"This is Theo," Karteris said. "He's an informer."

"Jesus!" Theo looked around, eyes wide. "Keep your voice down!"

"Sorry. Despite his many past mistakes, Theo is very keen to be a loyal citizen of the Administration."

Toreth couldn't help looking. Just looking, he told himself. "I'll bet. Want a drink?" He offered the ouzo and Theo took it with apparent gratitude.

Karteris's eyes crinkled as he smiled. "I'm too old for you, that it?"

Toreth grinned. "The hospitality is great, but it's really not necessary. I'm just here to do my job and go home."

The flash of surprise on Karteris's face made Toreth quite certain that someone in the local I&I had thoroughly checked out their visitor. He smiled into his drink. This might be fun.

Chapter Three

❖

The next morning, Toreth arrived to find a stunningly attractive female admin waiting outside the office. Toreth appreciated good skin care when he saw it, and he recognized the dedicated hard work behind her flawless complexion. Her thick, wavy hair probably sent another chunk of her salary down the drain.

"Senior Para Toreth? My name is Nikoletta Stefanides. I'm Para Karteris's admin, but he asked me to help you." She paused. "If you need me to."

Narrow waist, a light build that emphasized her generous breasts—unfair temptation.

"That'd be great," Toreth said. "I meant to ask about admins. I thought about bringing mine over with me, but she's too busy. It won't be too much trouble, will it?"

"Oh, I'm sure I'll be able to manage." She smiled brightly, revealing dimples that made her look practically edible. "It's pretty quiet in the section."

Toreth suppressed a grin. "I know. That's why I'm here."

Confusion showed plainly on her face, then she blushed. "Oh. It's not *that* quiet. I meant that things aren't too busy right now. Or..." She trailed off, then gathered herself. "Is there anything you want me to do, Para?"

"Not just now. If I think of anything, I'll let you know."

Forgetting his newly assumed role, he followed that up with a wink. She smiled again, obviously relieved that he hadn't taken her slip-up seriously.

"My office is right opposite," she said. "I keep the door open, so just walk in any time I can help."

Toreth watched her go, and sighed.

Toreth spent the day organizing the files he'd need for the review. A pity he couldn't have brought Sara, but he needed someone he trusted to hold the fort at I&I.

By midafternoon he had most of the depressingly large number of files arranged, along with the expert systems analysis of the statistical anomalies of which Vassilakis had been so dismissive. Despite the excellent summaries, it would take time to assimilate.

Toreth looked at the list of files he'd marked for close attention and frowned. He could just as easily have read through everything in the comfort of his own office in New London. Why the hell was he doing it out here? The reason, of course, was that the assignment was supposed to be a treat. A relaxing, low-pressure, high-expenses trip away that anyone would have jumped at.

Toreth amended that to "most people." Chevril wouldn't have taken it because it would've meant spending weeks away from his precious Elena. More fool him. Mind you, he could understand Chev's reluctance. Leaving someone as stunning as Elena alone for a couple of weeks was asking for trouble. Toreth might've put in a dinner invitation himself, just on general principles, although he'd probably be wasting his money.

In any case, he wasn't in New London with an available Elena. He was here, so he ought to relax and enjoy it, resolution of the previous evening aside. The work was probably optional. Maybe he should take a hand screen and continue the review on a beach, or at the very least on a lounger beside the pool at his hotel.

Karteris looked up from his desk, smiled, and checked his watch. "We usually go for a coffee about now, if you're interested."

Some things were the same Administration-wide.

In New London I&I, most serious business took place in the coffee rooms, and Athens seemed no different. This time Toreth's arrival caused a definite lull. At a conservative estimate, he'd been the subject of half the conversations in progress.

The group of Political Crimes paras went especially quiet, and Karteris gathered a couple of almost hostile stares when he brought Toreth over. Déjà vu again from Carnac's visit to New London; Toreth wasn't surprised when the group excused themselves one by one over the next few minutes, leaving him alone with Karteris, Manos, and Nikoletta.

Then Karteris's comm chimed. He listened, then sighed and stood up, beckoning to Manos. "George is in—he wants to talk to us." He turned to Toreth. "I'll see you back in the office."

As was about to leave, Karteris paused and laid two fingers lightly on Nikoletta's shoulder—not the first casual touch between them Toreth had noticed over the day. "You keep our guest happy while I'm gone."

"I didn't notice you around yesterday," Toreth said to Nikoletta when the other two had departed.

"I wasn't here."

"Skiing?"

She looked at him blankly, then laughed. "You mean like George? Oh, no. Nothing like that. My mother is sick, that's all. *I* can't afford skiing—I wish I could. Do you ski?"

"A bit. My—" He paused, stuck. Virtue was one thing, but he'd be damned if he was going to start calling Warrick a "partner" or anything ridiculous like that. "A friend of mine is a corporate director. I've tagged along with him on the odd business trip."

It didn't seem to strike her as strange. "That must be great."

"Yes. He's good fun, for a corporate."

"Are you married?"

No, I'm fucking the man I just described as a friend. "No, nothing like that. I'm—" Here if you want me. Hardly the right sort of sentiment for his new persona. Why the hell had he started this game? Nikoletta was looking at him expectantly, but all that came to mind were his usual lines designed to suggest availability. "My admin says I'm married to I&I."

There. That was fairly neutral, although Sara would laugh herself sick.

Or maybe not so neutral, because her gaze flicked briefly in the direction of the chair previously occupied by Karteris, then she said, "I understand."

On the way out of the coffee room, Nikoletta said, "Para? I was wondering if you'd like to go for a drink after work?"

The casual approach didn't fool him for a moment. The refusal was easy—he'd heard Sara go through the litany often enough. "I appreciate the offer, but no thanks. I like to keep my relationships at work completely professional. It makes things easier that way—no confusion."

Was that a touch of relief in Nikoletta's eyes? Not surprising if it was, since he'd bet any money that Karteris had put her up to this. Odd in itself, because he would've guessed there was something distinctly unprofessional between the admin and senior para. Maybe there was, and Karteris was happy to share in pursuit of a quiet life, although he hadn't struck Toreth as someone generous with his own possessions.

In any case, there was more and more obviously something going on in the section. Karteris wouldn't be taking all this trouble to make sure Toreth had a good time unless he had something to hide. Toreth put his beach office plan on hold, at least for a couple of days until he'd decided whether or not there was anything rotten in Political Crimes.

By the end of the next day, Wednesday, his opinion had shifted again, to an uncomfortably schizophrenic one. The investigation in progress reports, the arrests, and the interrogation records from the cases seemed perfectly in order for each example he looked at. It was only when he called up the summary figures for the statistical report that the improbability of the overall picture struck him.

Apparently, there were virtually no resisters in Athens. A handful of convictions, mostly of lone dissidents, for minor infractions. No groups, no major incidents. Could Vassilakis be right, and Athens simply be one of the happiest places in the Administration?

If so, it had citizens with too much time on their hands, because reports of suspected resisters by loyal citizens doing their duty (and maybe hoping to pick up a reward for informing) registered only fifteen percent below the Administration average.

Incompetence? Corruption? Subversion? One blindingly obvious fact was that if something was wrong in the section, then the odds of either Vassilakis or George spotting it were vanishingly small.

Toreth finally met the Political Crimes section head on Wednesday. George's second name turned out to be Makrigiannakis, making Toreth wonder if the widespread familiar name use came from the fact that none of the local I&I staff could pronounce his surname, either.

After a cursory ten minutes looking at the Political Crimes activity report which had sent Toreth to Athens, George insisted on taking him out for lunch. When Toreth looked at his watch, George laughed.

"Ah, yes. We don't move at the kind of pace you're used to, I'm sure. I was at I&I New London for a little while myself, for training. You used to work in Political Crimes there, right? We might know some of the same people."

"Possibly so, sir." And Toreth would *love* to know what PC had thought of George. Surely the man couldn't have been there long; he would never have survived the place. "But I'd like to go through the report today, if you have time."

"Plenty of time, of course. But is there any reason we can't read it while we eat?"

None that Toreth could think up, and really there was no point in spiting himself simply to keep up his puritan image. Following orders, Toreth decided, worked just as well as refusing for making him look like a good boy.

The lunch was spectacular, and George looked like a man who enjoyed something similar every day of the week and twice at the weekend. Skiing, Toreth decided, had to be a euphemism for something else. By the end of the meal, though, he changed his mind. As far as he could tell, George did ski. And sail—he owned his own yacht—and ride. He also played polo, and his wife bred horses for a hobby. A *hobby,* for fuck's sake. Somebody's nephew indeed, because he didn't fund his lifestyle on a section head's salary.

Despite all that, George was pleasant enough company. Overall, though, the meal did nothing to alter Toreth's opinion that the man was as much use to I&I as a pair of chocolate handcuffs. What George knew about his section could be written on the back of a postcard, and what he knew about resisters would fit inside the stamp. Worst of all, he seemed to rely entirely on Karteris, as his pet favorite among the senior paras, to run the section for him. When Toreth considered what he could get away with if Tillotson took that attitude, the possibilities for malfeasance in Athens Political Crimes seemed virtually limitless.

On the way back from lunch, Toreth bought a postcard with a picture of some ruined building or another on the front. On the back he wrote, "Weather sunny. Food great. Missing you sucking my cock," and posted it to Warrick at SimTech.

Karteris had produced an active case from somewhere—a near miracle, Toreth realized now that he'd had a better look at the section's records—and was absent from the office for most of Thursday. Just before lunch, Sara called.

"Problem?" Toreth asked when he saw her expression.

"Probably not. But I heard something and I thought you'd like to know. Mike Belkin was pissed off because you got the Athens job when he was supposed to be next in line for a cushy secondment. Davi—"

"Who?"

"His admin. New, again. Belkin's last new admin went on the sick. Stress, *again.* Anyway, Davi was chasing me, wanting to know how you swung it, so I told him you didn't do anything and to let me know if he found anything out. This morning at coffee he told me Belkin's dropped it because *he* heard that someone from outside the division insisted on you getting it and he didn't want to stir up trouble." She paused for breath. "Well?"

Toreth digested the tale for a moment, then asked, "Who from outside?"

"I've got no idea and neither does Davi or anyone else, which did make me wonder if there was anything in it after all. Might be complete crap—someone making it up to stop Belkin hassling them. You know how bloody-minded he is when he decides he's missed out on what he's due. But I thought you ought to know, in case there was something to it."

"Yeah . . . yeah, thanks." Just what he needed.

"Enjoying yourself?" she asked.

Toreth considered the question and decided there was no way of explaining it that made sense while sober. "Yeah. I'll tell you all about it when I get back. Actually, keep the comm open for a minute."

He called Nikoletta into the office for a brief consultation, making sure she passed in front of the comm.

"What do you think?" he asked Sara when Nikoletta had gone.

"I'd screw her," Sara said promptly. "And I don't really do girls. Should I be looking for another job?"

"I lost a data entry this morning—turned out she'd misspelled it and then tagged it with the wrong section code anyway."

Sara chuckled. "I'll put my CV away. Have fun. Oh—and ask her what she puts on her hair."

Chapter Four

❖

Coincidentally, when the call came through on Friday, Toreth was standing by the window, looking out at the city below. He wasn't sure whether it was pleasant to have no building facing him, or whether it was unnervingly open and unprotected. It would require a long, good shot, but a sniper could hit the building, and the glass didn't seem to be either tinted or bulletproof.

A fragment of his conscious awareness registered Karteris answering the comm. After a few sentences, the studiously casual tone made him pay closer attention.

"There's no need. Everything's fine. Okay. One fifteen, if we have to."

A time? An address? A room number?

Toreth stayed where he was as the call finished.

"I'm afraid I've got to deal with something," Karteris said, already rising. "It won't take long."

"Sorry?" Toreth turned, smiled vaguely. "Sure, go ahead."

Karteris didn't pick up his jacket, and it was barely ten o'clock. One fifteen must be a room number, Toreth decided as the door closed behind Karteris. Memories of the introductory tour suggested one of the ground floor meeting rooms.

Nikoletta was outside, and she'd probably report any departure to Karteris. The meeting would break up before he found it. The situation required a little lateral thinking, and the solution was right at hand.

Lucky thing that Karteris had a ground floor office, and that there was no flower bed outside to leave footprints in. Toreth eased open the window, swung himself over the sill—grinning at the ridiculousness of the situation—and set off along the side of the building.

The sloppy security proved a good thing. He quickly found an open fire door which let him back into the building only a few yards from his target. He checked the corridor both ways—clear. He'd decided to listen from the corridor if necessary, but luckily the next room along from the meeting room was empty and had a helpfully flimsy connecting door.

Toreth set his ear to the door.

"—not *my* fucking fault," Karteris said.

"So whose fault is it?" A voice Toreth didn't recognize spoke up. "You said you'd check him out."

"I did," Karteris said. "Maybe there's another Val Toreth at I&I and we got the quiet, serious one. What I heard was that he screws around, drinks, drugs, doesn't give a fuck about politics and likes a stress-free assignment with plenty of expenses and a good time. You know—normal."

There was muffled laughter, the edge of tension clearly audible.

"So who sent him? Who can *know*? Zavras, anything?"

"I've no idea, sorry." One of the juniors. "I couldn't even find out where the report came from. One minute everything was okay, the next thing I&I HQ was asking questions."

"But that doesn't mean anyone knows anything concrete." Toreth tensed as he heard a creak, before deciding it was Karteris standing up from a table or chair. "Probably just bored statisticians with too much time on their hands."

"So what are we going to do about it? About him?" Grammatopoulos, another of the seniors.

"Nothing," Karteris said. "He's not asking any questions about Grant yet, and he won't start if people keep their mouths shut."

"What about the others, though?"

"They've got even more reason than us to keep quiet. The timing's bad, but we'll get through it. He'll go home in a couple of weeks. Besides, it's probably a whitewash job—if they knew anything for sure, we'd have Internal Investigations tearing the place apart."

"Can't you ask him?" That sounded like Manos, Karteris's junior.

Karteris laughed. "Oh, sure. 'Excuse me, Toreth, are you here to officially ignore the fact that it looks like we can't catch resisters if they walk up to reception wearing a sign round their necks?' What the fuck am I going to do if he says no, genius?" Silence, then he said, "Is that it? Anyone else losing their nerve? Good. Then let's get back to work. And try to look busy."

Movement sounded in the room, and Toreth hastened to get back to his desk in time to appear suitably innocent for Karteris's reappearance.

To his surprise, Karteris didn't return at once. While he waited, Toreth considered what he'd overheard. Combined with Karteris's little meeting, Sara's call had become more alarming. Who had wanted Toreth assigned to the review? The idea of an unknown benefactor left him very uneasy. Was there something dangerous here that he'd be far safer not finding?

He had no objections to whitewashing I&I operational fuckups, *if* that was what was expected of him. It worried him that he didn't know. If there was a serious problem he was supposed to ignore, then standard practice was at least to drop a hint at the beginning of the investigation. Things didn't always work that way, of course. The mess with Psychoprogramming and Marian Tanit had practically given him white hairs—he didn't want to go through that again.

Then there was the other possibility, that the gift of an easy assignment had been given to him by someone who expected him to skimp the investigation and miss the source of the low conviction rates. In that case, Toreth would look like a prize idiot when whatever problems the section had later exploded into the open.

A thorough digging into Political Crimes had to be the best idea, he decided. As long as he kept a tight rein on what entered official records, he could always rebury anything particularly putrid that surfaced.

Glad that he'd transferred the files to his own hand screen, Toreth ran a search for Grant. Only one hit—a Theodora Grant, an administrative officer at the main university of Athens, who'd been reported as a suspected resister. When Political Crimes investigators arrived at her flat, they had found her recently deceased body, but no other evidence. The postmortem suggested suicide, although she'd left no note. Preliminary investigation of her family, friends, and colleagues had been unproductive and the case had been closed soon afterwards.

Apart from the corpse, the case seemed no different from many of the others. If it was the right woman, though, then there must be something there Karteris didn't want him to see.

Vigilante justice, being handed out to suspected resisters by paras who couldn't be bothered with proper investigations and paperwork? Possible, and not entirely unprecedented, although in that case he'd expect more corpses in the files.

Toreth stared at the screen, biting his thumbnail. Should he run a few more detailed searches on the unfortunate Theodora? For that he would have to use the local systems, or put a high-security connection through to I&I headquarters in New London. The latter option would put up a giant flag saying he was up to something, but it was better than anyone who was watching him knowing exactly what.

He connected to New London, then started by pulling Grant's security file. To his surprise, the request was denied. However, a five-second assessment of the message showed it was almost better than getting the file itself. The security-clearance rejection had a code which, from memory, belonged to Citizen Surveillance. If the Political Crimes paras had been tangled up in the death of a Cit agent—or even a suspect that Citizen Surveillance had put a "hands-off" notice on—it wasn't surprising they were nervous.

Why had Grant been here? To find out, he'd need the files from Cit. For that, while he was in Athens, he'd need to get authority from George and possibly even

Vassilakis. In either case it would inevitably attract Karteris's attention. Alternatively, he could investigate the lead more easily, faster, and far more quietly from his own office. A weekend return to New London wouldn't raise too many suspicions, certainly not with the happy accident of his newfound abstemious reputation.

A trip home, with the justification of inquiries at I&I, had another benefit. He could catch an afternoon flight back and be in Warrick's flat by early evening. Friday evening. Warrick in the cabinet would make a perfect setting to tell him about Toreth's week of virtue.

Still smiling, Toreth called through to Nikoletta and asked her to arrange a flight.

As he waited at the Athens airport, he called Sara. When she appeared on the screen, she looked at her watch at once.

"It's half past four there, isn't it?" she asked.

He grinned. "Yes."

"Great. Okay, I know what *you* want. How early?"

"I'll be in about lunchtime, I expect. But I'm sending a list of things for you to do before I get there." He activated the encrypted transfer. "Should be on your screen any moment."

"Long list?" she asked gloomily, sighing when he nodded. "So you spend Saturday morning in bed screwing Warrick, and I spend it here on my own?"

"That's about the size of it. You know, if you're going to bitch about it maybe I *should* think about making Nikoletta an offer."

"Yeah, yeah. Not that she'll want the job once I've warned her that you're a sadistic bastard who gets off on ordering his poor bloody admin to ruin her weekend plans."

He grinned. "What kind of language is that to use to your boss?"

"Memo me." She glanced to the side. "The list's here and clear. See you tomorrow."

Toreth picked up an extravagant box of liqueur chocolates at the overpriced gift shop before he boarded the flight.

Chapter Five

Warrick's flat was empty. Toreth stood in the darkened hallway, feeling the first twinges of irritation. All he'd wanted to do was surprise Warrick, and he was tired enough from the flight that being thwarted felt unreasonable.

Then he looked at his watch. Of course—he'd stupidly forgotten the time difference. Warrick was still at SimTech, that was all.

This time, he called Warrick's admin first, to check. No point wasting another journey.

"I'm afraid Dr. Warrick left three-quarters of an hour ago," Gerry said.

Toreth clicked his tongue with frustration. "Do you know where he is?"

"He has a dinner scheduled, but I'm afraid I can't give out the address without checking—"

"Forget it."

Toreth cut the connection and stood for a moment, frowning. Then he deliberately smoothed the expression away. A small setback in his surprise visit plans, that was all. He had plenty of ways and means at his disposal.

Carnac. Of all the people in Europe, it would have to be fucking Carnac.

Toreth stood in the entrance of the restaurant. He'd waved his ID to get in—it wasn't the kind of place that admitted men in casual clothes. Now he wished he hadn't bothered.

Carnac and Warrick, together. They were both in profile, intent on their conversation. Toreth stood, watching, time passing without him realizing it, until Warrick laughed and shook his head. Carnac reached across the table and patted Warrick's hand. Warrick shook his head again, but he was still smiling.

Were they talking about him, Toreth wondered? Were they talking about what they were going to do later?

Then Carnac looked around and Toreth's heart skipped a beat. Caught spying—how humiliating. However, Carnac's gaze passed blankly over him, eventually focusing on a waiter. As the socioanalyst beckoned the man over, Toreth stepped back towards the door, out of sight, to wait until the bastard looked away again.

On second thought, he kept backing until he reached the door, then pushed through it and strode out onto the street, wanting nothing more than to put distance between himself and the little tête-à-tête.

Bastard. Five fucking days away (five not fucking days away) and fucking Carnac was back. Had he known Toreth wasn't there? *How* had he known?

Then it hit him. Sara's comment, the coffee-room rumor—so obvious, with this last piece of evidence in place.

He'd been walking without really noticing where he was heading, and now he turned and went into a bar without noticing which one. He noticed the drink, though, although not for very long, before he ordered the second one, and the third one with it to save time.

Carnac. Of all the people it could have been. He downed the second drink and slammed the glass back onto the bar. Fucking Carnac.

Warrick, fucking Carnac.

Chapter Six

❖

Even through closed eyelids, the light was painful. Toreth dragged his arm out from under the sheets and laid it across his eyes. Slightly better.

Faint sounds of movement in the room but, thankfully, they stayed faint.

On a scale of one to ten, with one being "I had a few drinks last night" and ten being "someone please shoot me now," the hangover rated an eight. Maybe a nine—that would depend on what Warrick said when he noticed Toreth was awake.

Soft footsteps halted nearby.

"Warrick?"

A light laugh—male, but definitely not Warrick.

"No, my dear, I'm afraid not. Although I envy him exceedingly if you always wake with his name on your lips."

Oh, Christ. Where the hell had he ended up? Only the smell of coffee finally enticed him to open his eyes.

Not, by the look of it, a hotel room. Nor his own room, thank God, although he'd never been sufficiently far gone to take anyone back home. On the other hand, it wasn't the kind of room he wanted to wake up in with such a grim hangover. It was huge, high-ceilinged, and brightly lit. Every centimeter of the walls and ceiling was painted in trompe l'oeil—very good, but very unsettling.

There was no theme, no consistency. There were a dozen or more different styles of interiors, with startlingly realistic windows onto even more varied exteriors. It left him unsure exactly what was real and what wasn't, with the exception of the man smiling at him. He was very real, and Toreth temporarily forgot his hangover and the bewildering room.

Nikoletta was attractive, but the young man beside the bed was undoubtably one of the most beautiful human beings—male or female—that Toreth had ever seen: bottomless, liquid dark eyes; thick dark hair, curling to shoulder length; pale skin with a hint of Indian coloring. He wore a lemon silk robe patterned with tulips in a slightly paler shade, somehow managing to invest it with unquestionable elegance.

It was a measure of how bad the hangover was that Toreth even noticed the steaming mug the man held out towards him.

He struggled into a sitting position—or at least into a more or less vertical slump against the gold-embroidered lavender satin headboard—and paused to recover. "Who the fuck are you?" he asked once the pounding in his head had died down.

The man smiled, unfazed by the tone. "Think of me as a guardian angel. Or call me Paul. As you wish."

Once Toreth had taken the mug the man strolled over to a nearby small couch and draped himself over it, cat-elegant.

Toreth took a mouthful of the coffee—wonderfully thick and tarry—and tried to think. The latter part of the evening was a blur. The last thing he remembered was going into the kind of bar he'd never consider approaching while sober, or even normally drunk. He must have managed to get through the rest of the evening without mentioning his employer, though, as he couldn't feel any bruises or stab wounds.

When he looked up, the coffee-providing angel was watching him with a fascination that Toreth felt was probably unwarranted. He must look like shit. He studied the man in return and decided that his first guess had been wrong—he was nearer Toreth's own age than he'd thought initially.

Toreth ran his hand through his hair, trying to straighten it.

"How do we feel?" Paul asked.

"Absolutely fucking awful, but worse than that."

He laughed. "Regretfully, only to be expected."

Something needed clearing up. "Did we fuck?"

"Alas, beautiful creature, no, we did not."

Toreth felt obscurely relieved that he hadn't broken his resolution. Not that it mattered, if Warrick was—

Don't think about that. He felt bad enough already. "So what the hell am I doing here?"

"I found you in the street." Paul's voice lowered, sharing a distasteful secret. "Lying in the street, if the truth be told. Naturally I realized at once that higher powers had guided me there in order to render assistance to a fellow soul in distress. And while you told me many wonderful things, your address was not one of them, making you a creature of mystery as well as enchantment. So I brought you home with me."

He smiled, showing perfectly even, white teeth. "And here we are. If your inquiry was more metaphysical in nature, I'm afraid I must confess myself unable to help."

Pretty much what he'd imagined. "Thanks. That was, uh, very kind of you." Oddly, he felt more obliged to make some kind of a conversation than he would have done if they had fucked.

Paul brushed the thanks aside. "I woke you because you seemed like the kind of vision of loveliness who nevertheless has to suffer under the yoke of paid employment. And even though it's Saturday, when not even the meanest beast ought to toil in the fields..."

It took Toreth a moment to free the question from the tangle of flowery decoration. "I, er, yeah. I do have things I need to do. I'm a para-investigator."

Paul's already enormous eyes widened dramatically. "But how awful!"

Toreth blinked. "Sorry?"

"A dangerous job. *Dreadfully* important and public-spirited, of course, but so dangerous. Someone so exquisite shouldn't have to risk themselves like that merely to protect the rest of us."

No reply came to mind. Toreth had been complimented on his looks plenty of times before. Just never so... extravagantly.

"But no matter. There—" Paul waved a languid hand, silk whispering. "I never heard any such thing. However, if you are to make it to this frightening job you don't have, should you, perhaps, be leaving?" He leaned forwards a little, smiling again. "Although I assure you that nothing would delight me more than the happy prospect of your continued presence in my humble bed."

"No, I do have to go. Can I use your shower?"

"I see no reason why not—since you already have my heart. I shall summon a carriage for my prince while he avails himself of the facilities."

Paul glided out of the room. Toreth downed his coffee, then went in search of the bathroom.

It was also huge, richly tiled in turquoise and gold, and with an underwater seascape painted on one wall, populated with muscular fishtailed men and silver-scaled women who could have been mermaids if they'd looked in the slightest bit maidenly. One of them was fucking an octopus. The shower was big enough for a rather wet orgy, and the bath was one of the largest Toreth had seen outside the sim. He spent a while poking unselfconsciously through gilded cupboards, impressed by the variety of jars and bottles.

He set the shower temperature to as hot as he could stand, the water flow to fast, and the spray to stinging needles that soon started to wash away the worst of the hangover. He'd been in the shower for a couple of minutes when the glass door to it opened.

"All arranged, my foundling. Taxi in fifteen minutes."

Leaving the shower door open, Paul went to lean on the scalloped sink and watched Toreth with a faint smile and open appreciation. Water splashed onto the floor, but as it wasn't his flat Toreth didn't care. He carried on washing, taking a little longer than was strictly necessary since he had an audience.

"Exquisite," Paul murmured, then began to recite.

"I can love both fair and brown;

He whom abundance melts, and he whom want betrays;
He who loves loneness best, and he who masks and plays;
He whom the country form'd, and whom the town;
He who believes, and he who tries;
He who still weeps with spongy eyes,
And he who is dry cork, and never cries.
I can love him, and him, and you, and you;
I can love any, so he be not true."

He stopped, and sighed wistfully.

"What's that?" Toreth asked.

"A disgraceful transgendering of a delightful work by one of the greatest poets of the English tongue—John Donne." He tilted his head as though expecting a response, then sighed again. "No matter. The work bemoans the rise of unnatural constancy and praises the manifold joys of rampant infidelity."

Toreth had never taken much interest in poetry and, with a thumping headache, he didn't feel like starting now. "I'd rather do it than read about it."

"Wise words, beauteous one."

As Toreth stepped out of the shower, Paul picked up a towel. "Please—allow me."

So Toreth stood in the steamy room while Paul dried him gently, thoroughly, and silently, then he went back into the bedroom and dressed.

He'd had less strange mornings after. Or mornings not after, in this case.

On the doorstep to the apartment building, Paul stopped him with a gentle hand on his arm. With Paul a step above him, Toreth had to look up.

"I know I shouldn't even attempt to impose myself on you while you are in such a fragile condition, angel. However—" With a flourish, a small rectangle of lemon-yellow plastic appeared between his fingers. "Were you to call me, you would find me speechless with rapturous ecstasy at hearing your voice again."

Toreth took the card. "Okay. And, er, thanks."

"The pleasure, my love, was entirely my own. I shall remember you always." The melting smile again. "Or for at least a week. But do call, at any time, if you would like to remedy the tragic omission of last night."

He must have looked blank, because Paul laughed, then kissed his own forefinger and placed it briefly on Toreth's lips.

"Fucking, dear heart. Fucking."

And the door closed, leaving Toreth alone except for the waiting taxi.

The sheer strangeness of the morning—and the subduing effect of the hangover—meant that when he arrived in the office around ten o'clock and Sara cheerfully informed him that he looked like he'd been having fun, he didn't snarl at her. Instead he grunted something noncommittal, dropped the chocolates on her desk, and went into his office to brood.

Unfortunately, there was too much to do to allow a really good sulk—Sara had already found much of the information he wanted, and he had a job to finish, whatever Warrick was doing with his spare time. He'd barely read through the list of files when Sara came in with two coffees and a plate of biscuits. She handed him his cup and then pulled up a chair, obviously settling in.

"Did I get everything you wanted?"

"Yes."

Her eyebrow went up at his tone. "Nice time in Athens?"

"Fine."

"How was the flight back?"

He picked up a biscuit and dipped the end into his coffee. "Fine."

"How's Warrick?"

"F—" Distracted at the vital moment, Toreth left his biscuit submerged a fraction too long. A chunk of it broke off and sank out of sight. He picked up a teaspoon and fished vainly for it. "Fucking *hell.* I hate that."

She watched him for a while, not commenting, until he gave up hope of retrieving the biscuit. He threw the teaspoon back onto the tray.

"Don't you have any work to do?" he asked.

"Plenty." She stood up and reached for the tray.

"No. Look. Sit down." He took a deep breath. He mustn't piss Sara off, not when he had to go back to Athens and leave her to look after things here. "I'm sorry."

She nodded, accepting the apology, and sat down again. "Is he okay?"

"I don't know. I haven't fucking spoken to him, because—" He swallowed a mouthful of coffee, steadying his voice. "Because when I went to see him he was with Carnac."

"*Carnac*? The spook?"

"Yes."

"Hang on a minute. Is that 'with' as in 'in the same room as' or 'with' as in . . . ?"

He sighed and launched into the sorry saga. When he'd walked out of the restaurant, he looked up to find Sara staring at him in obvious bewilderment. "So they went to dinner?"

"Yeah. Very fucking cozy."

"But that's it? Dinner? Did you call his flat later or something?"

"No, I—" I made a huge fucking assumption on no bloody evidence whatsoever.

"Well, you know, maybe they were just—"

"Jesus Christ, Sara, I worked that out for myself. *Bollocks.*"

She smiled very slightly, and so briefly that he didn't have time to snap at her to stop it. "What did you do?"

"What do you think?" He rubbed his face. "I went off, felt sorry for myself, and got completely fucking wasted. Woke up in some bloke's bed with no idea of how I got there. *Fuck*."

"Oh dear. Well—" She stood up. "No harm done, eh? Shall I call Warrick, tell him you're back for the weekend?"

"No. No, I'll do it."

Halfway across the room, she stopped and turned around. "Did you . . ."

"What?"

"Did you really not screw anyone in Athens? For the whole week?"

Why the hell had he told her that? "If you say a word to anyone, I'll kill you."

Balancing the tray in one hand, she zipped her lips firmly. Then she grinned. "It's useless as gossip, anyway. No one would believe me."

When she had gone, Toreth sat and contemplated the extent of his stupidity. Christ, he'd sack any of his team who came up to him and tried to pass off something that weak as a plausible theory. It had probably been nothing more than a social meal, or even a business meeting. He should have thought of that in the first place—why the hell would Warrick's admins know about illicit liaisons?

Well, if he had to make an idiot of himself, at least it had only been in front of Sara.

He called Warrick—sound only. It would make it that much easier to lie to him. Between the effects of irritation, the hangover, and lingering embarrassment he'd need all the help he could get.

"Hello, Warrick. It's me."

"And very nice it is to hear you." Sounded like genuine pleasure. "How's the weather in Athens?"

"No idea. I'm back in New London. I got back last night. I called the flat, but you weren't in." Setting a trap.

"I'm afraid not." No obvious guilt. "Actually, I was having dinner with someone."

"Anyone I know?"

"Yes, indeed, although I doubt you'll guess who."

He played through the charade, guessing randomly, until Warrick finally said, "Carnac."

Deep breath. "Carnac? Fuck, really? What's he doing back here?"

Now there was a hesitation. "Working somewhere in the city, I think. Listen, I've got a meeting now. Are you free this evening?"

"Your flat?"

"Certainly."

"Fine. See you."

Toreth rested his chin on his hand and stared at the screen without seeing any of the work layered there for his urgent attention. *I've got a meeting now.* Warrick was working at the weekend, too? Not terribly unusual, and he had been expecting

Toreth to be in Athens. But why the sudden change in the conversation? What hadn't Warrick wanted to tell him?

He wished he could think of a reason beyond the obvious one.

"I can get a section head clearance, of course," Toreth said, "but it'll take me a couple of hours. Maybe more."

The man on the screen looked at his watch. "I'm supposed to be taking my daughter out for the afternoon, Para-investigator."

"I'm sorry," Toreth said with as much sincerity as he could fake. "The files I have give Theodora Grant as an alias for a Citizen Surveillance agent. I need the details of the operation in Athens she was working on when she died."

"Wait."

The screen blanked. Toreth leaned back in his chair. Working at the weekend had advantages and disadvantages. It had taken him an hour to track down someone over at Cit Surveillance who could give him the information he needed. On the plus side, it meant that everyone he spoke to was in a hurry to deal with his question and get on with whatever they were doing.

He sat up as the screen flickered into life.

"I'm sending the file now. Get a section head clearance to me on Monday."

"No problem." Sara could fight it out with Tillotson after Toreth was back in sunny Athens.

The file was short and perversely unhelpful. Two months previously, Cit Surveillance had assigned Agent #19710502 to act as an agent provocateur within the university in Athens. She had arrived, begun the process of sounding out potential resisters, and been discovered dead by Political Crimes investigators a month later. The operation had followed all proper procedures—thorough preparation of her cover, selective targeting of contacts, notification to other Int-Sec agencies, and a low risk projection.

How it could be connected to his own investigation wasn't immediately obvious. Karteris had mentioned her name, though, so there had to be something there. Had she been mistaken for a genuine resister? Had she discovered the reason behind Political Crimes's low arrest rate? The possibility remained that, despite the Cit connection, Karteris had meant another Grant, but as the name wasn't Greek the odds seemed low.

One thing seemed clear, which was that if Toreth hoped to get any further with the lead, he'd need help with some nonelectronic investigation when he returned to Athens. He had powers to take investigators from the pool there, but that involved, to put it mildly, conflicted loyalties. He needed people he could rely on, and who, more importantly, needed *his* good opinion for their future careers, not Karteris's or Vassilakis's.

Whom to choose? Barret-Connor, because the senior investigator did his job well and discreetly. Another investigator, or his junior para? He felt tempted to take Joielin Nagra, if she could be spared.

Nagra had been in Toreth's team for a year and a half, and she was the best junior para he'd ever had. Her only flaw was that she was bound to get an early promotion to senior, and she was good enough that he couldn't stop it. Not that it would happen for a number of years yet—talent had to be backed up by experience.

He called through to Sara. "How's Nagra's caseload?"

She didn't need to check, and once more Toreth wished he could take her with him. "It could be left with Wrenn and Morehen, if that's what you mean. The big one was the corporate extortion, and that's gone quiet—Systems are tracking leads but they don't expect results unless the corporation is contacted again."

"Great. Call her and tell her I've got good news. B-C, too. Sort me out flights for them both to Athens. The budget should stretch to it."

That settled, he returned to the files.

Chapter Seven

❖

I'm in the living room," Warrick called as Toreth closed the door to the flat. Toreth took his time taking off his coat. Carnac and Warrick had been having dinner, nothing more than that. Sara was obviously right. If he let himself worry about it he'd end up looking like an idiot in front of Warrick. As he set off down the hall, he took a deep breath—the flat smelled deliciously of curry. Special effort, obviously, for his return.

Was that a sign of Warrick's guilty conscience?

As he entered the living room, Warrick craned his neck to look over the back of the sofa and gave him a smile that under any other circumstances would have put a serious delay in dinner.

The picture flashed into his mind of Warrick's mouth on Carnac's. Don't, he told himself. Just don't even start that.

"Would you like a drink?" Warrick asked, not standing up.

"No." He knew what he ought to say, what Warrick expected to hear. "I'd much prefer you."

The smile widened. "Oh, *good.* Would you like to adjourn to the bedroom?"

Toreth came around the end of the sofa, almost stepping on the hand screen on the floor. "Not especially."

Still smiling, Warrick lay down on the sofa and offered his hand.

"This is a very pleasant surprise," Warrick said when they were comfortable.

"I had to come back to I&I. I'm heading back to Athens on Monday."

"We'll have to make the most of it, then. Thank you for the card, by the way. It arrived yesterday afternoon."

"Did you like it?"

His eyebrow arched wryly. "The admins certainly enjoyed it. They laughed so much that Asher came across to see what the fuss was about. If you hoped to embarrass me, you succeeded admirably." Warrick ran his fingers through Toreth's hair. "You were telling the truth about the sun, anyway."

"Yeah? I've not been out much."

"Still, it's distinctly lighter. Did you get to a beach?"

"Too fucking busy."

"Mm. Pity." Warrick's voice was muffled against his throat. "I have a sex-on-a-beach fantasy I'm very fond of."

Warrick was getting hard, squirming gently against him. It felt wonderful, but Toreth couldn't stop the thought from forming: is it me or is it fucking Carnac on the beach with you?

"I've been entertaining myself with it while you've been away," Warrick continued. "You know how it is—one becomes captivated by an idea for a while, a particular scenario. Or at least I do. Elaborating. Expanding. Adding new details." He ran his hand down Toreth's chest, then up again to start unfastening his shirt from the top.

Forget Carnac. "I swam in the pool every day—that's outdoors."

"Ah." Warm fingers traced down his skin as Warrick undid the buttons with his thumb. "Did you get sunburned?"

"No, I didn't. It's incredibly bad for your skin. Why do you want to... no, wait, don't tell me—sunburn turns you on."

"Yes, a little. Just the idea of a touch along your shoulders."

The wistful edge made Toreth laugh. "Sunburn." He shifted around, moving above Warrick, pressing him down into the sofa. "Sometimes you are so fucking weird."

It was a good thing that they'd done this so often, because it meant Toreth could devote most of his attention to looking for something different. Different responses, different movements, a different scent—something that would tell him beyond doubt that Warrick had been with someone else.

The downside of having done this so often was that after five minutes Warrick lifted Toreth's head up gently, one hand cupping his face, and said, "What's wrong?"

"Why the hell would anything be wrong?"

"If I knew, I wouldn't be asking."

"It's nothing."

Warrick wriggled out from beneath him and sat up. "If you're not in the mood, or you're tired, all you have to do is say so. Your company for the evening will be very nice whatever we do." He stroked Toreth's shoulder, straightening his shirt. "I don't expect performance on demand, you know."

Not if you've got someone else to do it for you. Toreth rolled onto his back and stared up at the familiar ceiling. "Carnac swung me the trip to Athens."

Warrick frowned down at him. "It's in English, and all the words make sense, but what the hell are you talking about?"

"Carnac pulled strings and got me assigned to the investigation in Athens."

"How on earth do you know that?"

"Sara asked around."

"For goodness sake. Office gossip—"

"Is about the most reliable source of information. If the admin network says someone from outside the division arranged the trip, then someone did. Who the fuck else could it be?"

"How should I know?" Warrick asked. "Internal politics at Int-Sec is hardly my specialty."

"Well, it's mine."

"Why would he do something like that?"

So he could fuck you. "I don't know. Carnac isn't *my* specialty. Why don't you ask him next time you see him?"

There was a brief pause before Warrick said, "I think you're perhaps being just a little paranoid."

"No, I'm not. Don't you think it's a bit of a fucking coincidence?"

"Yes. It's a *coincidence,* in the accurate sense of two unrelated events coinciding."

"Unrelated? He set it up so that he could take you to dinner and get you—"

He stopped, far too late, as Warrick's expression changed—slight smile, mostly around his eyes. "Toreth, I assure you it was nothing of the kind. We had dinner and that was *all.*"

A little exasperated and so fucking patient. If there was one thing Toreth hated more than that tone of voice it was the thought he was sure lay behind it. "You're utterly pathetic, but I can put up with it because I like your cock." Toreth sat up abruptly. Bastard. Unbelievable bastard. Sometimes, like now, he hated Warrick as he'd hated few other people in his life.

"He was fucking flirting with you at that restaurant," Toreth said tightly. "Or was that my imagination, too?"

"Carnac flirts with doors when he opens them. It's how he—" Warrick stopped dead. "How the hell do you know what he was doing there?"

No ready answer presented itself, so he settled for shrugging.

When Warrick spoke again his voice was quiet enough that Toreth reflexively leaned closer to hear him. "I hope the answer isn't that you followed us there."

Don't explain, you idiot. "I went straight to your flat from the airport, but you weren't there." With Warrick's gaze fixed on him, he couldn't manage to shut up. "So I called SimTech and they said you had a . . . a dinner meeting."

"A business meeting, yes."

"A business meeting. Right. So when you said you *thought* he was working somewhere in New London . . . ?"

Warrick sighed. "Yes. I'm sorry. He's at SimTech."

Toreth's hands clenched on the edge of the sofa. You *are* fucking him—he wasn't sure if he'd said it out loud or not.

"How did you find us?" Warrick continued.

"I ran a vehicle check on cars from SimTech. There was only one to a classy restaurant."

"Then you went to the restaurant, saw us, and left without asking for an explanation?" His lips twitched. "Not a very thorough investigation."

How could he be so casual? Probably because it really had just been dinner. "If he's working at SimTech, why didn't you tell me?"

"Because *no one* is supposed to know. He's carrying out a study of the corporation for an interested party. I'm afraid the details are confidential."

The seesaw of doubt tipped the other way again. "Very fucking convenient."

"And also true. Only the directors know why he's here—or even who he is. Publicly, he's a consultant psychologist."

"What's so fucking secret?"

"I can't tell you." Warrick sighed again. "I suppose I ought to be grateful that they didn't tell you the meeting was with Alex Welham."

Clandestine meetings under a different name—that certainly would have clinched it. "Yeah, I suppose so. Or maybe not. I mean, if I'd punched the fucker in the restaurant, it would've been sorted out then."

Warrick's expression iced over. "I hope that was a joke."

"Not really."

Warrick stood up, took a couple of paces away and turned. "Toreth, this study is important for SimTech. Very important. Production should start this year. We have customers waiting and a delay would be disastrous, both financially and for our reputation. I'm asking you—no, begging you—please don't do anything to endanger it."

"No problem. Just stay the fuck away from Carnac."

"You know I can't. Believe me, he wasn't my first choice, but the socioanalyst was appointed by the—by the interested party."

Yeah, right, of course he was. But Toreth didn't say it, because he knew perfectly well what it sounded like. Stupid, pathetic jealousy, and if Warrick got any more patient something very unpleasant would happen. Toreth ought to know better. He should've gathered enough evidence before he made his case. "Fine. Do whatever the fuck you like." Toreth stood up and began rebuttoning his shirt. "I'm going home."

For a moment he thought that Warrick would protest. It was a disappointment when he simply nodded and said, "Call me, if you have time."

Toreth poured himself another whiskey, looked at it, then left it on the table and went to the window of his flat. He opened it and leaned on the sill, breathing in the cool New London air. If his stomach would stop somersaulting at the memory of Warrick and Carnac eating together, he could manage to be properly angry about them.

The conviction had grown stronger all evening, as he tried not to think about it. Carnac had wanted Warrick the last time he'd been in New London. Now he'd arranged to get rid of Toreth so he could have him. Stupidly, the word adultery kept forcing its way into his mind. Stupid because adultery technically required a marriage registration. But Warrick had *promised,* and that ought to mean more than any fucking official stamp. After Girardin, he'd said never again, and Toreth had believed him.

For a moment he wondered what was worse—Warrick fucking Carnac or the way Toreth had been so stupidly naive as to think it wouldn't happen. Which was also a stupid thing to think, because of the two it obviously had to be the fuck.

If they were fucking, he told himself firmly. If. However sure he felt, he had no evidence. It was all bloody ifs.

Of course... it didn't have to be.

He'd thought about it before. Usually when Warrick had a conference, especially if Toreth had succumbed to the temptation of checking the attendees' names and found Girardin listed there. The only thing that had stopped him was the idea of Warrick finding out. Carnac was different. He was too fucking clever to leave things to trust, especially when Toreth had no choice but to return to Athens the day after tomorrow.

Returning to the table, Toreth contemplated the untouched glass of whiskey, then poured it back into the bottle.

Chapter Eight

The private detective firm hadn't expressed surprise when Toreth asked for a Sunday afternoon appointment. Perhaps, Toreth thought as the lift rose, they had a lot of customers who wanted to arrange a little surveillance of their unfaithful bastard fucks at the weekend.

Outside the office, he almost changed his mind. If Warrick found out then he would be unbearably difficult about the whole thing. Maybe if Toreth kept repeating Warrick's assurances that nothing was going on, he'd be able to get through the next couple of weeks. Then Carnac would leave, and everything would be back to normal.

But he still wouldn't know. Carnac would go on his way, and Toreth could never be sure that Warrick hadn't been assigned the part of personal liaison.

Would Warrick do it? Toreth snorted. With SimTech's future at stake? Of course he fucking would.

Hand on the doorframe, Toreth closed his eyes and imagined Warrick and Carnac together. It was so easy, since he'd fucked both of them. He could almost hear their voices, and even in his head he couldn't be sure whether Warrick was lying back and thinking of the corporation, or whether he was enjoying it. Wanting it.

Toreth opened his eyes. The detective firm was owed by Uche, an ex-I&I investigator who owed Toreth favors. The firm was discreet and reliable, and this was the easiest way to get rid of his exasperating uncertainty.

No problem, as Karteris would say.

The discussion had a relentless practicality that actually made Toreth feel more at ease with the idea. He wondered if Uche had different lines of salesmanship to use on different customers. This, presumably, was the Practical Guys approach.

"Prices depend on the resources we need to apply to the problem," Uche said. "If the target's high-level corporate for corporate information, that'll cost you more than if it's a noncorporate straying spouse."

"How about a straying corporate regular fuck?"

"That'll put it somewhere in the middle." He smiled, his slightly discolored teeth still appearing bright in contrast to his dark skin. "It depends on how close a watch you want and if you want it in office hours, too."

"Especially in office hours."

"Then you're back to corporate prices, I'm afraid, because we'll be dodging the same security. Do you have a second target in mind?"

"Yes. He's working at SimTech temporarily, under the name Alex Welham." Useful of Warrick to let that slip. "His real name is Carnac." Toreth had to think back. "Jean-Baptiste, I think."

"Corporate too?"

"No. Socioanalyst."

"A..." Uche stared, then laughed. "I'm afraid you'll have to wait for a few minutes while I come up with a whole new price scale."

It was a good job that he didn't have any expensive hobbies like skiing, Toreth thought as he emerged back into daylight. If he'd stuck to the cover story of Carnac being a consultant psychologist, perhaps Uche wouldn't have doubled the charges.

And perhaps, not knowing what they were up against, the watchers would've been caught. That didn't bear thinking about.

Back at his flat, the first thing that caught his eye when he opened the door was a yellow rectangle on the table below the mirror in the hall. Paul's card.

He picked it up and called the number. When it connected, the screen stayed blank.

"Paul?" he asked.

"On occasion," the musical voice admitted cautiously.

"It's Val Toreth." A pause, and he realized that it was entirely possible he'd never told the man his name. "You found me lying face down in the street on Friday night."

"Ah! My golden handsel!" Instant recognition, and unmistakable pleasure. "How may I be of service?"

Before he could change his mind, Toreth said, "I wondered if you'd like to have dinner tonight. With a post-dinner fuck."

Delighted laughter filled the air. "My dear! Refreshingly direct. But then, didn't I say 'any time'?"

"You said you'd be speechless, too."

"Oh, but I am, I am. All things are relative." Paul's voice developed a brisker, more businesslike tone. "Before you waste the price of a taxi, I ought to tell you that while I'm sure it will be my purest pleasure to accommodate your desires, I don't bottom. I sincerely hope that doesn't disappoint, angel?"

"No. Suits me fine." And the taxi was free, courtesy of I&I.

"Then I shall await your arrival in an agony of anticipation—no, first of all I shall put something on ice. Dry or sweet?"

To his surprise, Toreth found himself smiling. "Dry."

"I didn't doubt it for a moment. Later, my treasure—but not too much later."

Chapter Nine

Barret-Connor and Nagra flew back with him in the morning. They managed to book into the same hotel, and Toreth held an impromptu case conference in Nagra's room—even if Political Crimes possessed hidden depths of efficiency, they were unlikely to have every room in the place under surveillance.

Neither of his team members had any useful ideas about the case but they clearly appreciated the trip away. Toreth considered emphasizing that it wasn't a holiday, but decided against it. He trusted them, and besides, it still might turn out to be exactly that.

Back at Athens I&I, Toreth informed Karteris that he'd take the empty office and a couple of extra desks for the staff. Karteris seemed unfazed by the news, and provided accommodation two doors down. Had he known about Nagra and B-C's arrival in advance? Possibly. The question then was whether the information had come from the airport or hotel, or from the man's contacts at New London I&I.

The new office was close enough to allow Karteris to keep an eye on Toreth, but conversely it also allowed Toreth to keep tabs on Karteris. Advantage to the native, though, since he had Nikoletta to increase the effectiveness of the surveillance. Not that either B-C or Nagra were hard to pick out in the building, his pale blondness as unusual as her polished Caribbean skin. Pity he hadn't chosen people who'd blend in better. Used to the diverse ethnic mix of New London, it hadn't occurred to him that B-C and Nagra might be conspicuous here.

Toreth's research in New London had included a credit and purchase check for Karteris. It looked clean enough, but it gave him a list of regular hangouts to try for gossip. He assigned Nagra to that, as the more personable of the two. B-C would join the hunt through the case files, and also start investigations into the case files they hadn't been given, especially any that had been closed with the suspect's death.

Later that afternoon, Karteris appeared in the office doorway with Nikoletta beside him.

"Anyone fancy a trip up to the Acropolis dome this evening? See the sights. I don't know if you're interested, but I thought I'd offer."

Toreth had decided to stick to his new image, Carnac notwithstanding. However, sightseeing ancient monuments was taking being a boring bastard a bit too far.

"Is there much to see up there?" Toreth asked.

"At the Acropolis?" Nikoletta sounded shocked. "You've never heard of the Parthenon Casino? It's famous. And great fun."

"How did they get away with putting a casino in the place?" B-C asked.

"Ah." Karteris grinned. "Back in the days of petroleum cars, the air pollution was destroying most of the ancient monuments. Some anonymous corporate offered to pay for the restoration and then protect the Acropolis with the dome. No one knows who it was—supposedly he was part of the Mars consortium. Anyway, the city thought great, someone looking for a tax write-off, so they accepted. Turned out they should have read the small print more carefully."

Nagra laughed. "And they couldn't get rid of it?"

"Allegedly there are still Administration lawyers going through the contract with a fine-tooth comb, trying to find a way out."

The dome entrance, while not an actual airlock, still stirred unpleasant memories of Toreth's mind-numbingly dull secondment on Mars. There, however, the boredom had been compounded by the installation being dry. The Acropolis dome was anything but.

They stopped at a small building that housed a reception and bar, where Karteris paused to set up an account for the evening. He returned with three large bags of casino chips, which he handed out to Toreth, B-C, and Nagra. "Entertainment budget."

Toreth hefted the bag in his hand and debated, feeling the weight of expectant gazes, too. If he refused the chips, then B-C and Nagra would feel obliged to do the same, and the last thing he wanted to do was piss off his entire investigative team of two.

"Thanks," he said.

After acquiring drinks, they set off across the historical paving, following in the footsteps of millions. The Parthenon itself, brilliantly lit, dominated the dome. Toreth had no idea which of the white buildings were original, which were restoration, and which had been added to provide modern conveniences for the casino. As everything was under the protection of the dome, collections of slot machines and lower stakes tables sprouted in groups on the Acropolis hill.

The scene which greeted them when they reached the Parthenon would, Toreth thought, have induced collective apoplexy in the original builders. Good thing they'd been dead for more than two and a half thousand years. Although it was relatively early on a weeknight, patrons already thronged between the massive pillars. The gaming tables were in marble—whether real or fake, Toreth couldn't tell—and the staff circulating with drinks wore ancient-style dress. The lights blazed back in reflection from the golden clothing of a vast statue of a woman with ornate helmet and shield, which dominated the far end of the room.

"Well," B-C said after a while. "At least they didn't knock it all down to fit in a bigger bar."

Karteris gestured vaguely towards the floodlit heights of the building. "A lot of it's restored, but they brought some original bits back from a museum at your end of the Administration, sometime soon after the bombs. Athens was lucky, you know, not being hit then. There's a screen somewhere with the official story—don't know where, though. Come on."

They moved into the crowd.

Gambling bored Toreth, but he adored casinos, especially the expensive ones. Few places in the world came with such a rich assortment of neglected spouses who were not only bored to tears but actively resenting the person who'd dragged them there. Tonight, though, they were all off limits.

He turned to Nikoletta and rattled the bag. "Would you like to help me spend these?"

She glanced at Karteris, who had apparently been distracted by something on the far side of the temple. "That'd be fun, thanks," she said.

If he had to gamble, Toreth didn't mind playing poker. It was only really fun playing with people he knew, though, and it made for a poor spectator sport. They stuck to games where absolutely no skill was involved, betting small to make the generous expenses handout last even longer.

Toreth had his usual terrible luck. When the bag was half empty he handed it over to Nikoletta with a smile, and said, "Maybe you'll do better without me."

As he strolled off he caught sight of Karteris closing in to take his place.

Toreth wandered aimlessly for a while until he spotted B-C's blond crop through the crowd. He was seated at a blackjack table—not something Toreth would've suspected B-C of even knowing how to play. He seemed to be doing well enough, though. The neat stacks of chips in front of him looked to be more than double what Karteris had handed him at the start of the evening.

Nagra stood a little way away, watching.

"Not playing?" Toreth asked her in a low voice.

"Nope. My mother always said gambling was a tax on stupidity. And besides, I gave my stake to B-C."

"What the hell for?"

"We're not all on senior para salaries, you know. He's going to play for a while, then we're going to cash in what's left and keep it. He's counting cards," Nagra added confidentially.

Toreth snorted. "Or so he says."

"Well, he's winning, anyway." She frowned. "Except that he was supposed to quit if we ever made it fifteen percent up."

"Shall I get him away from there for you?"

Toreth moved to stand behind an empty chair opposite B-C, and waited until a brief break in the game, when the investigator looked up and caught his eye. As B-C nodded hello, Toreth smiled slowly, licked his bottom lip, and carefully mouthed, "Want to fuck?"

B-C flushed brick red, and for the five seconds it took him to realize what Toreth was up to, Toreth had never seen anyone appear so purely appalled. Then B-C looked down at the cards in front of him, over to the dealer's shoe, and shook his head.

Satisfied, Toreth strolled off to the bar and bought himself a cocktail that turned out to be fifty percent fruit salad. B-C joined him a couple of minutes later, his half of the winnings safely stowed in a bag with a print of a naked nymph, complete with friendly dolphin.

B-C sat down on the next stool. "You rotten bastard. Sir."

Toreth swirled the overloaded cocktail stick through his drink and sucked the cherry off the end. B-C colored faintly again, and Toreth knew what he was thinking about.

"Nagra told me you were supposed to stop at fifteen percent," Toreth said.

"Yes, but I was on a—" He paused, then nodded once. "No, she's right. Thanks, I suppose. You can buy me a drink, though, now I'm not playing. Lager."

Toreth grinned and beckoned the bartender over. After all, everything was on expenses.

"Where the hell did you learn to count cards?" he asked when B-C had his drink.

"I don't know if you remember, but when you had your six months on Mars, I got a secondment to Paris. While I was there, I went out with a girl who worked at one of the Atlantic coastal casinos in the summer."

"One of your interchangeable leggy blondes?"

B-C nodded, unruffled. "She showed me how to do it. Actually, it's a good way to keep your brain sharp, but the house always wins in the end, which makes it a bit expensive for me. So normally I do crosswords instead, with my mother. We generate them by hand for one another."

Sometimes Toreth couldn't tell whether B-C was joking or not.

They sat for a while, watching the crowd. Suddenly, B-C gestured with his glass and said, "Look over there, Para."

After a moment Toreth spotted Karteris and Nikoletta. It took him a moment longer to notice that Karteris's hand rested on his admin's backside as she leaned over a roulette table.

"Well done," Toreth said automatically.

"Para?"

"You just confirmed a theory for me." Either Nikoletta had a far more relaxed attitude towards personal space than Sara did, or Toreth had been spot on about their unprofessional relationship. One productive result of the evening, anyway.

Chapter Ten

❖

By Wednesday afternoon, B-C had ruled out another theory, too. Suicides and accidental deaths among citizens reported as potential resisters were, if anything, slightly lower than Toreth might expect—it wasn't unknown for those who feared they were about to be arrested to take desperate measures to avoid interrogation. If Political Crimes were killing resisters out of hand, then they were doing so in a highly ineffective manner. Not that Toreth was willing to discount that possibility, given what he'd seen so far. However, they certainly weren't killing enough suspects to account for their poor conviction rate.

Surprisingly, Toreth found that discarding that idea didn't discourage him. Being able to look up and see familiar faces made him feel more confident of eventual success. A small part of New London had been transplanted here—people he could rely on.

That evening, at the hotel, the confidence proved justified when Nagra brought him the first interesting result.

"It may be nothing, Para, but I'd consider asking for another full credit and purchase. There were a few regular taxi drop-off points on the list, with nothing spent at the other end. Not in the nice parts of town, either. I tried bars at the end of the most popular two routes, and an alternate name cropped up a few times when I showed people Karteris's picture. Taki Papadamou. All the places he was known at had gambling, some more legal than others, and this Taki is well known as a big spender. Speaking of which, I blew the budget you gave me for bribes."

"No problem." Damn, that phrase was getting to be a habit. Had he used it before he came here? He had a feeling he had, but now it was annoying him. "And good work. Call it through to Sara for her to arrange the c&p on both names. Use a personal comm, not the hotel one. Tell her to keep it quiet. Very quiet."

She raised an eyebrow, but didn't comment.

To celebrate the news, Toreth went for a dip before dinner. As he swam lengths in the fading light, he wondered where Warrick was, and whether Carnac was with him.

❖❖❖

B-C and Nagra were at lunch, leaving the office quiet except for distant noises leaking dully through the door. Toreth closed the daily report he'd received from Uche's detectives and looked out of the window over Athens basking in the spring sunshine. The report detailed Warrick's regular work schedule, nothing suspicious. Carnac had returned to his hotel after his day at SimTech and spent Wednesday evening alone in his room. Room service for one delivered at nine o'clock.

Toreth smiled and picked up his second lunchtime sandwich. The reports may have been pricey, but they had proved an excellent investment. He'd been stupid to worry about the idea. Maybe he should consider doing it more often. Warrick's trips to conferences might be a good starting point, when there would be no expensive socioanalyst bumping up the bill.

Or maybe not, because the undoubted satisfaction had an unpleasant aftertaste—an awareness of how pathetic this would look to an outsider. Sara would never let him live it down. Warrick would be horrified and livid. They'd both know that he spent his time fretting about what Warrick might be up to in Toreth's absence.

He'd call the agency from the hotel that evening and tell them to stop. After all, it was now Thursday—there had been three whole days with no action.

Of course, there was no way of telling what Warrick and Carnac had been up to in the sim. That wasn't a thought he liked, not least because he knew that Warrick would be able to say that nothing had happened with Carnac and believe it, because it was just work. Was there a way of getting hold of the sim schedule? At least that would show if the two of them had been in together. If they'd used any of the sex protocols, that would be recorded, too.

He was wondering how it might be possible to retrieve the records when the comm chimed.

Warrick.

Juxtaposed with his recent thoughts, his face on the screen gave Toreth a panicked second of fear that Warrick had found out about the surveillance, until he registered Warrick's smile. Still, an irrational touch of unease sharpened Toreth's voice.

"What the hell do you want?"

"Well, firstly, to ask if your temper had improved since I saw you last." On the screen, Warrick's eyebrow lifted slightly. "However, the answer to that question is clearly no."

"If you just called to be fucking sarcastic, I've got work to do."

"No doubt. So I'll be brief. I thought I might come out to Athens at the weekend, if you have no objections."

Objections? "Fuck, no. I mean—yeah, sure, come. That'd be—" He caught hold of the enthusiasm and damped it down. "That'd be fine."

"Wonderful. I thought, if you don't have to be in the city itself, that I might book somewhere quiet for us."

Toreth smiled slowly. "Somewhere near a beach?"

Warrick's answering smile was positively mischievous. "The idea had crossed my mind, yes."

"So I can—" Toreth was about to elaborate on the possibilities when he remembered Nikoletta. Friendly she might be, but there was no reason to assume that she wasn't passing information on to Karteris. Or that Karteris himself wasn't listening. No need to spoil his virtuous image with overly graphic plans. "I can get the weekend off, no problem."

When Warrick had gone, Toreth sat, twirling the comm earpiece between his fingers and thinking about the surveillance. If Warrick was coming here, there couldn't possibly be anything going on. Unless there was, and the trip was designed to diffuse suspicion. Would Warrick think of that? Carnac probably would.

In the end, Toreth decided to wait. One more day. He could call the agency tomorrow and cancel the surveillance then. Maybe.

Toreth finished his sandwich, brushed away the crumbs, and returned to the official investigation.

How long would it take Sara to manage the credit and purchase? Assuming Nagra had told her to keep it as discreet as possible, it might take longer than usual. Karteris obviously had some kind of contact in New London, but Toreth doubted that they'd be up to spotting Sara at her most sneaky.

Not that there was any guarantee that Karteris's gambling extravagance was anything to do with the dismal arrest record of the section. He shouldn't pin all his hopes on it, but it was difficult not to when it was all he had. He was no longer optimistic that he or B-C would come up with anything from the files.

For lack of other ideas, he found a few sheets of paper and a pencil and started making lists.

A few years earlier, Sara had tried to interest him in a decision-tree program on the I&I admin system. Toreth had killed a couple of hours with it, then abandoned it. It had too many flow diagrams with dozens of little circles and lines that gave him a headache. Sara loved them, but then she was better than him at holding twenty different things in her mind at once. It was, she had informed him airily, a female thing.

However, the first exercise in the training scheme had been binary lists, and Toreth had rather liked them. You knew where you were with a list—for one thing, all you had to do was look at the title at the top of the page.

He started one for Problems and Solutions. That lasted for ten minutes, until he reached the bottom of the page with Problems while Solutions was still a heading. He wrote "fuck 'em all and go home" underneath it, screwed up the paper and started again.

Dead Ends and Potential Leads started as badly. After a few minutes of pencil chewing, he unscrewed Problems and Solutions and smoothed it out.

That was the object of the exercise, after all—for every point you thought of, find at least one list where it fell in the positive half.

Nikoletta. A Problem if you wanted decent filing, or were trying to do anything without Karteris finding out. However, she might be moved over to Potential Leads, with some suitable persuasion.

The corridor was empty as he strolled the few meters to her office—everyone was still at lunch, and he wondered if she'd be there. She was, listening to something through headphones and reading from the screen. A white paper bag sat on the desk and she held a half-eaten cake of some kind in one hand. He caught a faint smell of cinnamon.

He waited until she popped the cake into her mouth, then stepped into the office. She looked up at once, lifting off the headphones.

"Doing anything tonight, Nikki?"

She waved her hand towards her mouth, chewed, and swallowed hastily. "No, Para."

"I thought I'd take you up on that offer of a drink. And maybe a meal." He smiled. "In a professionally friendly way, of course. You deserve an evening on expenses, and I could do with a change from the hotel. It's nice enough, but I've eaten there almost every night."

"That's very kind, thank you, Para. I'd love to." She licked her fingers, then offered the bag. "Would you like one? Loukoumades. Like doughnuts."

Far too sweet, but Toreth took one anyway. It was the friendly thing to do, and B-C or Nagra could eat it.

At three thirty he was alone in the office again when someone knocked on the office door.

"Come in," Toreth said.

"I brought you a file," Sara said as she closed the door behind her.

"Which—" Then it registered and he looked up. "What the fuck are *you* doing here?"

Sara's usual gray admin uniform had been replaced by a cream-colored shorts-and-halter-top arrangement that temporarily distracted Toreth from her reply.

"Sorry?" he asked after a moment.

"I said, I thought I'd bring it personally rather than send it, since you were so cagey about getting it in the first place."

"And Tillotson authorized the flight?"

"No, you did. Or at least you left me the code to sort out B-C and Nagra. I'm flying back Sunday night—that was the cheapest way to do it." She smiled brightly, radiating earnest truthfulness. "It was, honestly."

He grinned. "Did you know it's a statistical fact that people who use words like 'honestly' are usually lying?"

"You've mentioned it before. I *am* paying for my own hotel, though, and I booked tomorrow off as holiday." She waved her hand screen. "Now, do you want this file or not?"

"What is it?"

"Karteris's financial records. And either senior para pay is a hell of a lot better over here or there's something very fishy going on. He's spending—"

Toreth held his hand up. "Not in here. Let's go for a drink. I'll get hold of the other two."

They walked half a kilometer away from the I&I building and picked a café at random. Toreth bought three coffees, and a peppermint tea for Nagra, then they picked seats with a clear view of the tables around them.

"Show me what you've got," Toreth said to Sara, adding a suggestive twitch of his eyebrow.

Nagra snorted. Sara shook her head, then expanded her hand screen and set it out between them.

"I sorted everything by amount and location spent," she said. "All the money that goes into Karteris's account is from his pay here. No more, no less. Doesn't look like he gets any pocket money from his wife, unless she's funding his alias. Taki Whateverthehellhe'scalled gambles a heck of a lot, and loses badly. Despite that, he's got savings in six different places, and a third share in a pricey little boat. Doesn't spend as much as you'd think on food or clothes, though. And—get this—nothing spent at all on housing. No registered partner, either."

"He could be staying with a friend," B-C said. "No law against that, at least some of the time."

"Here's the killer," Sara said. "Taki's got a genetic profile, just as you'd expect. But the system doesn't throw up a fault if you query it with *anything*. Feed in any old DNA ID sequence, and it passes. Basically, he's a free-floating alias. As far as I could tell, he was set up about six years ago by someone at Justice in, uh—" She peered at the screen. "Salonika, I think you pronounce it. It was probably for a perfectly legit undercover operation, but they lost track of the alias and never shut it down. The files went dormant for a couple of years, then someone in Athens started using them."

Sara sat back, looking justifiably pleased with herself. "You should introduce Taki to Marcus Toth," she said. "I bet they'd get on well."

Toreth grinned at the reference to his own double. "Probably. So, we can get Taki shut down anytime we want to. Freeze the accounts, set up an inquiry with Justice. Tillotson will like that—we might get a cut of the funds. Sounds like we can find plenty of witnesses if we want to arrest Karteris."

"Maybe," Nagra said. "But I get that close-knit feeling. My bet is we'd need to interrogate. And I hate to say it, but none of this has anything to do with low arrest rates, except that Karteris doesn't need to work his nuts off trying to get a raise."

"So where's the money coming from?" B-C asked. "Bribes from resisters, maybe?"

"Good question." Toreth considered for a moment. "Okay. Taki's boat might be a weak point—Sara, when you get back to I&I, see if the other two partners are real or fictional. And if they're aliases, too, you can fly back out here to tell me." Toreth turned to B-C and Nagra. "And we can start financial checks on the rest of the paras in the section. It'll take time, but I think it's justified now, and it'll look less suspicious if we do the whole section."

On the way back to the office, Sara said, "I thought you could buy me dinner tonight—I know Warrick's showing up tomorrow."

He didn't bother asking how she knew that. "Great, except that I'm already taking Nikoletta out for the evening."

"Oh?" She glanced at him and raised an eyebrow. "Well, don't let me spoil your plans."

"No, that's fine." And the more he considered it, the finer it was. "You can come, too. I'm planning to take Nikoletta off on her own somewhere and try to get a handle on what's going on here. You can do the same with Karteris."

She stopped dead and pointed her folded hand screen accusingly. "Oh, no. You can stop *right* there. I don't screw paras, and I definitely don't screw paras as a favor to you."

"I'm not asking you to fuck him. Just show him a bit of attention. Butter him up. Dig for gossip. No body fluids involved." When she still hesitated, he added, "Dinner's on expenses—it'll be somewhere nice."

Chapter Eleven

❖

They're baiting hooks," Nikoletta explained. "They caught those fish during the day, and they'll be going night fishing—squid, I think. You need the right bait to get the right fish. Traditional fishery is all that's allowed these days. It's all strictly licensed by the Administration, to preserve stocks. They catch enough to supply the best restaurants, and the rest is for private sales, if you can afford it." Maybe Toreth looked surprised at the sudden flow of information, because Nikoletta smiled at him. "My mother's family were fishermen, in the old days before stock management."

The four of them moved off along the quay of the tiny natural harbor. Knowing exactly where his food came from had never appealed to Toreth, but he'd felt obliged to accept Nikoletta's suggestion that they take the public metro out to the Piraeus section of the city. He hadn't expected a double date, either, but Karteris had been surprisingly keen. Still, the strangeness of the situation appealed—him walking with Nikoletta while Sara walked beside Karteris, doing a passable imitation of interest in the man.

As far as Toreth could tell, there was no inch of the convoluted coastline which hadn't been colonized by restaurants and bars. The fishing boats bobbed against the harbor wall, setting off a vague unease possibly related to the smell of dead fish. Soon, Nikoletta turned back away from the water's edge and into a crowded taverna. Nikoletta and Karteris seemed to know the proprietors, and a table was found for them in a corner with, to Toreth's relief, no view of the sea.

"All wild fish," Nikoletta assured them as they sat down, as though it were a point of civic pride. "Nothing farmed."

Toreth was surprised to hear Greek being spoken by the older diners, or at least he assumed that was the language. Nikoletta must have caught his expression, because she smiled.

"This is a traditional place. They don't mean any harm by it."

Toreth exchanged glances with Karteris, who looked equally unconcerned. "I'm not on duty," Toreth said.

At least the menu was in English—Toreth felt happier knowing what he'd ordered. Service was slow, but that suited his plans. He kept up a constant flow of alcohol, refilling Nikoletta's glass as often as he dared. Karteris drank steadily to no obvious effect, and Toreth didn't worry about Sara—she could pace herself.

When the food arrived, Toreth had to admit that the fish was spectacularly good, the salad and other accompaniments simple but equally delicious. Fresh ingredients, which was exactly what Warrick always said was important. The proprietor came over and Toreth complimented the food enthusiastically, which seemed to please Nikoletta.

Toreth had to admit that it wasn't a bad evening. Karteris had a wide stock of work anecdotes, primarily about George and Vassilakis, which did nothing to raise Toreth's respect for them. Nikoletta must have heard them before, but she listened and laughed, and then listened with equal attention as Toreth responded with stories about Tillotson and other idiots at New London I&I.

The only irritation was Karteris's proprietorial air towards both women, which made Toreth grit his teeth. He didn't give a fuck how Karteris treated Nikoletta, but Sara wasn't *his* admin. It didn't help that Sara was showing every sign of playing the part Toreth had given her rather too well. When Toreth was engaged with Nikoletta, Sara and Karteris's conversation frequently dropped into lowered voices and laughter.

After the other three had rounded the meal off with desserts that seemed to be comprised entirely of nuts and honey—the mere smell of which was enough to make Toreth feel queasy—they left the restaurant.

As they strolled back into town, Toreth said, "It's still early. Would you like to get a coffee somewhere? Or another drink. I don't often feel like it, but...maybe it's the sea air."

On cue, Sara yawned. "I'd love to, but I'm shattered. I'll get the metro back."

A pause, then Karteris said, "I couldn't possibly let you go alone. I'll walk you back. You two stay, if you like."

"If you don't mind," Nikoletta said.

Karteris looked between them, then said, "Why would I? See you tomorrow."

When they had gone, Nikoletta said, "I know a bar—it's quite quiet, at least during the week."

As soon as they walked through the door, Toreth's estimate of his chances of success for the evening jumped sharply. He couldn't have picked a better place himself. Low lights, quiet music, medium busy with a relaxing hum of voices. Nikoletta steered him towards a secluded table.

He left her there and bought drinks at the bar, smiling to himself. Nothing like an air of reluctance or indifference to make a woman try to prove her attractiveness.

For the first hour or so, Toreth gave every appearance of listening with rapt fascination to a detailed if rambling recounting of Nikoletta's life, from her earliest memories. Which, from the time it took her to get through them, felt to start soon after conception. Only one thing was omitted—the blindingly obvious fact that she was fucking Karteris. He had hoped she'd mention it herself.

Even with his extensive skill in attentive not-listening, it made for a tedious evening. He checked his watch surreptitiously, and did his best to encourage her to drink a little faster. Finally, before boredom forced him to make a pass at her, she reached a sufficient level of intoxication to put the next stage of the plan into operation.

As he set a fresh pair of drinks on the table, Toreth forestalled a resumption of the Life and Times of Nikki by laughing quietly. It was sufficiently unprompted that Nikoletta would have to ask.

"What's so funny?" she said as he sat down.

"Nothing."

"Go on, tell me."

"It's just that—Jesus, was I an idiot."

She raised her eyebrows. "What?"

"Well—and you're probably going to throw that drink over me in about thirty seconds—here you are, nice respectable woman, great family, good career, and when you turned up outside the office that first day, I thought you were there to... oh, God." He smiled wryly. "I shouldn't have started this. Too much to drink. Forget I said anything."

"No, it's okay. You're right. I was supposed to be a—a distraction." She drank and put the glass down slightly too hard. "He told me to keep you happy—whatever it took. For the good of the section."

"Karteris told you to do it?"

She nodded, her olive skin flushing darker.

"Fucking—forgive me, but that is way out of order." Brief pause. "On his part, I meant."

She looked uncomfortable—as well she might, Toreth reflected, having just admitted to a man who'd told her he always kept his work relationships professional that she was willing to whore for her boss.

He patted her hand. "No need to look like that. Um, tell me if I'm overstepping the mark, but you and Karteris—is there something going on there?"

After a moment, she said, "Yes. And before you say anything, yes, I know he's married."

"Hey!" Toreth held his hand up. "That's between the two of you. Besides, he mentioned to me that he doesn't see much of her. Are they separated?"

"No. He wants to leave her, but he can't—his wife's family got him the job at I&I. I don't know what it's like in New London, but here you need a sponsor inside the Administration to get on. His wife's family are Administration and corporate. Everyone expects him to end up section head one day. Maybe local division head."

Now *there* was a frightening thought. Although to be fair, the man would be far more effective than the current morons in charge. "And that's why he's staying with her?"

"Yes. It's only until he's promoted. Then he's promised to leave her. Although sometimes I think..."

He nodded somberly. "I understand."

She sniffed. "No, you don't."

"You'd be surprised." Now she looked openly skeptical. "Oh, that sort of thing happens to men, too. Actually, okay, it happened to me. The difference is that men don't talk about it. Too embarrassing—not macho enough."

She smiled and poked his arm gently. "And you're not macho?"

He tried to summon a touch of color to his cheeks. "Hey, I&I's a male culture, you know that. Virtually all of the interrogators are men, most of the paras, more than half of the investigators. If you don't play the game, you don't get any respect and you don't get on." Pause to convey a touch of anxiety. He'd said too much. "Look—ah, hell. You won't say anything about this to anyone else, will you?"

"Of *course* not." After a moment she said, "Tell me about her?"

So she expected it to be a woman. "Well..." He finished his drink and, automatically, her attention fixed on him, she did the same.

"Let me get you another one," Toreth said, standing up before she could protest.

He took his time at the bar, running over his story a couple of times to ensure a basic level of continuity. With what he had in mind, it shouldn't be too difficult.

Back at the table he made a show of getting ready to tell all, under her sympathetic gaze.

"Her name was Dilly. Actually, I knew her brother first. Met him through a case, but we ended up good friends. Then I saw him with her, at the theater."

He paused, letting that collection of facts sink in. See, I go to the theater. Cultured as well as sensitive.

"And?" Nikoletta prompted.

"God, she was gorgeous. Dark eyes you could drown in. Blue dress, all the way down to the floor. I fell for her right then and there. But—" He sighed. "She had a boyfriend. Which she told me right up front." Sensitive, cultured, and fair.

"She said she wasn't interested?"

"Yes. Or rather—no, she didn't. She was interested, or at least bored. Her boyfriend was a structural engineer. Project management. He spent a lot of time off world. When I met her that first time, he'd left for Mars a week earlier. After she told me that, I offered to take her out for dinner. I could lie and tell you I didn't have any dishonorable intentions, but..." He grinned, and Nikoletta laughed. "Actually, I didn't have much except dishonorable intentions. And Dilly didn't exactly fight me off."

Good time for a pause, staring into his drink, rattling the ice. Clearly, the painful part was coming up now. As he expected, her voice softened. "What happened?"

"He was away for a year, and we had a lot of fun. I thought at the time there might be more to it, but—" He shrugged. "I kidded myself for months that the only reason she didn't tell the boyfriend that it was over was because she didn't want to hurt him when he was so far away. And then he came back."

She watched him intently, caught up in the story. "She didn't really want to leave him?"

"Not for a minute. Her family were old corporate money—they'd never have approved of her marrying me. It was never in the cards, not outside of my imagination. I was just something to pass the time. That's what she said to me in the end." He looked across the bar. "'There was never anything more between us than the physical,'" he said quietly, as if quoting.

"What an awful thing for her to do to you." Her voice had hardened. "If it'd been me, I'd have...well, I've have done something."

It *is* you, you stupid bitch.

"I nearly did." He looked down at the table, took a mouthful of his drink. Building himself up to the confession. "God. I went round to her flat, when I knew he was there. I was going to tell him everything—what she'd been doing for that year she'd been calling him on Mars twice a week. I got all the way to the front door, rang the comm, but when he opened it, I bottled out. I said I'd got the wrong flat."

She put her hand on his, squeezing for emphasis. "Maybe it was for the best."

"Maybe." Pause, look away, look back. "But, well, sometimes I really wish I'd had the guts to do it. D'you think it's wrong of me, to think that?"

"No, no. I understand." That had a pleasingly thoughtful ring to it. Silence before Nikoletta shook herself slightly and asked, "So what happened?"

He deliberately misunderstood the question. "I went out, got drunk, and woke up in the street the next morning."

She laughed a little. "No, with her."

"They married a few months after he came back. They've got kids now. He's a junior partner in her family's corporation. I still see her brother, he tells me how she's doing." He looked down into his drink, softening his voice. "She needed the kind of life I couldn't have given her."

He wondered if he was overdoing the sugar, but when he looked up again, Nikoletta's eyes were shining. "I think she was an idiot to let you go." Pause. "Has there been anyone else since?"

The touch of eagerness in the question sounded promising, at least from the point of view of getting her into bed.

"Well, I mean there have been women, but no one else...no one else like her." Poor damaged me, waiting for the love of a good woman to heal my broken heart. "I mean, when someone means that much to you, you can't cut it off. You can't stop loving someone just because..."

Her hand tightened. "You'll find someone, I know you will."

God, this was too easy, and the urge to move in for the kill, to take her back to the hotel, was becoming unbearable. With this amount of sympathy created, she'd be willing to do more or less anything—certainly any number of things she'd thoroughly regret in the morning. He was losing sight of his objectives, though, distracted down the well-trodden path of seduction.

She was looking at him, obviously expecting a response.

"Maybe. I suppose—" He sighed. "I suppose that, in the end, I loved her a lot more than she loved me. I believed what I wanted to believe."

She nodded. No light bulb over her head, though.

"Actually, I was just thinking that you're right." Make it her idea, disguising the non sequitur. "If you love someone—if you *really* love someone—then you do whatever it takes to make them happy. It shouldn't matter if you have to give things up. You do it."

Exactly like fucking Karteris doesn't. Can't you take a hint?

For a moment, he thought the point had missed her again, but then she frowned. "Yes. If you really loved someone you wouldn't worry about what your family thought, would you? I mean, you *loved* her."

He looked down into his drink, freeing her to talk without the pressure of his eyes on her. "God, yes, I did."

"And she just used you."

"Well..." Pause, a touch of reluctance to place any blame on the love of his life. "I knew from the beginning what I was getting into. Maybe I just wanted it too much. Read things into it—into us—that weren't there. I wouldn't want to say that she lied to me, as such. Things—" He gestured helplessly. "Things get said in the heat of the moment."

"Rubbish." Getting angry on his behalf. Good. "I bet she knew exactly what she was doing."

Another sip of his drink, then Toreth decided to layer it on thick. He slid down in the chair a little. "I suppose the bottom line is that if she did use me, it's because I let her. That's the way the world works. People abuse you if you let them. You give them what they want, open your heart, and they despise you for it."

Long silence. Longer than he would have liked, but he let it develop. Play the fish carefully enough and you'll land it in the end.

"Toreth?"

"Yeah?"

"What do you think of Karteris?"

Now there was a loaded question. "I think he doesn't appreciate his admin enough."

She smiled. "Thanks. But I mean...would you be surprised if someone said he wasn't completely honest?"

And another one. "Well, maybe not. Someone suggested that he might be spending more than he ought to be."

Silence, before she asked, "Who says?"

"I'm sorry, Nikki, but I really can't tell you that." But someone else has already shopped him, so it won't matter if you kick him while he's down.

She nodded slowly, chewing her bottom lip. Lipstick had smudged onto her top teeth and Toreth fought down the impulse to make it into an excuse to touch her mouth. Finally she said, "He's doing something at work."

Toreth held his hand up. "If you tell me about something specific, I'll have to do something about it. I'm here to look into the section."

"Good. I want to you do something. I'm sick of him treating me like a—like I'll do anything he wants and be grateful for the chance to kiss his shoes. I don't want you to have him sacked, or anything like that. Just..."

"Give him a hard time over it?"

She smiled, grateful. "Yes." She folded her hands on the table and took a deep breath. "Right. He's stealing drugs."

Not as good as he'd hoped for. He frowned. "Well, a lot of people do that, Nikki."

"No, he's stealing a lot. I know because I've seen him faking the drug returns. He sells them on."

"That's it?"

"Yes," she said, unhesitating. "Isn't that enough?"

He could hardly say no, since if she knew nothing else it would deprive him of the one piece of usable leverage he'd found over Karteris so far. "It's enough to scare him with, certainly." He needed to get her to do it now, before the cold and sober light of day brought her to her senses. "Listen, why don't you think about this? Sleep on it. Let me know in the morning if you're sure you want to, and then I'll see about finding some evidence."

"I *am* sure, and I've got all the evidence you'll need. I can give you the real drug returns. And I know the names of the dealers, too. They call him at home sometimes when—" She stopped abruptly.

When you're fucking him there, while his rich, classy wife is somewhere else.

She stood up, finishing her drink. "Come on. I want to do it now. Before I see him again."

"Okay." He stood, too. "If you're sure, Nikki."

Nikoletta's coffee was better than her filing, and Toreth sobered up with the thick sludge that passed for coffee around here while he read through the files.

The evidence was indeed comprehensive. So much so that Toreth wondered whether something like this had been in Nikoletta's mind for a while. There was no other reason why she should keep it all so neatly and conveniently at her own flat.

Karteris operated a simple enough system, variations of which went on all over the Administration. An interrogator signed out drugs, recorded them as being given to prisoners or discarded into the recycling systems, but then kept them for personal use or sold them. Toreth had done it himself from time to time, although he usually bought his supplies from Daedra Kincaidy in the pharmacy because he was too lazy to fake his own paperwork.

Scale made a difference, though. As far as Toreth was concerned, petty pilfering of drugs was no different from stealing office supplies or using his free pass every time he took a taxi. It was expected, a perk of the job. Karteris had been a little more ambitious. He must be turning a healthy profit, if not a skillful one. Unforgivably, the numbers didn't even add up. Paras ought to make competent thieves. This was frankly embarrassing.

The scam was not, however, enough to do much more than discomfit Karteris. And it would do Toreth's reputation no good at all to hand someone like Karteris over to Internal Investigations or, worse, Justice. A prime way to lose friends and credibility in I&I.

"Is that enough?" Sitting on a low couch opposite him, Nikoletta still sounded eager to see Karteris punished, which would make an exit with the evidence easier.

"Oh, I think I'll certainly be able to worry him with it." Toreth tucked his hand screen away. "Thanks for the coffee. Remember, don't say anything to Karteris about this—I'll make sure he doesn't know it was you who told me."

Even if she changed her mind about the betrayal in the morning, there would be no way for her to explain to Karteris what she'd done.

"You're going?" she asked.

Toreth crossed the room, bent down, placed his hands on her shoulders and kissed her cheek chastely. The urge to laugh rose up, almost overwhelming and far stronger than the temptation to stay and fuck her. "Yes. If I stayed, we'd both regret it in the morning."

Coming back to Karteris's flat had been a huge mistake, Sara decided. She'd overdone the flirting and then spun the so-far fruitless conversation out for as long as she could manage. Now she had the choice of either backing out in a way that would have to make Karteris suspicious or screwing the man, the idea of which made her feel rather ill. He reminded her too much of Toreth, except without his redeeming qualities.

Hell, maybe Karteris had the same redeeming qualities—if very deeply hidden—and this was simply how Toreth appeared to most people. That idea didn't make the prospect of getting intimate any more appealing.

At least the sitting room of his flat was nothing like Toreth's, except in size. The tiny room was clean, tidy, and very well decorated, if a touch too masculine for her taste—very obviously a bachelor place, however married he was. Presumably his wife lived elsewhere.

The furniture was new, and the place was in a good neighborhood, too, if her sense of social status hadn't been thrown off by the different city. It wasn't outrageously plush, but it fitted in with the suggestion of inexplicable funds. Or maybe this was all paid for by his wife. Was there a tactful way of asking?

Karteris returned from the kitchen with a chilled bottle and two glasses. Real crystal.

Then the door comm chimed. Sara thanked God silently while Karteris went to answer it. He returned at once. "It's my wife!"

Wonderful. Now the evening was turning into a cheap farce.

"What the hell do you expect me to do about it?" Sara snapped.

"Go out through the bedroom," Karteris said, with a speed that suggested practice. "The window opens onto a courtyard—the door opposite leads to the street."

On the way out of the room, Sara noticed the bottle and glasses. His problem, she decided as he hustled her through the bedroom door and shoved it closed behind her, catching her heel.

The window wouldn't open. Of course, Sara thought as she struggled with the catch. Noises came from the room behind her—closing doors and indistinct voices—and for a moment she was tempted to give up and stroll back and out through the front door. Serve the adulterous bastard right.

Finally, the window opened, but as she got a knee on the window ledge, the door handle rattled. Dive out or hide? The drop looked risky, so she ducked into a nearby wardrobe.

She was about to call out quietly to say she was still here, when she realized she had no idea who was out there. Walking out head high was one thing, being caught skulking in a cupboard would be humiliating. She listened to the footsteps cross the room, loud over wood, soft over carpet, loud over wood right outside. Then the window closed and the latch clicked shut again. Could things get any worse?

Loud, soft—and the footsteps stopped. "She's gone," Karteris said.

"Did you get anything from her?"

Surprise almost gave Sara away and she clamped a hand over her mouth to stop the squeak. *Nikoletta*?

"Nothing," Karteris answered, the question apparently causing him no surprise. "I don't think he tells her anything. How about you? Did you have to...?"

"No." Soft giggle. "Why? Jealous?"

"Of course. Weren't you?"

"Of that skinny, flat-chested Asian girl? Hardly."

Sara fumed.

A scuff of movement, then Nikoletta said, "Stop that, please. We need to talk."

"No. Come on. There's plenty of time later for that. Come *on.*" His voice was muffled now, with a note of pleading that made him sound suddenly younger. "It's been too long. I bought champagne—a good vintage, not the cheap rubbish next door." A sigh. "God, I want you so badly. Feel it."

A pause, during which Sara prayed they weren't doing what she thought they were doing. The mention of champagne had given her hope that they might leave. Then the unmistakable sound of bodies on a mattress made her press her hand to her forehead and groan silently.

When she saw Toreth in the morning, she was going to kill him. Or at the very least maim him. Emasculation sounded like a suitable punishment.

It went on for a long time. Hours, it felt like, although it was too dark in the wardrobe for Sara to check her watch. A wooden rail poked into her back, forcing her to lean uncomfortably to the left. As the volume from the bed rose, she risked moving. An ominous creak of wood stopped her, but at least she no longer felt as though her spine would snap.

Whatever washing liquid Karteris used stank of fake scent, of a variety that would probably be called "woodland fresh." Even though she held the clothes back away from her face, Sara's nose itched maddeningly. She pinched the bridge until her eyes watered, suppressing the sneezes. To complete the discomfort, that meant she had no hands free to put over her ears. Not that it would have done much good, as Karteris was loud and effusively complimentary.

God, this was almost worse than having to screw the man herself. Or maybe not. The idea of listening to it from a few centimeters away, rather than meters, made her feel queasy again. What time was it? Didn't these people need to get up for work in the morning?

She tried to concentrate on Nikoletta, but that barely improved the situation. For one thing, the woman was so *false.* Sara hadn't heard so much theatrical groaning and moaning since the last time someone had trapped Chevril into buying a round of drinks. She felt like opening the wardrobe door and yelling, can't you tell she's faking it? No, was the obvious answer, as Karteris finally came, with fervent protestations of eternal love.

Sara didn't know which of the three of them was probably most relieved.

Maybe they'd fall asleep. Maybe they'd go for a shower, or a drink, or *something,* and she could get out of here.

"Wake up," Nikoletta whispered.

Karteris mumbled something too low to hear.

"This is important, love. Are you listening? I've got some news you won't like, so please, just listen and don't be mad. I told Toreth that you've been dealing drugs from the pharmacy."

Moment of absolute silence, then a sudden creak. "You did *what?*" Karteris yelled.

"*Please* don't be angry. I didn't have any choice. They've been checking up on you, and someone told Toreth that you've been spending too much money. I had to come up with something."

"Why in God's name didn't you tell him it was from Stephi?"

"Because that would be too easy to check. Do you really think Stephanie would lie to protect you?"

"Nikki...oh, Christ. What the hell is he going to do?"

"Probably nothing. If I&I came down hard on everyone who stole a few drugs, they'd have to put half the paras and interrogators on suspension. George or Vassilakis will make sure he keeps it quiet."

The bed creaked again, and then footsteps sounded. Bare feet, this time, as Karteris paced.

"He's so bloody abstemious. What if he sends it straight to Justice, did you think of that? Justice wouldn't care what Vassilakis thinks. God, sometimes you are so *stupid.*"

"Please, love. I'm sorry."

"Listen, you silly bitch, do you have any conception of what happens to paras in prison?"

"You'd get a light sentence even if it came to that, which it *won't.*"

"It would only have to *be* a light fucking sentence, because I wouldn't live long enough to serve it. Even if I don't meet someone I interrogated myself, there'll be plenty of people in there with reasons to hate paras. If I'm lucky I'll last long enough to be gang-raped in the showers a few times before someone shoves a broken bottle up my arse or down my throat."

"Don't be crude."

"I will be killed if I go to prison," he said slowly and deliberately. "I'm not going to rely on Vassilakis to save my neck. Besides, even if it was just a charge, Stephi would divorce me and my career would go down the recycling."

Silence. Then the bed creaked again, and Nikoletta spoke in a low voice, in the same language Sara had heard in the restaurant.

"Speak fucking English," Karteris snapped.

"Okay. Listen, love—I'm sorry I didn't think of everything, but the important thing is that he thinks he knows where the extra money came from."

"I won't—"

"Shh." Voice lower still, and muffled. Sara imagined the devious bitch wrapped around Karteris, breaking down his resistance with her probably surgically enhanced tits. "Toreth isn't an idiot, and I bet he isn't half as pure and innocent as he makes out. *No one* got to be a senior by being *that* much of a goody two-shoes. Handing you over to Justice would be like...like career suicide."

"Nikki..." Weakening protest.

"He'll be here for a few more days, then he'll go away and everything will be back to normal. Didn't you tell the others that everything would be okay if people kept their nerve? You were right—you always are. You were right about Grant."

"Yes, but only because she died."

A pause, then Nikoletta said, "I mean, of course I know that we can't expect a lucky coincidence like that to solve *this* problem, but the point is that it worked out for the best, didn't it? You told everyone they didn't need to do anything and they didn't."

"Yes." Karteris sighed. "Yes, okay, you're right."

Sara was forced to listen to another round of noisy, wet kissing, then Nikki said, "Why don't we go and find that champagne?"

Chapter Twelve

❖

Early Friday morning, over a hotel breakfast, Sara spent half an hour listening to Toreth's account of the evening before, suppressing giggles with ever-increasing difficulty. When he reached the revelation about Karteris's drug-dealing, Sara summoned her best admin poker face and said, "I know."

Toreth stopped dead, a bread roll half torn in his hands. "You what? Karteris told you?"

"In a way. Actually, I overheard him discussing it with Nikoletta. When she turned up at his flat to let him know that you'd swallowed her act like one of those hooks. Right bait for the right fish."

At his expression of utter amazement, a warm flower of satisfaction began uncurling, petal by petal. Some compensation for the stifling time in the wardrobe—her sinuses still stung.

"The drug story was a cover to explain why he's been throwing money away," Sara said, when her first revelation had had a good long while to sink in. "He's up to something completely different. She must've thought last night was a godsend."

"But—" Toreth dropped the bread. "But she had the fucking evidence ready! And she must know I'll cross-check it with the pharmacy records."

"Then he's dealing *and* doing something else."

"So Karteris put her up to it?"

She couldn't remember him being so comprehensively wrong for a long time. "Nope. It was all her idea to tell you. Protecting her man, who wasn't very happy about it."

Silence. "Admins," Toreth said finally. "You're a devious fucking breed, aren't you? Remind me to keep an eye on you in future. Did you find out where the money's really coming from?"

"No, but she mentioned that some of the others were involved, too."

"Ah, fuck." Toreth sighed. "I suppose I'll have to do something about it, won't I?"

"You don't *have* to."

"And if it comes out later? I'll look like an idiot if it's something big and I miss it."

"Well..." God, if he insisted on pursuing this hard, there went her relaxing weekend. "You're here to look at efficiency, not corruption. If the whole section's involved in some scam, it won't be anything to do with conspiring with resisters, will it? How many paras have gone bad? Ever."

He thought it over. "Hardly any. And never a whole section."

"Right. It's far more likely to be gambling or contraband from outside the Administration—something like that. They're just worried about whatever you might find out on the side while you're working out why they can't close cases."

He nodded, still looking pensive. "I'll get Nagra and B-C to keep their ears to the ground over the weekend. I'd be a fuck sight happier if I knew what was going on, though. Pity you didn't overhear that, too." He focused on her. "Come to think of it, how the hell *did* you hear all this?"

"From the wardrobe in Karteris's bedroom. He thought I'd gone out of the window."

"What was it like?"

"Cramped. Noisy."

He grinned, then his expression turned thoughtful. "Were they speaking Greek?"

"A bit. When they were arguing about the drugs, she said something in Greek and he told her to use English."

"How about when they were fucking?"

He waited patiently while she thought it over, giving her all the time she wanted. "They might've been," she said finally. "Or she might've, anyway. A few words. I was trying not to listen too hard."

"Interesting."

"If you like women trying to win awards for bad acting."

"No, interesting that she'd know it. That he'd be angry with her for using it. There were a lot of people speaking Greek in that restaurant."

She hadn't looked at it like that. "That doesn't really mean anything, though, does it?"

"Well, you couldn't get a waiver on the strength of it, no. But it's an idea. Karteris runs the section, for all practical purposes. If there's any one person who could cut arrest rates to favor resisters, it's him."

"But... Karteris?" She tried to think of a tactful way of phrasing it. "I mean, he's a para. I can't imagine him being a resister any more than I could you."

He looked at her sharply. "Reminds you of me, does he?"

"I hadn't really thought about it." He was watching her with the penetrating, assessing gaze that won him so many confessions. It compelled some kind of reply. "I only met him the one evening. I mean... a bit, I suppose."

"A bit. You suppose. Hm." He picked the bread up again and started buttering it. "Get some fresh coffee, would you?"

Chapter Thirteen

Toreth had already unpacked, dumping his clothes into a drawer and throwing his toilet bag into the bathroom, which had taken him a total of forty-five seconds. Warrick, of course, was dragging his own unpacking out to ridiculous lengths.

Standing in the sunlit bedroom of the expensive villa, watching Warrick unfolding and refolding clothes, Toreth wondered again why he hadn't ended the surveillance. He'd called the agency, meaning to do it. He had told them that Warrick would be out of New London for the weekend, and not to bother trying to keep tabs on him for that time. Somehow, however, when Uche had asked whether he wanted the surveillance to resume on Monday, he'd said yes.

Why? It was stupid, really. He'd trusted Warrick with Marian, with his career—with his life, for fuck's sake. Not over this, though. Not over Carnac. Carnac was too fucking slippery.

As Toreth had half expected, Warrick hadn't brought any gear—no doubt he'd been too worried about security searching his case at one of the airports. Not that they needed gear to have fun. However, Toreth did catch sight of a package wrapped in gold paper nestled in the bottom layer of Warrick's case. Too small to be anything more than a gag, or narrow cuffs, or maybe a cock ring, but still promising.

"What's that?" Toreth asked.

"A present," Warrick said blandly as he set it on the bedside table.

"What kind of present?"

"A secret, for now." He smiled as he turned away—anticipatory, probably pleased that Toreth had asked. "But I think you'll like it."

"From the Shop?"

"That would be telling."

Unpacking done, Warrick led the way back into the main room. The villa had only a handful of rooms, but they were huge and beautifully furnished—spotless white walls, well-cushioned sofas, thick rugs, polished wooden floors to match the wooden beams. Of more immediate interest was an extensive collection of bottles on the sideboard.

He poured drinks while Warrick disappeared through another door. Then Toreth strolled over to sit on one of the deep window ledges and looked around the living room. It was larger than some flats he'd been in—hell, the screen on the entertainment center was practically larger than his own place.

Generous, expensive, tasteful, and so exactly Warrick's idea of a perfect weekend. However, something nagged at Toreth. It took him a minute to pin it down—the silence.

Or rather, not silence, but an absence of familiar noises. The boat trip out to the small island had taken less than an hour, but there was no trace of the sounds of the city. The sea hissed on the beach below the villa, and something insectile chirped in the fragrant bushes, but that was all natural. Gulls calling, wind in the leaves of the olive trees—it made him feel oddly exposed. When the hum of a boat engine rose in the distance, it was almost a relief.

He was listening to it fade away when Warrick reappeared through a doorway to his left.

"What do you think?" Warrick asked.

"Middle of fucking nowhere. No bars, nowhere to eat."

"Rubbish. Call a boat, we could be back in the city before it got dark. And there's all mod cons here, plenty of food and a beautiful kitchen. And—" he paused and smiled, "—no one around to hear anything."

Toreth snorted. "Doesn't usually bother you."

"Oh, it bothers me." Another pause, another smile. "I just can't help it, that's all. Come and look at this."

Rather to Toreth's surprise, Warrick didn't want to show off the kitchen but instead took him through to a courtyard at the back of the villa. Tall white walls screened it on three sides—from whose eyes Toreth couldn't imagine—and a woven roof provided a shaded area for a table and chairs. The fourth side was open to an olive grove, with glimpses of the sea beyond. Sunk in the center of the courtyard floor was a deep tub, sunlight making prisms of the fine droplets above the bubbling surface.

Maybe this wasn't such a bad place after all.

"Want to try it?" Without waiting for an answer, Warrick began to strip.

"Sure. Want a drink?"

"Mm. Please."

By the time he returned, Warrick was already in the water up to his neck, eyes closed, head back against a folded towel, and looking both blissful and eminently fuckable.

After setting the glasses on the rim, Toreth undressed and slipped in. A seat ran around the side of the tub and he settled onto it opposite Warrick, wriggling until he found some suitably entertaining bubbles. He reached out with his foot, stroking up Warrick's thigh, nudging his cock gently. Not uninterested, despite the warm water.

Not surprising, as it was eleven days since they'd done anything. Five days since Toreth had done anything with anyone at all. The memory flowed back of the night with Paul, the disconcerting walls of his flat muted in the shivering light of a startling number of candles. Champagne, and expensive smells in complex layers. Soap, shampoo, conditioner, moisturizer, a spicy scent, and underneath it all the warming musk of male skin. Lying on the bed, enjoying the smooth slide of fingers inside him and listening to Paul's unexpectedly filthy pillow talk.

Uncomplicated fun. He could have a whole weekend's worth of that here, if he could just forget Carnac.

Toreth relaxed into the embrace of the water, letting the swirling bubbles carry away the tension, the doubts.

"Well?" Warrick asked after a while, eyes still closed. "What do you think?"

"I think... I'd like you to fuck me."

"Mm. I could probably manage that."

Toreth was about to suggest they change venues to the bed when Warrick sat up and said, "Wait there."

Dripping water, Warrick climbed out and disappeared—into the bedroom by the sound of his wet, bare feet on the boards. He returned after a minute with a tube.

"Warrick, that won't—"

"Oh, yes it will." He splashed back into the water and flourished the tube. "Guaranteed waterproof lubricant."

"You're joking."

"Not at all. I read the brochure, and I thought we ought to be prepared."

Toreth slid off the seat, keeping low in the water, and moved towards him. "Fucking Boy Scout."

Warrick laughed, reached forwards, and ducked him.

If he'd been expecting it he wouldn't have panicked. He flailed out and his fist connected hard with something before he broke up from under the surface, gasping for air. He lost his footing, slipped, and disappeared under again, the rush of water in his mouth sweeping away the last shreds of control.

That was the last thing he remembered until he heard Warrick's voice, urgent and insistent. "Toreth? Toreth—listen to me. You're fine."

Where the hell was he?

He opened his eyes to find himself half out of the tub, the floor a few inches away from his nose, and his knuckles white as he gripped the rush mat. Bubbles still swirled around the lower half of his body and he heaved himself out. He struggled up onto to his hands and knees and stayed there, coughing up the last of the water. Its chemical tang mixed in his mouth with the bitterness of stomach acid.

Warrick crouched beside him, hand outstretched but not touching him. "Are you all right?"

Humiliation set his cheeks burning.

"Shut the fuck up." He staggered to his feet. "Don't say a fucking thing." He grabbed for a towel, missed, and stumbled out of the courtyard anyway, just wanting to get away from the water. He made it as far as the living room before his legs started shaking and he collapsed onto the sofa, still coughing.

Well done, he thought bitterly. Good start to the weekend. Very fucking sexy.

A robe landed on the sofa beside him and he managed to stand up for long enough to pull it on. By the time Warrick returned with a full glass, he had the shivering under some kind of control. Warrick handed over the drink and turned to go.

"Wait," Toreth said. "It's okay. Sit down."

As Warrick sat, Toreth looked at him properly for the first time and saw the scrape on his cheekbone with the bruise starting to swell up. His own knuckles were beginning to hurt, some indication of how hard he'd hit him.

"Jesus, I'm sorry," Toreth said.

"Don't worry about it." Warrick touched his cheek gingerly. "Makes me appreciate how restrained you are the rest of the time."

"The rest of the time is the game. That was... I wasn't thinking."

"I noticed," Warrick said dryly.

Silence. Warrick didn't ask, of course. He simply sat there, his expression guarded but his entire body radiating patience and concern. It was, for some reason, infuriating.

Toreth took a deep breath, trying to stifle the anger. He had to say something, so he should make it as quick and matter-of-fact as possible. "Remember when you tried to show me how to do underwater breathing in the sim?"

Warrick frowned. "I... yes. You wouldn't do it."

"Yeah." Toreth looked away. "Reason being, back when I was a trainee, the instructors had a little initiation ceremony for the new recruits." He swallowed down the sickness. "Ducking them in a bath. Cuffed. I wasn't very good with water—I never have been, since I was a kid. Anyway, the stupid bastards managed to drown me. No heartbeat, emergency resus, the full works. And now I'm *really* not good with water."

There was a brief pause. "But you go swimming," Warrick said.

"Yes, I do. I like it." But sometimes when I dive in, just for a moment... "It's not really water itself that's the problem. It's the idea of—" He swallowed again. "Of drowning. The actual process of... as long as I'm in control, it's fine. But what happened just now, or being underwater in the sim, or looking at drowned bodies. Or—fuck, I saw them doing it at Justice once."

He looked down, watching the ice starting to shiver in his glass. Perversely, he couldn't resist the urge to push the limits of the fear. "Totally fucking illegal, of course—no waiver, not that I reported it. Took three of them to hold him, with someone else counting seconds while they had him under. Up just long enough for a breath before—" Whiskey and water slopped over the rim, and Warrick removed the glass from his hand.

Toreth licked his fingers slowly. The spirit tasted thin, overwhelmed by the memory of cold, chlorinated water, fresh from the tap. If he concentrated, he could hear the laughter of the interrogation instructors as they demonstrated the effectiveness of their restraint techniques. He'd fought them, and it hadn't made the slightest fucking difference except to how quickly he'd lost the battle not to breathe, not to—

"This is what the nightmares were about?" Warrick asked.

"What?" Startled out of the grim fantasy, Toreth blinked at him.

"Gil Kemp?"

"Oh. Yes. That fucking river. River and the cuffs. Fuck, yes. The bastard couldn't have picked it better if he'd known. I should probably sleep in here tonight."

"Don't be ridiculous," Warrick said firmly. "I didn't arrange a secluded weekend so that you could sleep on the sofa."

"I won't sleep, and I'll only keep you awake." And I'd rather be pathetic on my own, thanks very much.

"You'll sleep if you're tired enough."

It took him a moment to realize what Warrick meant. "No. I'm not in the mood."

Warrick smiled slightly. "You're not in the mood *yet.* Wait here."

He stood up and left, heading for the bedroom. If he'd had anywhere to go, Toreth would have gone, too. Staring through the window he could see nothing except blue sea and sky and a single wisp of cloud, white as bleached bone. Miles and miles of fucking water and the realization brought back the nausea.

Odd that he hadn't thought about it on the trip over. Well, he was thinking about it now. Much too far to swim if anything had happened to the boat halfway across. Starting to head for the shore, watching it stay stubbornly far away, until the cramps started, pulling him down...

He turned away from the window, killing the thought deliberately.

Trapped, he had no choice but to wait until Warrick returned, carrying the gold-wrapped box. His cheek was coming up beautifully. Dillian would have a field day if she saw that, and God only knew what Carnac would think.

Warrick closed the shutters, sinking the room into twilight.

"Here you are." Warrick sat beside him and offered the box. "Go on."

With a sigh, Toreth took it and opened it—a data stick. "What is it?"

"A recording. Put it on and find out."

The screen stayed black at first. Toreth settled back on the sofa, and Warrick edged along, closer but not touching.

"What is it?" Toreth asked again.

"Wait."

Slowly, the darkness faded—not disappearing, but seeming to shift into the background and edges. There were suggestions of walls and floor, everything shadowy and indistinct, except for the man in the center of the screen. Warrick, dressed in a loose, dark shirt and trousers, his feet bare.

And then Toreth knew exactly what it was.

On the screen, Warrick stripped slowly, not making the amateur's usual mistake of looking at the camera. Of course, with the sim there was no camera to tempt him.

"That is the sim, isn't it?" Toreth asked as Warrick's shirt came off.

Warrick paused the recording and nodded, a little rueful. "That obvious, is it?"

"Well, how old's the body?"

"Thirty... no, all right. Twenty-seven."

A touch of smug satisfaction lightened Toreth's mood. "You know, I've got the same waist size I had when I was twenty-seven."

"It's from the first truly high-res bioscanning system we bought. I was the guinea pig—I remember lying in it for the test scans while Lew calibrated the system. Motionless for four hours, just for the first pass." Warrick contemplated the screen, tapping the remote against his unbruised cheek. "I had to process the file quite extensively to pull it up to the current standards, but it wasn't as bad technically as I thought it might be. The low lighting helps—I don't know how it would look in a high-illumination setting."

Toreth couldn't help smiling. "Very fucking seductive."

Warrick blinked, then grinned. "Sorry, no, it isn't really, is it? Not unless you're turned on by real-time spline reticulation."

"And are you?" Toreth reached out and found the back of Warrick's neck, massaging gently, then tightening his grip.

"Mmh." Warrick's head went back and he sighed. "Sometimes. If they're topologically interesting splines."

"Put it back on." Toreth released him. "And come over here."

Warrick obeyed both commands, moving up to sit against Toreth, shoulder to shoulder, thigh to thigh, as the figure on the screen came back to life, dropping his shirt and then slipping off his trousers.

Now he was clad the only in the briefest of black silk briefs, which for the moment remained in place. Warrick lifted his head slightly, half smile curving his mouth, and started to touch himself through the thin silk.

Toreth surprised himself with a gasp—he'd been unconsciously holding his breath in anticipation. Not wanting to look away and miss a second of it, he groped left, sliding his hand up Warrick's thigh. Warrick's hand came down on top of his, holding him still.

Watch, was the clear message.

Okay, fair enough—it was Warrick's present.

There was, however, a problem. Either it was going to be just Warrick, which would be nice but not that novel, since he'd seen Warrick bringing himself off plenty of times, or...or there was going to be someone else. The idea bothered him. It would be better, as porn, but right now it would be unbearable to see Warrick with anyone else.

Maybe he should ask what was going to happen next. Maybe he should just enjoy it and not worry. It wasn't as if Warrick didn't know him and what he liked and didn't like—far too well, indeed.

Well enough to know how to distract him from recent events. How long since he'd thought about the tub? He ought to be going over it, replaying the panic, working himself up to a good long night of bad dreams. Toreth shook his head sharply and concentrated on the screen.

It took him a while to notice the figures. To begin with he thought they were a part of the background, until the forms became solid enough to distinguish from the darkness. They weren't so much people as living shadows, featureless, androgynous, with a peculiar fluid grace. A dozen of them crouched or leaned against dimly visible walls, standing out only when they moved. They stayed back on the fringes, but as Warrick's eyes drifted closed they began to circle closer.

"Are those Yeses?" Toreth asked, whispering without meaning to.

"An unofficial outing, although we're restarting the program at the end of the year. Now, shh."

The restlessly prowling group inched closer. Toreth was torn between wanting to see what they were going to do and wanting Warrick to get on with it. As if he'd heard the thought, the figure on the screen eased the briefs down, exposing the tip of his cock, sighing as he touched bare flesh at last. Toreth was mildly embarrassed to find his mouth was actually watering.

Finally, one shadow, bolder than the rest, came up behind him and slid its arms around Warrick's chest, smoky and semitranslucent, and he seemed to notice them for the first time. Too late, evidently, because as his head turned and his eyes opened, the rest closed around him in a rush. A swirl of darkness, glimpses of pale skin, the view finally clearing to reveal Warrick struggling futilely in their grasp.

Darkness slid from their hands, binding his eyes and mouth, curling around his wrists and ankles to form manacles, around his throat to collar him. Shadowy chains with floating, tattered ends still managed to hold him, legs apart, arms up and out. With their prisoner bound, the figures drew back, leaving him twisting in the chains, breathing harshly past the black gag.

A small, slender shadow knelt in front of him, and Warrick jerked in the chains as it touched him, pulling down the briefs. A few minutes of stroking and he was hard again; a few more and he was twisting in the chains, thrusting forwards. Then Warrick stiffened, his cry muffled by the gag as he came, and a second later a dark blur rippled over his body, seeming to originate from the shadowy hands on him.

He was still hard—sim magic—and the shadow kneeling before him didn't stop its attentions. Four more shadows detached themselves from the silently watching pack and flowed forwards, hands reaching for Warrick. Slowly, with inexorable strength, they pushed him to his knees.

Androgyny seemed to be optional for the whatever-the-hell-they-weres, because the figure behind Warrick was now most definitely male. The rip of silk sounded unexpectedly loud as the shadow tore away the briefs. It knelt behind Warrick and placed its hand on his back with an oddly precise gesture. He stopped struggling at once, staying in place, trembling, as the rest of the figures drew away.

Warrick hissed, his back arching, as the shadow thrust into him hard. Protest or pleasure, Toreth couldn't tell. Probably pleasure to some degree, because he was still hard. The first shadow returned, lying on its side in front of him and swallowing his cock easily. The shadow behind him shifted, leaning in, fucking him harder, and Warrick bucked in the chains, moaning through the gag.

It took another few minutes before Toreth noticed that Warrick's body was becoming translucent—at first, he thought he was imagining it, but then Warrick shuddered, coming again, his head lifting. The darkness rippled over him once more, and when it was gone, Toreth could see the faint outline of the cock still thrusting deep inside him. The gag, too, was visible through his cheek, a thick tongue of black holding his jaws apart.

One of the shadows moved forwards and took hold of Warrick's head. Toreth barely noticed that its foot slid into the body of the shadow on the floor as it came closer still.

"Jesus fucking Christ." It took Toreth a moment to realize that he was the one who'd spoken. Warrick shifted on the sofa beside him, but didn't say anything.

The gag stayed in place—the shadow simply thrust through it into Warrick's mouth, the shape of its cock dimly visible as Warrick's throat spasmed. Acting, Toreth thought vaguely, because Warrick never choked in the sim. Not even underwater, when—

Easy to dismiss the thought, to focus his mind on the picture in front of him. God, he was hard—almost reaching the point of discomfort. Toreth shifted on the sofa, pressing down on his cock with the flat of his hand through the toweling robe.

"Want some help with that?" Warrick murmured.

"I wouldn't say no."

Warrick slid off the sofa, moving to kneel between his legs. Even as Toreth opened them wider, inviting, he couldn't help saying, "You'll miss the end."

Warrick smiled, hands sliding slowly towards their goal. "I've seen it before."

"You've seen that before, too—mmh."

Warrick's fingers closed around his cock, and he groaned, sinking back into the deep sofa.

On the screen, Warrick echoed the moan, hands clutching convulsively at the shadow chains as another orgasm shook him.

Fuck, Toreth thought, he must've had fun making this. And then, briefly, what a weird bloody present to give someone.

Coherent thought was becoming difficult, though, as Warrick's head dipped in his lap, breathing out over him, licking, breathing again, hot and cool at once.

"Please." Toreth lifted his hands to push Warrick down, changed his mind, and laced them behind his own neck instead, arching his back against the sofa and lifting his hips. "Please."

Mouth sliding down over his cock, and he was shuddering, too, eyes locked to the screen, enchanted by the combination of the muffled gasps from the recording and the real counterpoint from his lap. Too good to last for long, and no reason to try to delay it.

"Ah, Jesus, *fuck.*" He arched up again, eyelids closing as he came, Warrick's throat squeezing deliciously around him as he swallowed.

Afterwards, Toreth lay back, panting, watching the screen with rather less concentration than before. Warrick shifted around on the floor to rest his back against the sofa.

The scene had changed while his attention was elsewhere. The figures had drawn back, leaving Warrick alone in the center of the screen, as smoky and translucent as any of them. The chains dissolved, removing the last thing that differentiated the shadow that had been Warrick from the rest. Toreth tracked him by eye for a few seconds before he was lost in the restless crowd, and a moment after that the figures dissipated, spreading darkness over the screen.

Warrick rested one hand on Toreth's thigh and picked up the remote with the other, switching off the screen. "Not too arty?" he asked.

"Arty?"

"The present. For porn, I mean." Warrick looked around. "I have a broad understanding of the principles, obviously, but it's not my field and I've never tried to make anything before. I know it's rather short. I'm afraid I became a little caught up with the effects. The shadowing was—"

Just like Warrick to start a fucking inquest. Toreth leaned forwards and shut him up with a kiss. "It was fantastic. Just what I've always wanted. Do I get to keep it?"

"It wouldn't be much of a present if you didn't. I'd rather you didn't show it to anyone else, of course." Warrick raised a finger in warning. "And if I ever happen to flick on the screen and see it commercially available..."

Toreth grinned. "No fucking chance. Like I'd share that." Except with Sara, maybe. She'd love it.

They sat in silence for a few minutes, Warrick leaning against his leg, an enjoyable weight and warmth. In the postorgasm glow, even the silence of the island didn't seem so bad.

Eventually, Warrick levered himself to his feet with a grimace. "Are you hungry? We can eat outside before it gets too cool."

When Toreth followed him into the kitchen, Warrick already had the fridge open and was taking out cartons. Cold air from the fridge made Toreth belt up his robe. Then he stood and watched as Warrick laid out the food—ready-prepared salads and snacks, all delicious-looking.

"I asked them to leave one meal for us," Warrick said. "I'll cook tomorrow. It's possible to have full service with this place—there is a cottage at the back for a couple of staff. However, I thought a little privacy would be pleasant."

So that was who the wall was designed to keep out. Thinking about that brought back the memory of the pool.

"What was the present for?" Toreth asked, hoping to distract himself.

"For?"

"I mean, what occasion?"

"Ah. Nothing in particular. I had intended to give it to you for your birthday, but it took rather less time than I expected to finish it. Then I thought that now would be as good a time as any."

Feeling guilty for something? He squelched the thought.

"Bring the bottle and glasses." Warrick picked up the tray and started for the door to the courtyard. Then he paused. "Or would you rather—"

"I'll be fine," Toreth snapped.

Warrick raised his eyebrows. "Very well."

He wasn't fine. They sat at the table and ate, and the gentle bubbling of the water grated on his nerves like broken glass. He pressed on stubbornly, not tasting the food, barely aware of the conversation. He refused to let this overshadow the weekend. Bad enough that Warrick had seen it happen—no need to compound the embarrassment with a further display of nerves.

By the time they'd finished eating, dusk had fallen. It was only when Toreth looked up that he realized low lights had come up around the courtyard.

"Fancy another dip?" Toreth asked as he pushed his plate away.

"I'm not sure if..." Warrick hesitated, obviously not wanting to mention the earlier incident. "I remember that when we were kids, Jen used to threaten us with the direst consequences for swimming after meals," he finished lightly.

Toreth stood up before he let Warrick talk him out of it. "Well, I'm going in."

The touch of the water on his foot almost caused him to lose his balance and his dinner, but he fought the feeling down and lowered himself into the tub. It had been okay earlier. It would be okay now. He sat on the ledge, trying to relax, his muscles aching with tension.

"Are you all right?" Warrick asked from behind him.

Toreth realized that he had his eyes squeezed shut. He forced them open and leaned back, looking up. "Absolutely fucking fine. Get in."

Warrick opened his mouth, then closed it without comment and slid into the water.

A bloody good distraction, that was what Toreth needed. He reached out and pulled Warrick onto his lap, facing him. Steadying him with one hand in the small of his back, he took hold of Warrick's soft cock with the other.

Warrick smiled. "Something of a standing start."

"I like a challenge."

Not that much of a challenge, but it proved an effective way of avoiding thinking about what had happened earlier. Warrick's face, shadowed by the courtyard lights, reminded him of the creatures in the recording. He studied the changes as Warrick's arousal increased, lines smoothing away from his face, his eyes drifting closed. Loving the way his lips softened and parted as his breathing quickened, tongue flicking out once to wet them.

Finally Warrick was close to coming, and the words started, as if he could no longer control his voice. "God, that's good. That's so good..."

"Do you want to get out?" Toreth asked.

Warrick shook his head vehemently.

"It'll make a mess of the water."

"I don't care. It's filtered." Warrick's hands tightened on the rim of the pool. "If you stop...just don't stop." His head bowed. "Mmh—did you like the sim demo?"

For a moment the non sequitur threw him. Then Toreth smiled. "Yes. It was the most incredible fucking turn-on. You look so good in chains. Helpless. Being taken. Being used."

Warrick whimpered, thighs spreading wider as he pushed forwards into Toreth's fingers.

"That was only playing, though, wasn't it?" Toreth lowered his voice. "The sim. You could've snapped out of it whenever you wanted. Not like the real world." His free hand slid down to cup the base of Warrick's spine. The palm keeping him in place left his fingers free to stroke and probe gently. "Much better when it's me, isn't it? Isn't it?"

"Yes," Warrick gasped. "God, yes. *Please.*"

"Better when you can't escape. Better when the chains are real, when the pain is real, when you're mine, to do whatever—"

Whatever the fuck I want with. But the words were drowned by Warrick's scream as he came, shoulders bunching as his arms tensed, his cock twitching in Toreth's hand.

"Ah. Mm." Warrick slid down into the tub, onto the ledge, and collapsed against him, slopping warm water over Toreth's shoulder. "Thank God—no one around."

"They probably heard it on the mainland."

Warrick chuckled quietly. "You know, you were right before. I don't care." He sighed, then said, "House systems—courtyard lights out."

Darkness enveloped them. Darkness and silence, except for the bubbling of the water. Tension crept back into Toreth's neck and shoulders. For a moment he considered suggesting that they go inside, but that might be construed as running away from the water. He was supposed to be proving something here.

"Look at the stars," Warrick murmured.

Toreth leaned back obediently. Like diamond dust sifted thickly over the sky, the Milky Way blazed impossibly bright, unobscured by the reflected glow of city lights. More stars than he'd seen in his life. More stars than he'd ever imagined existed. Even the gaps between them looked different—a deep velvety blue only a shade away from black. The unexpected beauty of it held his gaze, leaving him unaware of time passing. He didn't look away until a moth, blundering past in the darkness, brushed his cheek and he started.

Stars. He blinked. I should tell Warrick to put it in the sim, he thought. If it isn't there already. The sim . . . and he thought of the recording again, and that made him smile. The sim demo and the sofa. This was going to be a perfect weekend.

Warrick still lay against him, light in the water, holding him securely to stop the currents from pushing them apart. He breathed slow and steady—very nearly asleep.

"Warrick?"

He pressed closer, face against Toreth's neck, and hummed sleepily. "Mm?"

"What the fuck is real-time spline reticulation?"

After a moment Warrick's head lifted slightly, and he started to laugh.

Chapter Fourteen

❖

What's that part of the city like?" Toreth asked.

"Traditional," Karteris said. "As far as anywhere in the main city is. Not like you might find out in the country, though."

Traditional. Elsewhere, that might mean not arrestable but worth watching. Did it here? "Safe?" Toreth asked.

"Of course. Under normal circumstances." Karteris took a breath, as if debating what to say. "I know what the note said, and I'm not trying to tell you what to do, but you're not going through with it, are you?"

"Vassilakis told me there hadn't been a major incident in the city for years. Was he talking crap?"

"Well, no, but... you should let me organize a team to come with you."

"No." Toreth pointed at the screen, where an anonymous note gave a time and place, and the single line "come alone." "They'll be watching—I won't get a sniff if they see a load of backup."

"Or if you don't trust anyone here, why not take your two?"

"Just let me do this the way I want to," Toreth said evenly.

"Well, it's your funeral." Karteris shrugged. "But Nikoletta won't thank you for the paperwork if you get killed or kidnapped."

"Who the hell in Athens would want to kill me?" Most of the likely suspects were in the I&I building itself. "I'll take a gun, though."

"Well, thank God for that, at least. Come down to the armory and I'll get one signed out for you."

Toreth leaned against the wall in the stifling heat of the enclosed square. With the sun high in the sky, only one side of the square was in shadow. That had seemed too obvious a waiting place, so he'd picked a doorway in the opposite wall.

His jacket lay over the rim of the small fountain at this side of the square—more an elaborate water trough.

Ten minutes had passed since the appointed time. How long should he wait? Despite the heat and the bright light, he kept scanning the square.

Movement, from up and right—a long shutter opening onto a balcony on the shadowed wall. Opening very slowly. Pots of geraniums hanging from the metal railing obscured his view as he squinted against the light. A soft sound floated down of metal hinges moving and the shutter stilled. Either the opener was trying not to wake someone in the room, or... Toreth stiffened.

Deliberately, he turned his head as if scanning the square again, keeping his gaze locked to the balcony. After a few seconds the shutter moved again, squeaking once more. This time, instead of stopping, it swung quickly back with a squeal of metal and he caught a glimpse of movement from the darkened room beyond.

White powder and chips of brick rained down even as Toreth dove left toward the marble fountain. He landed heavily, swearing, scrabbling for his own gun. He thought he saw a shape on the rooftop to the right, then a faint flash of light from the balcony opposite fractionally preceded another smack into the wall above. Toreth fired at the balcony, three quick shots, then scrambled completely behind the meter-high side of the fountain.

Something hit the cobbles with a crack and a crash of breaking pottery.

Silence.

Heart pounding, he tilted his neck and looked back. Nothing obvious on the roof. The holes in the plaster covered a spread of three meters, roughly at chest height if he'd been standing, and were large enough to make him glad of his cover. Marble and water should stop anything that simply made dents rather than demolished walls. Toreth edged cautiously along behind the fountain until he reached the best cover from the balcony and rooftop. His comm earpiece was still in place, and he tapped it left-handed to activate it. "Emergency comm."

There was an Int-Sec standard code for describing field situations—a letter denoting an armed situation, numbers to describe the details as economically as possible. Toreth was saved the difficulty of remembering it because the comm remained stubbornly dead. He tapped it again. "Emergency fucking comms. Come on, you lazy bastards." Nothing. "B-C. Nagra. I&I Athens incoming. I&I New London incoming. Sara."

Had he jarred it when he landed? Toreth didn't think so. He did, however, know that he'd left it in his jacket pocket at the armory when he was putting on the holster. Where had Karteris been standing at the time?

Run or stay? If he ran, the gunman would very likely get another shot. Accuracy didn't seem to be his strong suit, but he definitely had caliber on his side. Staying was superficially attractive, right up to the point when the gunman or his possible friend appeared at the end of the fountain... or above him.

An upward glance revealed more balconies, shuttered windows and flat roofs. It had certainly been a lovely setup. Toreth shifted position and peered cautiously around the curved end of the basin. Nothing. He moved another few centimeters from cover, and still there was no reaction.

A heap of soil, geraniums, and broken pottery on the far side of the square marked the results of his own shooting. Otherwise, the small square was still empty, the fountain trickling peacefully. Surely someone would come to investigate the shots?

Long time since he'd been in this kind of position. Usually his cases were less exciting. Toreth had never enjoyed being shot at—there were far healthier ways to generate adrenaline. The alley by which he'd entered the square was less than ten meters away. If he went quickly, he would easily make it. Toreth checked around the end of the fountain once more, crouching, readying himself for the dash.

And stopped.

Red and white flowers and green leaves, with dark splashes of soil between them. He replayed the sound in his mind. A crash—and a metallic impact as well? The black shape poking out from under the compost certainly looked like a gun. Interesting, but still better examined from behind a solid wall with an easy exit to hand.

One, two, three and—

The sprinting start would've impressed the hell out of the I&I gym instructors. Toreth slithered to a standstill ten meters down the alley, left hand on the wall, heart trip-hammering again.

No shots. No sound at all. He considered returning to the square, but whether the object amid the flowers was a gun or not, there was still the figure on the roof to consider. He was still thinking it over when he heard movement behind him.

As he spun away from the square, he heard B-C call, "Para!"

"Where the fuck have you been?" Toreth asked when the investigator reached him. "You were supposed to be waiting out of sight, not out of the fucking district."

"Sorry, Para. We were—" B-C stopped, then pointed. "Are you okay?"

Toreth had been vaguely aware that his left arm hurt—bruised when he landed, he thought. However, when he looked down, the upper part of his shirt sleeve was slowly dyeing crimson. Fuck. Still, the tear in the fabric was small and his arm moved freely—nothing worse than a scratch.

"I'm fine. Come on. And where the hell is Nagra?"

"We were trying to raise some backup," B-C said as they started down the alley away from the square. "As soon as the shooting started, Nagra called you and didn't get anything. So she stayed back to call the emergency comms while I came to look for you. It's only been a minute since we heard the first shots."

Seemed like a lot longer than that, but B-C was probably right. "My comm's dead."

"Where are we going, Para?"

Toreth paused at a cross alley, then turned right. "I'm trying to find another way into a house on that square." Too many narrow streets and irregular houses. He stopped and pulled out his hand screen. "Local map."

After a moment the tangle of streets appeared on the screen, with a dot to mark their location. At least the location mapping worked, which suggested that the fault was in the earpiece rather than the comms chip. "Okay. We're here, and we want to be there, so..."

B-C peered over his shoulder. "That way?"

"Looks good. Call Nagra, tell her where we're going."

As they approached the front of the building, the map screen went dead again. Intermittent fault? Not important, because he'd got a fix on the right one.

The shutters on the front of the tall, narrow house were also closed. To Toreth's bafflement, the door had no screen or card swipe. To his surprise, when he pushed the handle, the door simply swung back, revealing a dim corridor and a staircase.

They were still looking and listening when Nagra appeared. "Backup's on its way."

"I want to take a look before they arrive," Toreth said. "B-C, you wait down here. I don't want any I&I people going in there until I'm done, understand? Especially not Political Crimes."

"Where first, Para?" Nagra asked.

Toreth thought back to the square, to the stealthily opening shutter. Not difficult—the scene was still sharp in his mind. "Top floor. Quick check in the rooms on the way up."

Actually, there was little serious danger of being boxed in. Anyone in the house had had ample time to get out before the three of them arrived.

Leaving B-C by the door, Toreth and Nagra moved quickly up the stairs. The lights were out, so Nagra opened shutters on the landings, letting light in as they went. The house stood silent—the rooms they glanced into were dingy, even considering the lack of light, and plastic dust sheets covered what little furniture they held. On the top floor a single door opened on the side facing the square. It stood ajar, letting in light and a faint air current to lift the dust on the floor. Toreth caught the familiar smell of blood, and not from his arm.

Nevertheless, he and Nagra opened the door in approved textbook style—it would be highly embarrassing to be shot at this point.

The only furniture in the room was a bed, the plastic covering carelessly folded beside it. The body lay beyond it, by the open shutter which squeaked softly as the breeze nudged it. Blood pooled on the dusty floor.

Nagra waited by the door as Toreth crossed the room. A crumpled, grease-spotted paper ball on the floor by the bed caught his attention—a half-empty bottle of water stood beside it. Toreth sniffed again. Faint hint of some food under the blood. Obviously the man had been waiting for him.

In the center of the bed sat a matte black box, fifteen centimeters on a side, square except for one sloping face where a small control screen glowed dimly. Two steady green lights. Altogether, it looked like the kind of thing best not touched.

A faint noise distracted him from his inspection. It was unexpected enough to set his heart thumping again, and it took him a moment to realize what it was. A soft moan.

"Nagra," he called in a whisper.

"Para?"

"Get an ambulance. We've got a live one, for the moment."

A pause, then she said, "I can't get a contact."

He opened his hand screen and tried to call up the map again. Nothing. Toreth looked back at the box, considering. Maybe he'd been maligning Karteris, or at least wrong about the method of cutting off Toreth's communication—Karteris could still be behind this.

Leaning over the bed again, he inspected the device more closely. A switch at the back looked like power and was probably safer than messing with the unfamiliar interface on the screen. Unconsciously holding his breath, he clicked the switch. The lights went out and the screen faded. "Now?" he asked softly.

"It's back."

Toreth crossed the last couple of meters to the body, stepping awkwardly around the blood, keeping his gun trained on the still figure. The man lay huddled face down—from the smears on the floor, he hadn't moved very far since he'd been shot.

And a lucky fucking shot it had been, Toreth thought as he knelt. He wouldn't have staked a single chip on any of his shots having connected, but at least one clearly had. Exactly where was now his main concern. Carefully, he turned the man over and stopped, unaware of the wetness of the bloodied clothing under his hand.

DNA records, held on every citizen in the Administration from birth, would have revealed the man's name. For once, though, that wasn't necessary. Toreth recognized his victim—Karteris's pretty informer. "Theo?" he said aloud.

Theo, Alexandros thought as he sat down behind the roof parapet. Out of the sunlight, the breeze was cool enough to make him shiver, his face and neck damp with sweat. Five years in the resistance cell together, and he'd never known the man's name. Even now, with Member Two dead, the knowledge felt uncomfortable.

Was Theo—Two—dead? There had been no movement from the room since the first silenced shots, and no reply to the para-investigator's exclamation. Alexandros had seen Two drop the gun, seen him fall backwards. He must be dead.

It should have been fingerprints, not a corpse, providing a lead to the para-investigator, and Two should have been clear of the building by the time they were found. Cursing silently, Alexandros looked up at the sky, blinking back tears. Two had been a comrade—a friend, even, name or no name. At least now he could never be taken back to I&I.

He forced his gaze down to the gun in his own hands. It wasn't that he didn't know how to use it, but he was glad that it hadn't been necessary. No backup had materialized. Everything had gone exactly to plan, except for the bastard's unexpectedly good shooting. That wasn't his fault, or Two's.

The gun felt heavy and unpleasantly slick in his sweating hands. He remembered to click on the safety before he put it away in his jacket pocket. Then Alexandros made his way carefully along the roof, stepped across the gap to the next building without looking down, and went to leave a message for Member One reporting their success and failure.

The middle-aged I&I medic introduced himself as Eugenio Quattrone, lately of I&I Naples. Combined with his complete nonassociation with Political Crimes, that gave Toreth some confidence in the man.

"Aren't you going to tell me that a few centimeters to the side and I'd have bled to death?" Toreth asked Quattrone.

The man glanced up from his examination of Toreth's arm. "Para?"

"I thought it was a medic thing. I've been stabbed a couple of times and both times they told me—fuck!" Sudden pain startled him into the exclamation.

"Sorry. I think we have something in here. One moment." The man turned away.

Blood trickled ticklishly down Toreth's arm as he waited and he held his elbow away from his body, trying not to drip on his trousers. B-C had gone to the hotel to pick a shirt up for him, so that he'd have something less gory to wear once the medic finished.

"Now, if we can just hold still..." A hiss of a nozzle, and the pain slowly faded away. Now Toreth felt only pressure on his arm and a dull sensation of probing. "This wasn't done by a bullet, so I don't think a few centimeters would have made any difference at all. Except it would be harder to find whatever's in here."

Toreth decided that he'd rather not look. With his free hand, he picked up his shirt and examined the sleeve. Not much torn, but the bloodstain would be difficult to get rid of now that it had dried in. Perfectly good shirt as well, expensive and practically brand new—a New Year present from Warrick. Maybe he could get it repaired.

The probing stopped, and a few seconds later came the chink of something on metal. "There we are," Quattrone said.

Toreth looked into the proffered bowl. It held a small flake which seemed to be white underneath the coating of blood.

"Marble, I think," the medic said. "Although you know better than me how that could've got in there. Made a nice clean cut, anyhow. Keep still, I'll bond it together and we'll be ready to go."

As the medic started work, the door opened. Expecting B-C with the clean shirt, Toreth looked around to find Vassilakis. The division head appeared gratifyingly concerned. "I'm fine," Toreth said before he could speak.

"Thank God." Vassilakis came in and closed the door. He glanced at the medic, but Quattrone didn't visibly register his presence. Vassilakis frowned briefly, then said, "Toreth, I have no idea how this could happen. Or who could be behind it. No idea at all."

Tell me something I don't fucking know. "Athens doesn't seem like a very healthy place for Int-Sec outsiders, does it? Between me and Grant, I mean."

Vassilakis stared at him blankly.

"Theodora Grant?" Toreth said. "Cit Surveillance? She didn't have much fun here, either."

Vassilakis stiffened. "Hardly the same thing."

Interesting that he recognized the name right away. "Oh?"

"No. The woman deliberately mixed with criminal elements. Not surprising that it had unfortunate consequences."

"I thought Athens didn't have resisters?"

Vassilakis's normally affable expression hardened. "It doesn't, Para-investigator. She came looking for something that isn't here, and when she couldn't find it she pressed until she found something else instead. If Justice can't control the vermin running around in the city, that's no concern of I&I's. Now, if you'll excuse me." The door closed firmly behind him.

"That man," Quattrone said precisely, "is an idiot."

"Tell me about it."

He'd meant it rhetorically, but Quattrone didn't hesitate. "If you'll excuse me for saying it, para-investigators need to be supervised, and what this place really suffers from is too many people like Vassilakis not doing it. The section heads all take their cues from him." From the vehemence, it was a grievance the medic had been waiting for a while to air. "I've worked in five different I&I stations, and this is the worst. Everywhere else the paras don't trust each other, they don't trust the management, and the management doesn't trust them. Here it's all hands off. Too friendly and too laissez faire."

Toreth felt a sting in the back of his hand, and looked down in time to see Quattrone lifting an injector away. A thin, shiny line of wound sealant marked the near-invisible line of the cut on his arm. "Thanks," Toreth said, covering the treatment and the assessment of the division.

"We're all done here," the medic said. "It won't give you any trouble *if* you don't put too much stress on the join for the next twenty-four hours."

Toreth hoped Theo was enjoying a similarly easy time. Unfortunately, the I&I medical unit wasn't equipped for the required surgery, so Toreth had been forced to surrender his prisoner to the nearest hospital. Toreth had stationed I&I guards outside his room, and at the moment Nagra was keeping them company.

Karteris was waiting in Toreth's office. Toreth sent B-C away, not making even a thin pretense of an excuse.

"Glad to see you're okay," Karteris said as Toreth closed the door. "You should see the paperwork from getting internal reviewers killed. As it is, I've got more forms than there were bullets in that wall."

"Here's some paperwork for you to look at first," Toreth said.

The summary page he showed Karteris was simple—the discrepancy between the amount of drugs signed out of stores and the amounts used and discarded. Along with the names of the people he sold them on to, it was some of the best evidence he'd seen for a long while. Since it had been prepared by an I&I admin, it ought to be.

"Where did you get this?" Karteris asked, although he didn't seem to expect an answer.

"Aren't there enough legal drugs for sale?" Toreth had trouble keeping the smile off his face. "It's not like they're expensive."

"There's always room for more. Haven't you ever done it?"

"Of course I haven't," Toreth said with self-righteous indignation.

Karteris stared for a moment. "You know, I believe you. What the fuck *do* you do for fun?"

"Exercise and go to bed early." Time to be serious. Best not to mention his suspicions of Karteris's resister sympathies straight away. "Okay, this is the deal. I want to know what's going on in the section. What's important enough that you're willing to risk losing a nice little fuck like Theo to keep it quiet."

"Theo's nothing to do with me."

"No? He's your informer, and he tried to kill me."

Karteris shook his head firmly. "He's registered to General Criminal, not me—it's in his file."

"Fine. If you don't tell me... well, dealing is a Justice matter. Vassilakis won't be able to charm you out of that one."

"Justice?" Outrage, not fear. "You can't give me to Justice!"

"Watch me. Of course, you might want to risk it. You'll probably only get restrictive detention, not re-education."

"Don't you have *any* fucking loyalty to the uniform?"

He didn't dignify that with a reply. Karteris stared at him, expressionless now, and Toreth had to admire the man's nerve. From what Sara had said, jail was a real fear for Karteris. Toreth closed up the screen. "Up to you. I expect you'll like it in prison. Lots of men there who won't turn you down. Or let you turn them down. You might even meet someone you know—do you have a good memory for prisoners? I know I can't remember all the useless bastards I've interrogated. Bet they remember me, though."

There was a brief silence, then Karteris said, "You won't do it."

"What?"

His confidence had returned. "Hand a para over to Justice for doing something practically everyone in the division's done? You'd be stupid to try it, and I'd be even more stupid to believe you would. Forget it."

This was why Toreth hated being forced to bluff. And to be fair, it was no different from how Toreth himself would've played it. He had one card left—he wondered if Karteris knew he was holding it. "Okay. If you won't tell me what was worth sending Theo after me for, maybe he will."

Clearly Karteris had no idea. "I thought—I heard that you killed him."

"Where did you hear that from?"

"One of the admins."

And they'd know if anybody did, making it a good source to name even if it wasn't true. "I'm not that good a shot. I'm bringing him back here from the hospital later, and as soon as he's up to it I'll be interrogating. The first thing I'll be asking him is where he got his comm jamming gear. Unless you'd like to tell me something first?"

Karteris shrugged, composed once more. "Nothing to tell. Good luck with him. He's not easy. Took a good few days to crack the first time. Mind you, once he went…" He smiled, almost convincingly. "But hey—maybe you're more his type."

"Maybe." Toreth touched the comm, sending the signal to B-C. "Until I find out, you can wait in the cells here."

Karteris stared incredulously. "*Cells?*" Then he looked around as the door opened to reveal B-C and two I&I guards.

"I might not be willing to take the drug sales all the way," Toreth said, "but they'll do to hold you until I've had a word with your little friend. Shouldn't take long. And hey, if I'm wrong, I'll buy you dinner to make it up to you."

As Toreth argued with the hospital medic, Nagra stood nearby, looking twitchy. Outright attacks on I&I staff were rare enough, and combined with the possibility that it was an inside job Toreth couldn't blame her for a little healthy nervousness, especially given the slackness of the local I&I. The I&I guards themselves seemed merely bored.

"I have every legal right to do it," Toreth said to the medic, with as much patience as he could muster. "I want to see his medical records, right now."

"He's not fit to leave the hospital," the medic repeated adamantly. "Still less for anything else."

Toreth glanced at her name badge—something unpronounceable with far too many vowels. "I'll make that assessment. I have plenty of experience in scheduling injured prisoners for interrogation. Believe me, I don't want him to die any more than you do."

"I won't release him so you can—"

Toreth held up his hand. "I'm going to give you one chance to reconsider the end of that sentence, Doctor. Unless you'd like to accompany Theo back to I&I."

She stopped, jaw clenching. Toreth watched curiously, wondering if she'd have the guts to go through with it. They so rarely did. Finally, she nodded. "Wait here, please," she said.

Toreth looked at his watch and swore under his breath. It had taken until now, almost nine o'clock, to get to speak to the medic. In the end, he'd had to threaten arrests for obstruction. He hoped B-C had had better luck back at I&I.

Half an hour later, when the medic walked back into the room, the mixture of fear and defiance on her face told him what she was going to say before she spoke. Stupid of him to have let her go alone. The shooting must have shaken him up more than he'd realized.

"I'm afraid it won't be possible for you to speak to your prisoner," the medic said. "He died of complications from his injuries about fifteen minutes ago."

Bullshit that stank worse than the room he'd found Theo in. "Did he say anything?"

"Nothing." Her right hand clenched and unclenched. "Nothing at all."

"I see." Without taking his eyes from her face, Toreth said, "Nagra, I want the security recording from Theo's room. Just to make absolutely sure he didn't have any interesting last words for us."

The doctor's gaze darted to the door, and Toreth shook his head. "Try it, if you like."

She straightened. "I have nothing to be ashamed of."

He and Nagra watched the recording in the security center at the hospital. The unpronounceable doctor stood between them.

"I'm sorry. I couldn't do anything." She spoke softly, only just audible on the microphones. "I tried."

"Can't go back there." Theo's hand clutched at her arm, his voice weak. "Can't. Please. *Please.*"

Then Toreth could do nothing but watch as the medic gave the injection to his prize bloody witness and then stood by the bed, waiting, finally calling the resuscitation team. The irony was that Toreth had done it so many times himself, albeit under the unofficially official sanction of an annex order. How the hell had the woman imagined she'd get away with it?

"Want to tell me it was painkillers?" Toreth asked her.

She shook her head, eyes tearing.

"Get the guards down from Theo's room," Toreth said to Nagra. "I think we can trust them to process her. Tell them to put her in a cell until we get the results of the postmortem."

On the way out, he thought of Vassilakis. No fucking resisters in Athens, indeed.

Chapter Fifteen

Right, we've lost Theo, which is unfortunate. And now Karteris definitely won't play." The next morning, Toreth addressed his team of two back at I&I. "It's not hopeless, though. We have the lists of Theo's contacts from his first arrest. The lists are probably suspect, but it's the best we've got. What we do have is a general level four damage waiver for suspects associated with the attack on me. Vassilakis signed it himself, Justice are processing it now. We've got Theo to thank for that, for taking shots at an I&I officer, so we shouldn't think too badly of him."

"So we get cracking as soon as we bring them in?" Nagra asked.

"Yes. Arrests should be starting soon. We need help, so I've asked the General Criminal section here to lend us some investigators. Not ideal, but it's the best I can do for now. The alternative is to call in a lot more help from New London, and that risks Internal Investigations hearing about it and coming in to take the whole damn case away. B-C, did you find out anything yesterday?"

"Yes, Para. I went down to stores, and there's a comm jammer missing, all right, machine ID matches the one from the scene. But, big surprise, it wasn't officially signed out."

"Right. Well, it's probably a waste of time, but see if anyone will admit to anything. And then—"

Someone knocked on the door. "Yes?"

Nikoletta opened it, started a sentence, then stopped when she saw B-C and Nagra. "Sorry to interrupt, Para, but Section Head Makrigiannakis would like to see you. Right away."

George's office was even plusher than Vassilakis's. When Toreth walked in, he actually stopped to look down, because he thought he'd stepped in something unpleasant. In fact it was a deep-pile rug, fantastically patterned and exquisitely dyed. The wooden sideboard looked like it belonged in a mansion or—judging by the extensive range of drinks at one end—a restaurant.

"Did you want me, George?" Toreth asked.

The section head didn't ask him to sit down. "Why is Senior Para-investigator Karteris locked up on the detention level?"

If you'd been here yesterday, you lazy bastard, you'd know that. "Because I told someone to put him there."

The section head's eyes narrowed, which meant that they virtually vanished in his pudgy face. "The detention officer said that you ordered he be denied access to a Justice rep."

"I told them not to rush processing him, yes."

"He has a right to a rep. He claims that you've got him there because of a few irregularities with his drug sign-outs. Is that right?"

Toreth said nothing. After a few seconds, George asked, "What evidence do you have against him?"

Not as much as I'd like. "I'm afraid I can't discuss that. I have my reasons."

"This is my section, Para-investigator, and—"

"And I get my authority from I&I headquarters in New London, not from you. If you don't like the way I do my job, file a complaint." Without waiting for a dismissal, he left George spluttering outrage and went to start organizing the arrests.

Chapter Sixteen

❖

The next day, Toreth and Nagra met up in the canteen for a late lunch. They bought sandwiches and took them outside, where the chances of being overheard were lower. Probably a little late in the day now, since Theo's death and his acquaintances' arrests were hardly secrets, but Toreth thought there was no point in taking chances.

"Get anything?" Toreth asked as he unwrapped his lunch.

"Nothing, Para. And I'm afraid the second prisoner I worked on is in medical. But he didn't know anything. In fact, I doubt he had any more to do with any resistance than I do."

"Why the hell is he in medical?" Unlike Nagra to be careless.

"I made a mistake with the dosage. I'm sorry, Para. It was an old model injector and I missed a decimal point."

"Damn. Well, it's inside the waiver, unless he dies. Nothing else?"

"'Fraid not. I sent the third one back to the cells before I stopped for lunch. Nothing again, unless she was hiding it well. But you know how it is—quick, thorough, safe. Pick any two."

The news would have been less depressing if Toreth had had any better success himself.

"Para!" Toreth looked up to see B-C approaching at a trot. "Para! Karteris is gone."

"Gone?" Toreth wondered if he'd misheard. "As in dead?" Suicide?

B-C stopped by them, breathing quickly, and shook his head. "Gone as in not in detention."

"How the fuck can he be gone? How long?"

"Late yesterday afternoon. His twenty-four hours for a Justice rep to be appointed expired and G—Section Head Makrig—" B-C took a few breaths.

"George, right. Get on with it."

"The section head signed a release for him. The security officer said he brought it down in person."

"He doesn't have the authority. Not over an internal review. That would take a division head." A division head who was another member of the favored elite. "Vassilakis?"

"I haven't seen the release, but probably."

"Shit." There was nothing to be done about it now except make sure it was included in Toreth's final report. "I don't suppose there's any sign of Karteris?"

"As far as I can tell, he hasn't been seen since yesterday. I heard about it while you were in interrogation, and I've been chasing rumors round the building that he was still here somewhere. But I'd say Political have been covering up for him, although you'd never be able to pin it on them as deliberate. He supposedly left a lot of messages, saying he'd be in various places he hasn't been anywhere near. He's run, for sure."

"The alias? Taki?"

"That's the other thing. There's almost eight thousand gone from his accounts. Probably all he could get out on short notice, but nowhere near all of it. It's possible that he doesn't know we know, so he might be traveling under that name."

Possible, but not likely. A feeling based primarily on the fact that if Toreth had been in Karteris's place, he wouldn't have risked it. "Put out an arrest warrant for Karteris, under both names."

"He's probably outside the Administration by now," Nagra said.

"I know." Toreth closed his half-finished pack of sandwiches. "I'm going back to try again. The sooner we get on with it, the sooner someone will know *something*."

Mass interrogation was never Toreth's favorite technique. It was boring, took too much time, and smacked of desperation—something bad paras did when they'd run out of intelligent ideas. The fact remained, though, that there had been at least one more person at the square, up on the roof. Setting aside the small chance that it was Karteris himself—which would have been a monstrously stupid risk Toreth couldn't imagine the man taking—then it was probably someone known to Theo. Odds were that the name would be in the system somewhere. It was damned difficult to lose records, and the chances of Karteris having a Warrick at his disposal were fortunately small.

Of Nagra's three words, Toreth went for safe and quick for the rest of the afternoon's interrogations. The brief interrogations backed up his theory that the contacts listed in the file knew nothing about any resistance.

He was explaining the terms of the damage waiver to the sixth (and hopefully last) prisoner, when Nagra called him out of the room.

She was waiting for him in the office upstairs, standing by his desk. "You aren't going to like this, Para," she said. "Justice have Karteris."

Toreth stared. "Where? When?"

"The coast guard found him at lunchtime on a beach, few miles down the coast. Drowned." She looked at him, then said, "I said you wouldn't like it."

She was dead right, although she didn't know the real reason why. Toreth sat slowly, keeping his back straight, deliberately relaxing his abdominal muscles. Sickness is mostly tension, he told himself firmly. "What happened?" he asked.

"Someone reported a motorboat drifting this morning. Turns out it was the one Karteris owns a part share in. The engine was dead—mechanical failure. Unlucky for him that there weren't any oars or even a life jacket on it. The pathologist thinks that he tried to swim to the shore and just didn't make it."

"Why—" Toreth swallowed. "Why the hell would he try to swim?"

"He must've known he'd have been picked up the next day. It's so busy around there that the boat was spotted almost as soon as the sun got up. They found a suitcase on it. Clothes, but no ID—which is why we didn't hear about it right away—and no sign of the money. Probably at the bottom of the Med."

Toreth turned away, trying to look at the situation objectively. Did it make sense? A gut instinct said that something was wrong, but when he tried to pin it down it was washed away by the sickening idea of Karteris dead. No. Karteris dying. Of the water—

"Excuse me," Toreth said.

He managed to make it down the corridor at a walk, not a run, until he reached the toilet door. Then he was forced to press a hand over his mouth, fighting the choking tightness in his throat. He crashed through the door, pushing past a startled investigator, barely hearing the man's protest.

Toreth dropped onto his knees inside the cubicle, then he was lost in the darkness, surrendering helplessly to his body's memory, his stomach emptying in wrenching spasms.

Ten minutes passed before he could even straighten, never mind stand. He leaned against the wall, gulping air, muscles aching.

Three people in his life he'd known before they'd drowned. The first had been his brother, and they'd both been so young that the memories were no more than faded still photos. Yang had been a witness at SimTech, hardly a person at all. But Karteris he'd spent time with. Karteris he'd seen alive two days ago. Karteris he could imagine struggling, fighting the cramps, could imagine him going down, breathing in water like a kick in the chest...

His stomach turned over again, but there was nothing left to throw up. Stupid. He hadn't even fucking liked Karteris. And thank God that he hadn't fucked the bastard. Illogical as it was, that would have made the whole thing so much worse.

Outside the cubicle, he was relieved to find the room empty. Turn on the tap. Lean down and—cool, chlorinated water in his mouth. He forced himself to rinse and spit until the taste of vomit had cleared. Then he washed his face and left.

Nagra was waiting patiently. Toreth said nothing about his abrupt departure, and she didn't comment.

"Why did it take Justice this long to work out who he was?" Toreth asked when he'd sat back at his desk.

"No one recognized the body, and no one got round to doing the DNA check until this afternoon. I'd say laziness rather than malice."

"You'd think someone there would know him."

"There was damage to the body, including the head. Probably done by rocks when it was washing around, or it might even have been hit by a boat."

Something almost like hope made Toreth's heart rise. "Could he have been dead when he went into the water?"

"The Justice pathologist says not. Postmortem injuries only." She cocked her head. "You think he was killed to shut him up? Why? I thought he wouldn't play ball with you."

"I think—" I don't want to think about it at all. "I think we should forget him. Whatever he knew, we'll have to get it from somewhere else."

Toreth tried Nikoletta first. She was in her office, surrounded by a crowd of other admins and weeping copiously. He thought of Sara's opinion that the woman had faked enjoying fucking Karteris. That didn't mean the current grief couldn't be real enough, though. Guilt, maybe. In a way, her intervention might have triggered Karteris's plan to remove Toreth from the scene, and thereby, indirectly, his aborted flight.

He coughed. "Excuse me," he said. "I need to speak to her alone."

The group tightened protectively around its wounded member, but Nikoletta shook her head. "I'll be fine," she said in a tiny, brave voice.

When the room cleared, Toreth closed the door and went to crouch beside her chair. Better a nice, sympathetic interview here than in an interrogation room. "Nikki? How are you?"

Damp tissues littered the table like leaves. At his words she picked up a handful and burst into fresh tears. Toreth rubbed her arm sympathetically and refrained from sighing.

"It's all my fault!" she wailed. "I told you about the drugs. You talked to him, didn't you? It's all my fault for wanting to hurt him. And I can't even tell anyone because they'll all hate me."

Good summary of the situation so far, from a frighteningly selfish point of view. "Nikki, do you know about anything else Karteris might've been part of? Anything else that might've made him run?"

Tears dried, and she stared at him. "Anything else? No. Why?" The protective streak surfaced again, frown gathering. It would've looked good on her, except for the red eyes and dripping nose. "What are they saying about him?"

"Nothing. I was just wondering. Running like that seemed to be an overreaction to what I said to him, that's all."

He ought to have guessed her next words. "You mean, it maybe wasn't my fault?" The frown deepened. "But...no, I can't think of anything." She sniffed. "Nothing ever *happens* here, or it didn't."

Until I turned up. He was using the wrong bait, or maybe looking for the wrong kind of fish. "Did he say anything to you the last time you saw him? Ask you to do anything?"

To his surprise, she nodded. "He asked me to find him a current address. He said he had to leave the office, and he wanted me to find it and send it to him. The name was Alexandros Vasdeki."

"Did you do it?"

"Yes, of course."

"Good. Send it to me, now. Then go home, why don't you?" Her grieving presence was an irritating reminder of the cause of it. "No one will mind." And it's not like Karteris needs any misfiling done.

"I'd rather be here, at least for a bit. With things to do. Not stuck at home to think about him..."

The name had sounded familiar in Nikoletta's office, and when Toreth opened the file, he discovered why. Alexandros Vasdeki was the man who had considered Theodora Grant suspicious enough to be worth reporting to I&I. Not, however, listed as an official informer under Karteris's control. He was also listed as a known contact of Theo, his name marked as No Action. One of those who'd been considered so respectable as to be eliminated without interrogation.

Toreth asked the system to run a background check on Vasdeki again, using all the latest up-to-date information. Clean again—apparently a very well-behaved citizen.

On reflection, he should have guessed. It was exactly the kind of thing Toreth would have done, in Karteris's place—kept the important name well away from the lists of previously arrested and interrogated prisoners, if it couldn't be eliminated from the records completely. In fact, Toreth would've padded that list with innocent names to slow down exactly the kind of systematic interrogation approach they had tried, to give himself more time to get clear.

Which all added up to the conclusion that Toreth wasn't thinking clearly enough to get the job done. Karteris's fucking fault, for being stupid enough to drown himself in the—

Toreth sat back in his chair, rubbing his temples. Headache starting—that was too much coffee and too little food. Briefly, he considered finding something to eat, then decided to wait. He'd call B-C and tell him to arrest this Vasdeki, and then go back downstairs to try a couple more prisoners before he went back to the hotel. Perhaps that would make an effective distraction.

His coffee was growing cold, but the idea of touching it made Alexandros queasy. The pavement café felt horribly exposed; in the middle of the early evening crowd, it was as though there were a giant screen above his head, an arrow pointing him out to all.

Finally the young woman three tables over answered her comm, turning half towards him as she did so. Dark glasses and a scarf obscured her features, but he recognized Member One. When she stood up and walked away, she left a small briefcase beside her chair.

Walk over, pick it up, stroll away. Easy and natural—no one called out, or tried to stop him. By the time he reached a taxi, he was shaking. Why had he ever become involved? Why had he ever thought they might succeed?

He turned up the window opaquing and opened the case. A screen lay on top, and he sat back, holding it tightly as he read his instructions. Hard to get past the first lines, which drew his attention back repeatedly. His arrest had been ordered. He'd expected it—feared it—from the moment he'd heard that Theo had been taken away from the failed ambush by ambulance to the hospital, not the morgue. A stolen ID had paid for this taxi. Another lay in the case, along with an amount of money that under other circumstances he'd have been delighted to see. Even now, it lifted his heart because hopefully it meant flight, escape. Please, God, that arrangements had been made to let him leave now and take Gina with him.

He read on, a chill settling through him at the next sentence. "I can't explain and I won't order—only ask, and pray that you'll have the courage to do what's necessary..."

No swimming today. Back at the hotel that evening, Toreth forced himself to eat and then went up to his room and began pulling together the basics of the report on Political Crimes. The first few days—initial interviews, case reviews—included nothing that needed close attention, which was good because the words came off one file, through his brain and back out into the report without leaving any lasting impression. He had to keep reading back over what he'd written to work out what he needed to say next.

Something to do, as Nikoletta had said.

Even so, without the prospect of a weekend of dedicated fucking to distract him, his mind kept circling back to the news of the afternoon. Eventually he found himself staring out of the darkened window, seeing ocean. Black ocean. Cold, brilliant stars overhead. Night breeze, water growing colder. He pressed the heels of his hands against his forehead, trying to stave off the inevitable moment of imagining going under and—

Drink. He needed a bloody great big drink. He emptied the minibar of everything that looked moderately drinkable, lined the bottles up on the floor by the foot of the bed, and lay on his stomach, looking down at them. Start with the most palatable. The first two miniature bottles of generic whiskey went down easily, and he closed his eyes, concentrating on the warmth spreading from his throat down into his stomach.

Better. He counted the bottles again, deciding how many he could drink and still function tomorrow. However he calculated it, if he drank enough to blot out the nightmares, he would be far too hung over to work. When he'd just about resigned himself to a bad night, another source of distraction occurred to him.

He set the shadow fuck file playing and watched the first ten minutes. Concentrating on Warrick, trying to reach back to the memory of the sofa, to Warrick beside him, to the following two days of fun and fucking and olive groves and beaches. Beaches. No. Fun as recreating Warrick's beach fantasy had been, it was better to stay away from there, and from the courtyard.

The embarrassment of his panic in the tub felt distant now. All he remembered was the water, the overwhelming fear as it closed over him. Feeding into the image of Karteris struggling, of the unheard cries suddenly cut off by—

He switched the screen off and threw the remote across the room.

Another miniature bottle, vodka this time. When he'd finished it, he rolled over on his back and stared at the ceiling. This was going to be a bad one. Why the hell hadn't it all happened when Warrick was here?

I want him, Toreth thought, the admission sickening and weirdly comforting at the same time. I want him here, to make me forget all this crap. I want to fuck him until I'm too tired to dream about anything and fall asleep with—

Toreth looked at his watch. Ten o'clock. Maybe he could go down to the bar in the hotel and find someone—sod his virtuous image. Or... he pulled his comm earpiece out of his pocket and called Warrick before he could even wonder if he was with Carnac. Fortunately, Warrick answered immediately.

"Toreth?"

"Yeah, it's me. I just wanted—" And then Toreth couldn't think of anything to say.

"Is something wrong?" Warrick asked.

"Not really. I mean, yeah, I've had better days." He pinched the bridge of his nose, trying to focus, trying not to see Karteris. "Feels like I'm getting nowhere fast." Swimming for a distant shore. "I nearly had a suspect, briefly, one of the seniors, but they fished the stupid bastard out of the sea this morning, dead. So I'm back to square one."

"Ah." Amazing what a lot of meaning Warrick could cram into one syllable.

"Yeah. Ah. Look, can you make it out here this weekend?" He found he didn't care how pathetic it sounded. "Friday, or whenever." Tomorrow. Now.

"Damn. Toreth, if I could come, I would, I promise. If I could get on a flight tonight, I'd—" He stopped. "But I'm confined to my flat."

"What?" Confined to—what kind of a fucking excuse was that? "Why? Who by?"

"SimTech are assessing a security threat—someone has been attempting surveillance on the building, and on myself in particular. Until they find out who, they're treating it as a physical threat. I woke up this morning to find half the security team outside my door. I'm working from the office in the flat until they find out who's behind it." He sighed. "These things are always so damn tangled—corporations, independent surveillance companies, possibly sabotage teams. You know how it is. I can't see it being resolved by the weekend. And it would happen now, of all times, with the report and... everything."

Toreth heard a voice that sounded remarkably like his own say, "What a fucking pain."

"Quite so. Of course, you're more than welcome to come here, if you'd like to. I'm afraid it would be the polar opposite of last weekend, though." Toreth could imagine the wry smile. "Privacy is in short supply—the place is crawling with security."

"That's okay. I've got things to do here." Like kill myself.

There was a brief pause before Warrick asked carefully, "Will you be all right?"

Why the hell wouldn't he... oh. For a minute, he'd completely forgotten Karteris. "Yeah, sure, I'll be fine. Talk to you later."

After the connection cut off, he considered calling Warrick back and confessing. If he could've come up with a way of phrasing it that didn't make him want to die of embarrassment, he might even have done it.

Warrick, you're right, I *am* paranoid and pathetic. I had you followed because I thought you were fucking Carnac.

Oddly, that was the first time since the start of the call that he'd thought of Carnac and the name made him moan out loud. What if Carnac discovered what he'd done? He pressed his hands over his eyes, trying once more to block out an image, but this time of Carnac's delighted smile. The arrogant fucking bastard would really get off on the idea that Toreth thought Carnac was a... a threat. No. If Carnac found out, suicide *would* start to look like an attractive option.

If he could've borne the idea of her knowing, he might have called Sara and asked for her advice. Except that she'd probably say "tell Warrick straight away," because that was the kind of fucking stupid idea she usually came up with.

No. The sensible thing to do was to cancel the surveillance at once, warn Uche to beware corporate snoopers, and pray that Warrick never found out anything more about it. Eventually SimTech would drop the investigation. No one need ever know what he'd done. Toreth brightened very slightly as he spotted the silver lining. At least with Warrick locked in his flat and surrounded by security, he couldn't be playing personal liaison with Carnac.

Chapter Seventeen

Despite the combination of SimTech, Karteris, and too much to drink, Toreth woke in the morning surprisingly refreshed. His shoulders ached a little, say one bad dream's worth, but he didn't remember waking. Maybe the stresses had canceled each other out. Even so, hungry as he was after eating so little yesterday, he couldn't face breakfast.

When he arrived at I&I, Nagra was waiting in the office.

"More bad news?" he asked her.

"Not this time. Justice picked up Alexandros Vasdeki this morning."

"Alive, I hope."

"Yes. They caught him up at the station, trying to get a ticket out of the Administration. He had a fake ID, but it failed the security check. He tried to bribe his way out, but he was desperate enough that the station staff guessed he was running from something serious, and they held him instead of taking the money."

"A lot of money?"

"He had nearly five thousand on him. No accounts in his name missing that sum, so I expect it was a present from Karteris."

Interesting that Karteris hadn't simply killed the man—Toreth would have done, in his place. Again, the feeling nagged at him that there was something wrong with Karteris's death. Hard to see what, if he'd been alone in a small boat... Toreth closed his eyes briefly. Stay away from the whole damn idea. "I'll read his file one more time and go down."

It had taken two attempts yesterday before the guards managed to leave Toreth's prisoners sitting at the table rather than putting them straight into the interrogation chair. The second, more forceful explanation seemed to have sunk in, because Toreth found Vasdeki there, waiting with his head in his cuffed hands. He breathed harshly, sounding close to tears, and he didn't seem to hear the door open. Excellent start.

"Good morning," Toreth said.

With a startled exclamation, the prisoner looked up. Slighter than Theo, but good-looking in the same classically Greek way. He muttered something under his breath—a prayer, probably, but the desk microphone would pick it up for later examination.

Toreth sat down and placed a hand screen on the table to one side. "My name is Toreth. Senior Para-investigator Val Toreth, in fact, although I don't particularly care what you call me. I've heard it all before, anyway."

Vasdeki took a shaky breath, but when he spoke his voice was only a little unsteady. "What are you doing here? This isn't your country."

"It's a part of the European Administration, of which we're both citizens. Now we're here, citizen, to talk about—"

"Forget it. I won't tell you anything." Vasdeki stood up. "I'm ready. You can do whatever the hell you like."

Not protesting his innocence, then. Toreth smiled and waved the man back into his seat. After a hesitation, he obeyed.

"Oh, no, no, no. Not like that." Toreth pretended to consult the screen. "We're not here to discuss *your* interrogation. Your wife is called Gina, isn't she?"

Dead silence, the low purr of the air cycling systems seeming suddenly loud.

"She doesn't know anything," Vasdeki whispered.

"I'm sorry?"

"She doesn't know anything." And then the realization dawning that that didn't matter in the slightest.

"I'm sure I can come up with a reasonable suspicion that she does, which will be enough to get me a damage waiver. For example, she also works at the university. The case we're considering—a political case—has connections to there. Do you know what a section N interrogation is?"

When the prisoner shook his head, Toreth called the relevant section of the Procedures and Protocols up on his hand screen and held it where Vasdeki could see it. The heading, "Approved Sexualized Interrogation Methods," always caught the eye.

"I won't touch her myself, of course," Toreth said as Vasdeki read. "There are section N trained guards who I'll bring in to do all that. I'll be standing right next to you, so that when you want it to stop you can tell me."

The problem with section Ns was reliability. Some prisoners folded almost at once but, especially if both partners were active resisters, it could make them more determined to resist, to show no weakness in front of the other. An even bigger gamble here, since it was unlikely he really could get a waiver issued for the section N. Making a threat he couldn't carry out was a disastrous way to start an interrogation. Worth the risk, though, because it fell under both safe and quick.

No reply came from the prisoner. An outright refusal would have come by now. Toreth decided to test the water. "How long had Karteris been helping the resisters?"

Laughter wasn't a sound often heard in the interrogation room. Not even, as with Vasdeki, when it was ninety percent hysteria.

Finally he said, "Helping us? Oh, God." He shook his head, laughter still escaping in hiccups. "You have no—they've been *blackmailing* us. For years. And in return they've been 'protecting' us."

The ease and completeness of Vasdeki's surrender stirred suspicion. "You don't think they'll protect you now?"

Vasdeki looked down. "No. And if I don't talk you'll get everything you need from them. It might take you more time, but I know what they are." His head lifted and he extended his hands, displaying the cuffs. "You're cowards, all of you. Threatening Gina because of what I've done. Coward. Karteris was the worst of the lot. I heard what happened to him—I hope he took a long time to die."

Easier not to react here in the interrogation room, where his training held most strongly, but it still sickened him. Not so much the images he couldn't stop, but the thought of dozens of interviews to come with Karteris's name mentioned again and again.

He'd get through them, one at a time. Start with this one. "How did the blackmail work?" Toreth asked.

The lack of reaction to the insult seemed to quench the brief defiance. "Oh, we did all the work. A few people were registered as informants and they collected the payments for the bastards here. Cash, or goods and services, whatever we could give them. Wanting more and more . . . it couldn't have gone on for much longer."

Toreth felt his focus coming back as he kept the questions away from the danger topic of Karteris's death. "How did they find the resisters?"

"Whenever someone was reported, they'd drag them in and sound them out. See if they were guilty, and what they'd be willing to do. Sometimes if people were innocent they still might pay to have their names cleared completely. Even an accusation of anti-Administration activity is damaging."

Perhaps arranging a few extra accusations of suitably rich targets, too. An old scam, and one cracked down on by I&I management wherever it appeared, because it inevitably ended in tears when an ambitious para tried to strong-arm the wrong corporate. "But what about real resisters?"

"Nationalists." He shifted his wrists in the cuffs. "Sometimes the accusations were true. And from time to time they'd pick up someone who knew a few names, other nationalists, and they'd suck them into it, too. Theo was like that—he knew my name, I don't know why. If people wouldn't cooperate, they died under questioning or went for re-education."

"I need names, Alex. Resisters being blackmailed, who was doing the blackmailing. Give me that and if it all checks out—*if*—then Gina is safe and you're on reduced charges."

Vasdeki smiled grimly. "I can give you some of the bastards who work here. But not the rest. I don't know any of our names. We weren't stupid."

Of course, once Toreth had the names of the paras, the resisters would be easy. Whether Vasdeki hadn't thought about that, or was lying to himself about it, Toreth knew better than to point it out. "You can't give me any resisters at all?"

"Nationalists," Vasdeki repeated. "No—I know one name. Theo. And I only know because I heard you call him that."

"You were there?"

"Yes. On the roof." He lifted his head. "I thought he was dead, or I never would've left him."

As if Toreth cared. "Who was behind that?"

"Karteris arranged it all—I was there when he did it. Theo took me along, because it was set up in such a rush. He told Theo what to put in the message, he gave us the comm jammer. Just like he did with the woman. The Citizen Surveillance agent."

Exactly what Toreth had hoped for. "You were there when Theo and Karteris talked about Grant?"

"No. Theo told me about it afterwards." Vasdeki smiled bitterly. "Our first joint operation. We had as much to lose as they did, by then. Mutual destruction. Karteris told us she was there. I worked at the university, so I was chosen to keep an eye on her. I tried to steer her away from things that mattered, but she kept asking questions—she wouldn't stop looking."

"But you weren't there with Theo when the murder was arranged?" Hearsay, and so difficult to get a warrant on when corroboration from Theo or Karteris was unfortunately impossible.

The prisoner shook his head. "If you want to hear about it firsthand, Theo said another one of them was there—another para. Shorter, heavier build. Pale."

Easy description to match up, but Toreth waited patiently for the prisoner to produce a name unprompted.

"P-something, I think."

"You tell me."

Vasdeki closed his eyes. "Priftis. Emmanuel Priftis."

Toreth paused briefly, but prompting would be acceptable now. "Manos Priftis?"

"Probably. That's what Manos is short for. He went with Theo when she was killed. For all I know, he might've been the one who did it. Theo never told us the details."

Beautiful. Finally, a live fucking witness—the first crack in the wall. There would be more. "Well done. Gina will be grateful."

Vasdeki looked down, shaking his head.

❖❖❖

The next time Toreth opened the door to the interrogation room, he found his prisoner uncuffed and pacing the floor. The single guard watched; Toreth decided not to bother with a reprimand, which would only add to the resentment against him.

"Sit, please," Toreth said.

Priftis did as he was told. "What's going on?"

Toreth didn't answer. Instead he spent a minute or two checking the camera feeds and recordings, watching the junior para out of the corner of his eye. When he began to fidget in the chair, Toreth sat down.

"Okay, here's what I'll do. Straight, simple deal. I know that you can give me the names of the people blackmailing resisters, and the names of the resisters, too."

He said it with such matter-of-fact confidence that it took Priftis a moment to register what he'd said. Toreth watched horrified realization dawn before the junior struggled for control—too late, as they both knew. Even so, Toreth had expected Priftis to try to lie his way out of the situation. Instead he put his head in his hands and said, "Hell."

"I hope for your sake you can tell me how it worked, where the money went, and who else was involved. Do that, and I promise you'll get treated as leniently as I can arrange. I&I can't discipline the whole section. You know the drill. You can go to a new division with a nasty mark on your record, or you can be one of the scapegoats the Administration hoists up on high to show the good citizens we're serious about corruption." Toreth smiled. "I choose which."

Priftis took a deep breath and looked up. "I don't know where you're getting this crap, but I don't know anything about it."

Much too late. "If I were you, I'd be looking harder for friends than that, because the ones you've got already aren't doing you much good. Alexandros Vasdeki has pointed the finger at you." Toreth watched the name sink in. "Yes. He's made a statement that he spoke to you about the blackmail, more than once, with Karteris."

"The word of a resister?"

"He also said that you were there when Karteris arranged to have Grant killed. Remember Theodora Grant? She was a Cit Surveillance agent, Junior."

Priftis looked away, breathing more quickly.

"Suit yourself. If I don't clear this up soon, you know what will happen—Internal will hear about it. You can talk to me, now, here, or you can talk to Internal later, when they're holding a report saying you were an uncooperative prisoner. Or, who knows, maybe Cit Surveillance will get to you first."

Another pause before Priftis slumped back in the chair. "You're good at this."

"Yes—it's my job. Want to see my commendations?"

"It's no fun from this side." He sighed. "Okay. Christ, I feel like I ought to ask for a guarantee signed by my Justice rep."

"Names, please."

Priftis frowned at him, doubt still plain on his face, then nodded slowly. "Okay. No problem."

Toreth took Priftis and Vasdeki over to Justice and left them in cells there, where they would have a much harder time getting a message to their respective friends, and where the friends would have a harder time getting at them. Now that he had a brace of live witnesses, he intended to keep them that way.

Back at I&I, Toreth filled in Nagra and B-C on what had happened, then moved on to plans for the future.

"We still need more evidence than Manos's word. For one thing, he claims he knows nothing about Karteris arranging to have Theo take a shot at me, and I believe him because he spilled everything else. We'll get a team of investigators and interrogators from the pool in New London. Then we'll pull in all the resisters being blackmailed, and from them we get confirmation of the names of the blackmailers. From what Priftis says, everyone kept their own list of resisters they'd brought in personally. Karteris might've had a more comprehensive list, but we'll be lucky to find it—I'd have wiped it if I were him."

Nagra cocked her head. "Any chance Nikoletta would know about it?"

"Priftis says not—none of the admins were involved." Although that didn't quite tie in with Sara's overheard conversation. He must remember to get an official account of that for the case file. "Priftis couldn't know for certain, though."

"If she had known anything about the larger picture," B-C said, "why would she have given us Vasdeki?"

"Good point. Anyway, they seem to have put most of their effort into making sure no one here from outside Political Crimes heard about the extra cash on offer. The only non-Political person Priftis named is the head of security. He arranged camera-free interrogation rooms for them to soften the resisters up and make the blackmail threats."

"So he'd know pretty much everyone who was involved?" B-C asked. "If he blacked rooms out for them."

"Another good point. When the waivers come through we can start with him. I doubt it'll take too long to have everything wrapped up." And then he could go home and forget about the whole thing, most especially Karteris. "Lucky for us, because when Internal Investigations catch wind of what's going on they'll put half the division on a flight over here. If I had the choice I'd prefer to be long gone by the time those bastards arrive." Not that there'd be much chance of that.

Nagra nodded a vigorous agreement. However, Barret-Connor coughed. "Shouldn't we call Internal Investigations in anyway, Para, for something this big?"

How the hell had the man stayed so naive for so long? Almost endearing, in a way, but dangerous. "B-C, do you want to spend the rest of your career known as the man who handed over virtually an entire I&I section to Internal on a plate?"

B-C considered. "Ah—no?"

"Good choice. Me neither. Nagra?"

She laughed. "Not unless I get a pay rise big enough to make up for it."

"So we're agreed. This stays within the division for as long as possible. At the very least, we want to be well enough entrenched that they can't just kick us out and take over. Although..."

Although better still if they could ensure a clear distinction between their own investigations and Internal's probably inevitable involvement. Best of all, the change of plan offered a way to get back to New London all the sooner.

Nagra and B-C were looking at him expectantly.

"Just thinking." He pointed to Nagra. "Call Sara, tell her to organize everything but not to put anyone on a plane just yet. I need to talk to Vassilakis."

Despite Manos's assurances, Toreth hadn't been sure whether Vassilakis knew about the scam. It didn't much matter either way, but from his reaction to the revelations, the answer looked to be no. By the time Toreth finished talking, Vassilakis was ashen under his tan. His first words were everything Toreth had hoped for. "What should I do?"

"If I were in your place, sir, I'd take the initiative—suspend everyone under suspicion, maybe even place them under watched house arrest, and call in Internal Investigations yourself. Make clear you're doing it on your own initiative, no pressure from me. You found something out, you're reporting it."

Toreth hadn't thought it possible for the man to get any paler, but he did. "Internal? I'll be crucified!"

"Vassilakis, this has been going on right under your nose for years. I didn't have to bring it to you—I could've kicked off the whole thing and the first you'd have known about it was when you strolled in at eleven o'clock and found your office sealed and Internal scheduling the whole of Political Crimes for interrogation. More than likely, you as well."

"And you'll tell Internal if I won't?"

"I have no choice. They're coming anyway, at some point, and the last thing I want is suspicion I'm involved in a cover-up."

Tired smile. "But with my signature on the invitation, I take any heat resulting?"

Not quite as stupid as he looked. "Not at all. I keep my hands cleaner, you have a chance of salvaging some kind of reputation. In other words, we both win." Toreth leaned on the desk. "I had Karteris safe in custody, and George let him go. Who else's authorization is on that release? Internal won't just be looking at the seniors on this one."

Vassilakis stared at his immaculate desk, picking at his bottom lip. Finally, without looking up, he nodded slowly.

Toreth waited while Vassilakis made the call; the Athens division head didn't protest his insistence on staying to listen in. Toreth thought Vassilakis put up a decent performance, and he certainly engaged Internal Investigations's interest. By the time the call finished, Toreth could imagine the activity beginning to stir up at Internal headquarters.

No mention at all that the call was Toreth's idea. Good. The man could change his story later, but the first version on file would be the right one.

Outside the office, Toreth pulled out his comm earpiece and called Sara. "Ready?"

"Yes. I can have everyone on a plane in a couple of hours, whenever you want them."

"Great. Set everything up for the team to leave..." When? How long would it take Internal to get themselves organized? Not long. "First thing tomorrow morning will do." That should spread news of the operation within I&I. That might be useful later, if Internal got here sooner than he hoped.

Back in his office, B-C and Nagra were waiting.

"The team will be here in the morning," Toreth said.

"Will that be soon enough?" Nagra asked.

"I think it will be about damn near perfect."

Chapter Eighteen

❖

Nightmares woke Toreth four times. Not, however, the usual frantic recreation of real memories. Instead he struggled through far longer dreams of darkness, exhaustion, and the cold, bottomless pull of the sea. He woke panting, gagging at the salt taste of sweat on his lips.

He wanted it over, he thought as he stared at the stars through the window, muted here by the city lights. He wanted the case finished. He wanted to go home.

After the fourth dream, he didn't think he'd sleep again, but when the comm chimed at seven thirty it shocked him unpleasantly awake from deep sleep. Toreth groped for the earpiece, accidentally switching on the light. He groaned at the brightness.

Expecting Sara, he was surprised to hear Warrick.

"What the fuck do *you* want?" Toreth said, too dazed for tact.

"I would like you to read a file."

"Now? Jesus fucking Christ, it's—"

"Five thirty in the morning, here. Read the damn file, Toreth."

Finally Warrick's tone of restrained fury penetrated the mental fuzz of sleep. If he'd been more awake, he might have had the sense to close the comm link straight away. "Okay, okay." Toreth found the hand screen and fumbled to expand it. "Send it through."

Despite everything, Toreth still didn't realize what it had to be. The opening three or four lines were enough to tell him. By the time he'd read halfway down the page, his stomach cramped with the humiliation of being caught. "Warrick—"

"Finish it," Warrick said.

He slumped back against the pillows and obeyed. Everything was there: everything he'd arranged, everything he'd told them, copies of the reports he'd received. One line stood out. "The client has requested recorded evidence of any liaison." Which was true, he had. But written like that, laid out in black and white, it looked so pathetic. That was because it was. So fucking pathetic.

As soon as he got back to New London, he'd have Uche's license revoked. Client fucking confidentiality, indeed. Reaching the last page, he read slowly, not wanting to finish and move on to the next stage. "Discussion"—blazing row—and then Warrick closing the connection. He wished Warrick had just sent the fucking thing, not waited while he read it.

Eventually, he couldn't delay any longer. He closed the file and Warrick's face appeared on the screen. Too small and too far away, and he was almost glad about that. "I'm sorry." What else could he say?

Warrick let out a breath. "It's all genuine, then?"

Oh, fucking *hell.* Complete fucking *idiot.* A stupid, amateurish mistake he'd sneered at dozens of prisoners for making. Too late to take the admission back. "Yes, it is. Warrick, I'm really fucking sorry." Sorry SimTech caught me, sorry I was so stupid as to think they wouldn't.

No response, and for the first time Toreth realized how angry Warrick was, because he didn't look it. He didn't look anything—self-control so tight that it left not a crack through which any emotion could escape. He didn't look like he cared, and the fear went through Toreth like a knife. Say something, Toreth told himself. Anything. Don't let him go. But his mouth felt as dry as beach sand and he couldn't force out the words, even if he'd been able to think of any.

"Thank you for being honest, at least," Warrick said. "Rather too late in the day as it is. I'm sorry that you couldn't trust me, but the real—"

Suddenly, he found his tongue. "Why the fuck should I trust you? It's not as if you haven't done it before."

"Don't you *dare* try to use that as an excuse for this." Warrick's voice lowered, harsh with anger. "It has nothing at all to do with Girardin."

"Who said anything about that tosser? You fucked Carnac before. And you lied about why he was there."

"No!" Dull crack over the comm—Warrick's hand on the desk. "Enough. I have no intention of listening to you justify yourself. How the hell you can even..." With an obvious effort, he regained control, the anger subsumed beneath his mask. "I won't keep you awake any longer. I have a great many things to do, and—" his mouth twisted, "—a number of people to see. Damage control. I need some sleep beforehand, so please don't bother to call back."

Blank screen. Toreth stared at it blankly, paralyzed by the shock. Finally, the numbness dissipated sufficiently to allow him to panic. What the hell could he do? Here, nothing at all. Warrick was too far away for Toreth's usual tactic of fucking him out of a bad temper. Not that there'd be a makeup fuck for this even if Warrick were standing right in front of him. Probably not ever again.

Even so, even though Toreth couldn't imagine what the hell he could say to Warrick, the urge to go back to New London and find him was suddenly overwhelming. So overwhelming, in fact, that he spent a minute considering leaving

Nagra in charge and going anyway, before he acknowledged the impossibility of that. He was as stuck in Athens as Vasdeki and Priftis, locked in their cells.

By eight thirty, Toreth had been to the hotel gym and back. Exercising had blanked his mind for a while, but there were physical limits. Every muscle ached, and it barely blunted the edge of burning embarrassment. Caught, and in a weird way half of him hoped that Warrick would never call him again. The other half prayed for a call this minute—or the next minute—or the next one—

The comm chimed again while he was in the shower. He didn't even bother grabbing a towel on the way out.

It wasn't Warrick.

Sara's eyes went wide. By the time he'd switched to sound only, she was laughing. "What the hell is it?" he snapped.

The laughter cut off sharply. "Toreth, I'm sorry. Listen—everything's screwed up."

Fucking tell me about it. Toreth tried to focus. It must be the case. "What?"

"I'm at work and Internal Investigations are here, too. One of the receptionists called me when they showed up. They've put a hold on the team you wanted for Athens—they say they're taking over."

He let out a breath. At least something was going wrong according to plan. Someone could well be listening, though, so open relief would be dangerous. "Fuck. Would it help if I came back?"

"I don't think so. They've got Tillotson's agreement to the transfer of authority—not that he could've done anything about it. And I expect they'll want to talk to you out there. I just thought you ought to know."

"Thanks." He sighed. "Stupid of me to think I could keep it inside the division until we'd found out how far it went."

"I'm really sorry."

"It's not your fault." Sara was still apologizing when he cut the connection and went to find a towel. It was a pity to let her worry, but he could explain it all when he got back to New London. She'd understand.

Unlike Warrick. He stood in the bathroom, towel in hand, distracted by the thought of Warrick. It could take hours to get everything sorted out in Athens—days, maybe. He could only hope that Internal would live up to their reputation as high-handed heavyweights and crush his insignificant little investigation without a second thought.

Why hadn't SimTech security tracked that fucking idiot Uche down a couple of days earlier? If they had, then Toreth could've left Athens. He wouldn't have wrung confessions from Manos and Alexandros, and he wouldn't be waiting now for Internal Investigations.

If. Ifs were no bloody use to anyone, which was the same thought that had started the mess in the first place. Toreth took a deep breath, let it out slowly, and started drying his hair. He'd just have to deal with one thing at a time.

Toreth intercepted the Internal Investigations team as they arrived in the I&I Athens reception. There were more than two dozen of them, easily distinguished by dress from the local staff. Internal wore dark gray suits, an unusually civilian look for an Int-Sec division. On the other hand, the black I&I uniforms were meant to impress the public; anyone facing an invasion by Internal didn't need any extra intimidation.

The team head made him wait until the entire Internal group assembled before she would even speak to him. Arrogant wankers.

Toreth pretended impatience at the snub. Actually, he welcomed the delay. It gave time for the Athens branch staff to gather around the periphery of reception to watch the show. Out of the corner of his eye, he could see B-C and Nagra hovering, and Nikoletta—in tears again—handkerchief pressed to her mouth. Witnesses, dozens of lovely witnesses, ready to recount to all and sundry how this mess was in no way Toreth's fault.

Looking around, he spotted only two faces from the list of blackmailers. The rest were probably busy destroying evidence or already running. Much good either choice would do them. Or maybe Vassilakis had taken his suggestion about house arrests.

Finally, the senior Internal officer disengaged herself from conversation with her second in command and strolled over. She looked like a woman it would be a bad idea to play poker against. She didn't offer to shake hands, but her tone was friendly enough. "Senior Investigator Ransome, Internal Investigations." Ransome gestured at her companions. "And my team."

Whose names I don't need to know because I won't be here long enough for it to matter, Toreth thought.

"We have been called in by the I&I Athens division head," Ransome added.

Toreth resisted the urge to look around to check that everyone had heard that. "I have everything under control here. I have investigators on the way from New London."

"No, you don't. This branch of I&I is now under the supervision of the Internal Investigation Division, by authority of the Int-Sec Head of Department. You are ordered to hand over all information and prisoners."

Ordered. God, he loved that word. "Prisoners?"

"We know where the information came from."

Well, that was Manos fucked. Toreth pretended to debate the decision for a moment, then shrugged. "Of course, ma'am. If you come with me, I'll arrange the transfers right away."

The woman nodded. "One moment."

Another brief discussion with her number two—Toreth caught the words "begin the arrests"—before the Internal team broke up into groups and headed into the building. Most of the crowd moved off ahead of them, not wanting to attract Internal's attention. It didn't matter; they'd served their purpose. So far the plan couldn't have gone better. All that spoiled it was the nagging worry from last night.

As they walked to his office, Toreth asked, "Do you want me to stay on and help with the investigation?" He wasn't sure what he wanted the answer to be.

"That won't be necessary. We'll debrief you, and then you can return to New London. I've already booked a flight for you and your colleagues for this evening." Ransome smiled—a brief crack in the façade. "Sorry to spoil your little holiday, Para-investigator, but I think we can handle this on our own from here."

They were halfway across Europe, with the setting sun painting the clouds below them a vivid pink, when Toreth remembered that he'd never had Sara make a statement about the overheard conversation between Karteris and Nikoletta. Sloppy casework, because it was the only evidence they had that Nikoletta had any involvement in, or knowledge of, the scam. On the other hand, he didn't see why he should do Internal any favors. They'd only want to drag Sara in for an interview and she wouldn't thank him for that.

"Want the dessert, B-C?" Toreth offered the investigator the triangle of airline cheesecake.

"Thanks, Para."

Toreth contemplated rounding out the tail end of the investigation expense account with as much alcohol as the plane carried. Probably not a good idea to turn up to Warrick's flat paralytic, if he could manage to go through with it at all. Why the hell hadn't Warrick called to say what had happened?

"Sir?"

Toreth looked up to find a steward offering coffee. Caffeine was probably an even worse idea, but he accepted a cup. B-C had tea, and that made Toreth think of Warrick again. Coffee for relaxing, thinking, or waking up, tea for disasters. Must've been drinking a lot of tea over the last few days.

"Para?" B-C sounded concerned.

"Um?" Toreth looked around and frowned. "What's wrong?"

Pause, then he noticed a quiet bump and B-C's seat jerked slightly—Nagra nudging the seat from behind. "I was going to ask you that, Para. You hadn't even started pulling in resisters when Vassilakis called Internal. No one's going to blame you—us—for them getting involved."

"I know they won't. In fact, that was the whole point." Toreth grinned, briefly cheered by B-C's expression of confusion. "Why do you think I went to see Vassilakis? What do you think I told him? To call Internal, before I did."

"You weren't going to—oh." B-C's face cleared, and Toreth heard a suppressed snort of laughter from Nagra. He bet she'd guessed even before she put B-C up to asking.

"Sorry," B-C said. "Stupid of me. So now we're flying home and Internal will make all the arrests and take all the flak."

"Got it in one."

"But if that's what you wanted . . . ?"

Then why do I look like I'm flying to a funeral? Abandoning his coffee half drunk, Toreth reclined his seat and closed his eyes, deciding to risk the possibility of nightmares. "Wake me when we land."

Chapter Nineteen

❖

Warrick had apparently placed Toreth on the "unwelcome" list for the main door to his building. Toreth tried the system half a dozen times anyway, hoping he had simply made a mistake with the code. The failed attempts must have registered in Warrick's flat, because when he'd given up and was staring at the comm screen, trying to pull together the courage to press the button, Warrick's face appeared. He looked as though he'd been asleep on the sofa—hair tousled, shirt creased and unbuttoned at the neck.

Toreth rushed the words out before Warrick could speak. "Warrick, I came to explain."

"Explain." Flat voice, giving nothing away.

Slight change of tack required. "I mean to—to try and apologize. Look—" He glanced around. "Let me in. Please. If I'd wanted to do it over a comm, I'd have called from Athens."

"I was angry when I spoke to you this morning." The cool overarticulation might have made an amusing contrast to his sleep-rumpled appearance if the topic had been different. "I'm still angry now. However, not so much so I won't concede that you may deserve a chance to put your side. Since you've come such a long way to do it. Come upstairs."

Toreth spent the journey up in the lift trying not to think too hard. Should he disabuse Warrick of the idea that he'd come all the way from Greece just to say sorry? Did that look too desperate? Probably not half as desperate as he felt.

Once Toreth closed the door behind himself, Warrick stood, arms folded, waiting. Toreth considered asking if they could go through to the sitting room, or better still the kitchen, but he couldn't risk the refusal. Where the hell to start? Toreth took a deep breath. "Is everything…?"

The temperature lowered another degree or two. "The damage has been contained, yes."

"Who—" Oh, fuck. "Who knows?"

"Various people in the security department know the details of the investigation." Warrick's expression didn't alter. "I have no doubt that the contents will find their way into the office gossip system in due time. I had to tell Asher and Lew, of course. The head of security presented the report to them. I wanted them to know I hadn't concealed anything. Not my most enjoyable directors' meeting."

Of course Warrick would've been there—he wouldn't hide in another room while it happened. An image formed of Warrick, face like stone, staring at the wall as he listened to the report being read out.

The client has requested...

Asher and Lew. The rest of the time Toreth didn't give a fuck about either of them, but the idea of meeting them now that they knew he'd... and that wasn't the worst part. "And what about..." Toreth couldn't bring himself to say the name.

Warrick's mind-reading skills seemed to function in nonfucking situations, too. "Yes. However, he decided that it didn't impact in any significant way on his study and that it wouldn't be necessary to mention it in his report. Which, from Carnac, is a more significant concession than you are probably capable of appreciating."

So much for Carnac's vaunted fucking honesty when it was Warrick asking for something. Toreth supposed he ought to be grateful to Carnac—if the report had been fucked up, Warrick might've had SimTech security waiting outside the building to shoot Toreth on sight. Grateful to Carnac. Carnac, who now knew everything. The humiliation choked him, a thousand times worse than when he read the report in Greece. If Warrick hadn't been fucking Carnac before, he had every incentive now that the bastard had saved SimTech.

Was that it? Was that why Warrick hadn't tried to contact him? Carnac had already made a move and... He'd kill Carnac before he'd let him take Warrick. He'd kill Warrick. Rage spiraled up, frightening in its intensity. Dead—he'd see both of them dead before he'd even *think* of them together. He took a step back towards the door. "There's no point my fucking staying, I can see that. You can tell Carnac—" Toreth turned away, fumbling with the security.

"Oh, for God's sake." An exasperated sigh, then Warrick said, "Toreth, this one time you will listen to me, or there won't be another opportunity." His voice was quiet and absolutely serious. "Now, or never again."

He forced himself to turn, to look at Warrick. Don't think about it. Don't think about the two of them—"Okay. I'm listening."

"Very well." Warrick gazed at him steadily, his voice as dispassionate as if he were recounting a dull day at work. "Arranging the surveillance in the first place was bad enough. Continuing to conceal it when you knew that we were investigating the incident was far worse. If you'd told me, I could have called Security off with minimum fuss. As it is, you have damaged me professionally and deeply embarrassed me in front of my friends and colleagues. Worst of all, you endangered

SimTech at a critical time—something you knew full well could happen when you embarked on the enterprise, because I had explained the situation to you."

Endangered SimTech. All you fucking care about in the first place. The anger felt hollow now, though, a thin shell around the core of fear. Tempting to try another apology to fill the silence. After the cold, calculated listing of the damage, "sorry" didn't seem like much of a counteroffer.

"We both know that I'm not intolerant or unreasonable," Warrick continued. "However, some things are completely unacceptable. Much as I..." Warrick glanced down briefly, frowning, before he looked back. "No. What I mean is that I have no wish to—to finish things like this. But the possibility of a future repetition of this behavior would make it impossible for me to continue our association. Can you understand that?"

Meaning there was a chance this wasn't the end? Hating himself, Toreth grabbed at the thin thread of hope. "Jesus, I said it once already. I'm sorry. I'm really, really fucking sorry."

"To be perfectly honest, I don't care." No softening of Warrick's expression, no sign that he might relent. "Whether you regret it or not, it happened. What I need to know is that it won't happen again. I make—" Warrick hesitated. "I make very few demands of you, but I think I am entitled to make this one."

Could it really be this easy? "I won't do it again. Nothing like it. Ever. I promise." Not a chance in hell, after being caught once.

Silence, as Warrick looked at him measuringly. Toreth forced himself to meet Warrick's gaze, trying to transmit sincerity rather than fear.

"Very well." Warrick nodded. "Then the incident is closed?"

"Yes." Toreth stood, waiting for another comment, for Warrick to tell him to leave. The idea of a reprieve felt so unlikely. The silence quickly overcame his self-control. "If you want me to go..."

"No, I don't think so."

"Oh... okay."

Warrick raised an eyebrow. "Unless you'd rather go, of course."

"No!" His cheeks heated slightly at the speed of his response. "I mean, if you want me to stay, that's great. I just—" He shrugged. "I thought you probably wouldn't, that's all."

"When I said the matter was closed, I meant it. Over, finis, never to be mentioned again." Silence for a moment, then Warrick added, "I've had a hell of a few days and, since you're responsible for them, I think the very least you can do is try to make up for it."

Was that a joke? Hard as it was to believe, there was a small crease at the corner of Warrick's mouth. Relief flooded him. He turned away and ran his hands through his hair, composing himself. When he looked back, Warrick hadn't moved. "Sure," Toreth said. "Fine. What do you want to do?"

Now he was sure of the smile, catching it as Warrick turned and began to stroll down the hall towards the kitchen. "Well, first of all, you can watch me make dinner. I came back from SimTech and fell asleep before I could eat, or do anything else. And after we've eaten, I'm open to suggestions."

For the first time Toreth could remember, the kitchen was less than immaculate—the remains of a half-eaten breakfast sat on the table. Toreth picked up a plate, realized he had no idea what to do with it, and put it down as subtly as he could.

"Do you have to return to Athens tomorrow?" Warrick asked as he tidied up.

"I doubt it. Could happen, but Internal Investigations took the case away."

"Ah." The conversation had a brittle edge. "Is that bad?"

"Depends on who you are. Not much fun if you work at Athens I&I. And technically, for I&I as a whole, it's a bad thing, too. In reality, it's probably good. For me, anyway." There would be plenty of fallout to come, he was sure of that. At the moment, though, Athens seemed a long way away. "Too early to tell, really. I'll let you know when it's all shaken down."

"I&I internal politics?"

"Int-Sec internal politics—bigger version of the same thing. How—" He couldn't help pausing, even though Warrick had said everything was back to normal. "How's the thing at SimTech?"

Warrick turned away to open the fridge door. "The official report isn't complete. However, Carnac indicated to me that we had satisfied the concerns expressed by his employers."

"That's fantastic!" Slightly more enthusiastic than the comment really warranted.

"Indeed it is. Barring the unforeseen problems that always arise, there's nothing between us and the start of the first production run. Fame and fortune beckon."

Toreth watched as Warrick rifled through the fridge. From the look of the ingredients stacking up on the countertop, omelet was the most likely suspect for the meal. Not his favorite. Not, however, a problem. All Toreth had to do was activate his standard backup plan: distract Warrick, exhaust him, order something delivered.

"Have you got a copy of the shadow file?" Toreth asked.

A soft thump as Warrick dropped a block of cheese on the worktop. "Ah, yes, I think so."

"We can watch that later. In slow motion. You can point out all the really clever parts that I was too fucking turned on to notice the first time through. I must've missed plenty, with you in chains to concentrate on."

Warrick stood by the counter, ingredients ready, knife lying on the board. He didn't reply.

Toreth moved over, put his hands lightly on Warrick's waist, his fingers tingling at the contact. "Or we could watch it now."

"Or we could watch it now," Warrick repeated, his voice a little distant. Almost dreamy. Thinking about the shadow fuck, no doubt.

Toreth bent his head and pressed his face into Warrick's hair, inhaling deep and slow. After Warrick's long day it didn't have the freshly washed smell that always went straight to Toreth's cock, but it was still... inspirational. Watching the recording suddenly seemed like an unnecessary complication to the plan. "Do you know something?" Toreth murmured into Warrick's ear.

Warrick sighed, melting back against him. "A great many things. Which one do you have in mind?"

"We've never fucked in here."

"Really?" Warrick lifted his head from Toreth's shoulder. "I can't believe that."

"We've done every other room in the flat, and I sucked you sitting on the table once, but we finished that one in the living room. So, never in here. It's true."

"Mmm... no, not quite."

"What? When?" Toreth couldn't believe he'd forgotten.

"What you mean is, we've never fucked in here *before today.*"

Epilogue

❖

The comms unit—running highly illegal encryption code—chimed only once before Nikoletta answered it.

"Report." Nikoletta had no more idea of the name behind the man's voice than any of the other resisters who had heard it.

"It's finished." Nikoletta's own voice rang oddly in her ears, translated smoothly and instantaneously into the measured male tones of the leader of cell beta-one-forty-seven of the Hellenic resistance. "Alexandros was flawless—I've seen the transcript. Internal Investigations are here, the paras are being arrested."

"And the rest?"

"Some from the exposed cells will definitely be arrested, too." The awful price of breaking Political Crimes's corrosive hold over the Attican resisters. "We couldn't warn everyone in time, unfortunately."

"Unfortunate indeed." No emotion. "Although on the larger scale, perhaps it is for the best. If everyone disappeared it would lead to too many questions on the part of the authorities."

Another consequence of the inevitable arrests struck her. "And you'll be able to persuade the remaining cell leaders that we have to pull back and regroup. They'll have to agree now, with all the turmoil."

He ignored the comment. "And you, my dear. Are you yourself safe?"

The endearment gave her a twinge of fear. Despite her precautions, could the outsider know her sex? And if so, what about her identity? "As safe as I can be. Alex doesn't know my name, Theo and Karteris are dead, and as far as anyone else is concerned I never knew anything about Grant or the blackmail. The New London para might've suspected, but he's gone now."

"Karteris's disposal went smoothly?"

"Exactly like we planned." She smiled, thinking of the deeply satisfying expression of shock on Karteris's face as the men closed around them in the quiet alley. So busy watching them, ready to make a fight of it that it had been easy for her to use the injector. "The hardest part was persuading him to come down to Piraeus for the evening. Although it wasn't easy getting him to the boat. We should've just shot him."

"Then we would have had to provide I&I with a guilty party for execution. Complications of that nature are always best avoided. There have been no questions about the death?"

"No. We waited out there long enough for the drug to clear from his system, just like you said." The memory came back of fading curses from the water as they towed the stolen boat away, leaving him floundering. She'd felt a twinge of guilt then—more than a twinge—and if she'd been alone she might have turned back, to at least give him a more merciful end. But she couldn't show weakness in front of the men there with her.

"Can you be connected to it?"

"The people who helped me were from a secure cell. They won't be pulled in."

"Then everything is well. An unfortunate incidence of mass corruption which I&I will be eager to have closed as soon as possible. All to the good for us. Did you know," the man continued conversationally, "that admins have the highest proportion of convicted resisters of any grade within Int-Sec? Still a tiny percentage, of course, but it's a wonder that Internal Investigations don't pay more attention to them."

Somehow, Nikoletta kept her own voice even. "Really? I wouldn't know. If there's nothing else, I think we should end. Even this secure system is a risk."

"Good luck. And goodbye, my dear."

She sat, staring at the comm, suddenly cold in the stifling air. An unmistakable threat, a warning to keep in line. A threat against which she was utterly powerless. All she could do was trust and hope.

Ipsos Custodes

❖

In the end, Warrick decided not to meet Carnac at the airport. The socioanalyst's visit was supposedly clandestine; there was no point drawing attention to it by having consultant psychologist Alex Welham escorted into the building by a deputation of directors.

When Carnac arrived, early, Warrick kept him waiting for five minutes, then asked Gerry to show him in.

"I see that Toreth isn't an entirely bad influence," Carnac said, as Warrick rose to shake his hand.

"Oh?"

"You've lost weight." Carnac took a step back and made a more careful examination. "No, perhaps not. But there has been a definite redistribution. I feel humbled."

"What on earth for?" He didn't look a day different from the last time Warrick had seen him.

"I break few promises, even to myself, but two resolutions I make almost every New Year are to exercise more and to pay off my training debt. So far, I have been forced to renew them each January."

"Something to drink?" Warrick moved from behind the desk to the chairs by the coffee machine. Chairs that, for once, were clear of files and components.

"Herbal tea, if you have it. Nothing caffeinated, in any case."

Chamomile tea sat ready by the cups—he'd remembered that from Carnac's finickiness the first time they worked together.

"So how's the debt?" Warrick asked as they settled into the seats.

"Still onerous, but the end is perhaps distantly in sight. I'll be free of them, one way or another. By hook or by crook. Or, as seems more likely, by a great deal of tedious effort. Then I shall retire."

"Retire?" The idea was so ridiculous that Warrick laughed aloud. "You wouldn't know where to begin."

"Perhaps. But we all need our illusions to keep us sane." Carnac smiled distantly. "How is Toreth?"

"I'm glad to say he's absent, with leave." When Carnac raised his eyebrow, Warrick added, "On assignment in Athens. You'll be gone by the time he returns."

"Ah. A pity. I thought we three might have dinner together."

This time he frankly stared, before he recognized the subtle attentive tilt of his visitor's head—Carnac waiting to see if his victim detected the joke. Vital assessment of SimTech or not, Warrick didn't feel like humoring him over this point. "No," he said flatly.

"I was merely—"

"I know exactly what you were doing. Don't do it again."

"I see. You were more sanguine the last time we spoke."

"That was before you set about destroying Toreth's emotional stability for your own amusement."

"Now, that would hardly constitute a challenging pastime for me, would it? One might as well set about making lead heavy." Carnac's mocking smile entirely negated the semidenial. "I was simply intrigued by his . . . idiosyncrasies, nothing more. As you saw, he returned to you substantially unharmed when I left."

Although he knew he was responding exactly as Carnac wished, Warrick couldn't help the edge of anger in his voice. "Did you think I wouldn't notice?"

"Since we are being honest, yes, I did. I rather imagine Ms. Lovelady has regaled you with the luridly colored fruits of her overactive imagination."

"Does that make any difference to what you were doing?"

Carnac sighed. "I fear you overestimate my single-subject psychology skills. Or possibly underestimate my ability to resist provocation." Before Warrick could respond, Carnac looked pointedly at his watch. "And now, time is pressing and the Administration is paying for our personal conversation, albeit at a depressingly cheap rate. Shall we begin?"

Warrick nodded. "All we were told is that you're here because of concerns somewhere inside the Administration about the safety of the sim. I don't even know which department sent you. So I'm afraid we haven't been able to do much preparation for your visit, except what they asked us to do in the official notification. The staff know that a security psychologist is visiting and that they may be required to attend interviews."

"Most satisfactory. I also asked for a list of potential liaisons to be selected. Do you have it ready?"

"Yes. There's a summary here." Warrick sent the information over from his hand screen. "There are more detailed CVs there, too."

"One cannot help but notice that they are all female," Carnac said after a few seconds' scrutiny.

"I hadn't realized." Warrick kept his face deadpan. "I simply picked the staff I felt would be most suitable."

"I see." Carnac folded his screen. "Then I appreciate the time spent in your making the selections personally."

"There's also a document including a list of the highly commercially sensitive information that we won't disclose under any circumstances short of full legal compulsion."

"*Any* circumstances?" Carnac glanced at the closed screen as though contemplating checking the list, then laid it down. "At a rough estimate, how much of that is actually negotiable?"

"None of it. I thought it would save us both time if I gave you the short, honest list."

Carnac smiled. "And the consideration is much appreciated. I'm sure you don't wish to have me on the premises for longer than necessary."

"I want you here for as long as it takes for you to satisfy your—or your employer's—concerns. Do you have any idea how long that will be?"

"At this stage, I foresee spending about ten working days here, perhaps a little longer. It would have been much less, but I'm afraid the assignment came my way at rather short notice, and my preliminary reading has been cursory—so I will apologize in advance for any shortcomings in my technical knowledge. The socio-analyst originally assigned received the offer of a distressingly lucrative corporate contract and persuaded the division that his services could be spared."

No wonder Carnac looked sour. "So you're the second choice?" Warrick asked.

"In a manner of speaking." His expression cleared. "Rest assured that I won't let that interfere with my approach to the assessment."

"I know you won't. This assignment wasn't a punishment, then?"

"Not at all. Or a most ineffective one, which isn't entirely impossible, given the Administration. In point of fact, I may as well tell you that I volunteered quite forcefully when the assignment became available." Carnac smiled, his sudden animation and enthusiasm reminding Warrick of the time they had worked together in the Data Division. "Think about it, Keir. A substantial technical gap in my knowledge, and the dawn of a new psychological milieu for humanity—how could I resist? In this one case I anticipate a most enjoyable investigation. I would like to try the sim myself, at some point."

"Of course." Warrick found himself smiling in return. "I'll arrange someone to give you a demonstration."

Carnac hesitated, which was rare enough in itself to put Warrick on alert. "I had hoped that you would be able to show me the sim yourself."

"If you'd prefer. Any particular reason?"

Again, the slight, unusual delay. "You're the one who knows most about it—it will save us both time."

Warrick nodded. "I'll schedule a session whenever is convenient for you."

"Oh, no. At your convenience—I have no wish to interrupt any important work. I think I ought to form some personal opinion of the technology, but I confess that it's largely curiosity." Carnac smiled. "The Administration can afford to indulge me that much."

"I think I can free up some time on Monday."

"Excellent. Then perhaps we can meet with your fellow directors, and then I'm sure that you have a tour of the building planned for me. No assignment would be complete without seeing the coffee room, after all; I'm sure there's a paper to be written on the subject." Carnac stood, waiting until Warrick did the same, then smiled. "Oh, and one more thing. If Toreth is absent from the scene, perhaps you might wish to fill a lonely evening by accompanying me to dinner à deux. Business only, I promise—and at the Administration's expense, naturally. Tonight, perhaps? I will have had time to complete my reading of the basic background files by then."

Warrick managed to keep his sigh silent and internal. "Of course."

The cramped metal corridor echoed dully, the noise of their footsteps quickly baffled by the pipes and grilles. Carnac followed Warrick through the maze, occasionally pausing to inspect the details when Warrick pointed them out.

Warrick thought that he seemed preoccupied. Much the same, in fact, as he had at times during their dinner on Friday night. Warrick had wondered on the way to the restaurant if he meant to disclose something about the Administration's concerns over SimTech, perhaps even more than his remit permitted. Whenever Warrick had felt sure Carnac was about to say something, though, the conversation had veered off into another of Carnac's wicked anecdotes about past assignments, Administration and corporate. Warrick felt oddly as though he were being handled with care, or assessed, perhaps. Tested. For what, he had no idea.

Could some part of the Administration be planning a last-ditch attempt to gain control of the sim technology in the run-up to production? He wondered how much they would be willing to offer as a bribe to him, personally, to betray SimTech's secrets to them. Compared to some of the other possible reasons he'd come up with for Carnac's inspection, he almost liked it. At least it would be flattering to hear the figure he'd turn down. On the other hand, the idea of Carnac being used for something as tawdry as communicating a bribe was oddly depressing.

"I'm afraid I've never been in a deep sea installation," Carnac said. He paused and ran his hand over a pipe, rubbing the condensation between his fingers. "Which limits my appreciation of the verisimilitude of the model."

"I've had marine engineers tell me that if they didn't know better, they'd be sure they were in the real place." Even Dillian, who had finally cracked in her resistance to the sim.

"I find that... difficult to understand." Carnac looked around and sniffed critically. "There is a certain something, a lack of, ah, absolute solidity."

Psychosomatic, Warrick almost said, but didn't. "It's real enough for the failure simulations to give people nightmares."

"Of course they would. You are triggering a deep-seated fear. Even simple screens can achieve that."

"True."

The dismissive edge to Carnac's tone didn't concern Warrick. For people who thought they could see the flaws in the sim's reality, he had a well-tested surprise.

Through a thick, distorting porthole, a shark swam into view, fast, sweeping in from the deep-sea blackness to the arc of the installation's light. It shot head on towards the observers, mouth open to show off the rows of saw-edged teeth. Carnac didn't flinch, not even when it struck the glass with a dull thud before swirling up and out of sight.

Warrick snapped his fingers and the controls faded into view on a bulkhead. "Ending the session."

The room faded to black, and Warrick slipped a hand free and lifted his visor quickly.

In the other couch, a silently respectful technician was taking care of Carnac's visor straps.

"I was hoping for a rather longer demonstration. Thank you," Carnac added to the technician.

"My pleasure, sir." The man stepped back to let Carnac out of the couch. "Be careful when you get up—the first few times can make some people dizzy for a second or two."

"I'm afraid I took you at your word that you didn't want to interrupt any work." Warrick stood up from the couch, managing to hide his smile. "We can go in again another day. Actually, if you have a little time free now, there's something I'd like to take you to see—it's not far across the campus, and it had stopped raining the last time I looked out of a window."

Carnac nodded. "As long as it won't take more than forty-five minutes."

Outside the AERC the air smelled springtime fresh, full of recent rain and hints of flowers. The cream and blue-flowered daffodils planted around the edges of the courtyard had suffered from the poor weather, with broken stems and bruised petals. The granite blocks of the courtyard paving had begun to dry out in places, but most of them still glittered darkly in the sunshine.

"Look." Warrick gestured around, taking in the courtyard, the flowers, and the whole spread of buildings around them.

"The campus?" Carnac asked after a puzzled pause.

"The sim. We're still in the sim."

Carnac stared, then he shook his head, his mouth quirking into a faint smile. "I don't, ah—"

Warrick felt fairly certain that Carnac had been about to say, I don't believe you. Which was a common enough reaction.

"Watch," Warrick said, and snapped his fingers.

This time he'd varied the usual gin and tonics. The tray that appeared held a stone bottle of sake and two small cups. Getting the sake programmed into the system had been a last-moment rush, and he hoped it would stand up to scrutiny.

He set the tray down on the pedestal of a statue fountain—theoretically representing the flow of data through a network, although the water symbolism had never seemed very convincing given that the point of data transfer was *not* hopelessly to mix up the information—and opened the bottle.

When he turned and offered the cup, Carnac was no longer there. He was standing over by one of the flowerbeds, examining a broken-off blue daffodil.

"Is this setting accurate?" Carnac asked as Warrick came up behind him.

"This is an absolutely up-to-the-second representation of the area outside the AERC, barring any disturbances we make. Those will be corrected when we leave the sim."

"Ah, yes. The live shadowing described in the files." Carnac set the flower down, then accepted a cup and sipped. His eyebrows rose. "Very good indeed."

The real area outside the AERC had no seating, to discourage untidy loitering, so Warrick called up a couple of granite benches and a small table between them, which blended seamlessly into their surroundings. Carnac sat down cautiously, then relaxed.

"Padded," he said.

"Yes." Warrick sipped his own sake. "Form and function are only tangentially related. With a little tweaking, it can be exactly like the outside world or, perhaps, better. More suited to its purpose, at least. Texture, mass, strength—it's all just information."

"Indeed." Carnac leaned back on the bench and brushed his fingertips over the stone, then pressed at it gently. "All just information." He looked up. "I spoke to one of your team lead cryptographers this morning—a most impressive young woman—and she informed me that transfer of information between sim systems is highly secure. Possibly unhelpfully so. My opinion, not hers."

The sudden shift in topic made Warrick pause. Was this the reason the Administration had cold feet over permitting manufacture of the sim? It certainly came as no great surprise that they might fear the growth of a virtual world in which citizens could plot treason undetected.

"It's necessary if we hope to develop corporate applications," Warrick said. "We comply with all the legislation regarding information extraction and storage from communications systems, insofar as it is possible. The sim has a special dispensation due to the volume of data generated—Legislator Pearl Nissim championed the application. We separate out the information generated by the actions of the users and store that in a secure archived form."

"Is that system guaranteed to catch all user activities which might be used to transfer information the Administration would prefer to know about?"

"Guaranteed? No. We do everything practicable. The Communications Systems Assessment Division accepted that we cannot definitively detect intent, any more than their systems can pick out a normal message which uses a simple prearranged substitution code. And besides that, there are all the same confidentiality exemptions that apply to corporate bodies in any other data transfer situation."

"And here? Are the systems actively recording our conversation?"

"Right now? Yes. Although for ease and practicality the information extraction can be disabled—on the test machines, not in the final product."

"Then disable so, please."

Warrick called up the control panel. "Done. Anything else?"

"Your undivided attention, that is all. What is your opinion of the duty of care a corporation owes to those who use its products?"

"Safety legislation compliance is part of our—"

"No. I was interested in a less legal, more personal assessment. Let us remove the question from SimTech and place it in the realm of the hypothetical. It will make the underlying issues clearer. Hypothetically, then, if one came to believe that one was a part of an entity which caused harm by its very existence, which didn't care about the safety of those toward whom it had a duty of care, what should one do about that?"

Warrick felt as if the ground had shifted abruptly. In the end, he said, "I think it would be up to the individual's conscience. And, of course, the circumstances—what they could do about it, what harm they might bring to others by acting. It's impossible to generalize."

"Then we shall be specific once more. Marian Tanit."

Warrick had feared this since the beginning of Carnac's visit. Even so, it was an effort not to react. "What about her? The sim was cleared of all blame in that incident."

"I wonder what Dr. Tanit herself would have said about that? Regrettable that we cannot find out."

Thanks to Toreth. No—that was unfair. Thanks to both of them. "Very regrettable. Whatever she did to SimTech, and to her victims, I'm sorry that she died."

Carnac nodded, his expression absolutely unreadable. "I'm sure you are. Do you dismiss Tanit's reservations about the sim?"

"Not entirely. We have extensive psychological studies—you know, you've seen them—assessing the potential for the sim to harm individual users. The appropriate Administration regulatory bodies have seen the results, and accepted their validity. The chances of the sim causing addiction or inducing mental illness are no greater than for a range of other already legal products, and we've built in every safeguard to try to catch problems."

"And you began these studies after Tanit's death?"

"No, before. Although I won't deny we've pursued them more strongly. It seemed the least I could do to—" He stopped, appalled by how close he'd come to disaster.

"The least you could do to reassure the sponsors that you were vigorously protecting their investment? Please, I understand perfectly that commercial concerns can give an appearance of heartlessness when none exists."

Warrick felt as if Carnac were making it easy for him to recover from slips about Marian's death. Could he know the truth? All his carefully constructed protections would be useless if Carnac put the whole damn thing in his report, even as a suspicion without proof.

"When Marian was alive, I dismissed her concerns about the sim," Warrick said. "Perhaps I deliberately blinded myself to the strength of them, but she was convinced enough of her beliefs to do what she did. I think she was wrong, but we had to look even though it caused us difficulties."

"Intellectual honesty?" Carnac smiled at Warrick's nod. "Yes, it can be a costly and dangerous vice. Unhealthy, even. I did wonder... you may not remember, but I asked before how you coped with the knowledge of what Toreth does at work, and unjustly accused you of taking an ostrich approach. You said that you had seen an interrogation, and I wondered if hers was the one."

Thank God only the sim sensors could pick up his heartbeat. "Why would you think that?"

"It struck me that if you decided to put yourself through such an experience in the interests of gaining a fuller understanding of Toreth and I&I, then that is the one you would choose. The most personally distressing. A strong test case."

Warrick couldn't believe the relief didn't show on his face, but he did his best to keep it out of his voice. "You're right."

"Of course. Rather less theoretically—and please forgive my spoiling the illusion by explaining the trick—because I read the case file quite closely, and discovered that you were at I&I that day, as a public-spirited citizen, assisting our mutual acquaintance with his inquiries." The even, detached tone hadn't wavered, but he gazed steadily at Warrick. "Watching her unfortunate, accidental, death must have been very distressing for you. I quite understand why you're reluctant to talk about it."

Was that another let-off, Warrick wondered. Saying nothing, until he could even attempt to guess where Carnac was taking the discussion, seemed the safest option.

Carnac seemed quite happy to keep the conversation more in the style of a monologue for now. He drained his sake, then turned the cup over, checking the manufacturer's marks on the bottom. He smiled faintly. "Remarkable attention to detail. Absolutely delightful, verging on obsessive. I can quite see why the sim appeals to you, Keir." He looked up. "What did Toreth think of your, ah, presence as a witness?"

Warrick shrugged. "That's not the kind of thing that bothers him."

"True. Still, I have to ask, how did you find the experience?"

"Sickening." He mustn't forget who owned at least part of Carnac. "Although I realize that interrogation is perfectly legal and I don't doubt the necessity."

"Indeed." Carnac reached for the sake bottle and refilled his cup. He looked down into it, studying the patterns on the surface as he tapped the cup with the third finger of the hand holding it. "I have had doubts. More, recently, that ever before. Due in part, ironically, to your paramour. During the study at I&I, he showed me an interrogation that... I knew the theory, of course, but they are different in the flesh, so to speak. Far more visceral. So in one sense, a genuinely novel and fascinating experience."

Beneath the cool irony, Warrick heard the undercurrent of anger and remembered distress. It didn't surprise him. He found it unpleasantly easy to imagine the delight Toreth would have taken in making the interrogation as bad as possible for Carnac.

"Some day, I must thank him for it properly. Although to some degree, I have only myself to blame. I allowed myself to be drawn into a personal test of machismo, which is never advisable when dealing with someone with an overload of testosterone and the ethics of a shark. However," Carnac continued, still contemplating the sake, "it did lead me to question whether such things were truly a necessity, or if the imperative lay simply in the limitations and inflexibility of the system. That in turn caused me to consider other practices in which the Administration indulges merely in order to ease the perpetuation of its stranglehold on political power, and whether taking those tools away might ultimately result in a change for the better. And, more personally, it inspired me to reassess my part in all this, and whether serving the Administration unquestioningly is a conscionable act, or whether my role should perhaps be... redefined." He looked up. "What would you say to that?"

Warrick kept his astonishment in check. Formulating an answer took longer. Honesty felt dangerous, but he couldn't imagine Carnac going to all this trouble simply to trap him into a commonplace admission of anti-Administration feeling.

"I would... I would agree that the Administration might be better off without I&I, amongst other things. And I'd still say that anything you wanted to do about your part in it was up to your own conscience."

To his surprise, Carnac smiled warmly. "A sentiment I'm delighted, but happily not surprised, to hear. Thank you. However, there was a practical reason to tell you these things. I am here to pass judgment on SimTech and that colors all our interactions. Equality and openness are not possible where there is a severe imbalance in the power between the parties concerned."

"Nor consent?"

Carnac raised his eyebrow. "Beg pardon?"

"With, for example, a personal liaison?"

"Ah." Carnac smiled. "Simply because I understand the nature of the dynamic doesn't mean I cannot choose to abuse it when sufficiently bored."

"And are you doing this because you're bored?"

"No. SimTech is quite stimulating. Nor am I doing it in pursuit of intimacies on an equal footing. I wish us to be honest with each other. To facilitate that I am willing to make myself vulnerable to you. I have placed myself in your hands. If you report this conversation to my superiors, it will be believed, or at least not disbelieved. The consequences to myself will be... unpleasant and tedious."

"I won't tell anyone, you know that. You knew it when you told me."

"I believe I do know it, yes. Nevertheless, the leverage is there for you to use, to silence me at any point. And it will work; I have a very healthy fear of my superiors at Socioanalysis. Now, the reason for it. I know that you would lie to protect SimTech. And, indeed, do far more than lie—that isn't my concern now. All I need you to do now, for me and for SimTech, is to tell the absolute truth in response to my questions."

Warrick nodded.

"I could choose to focus a portion of my study upon Tanit's death. I have already made some preliminary inquiries in that direction. A consideration of the events led me to wonder whether a highly detailed examination might not reveal some things which would have as regrettable consequences for you as making public my distaste for the Administration would have for me."

Which, Carnac being who he was, probably meant that he knew everything. "Her death—"

"Was no doubt a very distressing time for everyone here. Another reason that it would be better for all concerned if my inquiries were limited."

No spontaneous confession required, clearly. Warrick nodded. "I'd rather people weren't reminded of it, certainly. Some valuable people resigned after the case was closed and I'd hate to lose more."

"Naturally. So, a few questions and hopefully the topic will be removed from my sphere of interest. Firstly, I came across—or perhaps was led towards—a rumor suggesting Marian Tanit discovered evidence that, at least at one point during its development, the sim was capable of inflicting serious neurological damage during normal use. True?"

Psychoprogramming stirring trouble? "Categorically no. If you've seen any such evidence, then I guarantee it's fabricated. And I have reason to believe evidence was fabricated previously, for others to discover before you."

“So there would be no unfortunate consequences to my speaking in detail to those involved with the sim when it was in Administration hands?”

“Feel free. They’ll tell you exactly the same.”

“As they indeed did.” Carnac paused to let that sink in, then continued. “Toreth’s investigation into Dr. Tanit’s death concluded that she was backed by unknown corporate entities which sought to destroy SimTech. Are they in fact as mysterious as he suggested?”

I have no idea of the names of any corporations behind her plan—a truthful if not honest answer that would probably bring disaster. “The whole thing was engineered by the Psychoprogramming Division.”

Carnac stared meditatively into the distance, quite unselfconscious with the silence as he considered the idea. “I see,” he said at length. “They planned to discredit the sim technology and remove it from the public arena.” Not a question. “Not because it posed any danger to users but because it threatens their monopoly on judicial brain manipulation. Once the sim becomes commercially available and sufficiently cheap, then places such as I&I will be able to use it, and Psychoprogramming will lose out in the Int-Sec power games.”

Warrick winced. “They won’t have it while I have control.”

“The sentiment is admirable, but the statement, I think, skirts dangerously close to violating your promise.”

Promise? Ah—to tell the truth. “I’ll fight them as long as I can. But if we don’t develop the sim, someone else will anyway—possibly Psychoprogramming themselves. People know it’s possible, and the payoffs are too large.”

Carnac sniffed. “The excuse of the innovative peddler of destruction throughout the ages.”

“And still true. We’re on the bleeding edge of the technology, and we have some proprietary neural interfacing systems that will be difficult for others to duplicate, but the concepts and the fundamental principles of the system aren’t secrets. They’ll get there in the end.”

“So, one way or another, your resolution is an empty one.”

“Perhaps. But, as you said, we all need our illusions. Carnac, why are you doing this?”

Carnac gestured around, taking in the simulated campus. “Because it would pain me exceedingly to have to destroy a thing of beauty, and still more so when it is such a remarkable technological achievement—and the beloved brainchild of someone of rare talent. You see—” He smiled at Warrick. “As my mentor at Socioanalysis told me more than once, sometimes I can still be unfortunately sentimental.”

Warrick was buttering his breakfast toast when the door comm chimed. Emma Queen stood outside, accompanied by four SimTech security guards; a dark-skinned woman it took Warrick a moment to recognize as Bet Johnson, a new member of the electronic security team; and finally Gerry Smith. Queen and the other security staff looked professionally serious, while the admin was glancing over his shoulder, checking the way towards the building entrance. Recovering from the surprise, Warrick stepped back inside the flat. "Please, come in."

He didn't ask for an explanation. There was no possible reason for the early morning visit which they could discuss in the corridor.

"Thanks," Queen said, then nodded to the guards and Johnson. One of the guards remained on duty at the door. The others disappeared into the flat, Johnson in the lead, already pulling out hand screens.

It had been a few months since they'd had a serious security alert at SimTech—Queen's highly efficient protocols caught most corporate sab attempts in the early stages—but this didn't feel like a drill. Gerry was fidgeting, no doubt at the interruption to his schedule and the prospect of more disruption to come.

Warrick raised his eyebrows, and Queen shook her head and placed her finger on her lips.

"I'm just making breakfast," Warrick said. "I'll put some extra coffee on."

They'd drunk the coffees, the three of them sitting in silence at the kitchen table, and Warrick had brewed more, by the time Johnson reappeared. "There's no sign of any physical tampering in the flat, no surveillance equipment we can find, nothing in any of the systems which shouldn't be there, and nothing we can pick up in line of sight from any of the windows which looks suspicious. Of course, they could have seen us coming in, even through the back door."

"Thanks," Queen said. "The office security, particularly?"

Johnson smiled slightly, as though she'd expected the question. "We went over it twice, with everything we have. No one's been in there, and no one's accessed any of the data there. Or if they have, they're far better than us."

"Which is always possible," Queen said. It wasn't an aspersion on the abilities of the SimTech team, Warrick knew, just simple fact. Corporate espionage was an arms race, and it was always possible someone else currently had the edge.

"May I ask what the problem is?" Warrick asked.

"Yes," Queen said. "But first—Johnson, go do anything you think is necessary to improve the systems and the physical security."

The expert nodded and left, smiling gratefully as she took the coffee Warrick offered. She looked tired, as they all did, and Warrick wondered how long they'd been dealing with the situation before it was considered time to disturb him. "Carry on," he said.

Queen leaned forwards. "Warrick, who is this psychologist? Is there something about him the directors didn't share with the rest of us?"

"Why?"

"Because someone is trying to carry out surveillance on him, and possibly you. At SimTech, his hotel, and maybe here." She pushed a hand screen across the desk. "I didn't want to use the comm, not even a secured connection, while I don't know the full story."

Warrick took the screen, and glanced through it only enough to be polite. He trusted Queen's assessment. "It's definitely targeted on him?"

"Definitely? No. The best information we have right now points that way, but not strongly enough to be sure. The apparent surveillance on you may still be entirely incidental, but I don't take stupid risks based on maybes."

"Corporate?"

Queen grimaced. "That's the nasty part. It's hard to say. You can see there, we think we have the name of the surveillance contractors. It's a small, single-owner outfit, but from what we can gather they take very well-paying work, private, corporate, and, so it's suspected, rather more clandestine Administration jobs." She raised her eyebrows. "Obviously, *I* don't have any information to suggest it's anything other than corporate."

And her suspicions about missing information made her unhappy, which was why she was such an excellent head of security. Warrick wished he could reassure her; in fact, anything he did tell her would have quite the opposite effect. This looked like a secondhand, disownable investigation, perfect for semiofficial surveillance on someone who should be untouchable and above suspicion.

Corporate espionage was one thing. If the surveillance were being run by a branch of Int-Sec or, perhaps worse, by Socioanalysis itself, then it could mean major problems for SimTech. However innocent the corporation and its directors, the mere fact that Carnac was here on an assignment he had elected to take could be disastrous.

That wasn't the only problem. Only a few days more at the most, and Carnac's visit would be over. If the watch was on Carnac, they could lose their chance to find out why when he went. Unresolved security issues were the worst kind.

"What do you want me to do about the surveillance?" Queen asked, watching him carefully. "We can dig deeper, try to find the client, or start an active counteroperation right away. Personally, I don't think we know enough to go in heavy."

"I agree. Dig as deep as you can, and try to limit the corporate information lost to them without arousing suspicion. I want to know more before I talk to Welham about it."

"Thank you," Queen said, although she didn't look happy at the prospect of sharing the news at any point with the mysterious outsider. "We'll be as discreet as we can—we're fairly sure they don't know yet we've spotted them."

"Good. Do your best to make sure it stays that way. So what's the plan?" Warrick glanced at the admin watching the conversation with silent attention. "Since Gerry's here, I assume that you want to confine me to the flat?"

Gerry nodded. "I can work from here for as long as necessary."

Queen looked relieved when Warrick didn't immediately protest the measure. "It's the easiest place for us to ensure your physical security, and for you to still have access to SimTech materials. We'll keep it all internal to security, tell the directors and no one else what the real situation is. It shouldn't take more than a few days, and we can tell everyone you're not well."

"Or I could sleep at SimTech," Warrick said. "I've done it before. I don't want the—the psychologist's visit disrupted."

"But if you're here, and Welham is at SimTech, then we can definitively assess the surveillance target."

"Ah, of course."

"Warrick, I have to ask—who is Welham?" When he hesitated, Queen sighed. "If you can't tell me, you can't tell me. But I'm asking because it makes it damn hard to do my job when I don't know what the security situation really is."

Warrick nodded. "All right. This is absolutely confidential, you understand? You mustn't tell anyone without clearing it with me first."

"Of course," Queen said.

Gerry nodded, too. Since he'd dealt with the arrangements between SimTech and Socioanalysis, he was perfectly well aware of Carnac's real purpose, but the knowledge didn't show on his face. That was one of the reasons why Warrick paid him as much as he did.

"He has been sent here to assess security in the sim—that's quite true," Warrick said. "But it's for the Administration, not for an investor. He's a socioanalyst."

Her only reaction was a sharply indrawn breath. After a few seconds she nodded. "Thank you. I'll be sure to keep that in mind."

After two days of frustrating confinement, Queen could report nothing more than that they'd been unable to establish further details of the surveillance firm's client. On the evening of the first day, Toreth called quite unexpectedly, and to Warrick's utter astonishment had invited him to Greece. Of course, Warrick had had to refuse, and when the call had ended he roundly cursed whoever had chosen this particular time to kick off another session of corporate game-playing. Their timing was immaculate in the most infuriating way.

Warrick didn't know what was worse—the uncertainty of the situation, the corporate house arrest, or the idea of Carnac loose and unsupervised at SimTech. Asher and Lew were supposedly keeping an eye on him, but it was impossible to convey to anyone who didn't know him well exactly how dangerous Carnac was. Impossible, too, to explain the full extent of the security threat without betraying Carnac's confidence. Who on earth would believe that a fully trained socioanalyst might be harboring anti-Administration sentiments? Warrick sincerely hoped no one would—and so no one would have any reason to watch him.

It was only late on the afternoon of the second day that a possible route to a solution occurred to Warrick. SimTech had a socioanalyst at its disposal, and one who would have every reason to want to untangle the surveillance web. Why not set Carnac to work on the problem? He called Carnac, and suggested he drop round to the flat in the evening. Carnac sounded suitably intrigued at what must have seemed like a very unexpected offer.

The least he could do, Warrick decided, was provide dinner. The weather was still cool and rainy, so something warming seemed suitable. Hoping to steer Carnac into a receptive, helpful mood, Warrick decided on a French recipe. French, and something he could prepare without having to rely on someone else to go out and select the major ingredients for him. The cassoulet was in the oven when the SimTech security guard let Carnac into the flat.

Carnac gave the man an appraising glance as the door closed. "I had wondered why you were absent from the office." Carnac smiled. "Even when unwell, it seemed rather out of character of you to allow me to run rampant without your close supervision, so I imagined there was some emergency. Corporate security issues?"

"Maybe, or maybe not."

"The cryptic really doesn't suit you, Keir. I'm quite sure this wasn't an elaborate charade to win the pleasure of my company for an evening. For one thing, as you well know, I always find dinner with you delightful."

"I think this might be the exception. We're under surveillance—or rather, you are."

Carnac's well-practiced control couldn't stop the alarm from showing on his face. He glanced around Warrick's hallway, as though considering whether they might be observed here. Then he smiled and offered the bottle of wine he was holding. "I thought I should play the part of the good guest in any case. From the rather delicious smell in here, I think I can manage to make a decent guess at the menu. Regional cuisine appropriate to one's guest, to put them at ease, prepared with dedication and attention to authenticity—a charming quirk I recall from our original time together."

Warrick looked at him curiously. "Don't you ever stop?"

"I can't," Carnac said as he followed Warrick into the kitchen. "Although, believe me, at times I have devoutly wished it were possible. So, open the wine to let it breathe, and then you can tell me about our mutual problem. I must say, I'm surprised that you didn't suspect me—or is that the reason for tonight's invitation?"

Warrick paused, hand over a kitchen drawer. "You?"

"Certainly. What better way to remove you from the office and allow me to carry out my nefarious plans?" Carnac smiled. "Really, Keir, if you didn't think of it then I'm disappointed."

"Not for a moment. For one thing, I can't imagine you'd find having me in the building enough of a hindrance to go to all that trouble."

"Both disappointed and flattered, then."

"Can you think of anyone who'd be watching you here?" Warrick asked as he took the corkscrew from the drawer.

"Keir, I can think of many, many people who might be watching me anywhere. And I'm sure I don't need to tell you that a number of them are persons neither of us would wish to have closely involved in our affairs. Although . . ." He stopped, head cocked like a broken automaton, then clicked back into life. "Affairs. You do raise an interesting point. Someone who might have a unique motivation to watch me here." Carnac held out his hand. "I assume you have the SimTech security reports available. May I see them?"

Warrick handed his screen over without hesitation. When Carnac had the power to take the SimTech systems apart at his leisure, there was little point in worrying about him catching a glimpse into the workings of corporate security.

Carnac took the screen and sat at the kitchen table. Warrick, who'd planned on keeping the evening in the more formal setting of the dining room, hesitated, then sat opposite.

"Mm." After rapidly scanning a few pages, Carnac paged through more of the report as though looking for something specific. Then he smiled very slightly. "A point of curiosity—Toreth returned to New London the weekend before last, did he not?"

"Yes. But he's back in Athens now. I visited him there myself last weekend."

"Yes—you were out of New London and unavailable. Also a point of interest. I noticed your tan when you returned, by the way." Carnac raised an eyebrow. "And the interesting bruise you are covering over quite effectively. How fortunate that your delightful sister isn't in a position to notice it also."

Warrick gritted his teeth. "That was an accident."

"You walked into a door?" Carnac grinned, a brief flash of devilish mischief, then sobered. "Don't worry, I believe you. Toreth has far too much professional skill to leave so obvious a mark intentionally, and I doubt that your mutual pathology has progressed so far that—"

"Jean-Baptiste," Warrick said.

The personal name proved as effective as he'd hoped. Carnac blinked slowly, then nodded. "Quite so. You're still alarmed over the question of our unknown spy, which shortens your temper. Well, perhaps this might set your mind at rest—in one way, anyway. 'Curriculum vitae' means, in a literal translation, 'course of life.' And invaluable sources of information they may often be, in discerning where the rivers of existence have meandered and met. See—the dedicated Ms. Queen has acquired a CV belonging to our corporate voyeur. A Mr. Uche, who possesses a rather interesting employment history."

As Warrick took the screen he thought for a moment of Marian Tanit, and her concealed past. Then the display wiped the comparison clean from his mind. The information was tucked away, of no real interest to the threat assessment, but in this case wildly significant. "He used to work for I&I?" Warrick said.

"Interesting, isn't it? Certainly not uncommon for a private surveillance contractor, but in this case, I suspect, rather more than a statistical coincidence. A moment, if you don't mind." Carnac opened his own screen, and spent a minute or so examining files. "Yes. Even a brief perusal of the relevant portions of their files shows that he worked in the General Criminal section, and the two of them shared cases several times. Would you like to see?" Carnac offered the screen. "Of course, the security files of I&I employees—and even ex-employees—are highly confidential, but I'm sure I could stretch a point."

"I'll take your word for it," Warrick said.

"And save me from abusing my security clearance. How thoughtful of you."

He closed the screen while Warrick contemplated the immediate future. He would have to get Queen to investigate further, but he knew Carnac's assessment was very probably right. Without the fear of a major corporate or Administration backer, they were dealing with a relatively minor operation; Queen could hit back hard, and on her past track record he would be very surprised if she didn't have a full report in a few hours. He would have to call a directors' meeting first thing in the morning.

The planning both helped him keep calm, and stoked the anger building inside. Of all the times—of all the damn stupid selfish times—Toreth had chosen now to do something Warrick had long feared he might try. "Toreth," Warrick said, with a combination of acknowledgment and exasperation.

"I'm quite sure you won't believe me, but seeing you embarrassed by him like this brings me no joy." Carnac stood. "I'm sure that you have things to do, and I doubt the rest of the evening would be pleasant for either of us if I were to stay, so I'll take myself off to my hotel. I have quite enough to keep me busy."

Warrick nodded heavily. "Thank you."

On the way out of the room, Carnac touched him briefly on the shoulder. "Drink the wine, at any rate. It should be excellent."

Anger kept the edge of adrenaline high. For the whole of the conference he'd made sure he was meeting someone's eyes—Asher, Lew, Emma Queen. Queen had read the security report summary aloud, with a professional neutrality for which Warrick was indescribably grateful. He'd had the idea that it would be best to get it over with at once, in the worst possible way, but by the end of the meeting he wished he'd simply sent copies to the other directors and taken a flight to somewhere a hell of a long way away.

Not Greece, though.

Finally, Queen folded her screen, and braced her hands on the edge of the table. "If you don't have any questions about the investigation, I'll leave you to talk it out."

Lew looked up. "I think that was everything we needed to hear. Thank you for your work; we all appreciate it."

"Thanks." Queen nodded and rose. "I do my job. I can't say I enjoyed it this time." She paused, still by her chair, and met Warrick's eyes. "But thanks for bringing it to me as soon as you found out, Warrick. It saved a lot of time and effort."

A comment aimed more at Lew and Asher than him. Warrick nodded. "I'll always do what's best for SimTech."

"So what's to be done next?" Asher said when the door closed behind Queen. "On the one hand, I suppose it's a relief. On the other... I hate to say it, Keir, but you have to deal with this. With him. Even if the surveillance wasn't targeted at us, they still could've picked up something of value—something which could've seriously damaged us."

"Toreth already said that he's sorry," Warrick said.

"Do you believe him?" Lew asked.

"Yes, I do. Or rather, I'm quite sure he regrets it happened, although I freely admit I'm not an entirely objective judge of his behavior."

Lew smiled sourly. "Meaning I'm not either, I suppose. True—I can't say that he left a good impression. Memorable, but not good."

"That was one unfortunate incident at a difficult time," Warrick said.

"And I brought it on myself." Lew flicked his hand sharply. "I learned my lesson, and I'm grateful you both gave me the chance to prove it, but my stupidity doesn't cancel out his."

"Lew, I—that isn't what I meant, at all," Warrick said. "I can promise that no one is taking this more seriously than I am."

"I know you are," Asher said. "But ultimately it isn't down to you, is it? Can you control him? That's the real question. Can you stop it happening again."

Warrick gave the question long and genuine consideration. They deserved nothing less. "I hope so."

Asher leaned forwards, her voice regretful but firm. "Hope isn't good enough, I'm afraid."

"I know. I've only spoken to him once, so far, and it was somewhat heated. But when he gets back to New London—" Warrick took a deep breath. "I'll make sure I'm satisfied there's no chance of a repeat performance, or I will terminate our relationship. For good."

Lew's eyebrows rose; Asher drew in her breath sharply.

"Keir—" she began.

"No. In this, SimTech has to come first. One way or another, this won't happen again, I guarantee."

Lew nodded and stood up. "Well, I wouldn't take his word on this or anything else, but you've never given me any reason not to take yours, Warrick. And—please don't make this the first time."

Asher watched her fellow director departing without a backwards glance, then shook her head. "I'm not sure if I ought to say this."

"Well?"

She sighed, sounding almost wistful. "For all the conferences and business trips I've been on, Greg has never even been suspicious."

On the other hand, she had probably never slept with anyone at a conference and told Greg about it in unnecessarily graphic detail afterwards. Not that, as he'd told Toreth, it was an excuse, but he was willing to acknowledge a degree of cause and effect. "You ought to be grateful to have someone who trusts you."

"Oh, I am. But in an odd way, it must be nice to know you're loved."

The unlikely suggestion almost startled him into a laugh. "No, that's really not the reason he did it. Jealousy's something quite different. Believe me—I know."

The room dismally failed to have its usual calming effect. The gentle, salty breeze, the rush of waves on the beach, the warm, soft sand under his hands, all made him think of the weekend in Greece. Warrick had just made up his mind to change the program, when Carnac appeared on the beach. He blinked and looked around, bringing his hand up to shade his eyes. "Goodness. How abrupt!"

"Didn't they tell you where I was?"

"No; I never asked." Not waiting for an invitation, Carnac sat down on the sand beside him. "I take it that Ms. Queen has confirmed the source of the surveillance?"

Warrick nodded. "Toreth, just as you said."

"Ah."

"I spoke to him this morning. Well. Perhaps 'ranted' might be a better description."

"With every justification. It may even do some good. Even those with a severely stunted level of emotional development are sometimes capable of modifying their behavior in response to clear, consistent cues." Carnac picked up a handful of sand and let it trickle through his fingers. "This is a curious place, you know. I manage to convince myself that I can see the flaws, that I can tell the difference between reality and fiction, but at the same time you thoroughly proved to me that I'm deluding myself. The mind is a powerful thing."

"Thank you," Warrick said precisely, "for not telling me that you were right about him."

Carnac smiled. "Will you accept his apology when he returns?"

"A bit premature, don't you think? I don't know if I'm going to get one."

"Oh, of course you will. 'Sorry' comes very easily to him, as it means nothing. It's a magic formula, nothing more than a word he's learned works on inferior beings. Still, when you accept, be sure you don't let him doubt you mean whatever threat you intend to hold over him to prevent future repetition. Dangerous wild animals can unerringly scent weakness." Carnac's eyes narrowed, more thoughtful than squinting against the sunlight. "And I hope you've judged the threat nicely. Another, sadly often forgotten, fact is that when we foolishly choose to treat dangerous animals as pets, the only thing which matters a damn is their whims. Provocation often ends badly."

Warrick tried to keep his voice level. "I think I can manage without your advice. And I certainly don't want it."

"Want. There's an archaic meaning of that word which fits the situation perfectly. However..." Carnac brushed sand from his hands. "I came in here to let you know that my business with SimTech will be concluded by the end of the day—I shall return to Strasbourg tonight."

"The report..."

Carnac waved the half question away. "The report will tell the truth, of course, insofar as it is relevant to the questions posed me. If not all the possible questions were asked, that's not surprising—time is finite. Incidents involving Toreth, current or historical, certainly don't fall within my terms of reference as I choose to interpret them."

"I'm in your debt."

"I wish you were. But if anything, the obligation is on my part." He paused but, when Warrick didn't ask, he continued anyway. "Our previous conversation in the sim was much appreciated."

With a quick mental command, Warrick stopped the sim recording. "I didn't realize I'd done anything. I rather hoped I hadn't."

"A little validation from someone whose opinion one respects goes a long way. And I have to try so hard to find anyone who fits that description."

He touched the back of Warrick's hand with two fingers, a brief brush of contact, then shook his head.

"Quite remarkable. It must be so tempting, sometimes, to stay here, where everything can be controlled with mere thought."

"Isn't that what you do out there?" Warrick asked.

"Hah. If only it were that easy. Controlling myself is difficult enough without considering the rest of the world." Carnac shook his head. "To be serious for a moment, self-doubt of the magnitude I've experienced recently would be very unpleasant for anyone. I don't wish to overdramatize, but for me it's . . ." He frowned. "Difficult even to consider the existence of the questions. 'Painful' would not be an exaggeration. To then allow those thoughts to generate actions should be impossible. Do you understand?"

"I don't think so."

"Mm. An analogy might serve, perhaps. A moment."

Carnac gazed off across the glittering ocean. He was sweating lightly, and Warrick reduced the temperature of the sun a little. Finally, Carnac turned back to him, his blue eyes as vivid as the imaginary sky. "You are very close to your sister, are you not? Also your mother and your aunt. Imagine them, if you can, murdered—raped, strangled, their bodies cut into pieces and thoroughly defiled. Now imagine doing those things to them yourself, with your own hands. I mean the exercise literally—imagine it, now."

His voice was still quite calm and neutral. Warrick stared at him, part of his mind unwillingly following the instructions. Suddenly the clarity of his sim-trained imagination became a curse, and he almost gagged.

Carnac smiled slightly. "Socioanalysts are very heavily indoctrinated into our loyal service to the Administration, during childhood and throughout later training, and knowing what has been done to one does not negate the effects. Conditioning is another word for it, and while I flatter myself that I'm a little more complex than a rabbit, it nevertheless remains true that with judicious application of electric shocks, a rabbit can be trained to starve itself to death while food sits ready to be eaten." Carnac shrugged, as though to negate the weight of his words. "So the oft-repeated story goes, at any rate. I confess I've never bothered to locate the original research. Perhaps I'm simply looking for excuses. Middle age is never the best time to find oneself questioning one's whole raison d'être."

"But I'm not the only one suffering from an unhealthy degree of intellectual honesty?"

"Quite so."

Warrick dug his hand into the sand, through the sun-warmed silky surface, down to the cooler, damper, grittier layer below. "Is that why you were talking about retirement? Could you really give it all up?"

"No, truthfully, I don't think I could. Besides, there's still the sticking point of my training debt, and attempting to leave with that unsettled would be unlikely to end well." Carnac flicked at his trouser leg, removing some clinging sand. "Who knows, perhaps there is some less-than-unhappy medium to be found. In any case, you have brightened the light at the end of my tunnel, for which, as I said, I thank you. If I can do anything in return at any point, don't hesitate to ask me."

"I know you won't take it personally when I say that I hope I'm never in a situation serious enough that I need your help."

Carnac inclined his head. "Indeed. Socioanalysts can be something of an overkill response. Nevertheless, I will remain at your disposal, gratis. Now, if you will excuse me, I have one or two things to tie up and a report to begin. Good luck, and I hope to see the sim in production soon—who knows, perhaps when my debt's discharged I'll buy one."

Carnac left him there, still looking out over the sea. Now the rush of waves had its old tranquility restored, and the warm sun soothed his skin. Peace had come back to his sim. Warrick wished his clothes away, and lay back on the yielding sand.

Psychosomatic, indeed.

Gratuitous Kink

❖

Silence reigned at the table, while all around them the café buzzed with conversation. Toreth had chosen one of their regular places, not too far from the edge of the Int-Sec complex, on the side nearest the university. During the summer, the café expanded out onto the pavement. The striped awning overhead provided relief from the hot sun, and the checkered tablecloth flapped gently in the breeze. Even if it was a bust, Toreth thought, they'd still had a nice lunch out of it.

Toreth forked through the remains of his pasta, dividing his attention between the plate and the man opposite him. Not surprisingly (since he hadn't said flat-out no), Warrick was taking his time thinking about the proposal. Toreth waited, braced for a refusal and already half wondering how best to change Warrick's mind. Not that it really mattered if he said no. When the invitation had arrived, he'd nearly deleted it without a second thought. Only a whim had made him call Warrick and set up lunch to ask him.

"Do you really want to go?" Warrick inquired at length.

Toreth shrugged, noncommittal. "I thought it'd be different, that's all."

Warrick smiled slightly. "And the answer to the question?"

"Yeah, why not? I'd like to. It'll be fun."

Warrick closed his eyes for a moment, tilting his head back. When he looked back at Toreth, his expression was serious. "Very well. But on the understanding that we'll leave if I don't enjoy it. Both of us will leave."

"Of course."

"And that you also understand that's probably what will happen."

"Sure. I know."

"I don't want you to be disappointed, that's all."

"I won't be." Then, as Warrick's eyebrow quirked, he added, "Of course I will be. But I won't go on about it."

"Perfectly acceptable. One other thing—I'm assuming that, the Shop being the Shop, there will be a certain amount of sexual activity going on."

Toreth smiled inwardly at the tone. Warrick's best sim fuck research voice. "Yeah, probably."

"So, if that proves to in fact be the case, the options are that neither of us will have any contact with anyone else, or that both of us can—if we decide we want to, of course. The point is that I have no intention of escorting you to an all-you-can-eat fuck buffet and standing on the sidelines, watching you fill your plate."

Toreth noticed a silence at the next table and glanced around, slowly and deliberately. The three young women colored furiously, and looked away when he smiled.

Now it was his turn to think something over. Saying "neither" would put a terrible crimp in Toreth's own evening. On the other hand, the idea of Warrick... even the idea of the idea of it banished the warmth of the café. "Neither" was by far the safest. But on a third hand, Toreth would be there with him, to keep an eye on whatever went on. Odds were Warrick wouldn't want to anyway—he didn't like doing anything in public.

Suddenly, he thought of a compromise. "Start off with neither. Then if either of us changes our mind in midparty, let the other know and then it'll be either." Then Toreth could fuck whomever he liked, as long as Warrick didn't see. Better yet, if Warrick *did* catch him, it would still be inside the rules. Toreth could just claim he'd meant to tell him when it was over. Perfect.

Warrick regarded him thoughtfully for a long moment, and Toreth had the uncomfortable feeling that he'd been seen through. He held his ground, keeping the suspicion off his face, until Warrick nodded. "Very well." He lifted his glass. "To an interesting and unusual Saturday evening."

"I thought I said don't get dressed until I arrived?" Not that Toreth really minded, because Warrick in black and white was his next favorite thing to Warrick naked. Fuckably irresistible, dressed or undressed.

The guilty party turned around from the bedroom mirror, where he'd been tying his bow tie. "I'm sorry. I thought it would save some time, since we're running late. Didn't your invitation say formal?"

"Yes. But that's formal for the—never mind. For me. You have to wear these."

Warrick's eyebrows disappeared up under his fringe as Toreth opened his bag and handed over the contents. Black leather—although not a great deal of it—and a short length of chain.

Taking the things, Warrick laid them out on the bed. Leather wrist cuffs, locked together by the chain. A key for the chain, on a fine plaited leather string, long enough to wear around the neck. Leather collar. Leash. A thong that redefined skimpy. He contemplated the assortment for a while, and then shook his head firmly. "Where did you get this?"

"Fran found it for me. She thinks it's all your size."

"Helpful woman."

To be honest, Toreth didn't rate his chances of persuading Warrick to do this part. He'd been antsy enough about the mere idea of a party at the Shop, and Toreth had been deliberately vague about the details. Deliberate bordering on deceptive, in fact. However, the idea of maybe having the power to make him do it, and of showing Warrick off, of marking him so clearly as *his,* compelled him to try. "You'll look great," he said.

"Mm." Warrick picked up the thong, dangling it from his forefinger. "Is this compulsory?"

Not at all, unfortunately. "In a way. It's traditional for the anniversary parties—so Fran said." He smiled, hopefully disarmingly. "There'll be plenty of other people wearing the same kind of stuff."

From Warrick's expression, that wasn't a helpful argument. "I don't suppose that *under* the DJ is an option?"

"Nope. Not in the spirit of things."

"Of course not." Warrick dropped the handful of leather on the bed, and then sat down beside it. "Come here," he ordered.

Really not in the spirit of things. Still, Toreth went over obediently. He did try to salvage something by pushing Warrick back onto the bed. Caught by surprise, he went down easily, and Toreth knelt over him, straddling his chest, pinning his wrists above his head. "Yes?"

"It's a question of what I enjoy," Warrick said, as calmly as if he were the one on top. "I enjoy domination. I like to feel controlled—to feel a loss of self. To that end, I like pain. What I don't want or need is public humiliation."

"Humiliation?"

Warrick sighed. "Off." One eyebrow arched. "I mean it."

Toreth clambered off, and Warrick sat up. "You put it on," he said.

"I don't think—"

"Obviously." He offered the thong. "Put it on."

About to refuse, Toreth changed his mind. Warrick was betting he wouldn't, and then Toreth would have to drop the whole idea. Not a chance. He stripped quickly, under Warrick's appreciative gaze, and donned the leather thong. It wasn't uncomfortable, but he had to admit there really wasn't a lot to it.

As he turned around, he heard metal jingling. Warrick was unlocking the leather cuffs from their chain. "Give me your wrists."

Toreth held them out.

"There we go." Warrick fastened the straps and then pointed to the mirror. "Over there."

Seeing himself, Toreth had to acknowledge that it looked very peculiar. Especially with Warrick standing beside him in full evening dress.

"Kneel," Warrick said, slightly husky. His eyes were bright, and it was only then that Toreth remembered. Yes, Warrick would enjoy this.

Step two of his plan had always been to get Warrick hot enough to agree despite himself, and this would be as effective as anything else he'd had planned. In fact, he'd be willing to bet that he could pull it off now. Twenty euros says I can make him do it, he thought as he dropped to his knees.

He tensed his muscles slightly, watching the results in the mirror. Not bad at all, even if he did say so himself. Grinning, Toreth shook his head, aiming to mess his hair a little. It was only after that, glancing to the side to see what effect it was having, that he noticed the collar and leash in Warrick's hand.

"Hang on a—"

Warrick's finger, laid across his lips, silenced him. "Shh."

A second's hesitation, then Toreth lifted his chin, offering his throat. He watched Warrick's face as he fitted the collar, a tiny frown creasing his brows as he fumbled with the buckle. Maybe, Toreth thought, they should skip the party and spend the evening here. Then Warrick clipped the leash into place and straightened. "What do you think?"

Returning his attention to the mirror, Toreth contemplated his reflection. To be honest, it looked ridiculous—on him, anyway. On Warrick, it would be mouthwatering.

Warrick wrapped the leash around his hand and pulled gently, until Toreth's head lay against his hip. "Well?"

"It looks fine."

"You'd be quite happy to wander around like that, exposed for everyone to see?"

Toreth shrugged, watching his shoulders flex. "Sure," he said.

"In public, at a party full of strangers? With a collar? On a lead?"

Another shrug, purely for the effect, giving most of his attention to the play of his muscles under the skin, tensing his stomach to complement it. Made all that time in the gym seem worthwhile. "Yeah, why not?"

"Very well." Warrick dropped the leash. "You can wear it, then."

Toreth blinked at his reflection, and then saw himself smile at the expression of shock on his face. Neat trap, Warrick, but it wouldn't work. "I—" Come on, think, Toreth told himself. There had to be an argument somewhere. "I don't want to." Oh, yes, very convincing.

"No? But I'm *sure* you just said you wouldn't mind." Warrick's voice, silky smooth, held a note of unfortunately justified triumph. "Didn't you? Or did I mishear?"

"Yes. No. I mean..."

"And I thought you said that it was traditional. Surely *one* of us ought to wear it? Wasn't that what Fran told you?"

Maybe if he called his bluff, Warrick would give up and behave. "Fine. I'll go like this."

To his surprise and discomfort, his acquiescence generated a broad smile. "That's settled, then."

"But—"

Finger on his lips again. When he'd quieted, Warrick ran his finger over Toreth's chin, down his throat, over his Adam's apple and along the line of the leather below. Toreth swallowed, finding his eyes drifting closed. He forced them open. This was not part of the plan.

Warrick traced a line out along his shoulder and back again, and then slipped his finger under the collar. He tugged gently upwards and Toreth rose. Warrick glanced up at him, and then turned his attention down to Toreth's chest. The finger ran downwards, outlining his muscles, flicking over his nipples.

It seemed to take a long time to get anywhere, but the general trend was downwards. By the time it skimmed once inside the upper edge of the thong, the stitching was being put through its paces, and Toreth's breathing had a ragged edge he couldn't control. Get him too hot to object, he thought vaguely.

"I must say that it's convenient," Warrick murmured. The teasing finger returned, running back and forth, and he couldn't help rising on the balls of his feet, trying for more contact. He gasped as Warrick's finger brushed the tip of his cock and then withdrew. "However—" Warrick looked at his watch. "We ought to get going."

Toreth shook his head again, this time to clear it. "Don't be stupid. I'm not going like this."

"Really? Why?"

Because... because... Pathetically, the only thing he could come up with was, "What am I going to wear down to the car?"

Warrick smiled, with a distinctly malicious edge. "What did you plan for *me* to wear?"

"I, uh..." Bastard. In the end, he had to confess, "I hadn't thought about it."

Warrick picked the chain up from the bed and dropped it into his pocket. "Well, then, I suggest you think about it now."

For once the entrance to the Shop wasn't entirely anonymous. Large, elaborately filigreed metal lanterns hung on either side, one gold, one silver, and the door itself was covered by a thin screen displaying a large "21" in shifting metallic shades on a dark blue background. The age of the Shop, Toreth guessed.

Inside, the reception desk had turned into a cloakroom desk. Toreth stripped off his shirt, trousers and shoes, handing them to a staff member he vaguely recognized. The woman took them without any surprise, although Toreth earned a lingering glance before she turned away. That made him feel slightly better about the stupid costume. Then he remembered. "Oh, shit. Hang on."

The attendant turned back, and Toreth retrieved his trousers and pulled a blister strip out of the back pocket. "Thanks."

He swallowed a couple of tablets and offered the strip to Warrick. "Want one?"

"What is it?"

In the unofficial I&I pharmacopoeia, it was listed under "fuck drug." "Very long name, but Sara says it gives you a golden glow. Speeds up alcohol clearance, too." In view of the arrangement, it seemed better not to mention its main purpose of stamina-boosting.

"Mm. All right. Just one, thank you."

That was a surprise, because Warrick didn't usually indulge. A promising sign for his getting into the spirit of the evening. After dispensing the tablet, Toreth went to put the strip in his pocket and stopped, dismayed.

Warrick smiled. "Would you like me to look after that?" He tucked it into his jacket's inside pocket, and then took hold of the leash. "Come on."

Opening the familiar door, they paused at the top of the stairs. Instead of the cool silence of the Shop, noise rose to envelop them, muffled and distorted by distance. Voices, music, and laughter—it sounded like quite a crowd.

As Toreth took a step forwards, Warrick held up his hand to stop him. "Before we go down—are you quite sure about what we decided?"

"Either or neither?"

"Exactly so. Because I have no special preference."

Now that it came down to it, Toreth wasn't sure. Too late to back out, though—and did he really want to waste the evening hanging around exclusively with someone who didn't fuck in public? If Warrick was asking again, that probably meant that *he* had no plans to play away and wanted to hook Toreth into saying a firm "neither."

"What we agreed's still fine by me," Toreth said. "Start with neither, see how it goes."

Warrick nodded. "Very well." He didn't move, though.

Toreth nudged his shoulder. "Well—don't just stand there."

The noise rose as they descended, and Warrick began to have second thoughts. Still, he had the promise to leave, and besides it would be unfair in the extreme to drag Toreth away before they'd even seen the cellar. He stole a glance at Toreth beside him, padding down the stairs on bare feet, apparently as relaxed as if he were wearing his dinner jacket.

Warrick slipped his hand into his pocket, fingering the chain, wondering whether Toreth would agree to put it on. The idea, as always, set his heart thumping, even though the reality had never worked out satisfactorily. Before now, though, they'd always tried it in private, where it eventually had to lead to something—a change of scenario, or submissive sex that Toreth didn't particularly enjoy. Here, where it could stay an image, a living picture, Warrick thought it would be different. Perhaps he was going to enjoy the evening, after all.

As ever, when he pushed through the curtain and entered the first room Warrick paused to check if the rack had been sold yet. It hadn't. Lengths of chain decorated it, sprayed gold and hung with silvery lights. As ever, he got as far as thinking, "I could buy—" and then stopped himself. He couldn't. It was ridiculous. It was completely over the top. It was insanely impractical. It simply wouldn't fit in Toreth's flat and if he had it at home—well, if Dilly saw it, she'd have him committed. It was, in short, impossible. Every time he hoped it would be gone, to remove the temptation for good, and every time he was pleased to see it still there. Impossible—he'd thought that about Toreth once. He knew that if he tried, he could get around the problems, and sometimes he wondered why he hadn't done so yet.

Then, welcome distraction, Fran appeared beside them. Her usual outfit of multilayered dark blue and silver had been embellished with a trailing gold scarf in fine silk and a silver "21" badge pinned to her chest, presumably in honor of the event. For the first time ever, she looked openly surprised when she saw them, and it took him a moment to realize why. By the time he did, she had recovered.

"Welcome to the party. I hope the chain didn't break?" she asked.

"He's got it." Toreth nodded towards him. "Everything's fine. Luckily, it's one size fits all."

"Indeed. Well, I must say that you make a very decorative addition to the evening."

Warrick couldn't have agreed more.

Always open to flattery, Toreth grinned. "Thanks." He looked Fran over and added, "You've changed your hair. Looks nice."

It always surprised Warrick when Toreth did that, considering that on a personal level he cared so little about casual acquaintances. Looking more carefully at Fran, Warrick still couldn't see the difference, but she smiled agreement. "Thanks."

While they'd been talking, more guests had descended. Fran stepped back and addressed the group. "A very warm welcome all, from Shel and myself, to our twenty-first anniversary party. The Shop comes of age tonight."

Smattering of applause, and Warrick joined in.

"Thank you. Please, make yourselves at home. There's food towards the back, drinks to the left, pharmaceutical pleasure to the right, somewhere, although the volunteers were looking a little hazy when I last saw them. You can pick out the staff by their badges. Staff with black collars are available to fetch plates and glasses, take messages, and supply toys. Staff with red collars are additionally available for extra requests, at their discretion. Other guests are guests, and I couldn't possibly generalize about them." She waved them forwards into the cellar. "Enjoy."

With Toreth close beside him, Warrick moved off into the crowd.

"Do you think she's wearing a collar?" Toreth asked as they left the entrance room.

"Fran? I didn't notice. I suppose she could have been, under the scarf."

"Yeah. I wonder what color it is."

Warrick glanced at him. "Is that an 'either' already?"

"What?" Toreth looked at him blankly before understanding dawned. "Fran? God, no. Too fat for me. I was just curious."

The Shop had certainly gone all out for the event. Except for the distinctive low-vaulted rooms, it was hard to recognize. Sparkling strings of small lights in silver and gold, like the ones on the rack, interspersed with brighter spotlights, replaced the usual dim ceiling lights. The doors in the outer walls, always kept closed, were now mostly open, spilling light of various colors out into the main area.

Although the majority of the merchandise had been packed away somewhere, the large pieces of equipment, too bulky to move easily, remained in place. The Shop being the kind of place it was, they were in full working order. The multidrawered cabinets still lined the walls, although thin, flexible screens displaying abstract designs concealed most of them. If Warrick stared at any one screen for long, naked bodies enjoying chains, cuffs, and more exotic items seemed to swim into focus out of the patterns. When he looked away and back, they were gone, and Warrick wondered how they were measuring viewer attention.

A few cabinets had been left bare, drawers unlocked, and Warrick caught sight of guests liberating the occasional toy. On their previous visits, there had never been more than a dozen customers on the premises. Now the place was packed, with a broad cross-section of the ethnic mix of New London. Dress ranged from dinner jackets and formal evening gowns to leather, rubber, metal, fur—just about every material from which it was conceivable to create clothing. There was also a great deal of skin on display, some elaborately decorated. The normal, nerve-shivering scent of age, steel, and leather was still there, but overlaid by warm bodies, alcohol, and a light, pleasant, but impossible-to-identify incense.

Warrick thought he recognized the occasional face, but as he rarely—perhaps never—spoke to other customers, he wasn't sure whether to greet them or not.

They wandered for a while, getting their bearings. Eventually Warrick ground to a halt at a small group gathered in one of the edge rooms. Guests—and occasional staff—seemed to be taking turns to recite poetry. Primarily poetry with a lot more sex involved than Warrick remembered from school, which was the last time he'd had much to do with anything that rhymed.

It was clearly impromptu, rather than any form of organized entertainment, and Warrick found it oddly engaging. People having fun, without caring what anyone beyond the group thought. When his presence registered, a couple stepped aside, making a space for him, then turned their attention back to the current speaker.

"Do you really want to listen to this?" Toreth demanded from behind him.

"I wouldn't mind. For a little while."

"Okay. I'll go get us some drinks." Without waiting for an answer, Toreth began to shoulder his way through the crowd. Warrick watched him go, wondering whether he'd be back or if this was the start of his probably inevitable exploration of the fuck buffet. Then he dismissed the thought and returned to the recitation.

Toreth had expected to find his unplanned costume rather cold, but the air in the cellar had been warmed by the presence of so many bodies. Only the smooth stone flags under his bare feet were still cool.

So *many* bodies. He examined the crowd as he worked his way across the cellar, gratified to draw so many interested and openly admiring looks in return; probably there were more than he would have drawn in the DJ. He wasn't the only one modeling the minimalist slave look, although in his opinion he was one of the most striking examples.

As he waited for a space at the makeshift bar, Toreth felt a prickle down his back. Someone watching him? A safe bet, really, but when he turned, he spotted the source of the scrutiny at once.

The boy was certainly eye-catching. He wore a skintight black-furred outfit with a white patch on the chest: a literal cat suit, complete with white-tipped ears, curling white whiskers, and gloves showing the gleam of claws at his fingertips. He also had a long tail, with some kind of control system installed. It held itself in a curve behind him, the white tip flicking from side to side like a metronome as he strolled over.

Even close up, the short glossy fur looked so natural it could've been growing from his skin. The suit was a dark chocolate brown rather than true black, with the faintest of tabby markings; it looked like Bastard in strong sunlight, if Bastard had been around one-seventy-five with a lithe, late-teens body. And, unlike Bastard, someone had collared this cat, with a silver band bearing a name tag.

The cat mask was beautifully crafted, and thin enough to show the expression beneath. It swept down beside the boy's mouth and along his jawline, leaving bare his lips and chin. Apart from that, the mask hid everything except his eyes, a vivid and unnatural green with wide pupils.

With the air of someone trying out a line for the first time, the boy said, "If I said you had an incredible body…" Then he dried up, the visible parts of his face and throat flushing.

Even if it was deliberate, which Toreth half suspected, it was still irresistible. The voice—light, with a distinctive hissing lisp—also confirmed his guess as to the boy's age.

One white-tipped ear flicked in irritation, and he started again. "If I said—"

Toreth shook his head. "Don't bother, I've heard it before. It's old enough to have whiskers."

The emerald eyes widened. "That was clever."

"It's practice, that's all. You can have another go if you like—try something original."

"Okay. Do you know why cats scream when they fuck?"

Well, that won points for a fresh approach. "Go on."

"Because the toms have spines on their cocks. They tear the queens inside—the pain makes them ovulate." He sighed. "I don't have spines, though. Not yet. I'm saving up for implants."

Toreth winced. "That'll limit the available field."

"I'll find someone." He cocked his head, disturbingly catlike. "How was that?"

"Awful. One more go."

"Mmm." Twitch of the tail. "Can I lick your cock?"

Toreth grinned. "Much better. Although suck is more traditional."

"Most people prefer me to lick." For the first time, the boy smiled, revealing the source of the lisp.

In the face of the spectacular display of ice-white fangs, Toreth nodded. "Lick it is. Although, to be honest, I'd rather fuck you."

The tail lashed enthusiastically. "Sounds *great.* I bet you wouldn't need spines to make me scream. But…I can't." He stroked his flank. "I'm stitched in. Zips spoil the lines and nothing else holds it tight enough. I haven't had anything to drink since lunchtime."

It sounded spectacularly pointless from Toreth's point of view, although he wished he'd thought of it for Warrick's costume. "Why come to the party at all, if you can't fuck *or* drink?"

"I like it here. It's a great place to play. Besides, my owner'll let me out later…if I'm a good kitty. See?" He flicked the tag. "I have a home to go to. It's great, having somewhere to roam from." Reaching up, he stroked the back of a claw around Toreth's own collar. "You know, you don't look like something that lives on a leash."

"Not usually, no. I lost a bet."

"With your owner?"

"With myself."

The tail curled into a question mark. "Can I ask you something else? Something personal?"

"Go ahead."

"How old are you?"

"Thirty-five," Toreth said, which was still true for another couple of weeks.

"*Really?* You don't look it."

"Thanks. Why do you want to know?"

Another fangy grin. "Curiosity. Well?" A pawful of claws raked very lightly down his chest, then batted at the trailing end of the leash. "Can I?"

Curiosity of his own prompted Toreth to ignore the request and take hold of the boy's hand, examining the claws more closely. The backs of the gloves were furred, but the palms were dark brown leather. The claws showed through slits in the fingertips.

"Watch," the boy said. He flexed his wrist back, and then curled his fingers. As he did, the claws extended, sliding smoothly out of the leather. They gleamed in the gold and silver lighting, long and obviously sharp. "Aren't they great?"

Toreth shifted his grip, feeling the fingers through the glove, but found no tangible sheath. "Implants?"

The boy nodded. "The second big thing I had done, after my eyes. Do you like them?"

Not having an opinion one way or another, Toreth settled for saying, "They're very realistic."

That provoked a delighted meow. "Thanks. I think they're just the *best.*" Another flex of his fingers, and the claws retracted. Then the boy stroked him again, this time using the back of his hand. The fur shivered Toreth's skin into goosebumps.

"Can I?" the boy asked. "Please?"

"Be my guest. But—"

Already kneeling, the boy froze and looked up.

"Just watch what you're doing with those teeth. And claws. If I need a tetanus jab afterwards, I'll neuter you."

"I promise." He rubbed his head against Toreth's thigh, whiskers tickling and the fur silky soft. "Not a scratch."

Unhooking the thong, he took Toreth's cock in both hands, the palms of his gloves beautifully smooth. "Mmm," he said, and began to lap busily, his paws stroking in a matching rhythm.

It was a peculiar technique, but perfectly adequate for Toreth's drug-primed system. He narrowed his eyes, enjoying the attention, but not entirely letting his vigilance lapse—Warrick could be along any minute, and this was as compromising a position as could be imagined. It was far too early in the evening to ruin the plan.

Glancing around, he noticed gathering spectators—hardly surprising, considering they were on the edge of a busy space. Even so, though, most people around them were intent on the bar, or concentrating on carrying drinks away. Odd to be able to do this so publicly—to feel the hands and tongue on him—and not to be remarkable.

Toreth looked down at his feline companion, although he tried to keep his gaze away from the glints of claws. The boy clearly hadn't been faking his enthusiasm for the idea of sucking—licking—him off. As Toreth watched, he wriggled his hips, dropping a hand briefly to tug at the front of the suit. With a new, drug-hazed sympathy for the problems of erections in tight leather, Toreth shifted his weight and pressed his shin forwards between the boy's legs. With a throaty purr, he began to rub against it. He had a cat's physical coordination, at least, because he didn't falter in his attention to Toreth's cock.

As time passed, Toreth found himself clenching his fists, resisting the reflexive temptation to drive forwards, to grab the boy's head and thrust deep. He didn't have to fight it back for long as the flicking tongue carried him over the edge. Not the slightest prick of teeth as he came into the fanged mouth. A *very* good start to the evening, he thought fuzzily.

To his surprise, the boy stopped moving and looked up, licking his lips, obviously asking permission. Toreth nodded, too breathless to speak, and the boy grinned. "Yesss!"

Furry arms slid around his waist, half steadying him and half providing support for their owner. The boy pressed his face against Toreth, his claws pricking lightly into the small of his back as he rubbed faster. His tail lashed from side to side in a frenzy. "Scratch my ears," he panted.

Bemused, Toreth considered the options, and then chose the ears molded into the top of the mask. They twitched as he touched them. A dozen or so hard scratches at the base, and the boy yowled ecstatically, thankfully not digging in his claws as he ground his hips hard against Toreth's leg.

After a minute, Toreth disentangled the arms from around him and helped the boy to his feet.

"Thanks." Once upright, he shifted, gingerly rubbing the thin fur above his crotch with his knuckles. "Oh, man. That is going to be *so* disgusting."

"Serves you right for being a bad kitty."

Flash of sharp white teeth. "But it was *great,* it really was—thanks ever so much for playing." He leaned forwards and licked Toreth's shoulder lightly with the tip of his tongue, then grinned again. "See you later."

As Toreth watched the swaying hips and flicking tail disappear into the crowd, he heard a voice behind him say, "What happened to the drinks?"

Toreth remembered to look down before he turned—thankfully, unlike Bastard, the cat-boy had mastered the art of closing access points behind him. "I ended up talking to someone."

Warrick raised a politely disbelieving eyebrow. "Oh?"

"Yeah. We were comparing collars."

As effective a distraction as he'd hoped. Warrick looked at his throat, then down to his wrists. What the hell—since he was wearing the gear, he might as well give Warrick the benefit of the full effect. "Do you want me to put the chain on?" Toreth asked.

"That would be... yes, I do."

"Front or back?" he offered, before remembering that they were supposed to be finding drinks. Ah, well, he could wait for a while.

To his relief, Warrick said, "Front."

After he locked the chain into place, Warrick stepped back and looked him up and down.

"Well?" Toreth asked, although the result was obvious in Warrick's smile. Worth playing the game just for that—and for the thought of what he might be able to extract in the future as payment for this indulgence. Maybe he hadn't lost the bet, at that.

Finishing his examination, Warrick shook his head. "Rather better than that. Now—what would you like to drink?"

Toreth lowered his gaze. "Whatever you think I ought to have."

Warrick was enjoying the party more that he'd anticipated. Of course, a great deal of that could be assigned to the scene in his flat at the start of the evening and the near-naked man beside him but, beyond that, the atmosphere wasn't as he'd imagined.

Clothing aside, and sexual license aside, it wasn't so very different from any other social gathering where all the participants had at least one thing in common. The crowded rooms had the same friendly, open atmosphere as a conference. Talk to anyone, and the Shop unified, even where kinks diverged. All the guests, as far as he discovered, were customers of at least a year or two's standing.

Assumptions, made and subverted, formed a substantial part of the entertainment. Their respective costumes were a clear cue to those they met, despite Toreth's endearingly unconvincing attempts to stay submissive. People addressed him, not Toreth, and it was so different from their normal visits to the Shop that Warrick found himself wondering about the cues he must give off at other times. It was all part of the fun, of the otherworldly strangeness of the evening—novel and a little disorienting.

To his surprise, Toreth didn't seem to mind his demotion to silent partner. Playing the game—a gift, and a much-appreciated one. Every glance at the cuffs sent a thrill through him, and several times he even caught himself looking for a dark corner. Later, he told himself. He had plans for that.

They had been wandering through the rooms for over an hour when the thing he'd worried about ever since the first visit to the Shop finally happened.

"Dr. Warrick? I didn't know you came here." A woman's voice. Dreading who it might be, he turned slowly.

In fact, it took him a long few seconds to put a name to the face, partly because of the distracting leather outfit, which consisted primarily of studded straps, concealing nothing at all. The plump brunette was definitely familiar, though, and, just as he thought he would have to ask, he realized who it was.

Funny that he'd earlier been comparing the party to a conference, because the last time he'd seen Eve Sanderson had been at a nerve manipulation trade show, where she and her husband had been pushing Peripheral Induction Technology's latest products. Of all the people he might have expected to meet here, Eve would have come nearly at the bottom of a list of guesses. From her expression, she might have said the same thing about him. Warrick paused briefly to thank God that he hadn't suffered a brainstorm and worn the thong.

"Hello, Eve. Lovely to see you." Then, automatically, because he'd thought about the show, he added, "Is your husband with you?"

It could, he reflected, have been so embarrassing. As it was, Eve merely shook her head. "Bastien's at home. He caught some really grim stomach flu, and he's been throwing up for the last two days."

"I'm sorry to hear it."

"He insisted I come, the sweet old thing, instead of staying there to nurse him. Even made me promise to have fun without him. So I'm out on my own, with no one to keep me in order."

That was a definite offer, and Warrick shook his head, smiling, conscious of Toreth's suddenly attentive silence. "I'm afraid I've got my hands full."

She looked at Toreth, who returned the scrutiny stonily, and she laughed. "I'll bet. Listen, if you don't have anything else to do, would you like to meet some friends of mine?"

"Ah..."

"Kind of work friends. All involved with the sexual leisure market in one way or another, anyway. I'm sure they'd love to meet you—SimTech is *the* big name at the moment, after all. Come and tell them about the sim."

Warrick turned to Toreth, who hesitated for a moment. Warrick noticed him give the briefest glance in Eve's direction. Then he shrugged, doing a passable imitation of placid acquiescence. "Whatever you like, of course." Competitive submission.

Eve took them to the far side of the cellar, where an open door led into a small room with, to Warrick's surprise, a thick, dark red carpet. Sturdy rings, set into the brickwork, dotted the walls. A part of the Shop he'd never been into before. Half a dozen men and women sat in a circle of low chairs. Eve introduced him to the group and, as she'd predicted, his name caused a flattering stir of interest.

There were two spare chairs, but Toreth sat down cross-legged on a cushion on the floor beside Warrick's chair, chained hands in his lap. As the group summoned over a collared staff member and ordered a round of drinks, Warrick leaned down and said quietly, "Thanks."

Toreth grinned and kissed him. "No problem. Enjoying it?"

"Yes. Yes, I am. It's . . . different."

"Told you. It's doing it in public, isn't it?"

"I think so. You look incredible."

The smile broadened. "Good. Because I feel like an idiot."

Even though he didn't actually sound upset, Warrick said, "Do you want to take the collar and cuffs off?"

"Nah. Not if you're having fun. I'll let you know when I've had enough." His smile turned sly. "You can pay me back for it later—I'll think of something I want."

Then, in the middle of a supposedly debauched party, Warrick found himself involved in a discussion on the technological future of the sex industry. It seemed oddly appropriate—sitting on wooden chairs, drinks resting on a variety of surfaces designed more for intimacies than for refreshments, and talking about the computers that would make it all obsolete.

Or not quite all, he mused, as he listened to Eve bemoaning the stresses of hunting for contracts with Administration Leisure Centers. Some things the sim couldn't do yet. Some things it perhaps never would be able to, much as he hated the idea. Without thinking, he reached out and ran his hand over Toreth's shoulders.

Toreth glanced up at him, then leaned on the armrest of the chair and rested his head on Warrick's arm.

Some things could never be replaced, or duplicated.

The conversation went on, and more drinks were ordered. Eventually, Toreth yawned, and then stood up. "I'm going to stretch my legs. Take this bloody chain off."

The first time he'd spoken since they came in here. Out of the corner of his eye, Warrick caught the surprise on his companions' faces, and he heard one indrawn breath. Breaking the role. It was much too tempting to resist. Warrick leaned back in the chair and said, "Ask nicely."

To his astonishment, Toreth's expression barely registered surprise before he knelt gracefully and offered his hands, palms up. "Please," he said in a most un-Toreth-like voice. "Would you be so kind as to remove the chain?"

Warrick grinned and fished the key out from under his shirt. "I could get used to this," he murmured. "Shouldn't you say 'master'?"

Toreth bowed his head. "Don't fucking push it," he growled softly.

Already reaching for the cuffs, Warrick withdrew the key. "I beg your pardon?"

The glare he got in return was murderous, and it whipped the gentle warmth of the drug he'd taken up into a sudden inferno. Warrick held the key up and raised his eyebrow. "*What* did you say?" he asked again, trying to provoke.

Of course, once he'd made that clear, Toreth had no choice—in this context, not playing the role properly was tantamount to losing the game.

"Nothing." The sweet, submissive expression returned, and Warrick barely held back a laugh. "I'm sorry. Please take the chains off." Pause. "Master."

Enough was enough. He opened the locks, and Toreth dropped the chain into his lap, then leaned forwards. Warrick felt his hand in his jacket pocket—presumably filching more golden glow.

"I can see I'm going to have to remind you how the game works," Toreth breathed into Warrick's ear. "When we get back to my flat, I'm going to chain you to the wall, on your knees, and make you very, *very* fucking sorry for that."

Warrick jumped in his seat as Toreth's tongue flicked into his ear. Then Toreth stood up and vanished through the door, back into the crowd.

After his departure, Warrick found his attention wandering from the conversation in progress. He felt strangely lightheaded, and wondered if it was a reaction to the drug or to Toreth. Or perhaps just having had more drinks than he usually did on an empty stomach. After a while he excused himself from the group and went in search of something to eat.

He'd passed through two rooms in the general direction of the buffet when a flash of gold attracted his attention and he turned, catching his breath unconsciously as he saw the couple.

A blonde woman in a golden floor-length gown—the source of the reflected light—leaned against the wall, one leg bent at the knee. A hip-high slit at the side of the skirt gave easy access for Toreth's hand, the metallic cascade of fabric shimmering as his arm moved. With his free hand, he kept his companion's wrists pinned above her head, and judging by her expression Blonde was having a very good party indeed.

Warrick had to acknowledge that it made an impressively erotic image: the gold of the woman's hair and dress catching the light, the clean, sculpted lines of Toreth's virtually naked body broken by the black stripes of the thong and collar. Toreth's head was bent down beside hers, his hair a shade darker, and, over the music, Warrick could hear the tone of his voice, if not the words. Even under these circumstances, it sent a thrill through him.

With the boy, he'd arrived at the end of the proceedings. Here things were definitely still in the middle. The woman's lips moved, and although Warrick couldn't hear the words, he could read them.

"I want you."

For a moment, he thought that they'd spot him as they changed position, but Toreth didn't look around and if Blonde noticed him, she didn't say anything. Well, she was hardly the naturally shy type, was she? The woman lifted her leg higher, thigh pressing against Toreth's hip as he eased into place, and started to thrust.

He ought to go, Warrick thought. He really ought to go. Instead, he stayed where he was, watching, just this once. This was what Toreth did with his time alone. The time he needed to keep apart so that, in the end, he could stay. One more anonymous fuck in the middle of a very long line that stretched back through the past and inevitably out into the future. Their future.

Soft voices.

"Yes. Hold my wrists."

Snatches of words.

"—like silk. Like fucking silk."

It was something he'd thought about, from time to time. Rather a lot at certain points. How would he feel if he actually found Toreth with one of his casual partners?

The answer turned out to be, slightly annoyed. Of course, this evening wasn't a fair test—he'd been prepared for it. They'd agreed things before they arrived, although Toreth had broken the agreement almost immediately. No more than Warrick had expected, but still irritating.

Now that he had seen it, though...it could have been a lot worse. Without waiting for the finale, he resumed his search.

Eventually he came across a quiet corner room—the only other person there was Fran. The Shop's co-owner was struggling with an apparently recalcitrant coffee maker and swearing under her breath. Beside it stood a tall rack of cups and saucers, and a small table set with plates of cakes and biscuits. The sight seemed oddly mundane for the party, an out-of-place corner of corporate hospitality.

Grateful for the distraction, Warrick asked, "Can I help?"

Fran yelped and dropped a cup and saucer. Amazingly, the cup bounced on the stone floor and rolled to a stop at Warrick's feet. The saucer, less lucky, smashed into pieces.

"Oh, *bother,*" Fran said fervently.

"Sorry." Warrick picked the cup up and offered it back.

Fran inspected it and shook her head. "Not a chip." Then she gestured to the floor. "I need to find a dustpan before someone steps on that lot and cuts themselves." She looked up at him. "I don't suppose—"

"I'll wait here and warn off the barefoot."

"Thanks."

As she hurried away, Warrick took a cake and then turned his attention to the coffee maker—antique and beautiful. Far too large for a home machine, it must have been made for a long-closed café. Glass and blued steel, with chrome trimmings that were unfortunately worn in places. After a little effort, he located the source of the problem and finally persuaded the machine to produce coffee, which was excellent. Taking a cupful for himself, he set the machine to fill the four large, elegantly-curved glass jugs nestling in niches at the front. He was still admiring it when Fran returned.

"Do you like it?" She knelt down and began to brush up the shards. "Shel brought it back from an auction trip. Went for antique branding irons, came back with a coffee machine—Shel isn't always very reliable for things like that."

"It's a classic design."

"Temperamental is the word I'd use. There." She stood up. "Oh—coffee!" She sounded genuinely surprised. "Well done!"

"Would you like some?" he asked. "Why don't you sit down?"

"Well, I—" She looked around. "Why not. But I'm hyped enough without the caffeine. Herbal tea, please. The stuff in the purple jar on the left." She abandoned the dustpan and sank into a nearby chair—heavy dark wood with wrought iron restraints. "They can manage for ten minutes without me."

Warrick opened the jar, amused by the sudden role reversal between host and guest.

"Ah—you're a lifesaver," Fran said when he handed over the cup.

He dragged over a three-legged stool that had no obvious sinister function and sat beside her. Once settled into place, he found himself remembering Toreth's question from earlier. Trying not to stare too obviously, he examined the scarf around her neck.

She must have noticed the scrutiny because she smiled and lifted the scarf to reveal her bare throat. "If I took requests—of any kind—I wouldn't have time to do all the things I'm supposed to do. Although I'll definitely make an exception for offers of tea." She took a deep lungful of the rising steam and sighed. "I was about willing to kill for this. You've definitely earned yourself a discount on your next purchase. So are you enjoying your first party?"

He'd wondered if she remembered him, but clearly she did. "Actually, yes, I am."

"Didn't I say you would?" She blew on the tea. "Are you surprised?"

"A little. It's not really my . . ."

"Your scene." She nodded. "That's fair enough—" As she hesitated, he realized that she'd never used his name.

"Keir Warrick."

She snapped her fingers. "Oh! Of *course*."

"What?"

"Oh, dear." Surprise turned instantly to embarrassment. "I'm afraid I've just been terribly rude, although you might not have noticed. I recognized you, and we have a strict policy that our customers' lives outside the Shop are absolutely private. Please—forget I said anything."

"I don't mind." He did, a little, but he was also intrigued. "Where do you recognize me from?"

"I went to a lecture at the university a few months ago, on computer simulation. I only managed to get a seat at the back, or I would've realized who you were before and not said anything. It was very interesting—you spoke very well."

"And I don't tend to say much here?"

"Perhaps that's it." She shook her head slightly. "Shel would dock my pay, and quite rightly, but... may I ask you something?"

"Go ahead," he said with a certain degree of trepidation.

"Can it really do everything you described in the lecture?"

"The sim? Certainly." He couldn't remember exactly what he'd said at the event, but it had been years since he'd needed to pad talks with future work.

"Amazing. A whole other world. Worlds." Her voice was a little wistful.

"Yes, it is. Amazing—I never get used to it. You must come and try it." Then a vision of trying to explain to the technicians at SimTech how he knew her almost made him wonder how to retract the offer. Her face had lit up, though.

"Oh, could I? That would be *wonderful.*"

Dismissing the doubts, he said, "I'll arrange something. May I ask a question in return?"

"Of course, as long as it's not about another customer."

"No. I was wondering how much Toreth paid for the tickets." He swept his hand around to indicate the whole cellar. "It's rather more extravagant than I imagined."

She shook her head. "The evening is free. Shel's idea. A thank-you to our loyal customers. We put a percentage of profits aside, every month, and use them for the party."

Sound customer relations, if expensive. He wondered if she and Shel were simply very generous, or if the Shop was more profitable than he'd imagined. "Is everyone invited?"

"Oh, no, not at all. Shel sends out the invitations." She didn't expand on the selection criteria, and he had the strong feeling that asking would get him nowhere.

"I didn't actually think that you had this many customers," he said.

"You tend to come in at our quiet times. Saturday afternoons are always slack. We're busiest in the evenings. Actually, Shel thinks we have too many customers at the moment, but at the same time our policy is not to turn people away for that reason only, so we're stuck."

"Stop advertising?"

"We never started. We're not even commercially listed. It's all word of mouth." She smiled wryly. "Too many satisfied customers."

He wondered if Toreth had been spreading the word. "Do you have many from I&I?"

"No... in fact, Toreth's the only para-investigator—or interrogator—amongst our customers. We've turned away several; you might almost call it a rejection criteria. There were some unfortunate incidents in the early days. As a group they're not good with rules, and we have a number of those. More than Shel would like."

"So what made you take Toreth?" he asked, curious.

She narrowed her eyes.

"If that falls under customer confidentiality, I'm sorry."

"No. In this case, I can probably stretch a point. He came here looking for a gift for someone else—for you. That was unusual enough for Shel to investigate more carefully. Of course, that applies to all our customers."

"Oh?"

"Yes. We carry out a full credit and background check after the first visit. It's policy. You see, with our particular retail philosophy—that's Shel's description, by the way—we have to be certain that our new customers are...suitable. We match the people to the Shop, you might say."

"What about me? You didn't even know my name."

"Toreth vouched for you, so we have no personal details about you at all."

"Vouched for me?" That was news to him. "Because I'm his—" He stopped, uncomfortable with any of the words he might have put there.

"No, not at all. Relationship and role are irrelevant." She sipped her tea. "And I try not to make assumptions on either score, although sometimes I still do."

"And sometimes it's obvious." Then he remembered the couple he'd seen on his very first visit here. He'd made assumptions and in the end been left with no idea at all. "At least, I imagine that it is with us."

"Well, I made a guess and I admit I would've been surprised if I'd been wrong. But I'm regularly wrong and regularly surprised, so I try to remain open-minded and treat people equally."

"You never spoke to me."

She smiled. "Ah, but *you* never spoke to *me*."

His first thought was that he must have done, but thinking back, he couldn't produce a single instance. "No, I suppose I didn't. A very fair point."

"Customers' self-imposed boundaries are far more important to us than any we might be forced to apply."

"Shel again?"

She nodded. "Shel would prefer to lift all the limits on what can be done in the Shop. So far I'm managing to hold the line against the idea."

Shel—no pronoun given, with apparently deliberate care. Ask or not? In the end he decided against it. "How does vouching for someone work?"

"We would never disclose the identity of any customer, at least not voluntarily, but people may require more protection than that to feel comfortable here." She took the trailing end of her scarf in one hand, twining the end through her fingers. "Shel wanted to dispense with the background checks altogether, to avoid excluding those people who perhaps needed the Shop most in the first place. The compromise is that a customer who has disclosed their name may vouch for a small number of others who have not, accepting full responsibility for everything they do on the premises."

Toreth hadn't said anything about it. Of course, he wouldn't have.

She smiled again, a little self-deprecating. "More than you wanted to know, I expect."

"No, it's very interesting. I'd never considered the practicalities of the business before. SimTech has... well, some related problems, if not quite the same. Choosing volunteers for trials—especially the sex-based trials. Ensuring there's no possibility of junior staff being abused by those in positions of power."

"Yes, of course. I must admit, I did think of that at the lecture. In fact, I tried to ask a question on those lines."

"I'm sorry I didn't have time to answer."

She shrugged. "As I said, I was right at the back."

They drank in silence for a while, and Warrick helped himself to a handful of biscuits. From all around the Shop came the sounds of people enjoying themselves in the widest variety of ways possible. For most people, limitless pleasures meant only excess, but it seemed very like the Shop that there would be a bar, drugs—and also tea.

Eventually Fran said, "If you don't mind me asking, do you still have the cabinet?"

"Yes," he said and inhaled a mouthful of crumbs. When he'd finished coughing, Warrick waved away Fran's concern and asked, "Why wouldn't we?"

"Oh, we've had it returned several times." She settled back in the chair. "In fact, it's probably spent more time in the Shop than out. You've had it a long time now, relatively speaking. People seem to find they don't like it after all, or that they like it too much."

"Mm. I think I can see that." He thought of the first months, how stupid he'd been about the whole thing, and despite that, he still couldn't resist the shiver of excitement that ran through him at the thought of it. A twinge of phantom pain in his wrist rattled the cup in the saucer.

She was still playing with the scarf. Silver threads which he hadn't noticed earlier caught the light, flickering hypnotically. Thinking of the beautiful, impractical dream in the entrance room, Warrick said, "We should buy something else. A contribution to the party budget for next year."

Fran nodded, releasing the scarf as her manner changed subtly to saleswoman advising a client. "I would suggest the rack," she said. He stared at her, astonished, and she smiled. "Someone offered a price for it last week. I turned them down."

"Not enough?" What if they came back?

"On the low side—it might have been acceptable from a different customer, but they wanted it for display, not for use. Besides, I'm saving it for someone."

"Who?" he asked, before he remembered the privacy policy.

"You."

Temporarily speechless, he covered the surprise with a sip of cooling coffee, but he didn't imagine for a moment that she hadn't noticed. "Why?" he said eventually.

"I saw you looking at it the first time you came here. I thought then that you wanted it. We're willing to wait, for valued customers—Shel insists, in fact. It takes some people a long time to make up their minds."

"I don't want it."

"The customer is always right, of course."

That seemed to be the end of it, as far as Fran was concerned. He'd rather hoped she would argue, so he could resist for a while and then admit it. Now he was afraid that his blunt statement might make her sell it to the next interested customer. "That is . . . I don't know whether I'd like it or not."

The change in position went unremarked. "If you'd like to try it, you're more than welcome. I could arrange to have it moved to one of the side rooms if you'd like some privacy."

Unfairly tempting. "It's not very practical."

"Large pieces of genuine antique torture equipment seldom are."

That gave him pause. "I hadn't considered it in those terms," he said eventually.

She nodded. "The idea makes a lot of people uncomfortable. It's different to many of the things we have here—it was designed to kill, to maim, and it has done. It's hurt a great many people and been responsible for a great deal of misery. But, to my mind at least, that doesn't mean it can't now bring pleasure to someone."

Some metaphors, he reflected, have the subtlety of a punch in the mouth.

"I don't like to limit things, or people," Fran continued. "I'm not as fanatical on the subject as Shel, but it is our fundamental philosophy here. Have you heard the saying, 'An it harm none, do as you will'?"

"No."

"Aleister Crowley, I think. We have some of his books in the middle room. As a general philosophy it's terribly impractical, in my opinion anyway, but I think that for sex it works very well."

"But Shel wants to live like that?"

She shook her head. "Shel *does* live like that, and it's—" She looked away, past him. "It's not a safe way to live, in this world. There are too many laws that violate that one law. I worry that . . . " She sat up, and out of the corner of his eye he saw a leather-clad staff member waving discreetly. "I'm sorry—disaster somewhere, I expect. Thanks for fixing the infernal machine."

"My pleasure."

She set the cup down and paused. "Shall we keep it?"

She didn't mean the coffee maker. He considered, seriously, swirling the dregs in his cup. In all honesty, he didn't want to own the rack, but neither did he want it sold. He'd wanted it, somehow, to be *possible.* Now he had to make a decision, and that was something of a relief. "No," he said finally. "I won't say I'm not tempted. But... Toreth wouldn't like it. It's too... too impersonal. He—" He needs to know that he's the reason why it's so good. That I need him. "He likes to be the main attraction."

Fran nodded. "Then I'll take it off the list."

He hadn't meant to say so much—partly because he hadn't pinned down the source of his reluctance before. "I'd appreciate it if you didn't say anything about it to Toreth."

She smiled. "Of course not."

Overall, Toreth thought, the evening had more than lived up to his expectations, despite the fact that there had been none of the careful stalking of prey that he usually enjoyed before a fuck. This kind of easy availability would bore him eventually but, as he'd said to Warrick, for one night it was different and fun. He'd started off keeping track of how many times he'd broken their either-neither agreement, but he lost count somewhere around the fourth partner. Or had it been the fifth drink? Thank God for the golden glow, anyway.

Eventually, Toreth chanced across Warrick again, still looking every inch the immaculate, well-tailored corporate. He stood with a group of people watching a couple doing, in Toreth's view, some rather eye-watering things with large hooks and lengths of chain. Warrick wore a distant expression—one that Toreth had seen before.

He worked his way silently around to Warrick and slipped his arms around his waist. Warrick didn't even look around, merely leaning back against him and folding his arms over Toreth's. "Hello again, slave," he murmured.

He knew it was me, Toreth thought, getting an unexpected kick from the idea. "Thinking of adding it to the sim?" Toreth asked.

"Indeed. Coding in my head as we speak."

"I guessed." He stood for a while, watching the performance, wondering idly how it could possibly be anything other than unpleasantly painful, and what level waiver he'd need to do it at work. Most of his attention, though, was occupied by Warrick, by the soft scratch of fabric against his skin. Good, but less clothing would be far better. The feeling coalesced into a plan: take Warrick home, fuck him, and then pass out until Monday morning. Sounded good.

"We could try it in the real world sometime, if you'd like to," Toreth said eventually.

"Mm... no, I don't think so. Too much tissue damage. And think of my poor carpets."

"Plastic sheets?" Toreth suggested, secretly relieved. Dillian would have him in prison before the stain had come out of the pile.

Warrick laughed, warm and lazy. "*Not* very romantic."

He sounded drunk—not too drunk, but enough to make Toreth wonder whether he might be persuaded into a fuck here. He slid his hand into Warrick's jacket pocket, fished out the strip, and took another one of the diminishing stock. He offered the strip to Warrick, who surprised him again by taking a tablet.

"Been having fun?" Warrick asked after the tablets were back in place.

"Yeah, lots. You?" He paused as Warrick freed himself, turned around, and kissed Toreth just as if they weren't in the middle of a crowd. It went on for a long while, Warrick's hands roaming freely over him, and when Toreth touched him in return the fact that Warrick was fully dressed was maddening and incredibly arousing. Toreth ground against him and Warrick hummed appreciatively into his mouth.

Okay, Toreth thought, as Warrick traced the thong down between his buttocks. Definite revision of the plan. Fuck him here, *then* take him home. Would Warrick be willing to play along?

"In a very virtuous way," Warrick said when he finally broke the kiss.

For a moment, Toreth thought it was an answer to his unspoken thought. He shook his head to clear it. "Huh?"

"I've been having fun, in a very virtuous way." Warrick began walking, away from the couple and towards an invitingly empty alcove. "Mending coffee machines for our host."

"And I've been saving myself for you," Toreth said with his best heartbreaking innocence.

Warrick smiled slowly, not looking around. "Oh?"

"Yeah. Haven't touched anyone all night. Just looking. I've been so good, it hurts."

"Does it really?"

Now Warrick looked at him and licked his lips, one eyebrow raised. Toreth nodded, surprised and delighted by the offer. Before he could lean against the wall, Warrick took his arm and turned him around. Toreth heard the chain, and helpfully placed his wrists together behind his back.

Cuffs secured, Warrick pushed him gently forwards. "Back there a bit. Where it's darker."

Nerves humming with anticipation, Toreth stood where he was bid. Pressed against the painted brickwork, the links of the chain made a line across his buttocks, and there was something else there too, in the small of his back—it felt like a hasp in the wall. Never mind. This probably wouldn't take long enough for things to get uncomfortable.

Warrick took off his jacket, folded it carefully with the lining outermost, and then knelt on it. "Hard floor," he explained.

"Not the only thing."

Warrick laughed and slid his hands up Toreth's thighs to frame the front of the thong. "So I can see."

He'd expected Warrick to rush, to get the treat over with before anyone spotted them. He didn't, though. For all the calm, unhurried concentration he put into it, they might have been safely back at the flat. Toreth shifted his feet on the floor and braced his shoulders, pushing forwards into the spine-curlingly wonderful enclosure of Warrick's mouth. "Mmh. That's good," he murmured. Keeping his voice down, for Warrick's sake.

Toreth barely even registered the clink of metal on metal as Warrick fastened the chain between his wrists to the clasp on the wall. So that was why he'd moved him. Toreth smiled, not opening his eyes. Not caring. If Warrick kept doing that with his tongue, he could chain him to any fucking thing he wanted to.

The warm flush of the fresh drug, working beautifully, sharpened the need. How many times this evening? He couldn't remember, only knowing that he ached, so ready, and he thrust forward again. Warrick shifted his hands to his hips, gripping hard, pinning him back. Get on with it, Toreth begged silently. Please. Get—

Noise penetrated the dizzying tide of sensation. Voices and laughter, loud and close, and he forced his eyes open.

The deserted alcove was deserted no longer. People surrounded them. A small crowd, in fact. Spectators.

"Warrick." He tugged on the chain, then nudged Warrick's chest with his knee. "*Warrick.*"

Warrick lifted his head, the rush of his mouth withdrawing quickly proving almost too much. Oh, God. Why had he said anything? Warrick would—

To his astonishment, Warrick glanced around, then smiled up at him. "Do you want me to stop?"

Intending to think about it, Toreth found himself shaking his head fervently.

"Very well."

He moaned as Warrick renewed the assault, choking the sound back as best he could. How much noise had he made already?

It took a minute or so before the change in technique registered. Warrick had been playing with him before, stretching things out. Teasing. Now, the teasing had slipped into outright torture. Too light, too shallow. It would have provoked a sinking feeling, if his nervous system had possessed the spare capacity.

Once—oh, God, a long time ago now—Warrick hadn't been quite so good at this, at least not in the real world. Never bad, never even average, but not as incredible as he was right now. He didn't know whether it was the drugs, or the evening, or the people watching (and he couldn't help looking down, just to see Warrick on his knees in front of an *audience*), but this was good. This was better than the sim, which considering Warrick didn't need to breathe in there was pretty fucking…

Then Warrick's head dipped forwards, taking him all the way in before pulling back quickly, and Toreth couldn't stop the moan. He bit his lip, eyes squeezed shut, head back against the wall. Clenching his fists, he tried to concentrate on the shapes the bricks made, pressing into his back. Not here. Warrick wasn't going to make him do it here. In the sim, yes, and sometimes in the real world, but never when anyone else could hear. Things he didn't tell Sara.

Why had he taken another one of those bloody tablets?

"Please." Christ, that was loud. Had it been him? Couldn't have been. *That* was him, though, panting for breath. He licked his lips and tasted salty sweat. It seemed as if the crowd heated the space around them and sucked the oxygen from the air. It had to be soon, or he was going to... he was...

"Warrick, please." Trying to keep his voice low. Was that a muffled chuckle in return? The plea certainly earned him a few sweet seconds of deeper, firmer suction, before Warrick pulled back. Toreth had never previously imagined circumstances under which you might regret teaching someone to deep throat.

There was... such a thing... as being too good a teacher. Still, at least it left no doubt that this was quite deliberate. No doubt as to what Warrick wanted.

Toreth could say the safe word. Warrick's safe word—he'd never needed one of his own before. Or the sim cut-out word—that might work. If he'd thought of it five minutes earlier, he might have tried it. Now, desperate messages from his cock seemed to be short-circuiting the neurons he needed to articulate the words.

"Please." He didn't have any trouble saying that, though.

What Warrick wanted. Oh, God. All he had to do was *ask* and who the hell cared if there were people watching? Not him. He only cared that they were listening. He couldn't. He gritted his teeth. No, not couldn't. He *wouldn't.*

What I don't want or need is public humiliation.

This was exactly Warrick's idea of suitable payback. Unfair, when Toreth hadn't even—

A noise pulled him back to greater awareness. Whimpering, escaping through his clenched teeth. Oh, God. Was that as bad as begging? Worse? Did it mean that now he finally could—?

Fight it. Keep fighting it.

"Jesus fucking *Christ,* Warrick, please. Finish it. Please. Mmh, *yes.*" Deeper with every word, Warrick's mouth moving faster. Worth any amount of humiliation, and even as he paused to think that, he felt Warrick draw away again. The chain snatched at his wrists as he reached to stop him. "God, no. Don't stop. Please. Keep it... don't stop. Keep going. Let me. Let me, please. Don't. Keep... more. Yes, Warrick, please. Please. *Please.*"

On and on, stumbling over the words, dimly aware that he wasn't making much sense, and that it didn't matter because even if Warrick stopped, it would soon be far, far too wonderfully late—

Now.

Toreth arched against the wall, bound hands scrabbling at the smooth bricks as he felt Warrick's mouth tightening around him, swallowing. The desperate effort not to scream as he came made him certain his head was about to explode. Moaning aloud, anyway, through the aftershocks, until it was finished, and he slumped back against the hard bricks.

He felt the chain give as Warrick unclasped it from the wall, and he slid gratefully to his knees, leaning heavily against his tormentor. Warrick's hands caught him and steadied him, stroking down his back.

Inhale. Exhale. Suddenly very complicated.

Toreth couldn't manage to keep his head upright—he pressed his face into Warrick's shoulder, panting for breath, the applause from the audience sounding dull and distant. Christ, it felt so fucking good: golden haze of the drug, the flood of endorphins, and Warrick's delicious, unmistakable smell.

"You bastard. You complete fucking bastard," he whispered once he could speak.

"Me?" Warrick said in mock surprise.

In the background, the applause had fragmented and stuttered into a hum of conversation. Just another ten minutes' entertainment. They didn't even bloody *care.*

"That wasn't fucking funny."

"I thought you enjoyed it." Warrick kissed his collar. "You could've said stop."

"No, I couldn't."

"So, was it worth waiting all evening for?" Warrick sounded so smug that Toreth was tempted to tell him he'd done nothing of the kind. Bit late to change the story now, though.

He took a deep breath. "Know what?"

"What?"

"I hate you." He tried again, struggling for conviction. "I absolutely fucking hate you."

"Really?"

"No." Another breath, his heart finally steadying. "Have they gone?"

Warrick's shoulder shifted as he looked around. "No one's particularly watching us, if that's what you mean."

Toreth sat back on his heels, fully intending to be furious just as soon as the treacherous, mellowing effect of the orgasm faded. Tuesday, maybe. "What time is it?" he asked inconsequentially.

"Ah . . . a little after half past two."

That late? Toreth tried to add up the hours they'd spent there, and failed. He struggled to his feet. "Let's go."

"Very well." Warrick stood, too, picking up his jacket and brushing it down. "But first . . ."

"What?"

"Well, the entertainment this evening has been rather one-sided." Warrick looked around the room. "And we did agree either, if either of us wanted to."

The chill Toreth had felt in the restaurant settled over him again. "*I* haven't touched anyone else."

"Your going first was part of the arrangement, was it?"

"Y—no, it wasn't." No way would Warrick genuinely forget something like that.

"In any case, I think the blonde in the gold dress and the boy with the cat mask have rendered the entire question somewhat moot." Warrick's tone didn't change in the slightest. "Along with, I imagine, various others."

Oh, fuck.

"How *old* was he, incidentally?" Warrick asked.

"I—" Toreth swallowed, trying to work up some saliva. "I have no fucking clue. Old enough to have had all his jabs and be let out at night."

"I see. Anyway, I think that the 'either' phase of the agreement has been thoroughly invoked." Another survey of the cellar as he put on his jacket and straightened it meticulously. "If I can find anyone willing, that is."

If? He looked at Warrick, once more perfectly—irresistibly—dressed. Dark hair only slightly disarrayed, thoughtful expression, lips still a little moist and... Jesus, they'd be trampled in the stampede.

Trapped by his own plan, Toreth stood chained in miserable silence, watching as Warrick eyed up the crowd with every evidence of serious intent. All his own stupid fault for making assumptions. He wanted to say, please, don't. To beg again, if that was what it took. Anything so he wouldn't have to watch Warrick being pleasured by someone else. Hear him coming for someone else. Why the hell had he been so sure Warrick wouldn't want to?

He could walk away and wait for Warrick to do it and find him afterwards, but that would be even worse, because then he wouldn't know what or who. The picture built quickly in his mind—someone just like him, tall and blond but fifteen years younger and hung like a horse. Warrick against the wall, or kneeling, or—

Toreth took a deep breath. "Come home and *I'll* fuck you." Even if it took extra chemical assistance, which after that it might well.

Warrick turned back to him, shadowed eyes unreadable in the dim light. "Mm?"

"I'll fuck you. Or you can fuck me. I'll do whatever you want. Suspension fuck. Gag and blindfold. Fist fuck. Hours in chains. Anything." The things Warrick wouldn't do here, not even in a private room. At least Toreth hoped not—right now he wasn't so sure. "I'll wear this fucking collar all night, if you like."

After a long moment, Warrick returned to his survey of the room. "I have a confession to make."

Please, God, no. Not already. Toreth waited, not wanting to hear it, until the silence forced him to ask, "What?"

"I called the Shop and asked Fran about the dress code."

Taken completely by surprise, Toreth stared. "You did *what?*" he asked eventually.

Warrick turned back to him, a smile twitching the corner of his mouth. "For some unfathomable reason, the request to wait until you arrived before I dressed made me suspicious. So I decided to establish the ground rules for the evening from source."

"Hang on. You knew all along I was—" lying, "—wrong about it?"

"Quite so."

"But you didn't think you'd tell me?"

"Also true."

Toreth looked down at the thong, and at the leash trailing down his chest. "So you got me to—" He looked up sharply as the logical conclusion hit him. "You never meant to fuck anyone else, either, did you?"

"Now, that I hadn't quite made my mind up about." Then Warrick smiled. "But no. Not since we arrived."

"You . . . " You bastard.

"After all, with you here, I'm hardly likely to find anyone who appeals more, am I?"

The sheer relief—and outrageous flattery—did a lot to cancel out the anger, and the knowledge that Warrick must have been counting on that didn't make the slightest difference.

Still smiling, Warrick rested his wrists on Toreth's shoulders, linking his hands behind his neck. After a long, thoughtful inspection, he said, "So . . . still think you need to remind me how to play the game?"

Toreth laughed, a little unsteadily, not yet entirely believing the reprieve. "No. You win. This time."

"Mm. And do I get a prize?"

Oh, yes. Oh, very definitely yes. He didn't need to say anything, and after a few seconds, Warrick dropped his gaze and shivered.

"If you turn round," Warrick said, "I'll undo the cuffs and we can leave." Not a bad attempt at steadiness, but Toreth knew him much too well to be fooled.

"Sounds good to me."

As Toreth turned, the hasp in the wall caught his eye. He smiled, thinking of the chains back at his flat, or of the cabinet at Warrick's—planning a suitable reward for such a comprehensive victory. They hadn't played like this for a long time.

After Warrick unbuckled the cuffs, Toreth turned back slowly, rubbing his wrists, and then held out his hand. "Let me have them." Warrick surrendered the bonds, the links rattling as he shivered again. Toreth took a step closer. "Take off the collar, too."

A brief hesitation—one last, lingering look at the collar in place—then Warrick obeyed.

It was, Toreth thought, nice to be off the leash again. "Good. And now..." Toreth darkened his voice, drawing out the pause as he watched Warrick's eyes widen, his lips part. "Now *you* put it on."

Gratuitous Epilogue

Even though he couldn't move, it was a lovely dream.

All his limbs heavy with the paralysis of sleep, but nothing frightening about it. Usually, not being able to move in a dream made it a nightmare. This was nothing of the kind. He couldn't run, but that was okay, because he had no desire to do anything of the kind.

"Mmm. 'S nice."

Toreth had no idea where he was, or what time it was, or even what day it was. In fact, he had no idea who was kissing his chest, licking his nipples, nibbling gently along the curve of his ribcage, but he thought they deserved some encouragement.

"'Gain."

He shifted a little on the bed—was it a bed? It felt pleasantly warm and soft, whatever it was. Why had he wanted to move? What had he meant to do? Open his eyes? Lift his head? Reach out and touch whoever was—

Then he gasped, deliciously surprised as the lips he had lost track of touched his cock. He squirmed again, sighing, feeling himself hardening under the gentle mouthing. Careful, clever, caressing tongue.

Mmm. Alliterative, too.

Clever, caressing tongue, carefully coaxing his cock to...to...Toreth ran out of words.

He appreciated the care, though, because now that he'd inched that much closer to waking, he didn't feel too spectacular. It wasn't the slow, thrilling sucking—oh yes please more—nothing at all wrong with that, but the rest of his body began to send in complaints for central processing. Cotton-wool mouth, slight headache, a bit queasy, aches in his back, shoulders, thighs, and calves.

What *had* he been doing? Maybe later he'd remember in more detail if the night before had been worth the morning after. Yes, probably, because he definitely remembered fucking. Lots and lots of fucking. Bright green eyes. Leather and chains. Of course—the Shop. Vague recollection of pills, too, so it was probably nothing more exciting than the comedown from those that left him so washed out and exhausted—a not-so-golden afterglow.

Fortunately, it was impossible to concentrate on the not very nice while the very nice indeed was still happening to him. Neither did he want to think about things too much. If he wasn't careful, he might wake up, and he'd hate to miss the end of the dream.

Hands and mouth on him, body moving more urgently against his, someone—two someones?—moaning. One of them sounded like him. Someone was whispering some very complimentary things about him, and he tried to mumble a thanks. Everything all mixed together and it didn't seem to matter that he still hadn't moved. Someone sitting astride him, hand on his cock, then shifting forwards and down, impaling themselves on him and ah, God *yes* that was good. So right and wonderful and perfect.

After that, Toreth rather lost track of events until the sweet rush of completion, hearing himself crying out to the distant accompaniment of the mystery someone gasping his name.

They sounded to be having fun, too. Good. Maybe they'd do it all again in a bit.

All quiet now.

Hm.

Was he awake yet? Probably. A heavy weight still pinned his hips, so it was either a very tangible incubus, or...finally, he managed to force open his eyes.

Warrick, of course, which he'd known all along if he'd been awake enough to realize it.

"Good morning," Warrick said, panting somewhat. "Or rather, good afternoon."

Toreth blinked up at him, trying to remember how to focus. Usually happened on its own, he thought. "Afternoon?"

"Mm-hm."

He blinked again. The light in the room did seem wrong for a morning in his own bedroom. Looking around, he discovered that he lay on the sofa in Warrick's flat. "Uh, what time is it?"

"Four o'clock." Warrick took a deep breath and looked at his watch, which led Toreth to notice the bruises on his wrists. "No, it's quarter past, now."

Fifteen minutes. Was that how long it had taken? Toreth frowned, looking again at Warrick's wrists. There was something he ought to remember, something to do with why he was here instead of in Warrick's very comfortable bed.

What had happened last night? They'd come back from the Shop and in the end they'd settled on a suspension fuck, after Warrick had asked nicely. Very nicely. By the time he'd finished begging—Toreth wrenched his mind away from that memory, pursuing the course of events.

Warrick in the cabinet. Then Toreth had gone somewhere...he'd left Warrick in the chains and gone to get a drink of water because the glow had started to fade and the effects of several hours of drinking and fucking had begun to slop over the top of the pharmaceutical dam. What next? Standing in the hall, looking at the glass, wondering if he ought to take another tablet, then distracted by the sickening feeling of the night rushing up to hit him, and then . . . and then nothing. Blank.

Didn't take fifteen years' experience at I&I to work it out, though.

"Oh, *shit.*"

Warrick raised an eyebrow.

"Yes?"

"I just remembered. I'm so sorry. No, really—I am."

Warrick shook his head. "The timers opened the cuffs after three-quarters of an hour or so. No harm done. I was a little concerned about *you,* but when I found you in here the snoring sounded healthy enough. You didn't seem interested in regaining consciousness for long enough to get to bed, so I covered you up and left you."

"I needed the rest." Well, Warrick genuinely didn't sound too upset, which saved a lot of tedious apologizing. Toreth's arms seemed to be responding again, so he stretched and yawned. "I don't think anyone's ever fucked me in my sleep before."

"I did try to wake you first. Hourly, in fact, since eleven. However, I can only wait so long." Warrick grinned sheepishly. "I tried wafting coffee under your nose several times, but even that didn't work. So in the end—" He shrugged.

"God. You're—" What was the word he wanted? Warrick would know. "What's that word? The one that you are."

Warrick's smile widened. "Insatiable?"

"That's the one. You're it." He pushed ineffectually at Warrick, in a way designed to suggest that he could stay there all damn day if he wanted to. "And it's not even as if you'll get the I&I death-in-service money after you've fucked me into an early grave. I signed that over to Sara years ago."

"Sorry," Warrick said, not sounding it. "If it's any consolation, there's plenty of hot water for the shower, and headache tablets, fresh coffee and bacon sandwiches, all ready for you." He smiled again, with a wicked edge. "So you can get your strength back for later."

Toreth closed his eyes, because sometimes, like now, Warrick was too much to look at. It felt too . . .

Had he ever had such an enjoyable hangover in his life?

Then and Now

❖

Toreth had been quiet all day—in the morning, at the gym, at the restaurant they'd had lunch in. So the question, asked out of the blue as they sat reading in Warrick's living room, surprised Warrick.

"Warrick, have you been in the sim lately?"

Warrick looked up to find Toreth still slumped in the armchair, one leg resting over the arm. Warrick bit back a comment—at least he'd taken his shoes off. The screen Toreth had been reading lay flat on the back of the chair.

"Not recently, no." He thought back. "Not for about three weeks. The last time was with you, in fact. I've been too busy with other things, and sadly I don't have as much direct involvement with testing as I used to. Although once the Yes program is up and running again, I hope that might change."

Toreth nodded, frowning slightly. Then his expression changed to one of determination. "How many men have you fucked?"

It was such an uncharacteristic question that Warrick couldn't believe he'd heard it correctly. The phrasing left no room for misinterpretation, though. Toreth was looking at him expectantly.

"I beg you pardon?" Warrick asked, playing for time.

"You heard me. How many men have you fucked?" Toreth tilted his head, then grinned suddenly. The effect wasn't reassuring. "I'm not planning to hunt them all down and kill them for not psychically deducing that however many years later you'd be fucking me."

Warrick raised his eyebrows, and Toreth swung his leg down and sat up. "Oh, come on," Toreth said. "Melissa's still alive and well, and I know where she lives."

"Do you?"

"Yeah. Flat seventeen, Symphony-Parker Building. With her husband and their shiny corporate kids."

"How the hell do you know all that?"

"It was in the SimTech investigation file. Ex-wife, former shareholder, that made her a pretty unlikely but potential suspect with inside knowledge and a potential for holding a grudge. The address stuck in my mind. Come on, how many?"

"Why do you want to know?"

"I'm curious."

Perhaps that was all, but Warrick doubted it. For one thing, the question was too sudden and too out of character for a man who usually cared little for anything beyond the immediate here and now. For another, Toreth making a joke of jealousy meant he was hiding something about which he felt even more uncomfortable.

Warrick closed his hand screen and patted the sofa beside him. After a moment's hesitation, Toreth joined him.

"Very well," Warrick said. "I will tell you, *if* you tell me why you want to know."

Toreth stared at him, clearly trying very hard for an expression of puzzlement. Then he equally clearly realized Warrick didn't buy it, because he looked away and ran his hand through his hair. When he spoke again, all the studied casualness had gone and his voice was tight with anger. "Who's Tim?"

Warrick stared. For a moment, the name genuinely meant nothing to him.

"Because I woke up this morning," Toreth said as if he'd asked, "and you were still asleep and when I reached—when I moved, I touched your arm and you turned over and said 'Tim.' And some other stuff that made it pretty clear you've done more than code with him. So who the fuck is he?"

Daylight—and recognition—dawned. "A name from the very distant past. He was, in fact, the first man I ever had sex with. Or boy, I should probably say."

Toreth's gaze searched his face, then the tension suddenly drained out of him and he flushed slightly. "Okay."

Warrick rested his elbow on the back of the sofa and leaned closer. "You know, you could just have asked me."

"Yeah, well . . ." He shrugged. "I'm a para-investigator. 'Just ask' isn't the way it works."

"Do you want to search my bedroom for evidence while you're at it?"

"'Course not—I trust you." Toreth looked at him more closely, then closed his eyes briefly as Warrick raised his eyebrow. "Fuck. How could you tell?"

"I've found things moved from time to time. Mostly it was a guess. You turned the place over the very first time I left you here alone, so I assumed you'd done it again since."

Toreth flushed. "You could have fucking said something."

"Why? It doesn't matter." He didn't keep much in the flat that he minded Toreth seeing, and if the security on the study was good enough to satisfy SimTech, then it was good enough to keep Toreth at bay.

"So what about the answer to the other question?" Warrick asked. Toreth blinked at him. "How many men? Do you still want to know?"

"Oh. No, not really. Or rather—" Toreth stood up abruptly and walked over to the window. When he turned, the light behind him hid his expression. "Yes." He didn't sound at all sure.

"Mm. In that case I'll just say that, excluding professional contacts in the sim, you'd probably find it a reassuringly small number. I could invite them all to dinner, along with their female counterparts, and have no problem fitting them round the dining room table."

"Yeah?" Toreth sounded cheered, as Warrick had expected. After all, it wasn't a very large dining room. "Too busy with SimTech?"

"Quite so." Simple agreement was easier than attempting to convey to Toreth the alien concept that a constant stream of casual sex wasn't everyone's idea of fun.

Warrick hoped Toreth would drop the conversation. And, indeed, he didn't say anything straight away. After a moment, Warrick expanded his screen and started reading again. He couldn't concentrate on the words, though. He watched out of the corner of his eye as Toreth strolled over to the mantelpiece and picked up one of the ornaments—a small copper sculpture of a hissing cat—and turned it over in his hands, apparently absorbed in study.

Warrick looked deliberately down at the screen. He invited Toreth here, he wanted him here. He had to accept that Toreth touched things, and not always with what Warrick considered a proper degree of care. Most of the time Warrick coped perfectly well. He no longer even minded that Toreth only remembered to pick up towels from the bathroom floor two times in three; looked at from the correct perspective, a sixty-six percent success rate was something of a triumph.

Some things still bothered him, though, even after all this time and despite his best efforts. The ornaments was one of them. Warrick didn't have many, and every one meant something—they were gifts from close friends and family, or things he had bought because he liked them enough he couldn't help it.

"This is pretty good," Toreth said, running his fingertip over the delicate whiskers.

Warrick suppressed a wince. "It's one of Cele's pieces. Actually, it's a copy of a much larger bronze. I saw the original in her studio and asked if she could make another, but unfortunately the purchaser had commissioned it as an exclusive piece."

"So what was this? A model for it or something?"

"Not quite. She made it as a surprise for my birthday. Because it was a gift in a different size and material, it slipped through a loophole in the contract. Or so she said." He vividly remembered opening the box to find the tiny, perfect miniature copy glowing in its nest of tissue. "Actually, I prefer it to the larger one—the copper is so beautiful."

After a minute, Toreth set the cat down again, out of place on the wrong end of the mantelpiece. Warrick knew it wasn't deliberate; it simply didn't occur to Toreth that it mattered exactly where the cat stood, and of course he was right. It didn't. It was a purely decorative piece of metal. Now with finger marks that would need polishing off before the copper tarnished. Warrick bit his tongue. He could clean the cat later and put it back in the right place. A little disturbance was good for him.

"So tell me about Tim," Toreth said. "Was he good?"

Warrick sighed and snapped the screen shut. He'd known that the topic wasn't closed. "He was a friend. Of Dillian's first, so he was a year younger than me. He had a sister who was two years older. Than me, that is—three years older than him. I had an absolutely hopeless crush on her." Even now, the memories brought a twinge of something, a shadow of the blind intensity of desire. "You know how Dillian and I share a strong family resemblance?"

Toreth nodded.

"Well, Tim looked *nothing* like his sister at all. Dark where she was blonde, rather skinny while she was—" He looked past Toreth, unfocusing his gaze to sharpen the image in his mind. "Athletic. She played tennis to a fairly high standard."

"Sounds nice."

"Extremely." He looked back at Toreth. "Poor Tim was really no competition. However, he lived in the same house as her, which was a good enough reason to visit him. She'd barely even speak to me, of course, but I'd get to spend some time with her. She'd tolerate our presence, if she didn't have anything better to do."

"And?"

"Well, I'm sure you can imagine how a few hours in the presence of someone who put all my hormones into overdrive left me."

"And he was a handy fuck." Toreth sounded thoroughly approving, which made Warrick uncomfortably aware of a dynamic he'd often felt guilty about.

"He was always very accommodating, yes. Because—" He hesitated, then plowed on. "Because, I suspect, he felt about me the same way I felt about Tamara. I treated him very badly without thinking anything of it, as one does at that age. Once she went to university, I stopped going round to see him. I've wondered since if he knew why—he must have done, I suppose."

"No one tied him up and forced him to fuck you." Toreth paused. "Or did you?"

"Good God, no. Nor he me." That was a conversation he didn't want to pursue right now, so he looked for a distraction. "Who was your first—" He shied away from the word 'lover' just in time. "Fuck?"

Toreth shrugged. "I don't remember."

"You must do."

"Honestly, no." He went back to his original chair, lounging back into his original position. "And anyway, it depends what you mean by first. Handjob, blowjob, fuck, what?"

He hadn't considered that for Toreth the acts would be so separate from any kind of relationship. "Well, any of them."

"Okay." Toreth rubbed his nose. "Well, when I was thirteen, I was sent to a Retraining Center. Juvenile prison, really. It'd be in my security file—you must have seen it?"

Warrick nodded, despite a sudden chill of premonition.

"Right. I was there until I was sixteen, so the first time I did pretty much everything, I did it there." He closed his eyes. "Blowjob, giving, that would be one of the guards. Same for a handjob. Getting both of them would be one of the other kids in there. Fucking...being fucked, guard again. Fucking a grown-up was with one of the teachers, although I maybe did some of the other kids before that. I don't remember for sure. And I don't remember any names, except for the teacher: Gee Evans, who was a complete fucking fruitcake, but other than that not a bad bloke."

He opened his eyes. "That was all men, of course. Women were later, after they kicked me out for being bright enough to dress myself. Well, to pass exams, actually."

Toreth paused, watching Warrick expectantly, waiting for a reaction. Warrick had the sudden feeling of a test in progress.

He had read the words Retraining Center in Toreth's file, but he'd never stopped to think through the possible consequences. If he had, this conversation would never have happened. He'd asked Toreth to reciprocate, though, so it was up to him to live with the results.

"It must have been—" Warrick ran up against a locked-down security door. What the hell *would* it be like to be Toreth, at any age, whatever was happening? He did know that getting the wrong answer would, at best, lead to an awkward weekend, if not a full-scale vanishing act.

Toreth still hadn't said anything.

"It must have been very boring—frustrating—being locked in a secure facility."

"Yeah." Toreth sounded surprised and possibly relieved. "Very. Maybe that's why I like walking everywhere, huh?"

"Possibly."

After a brief silence, Toreth shook himself, shedding memories like water, and said, "I can do the first time I fucked a woman, if you'd rather. I can even remember her name. Or at least I can remember the name on the card someone gave me, which was 'Chastity.'" He snorted. "Talk about false advertising. Good, mind. Value for money. She was about the only time I've ever paid for it, as well."

"Why did you then?"

"Practice. I like to do things properly and it's a hell of a lot easier to do intensive training with someone you're paying."

Warrick laughed, and Toreth frowned slightly. "What's so fucking funny?"

"It's—" It took a few more seconds to rein in the amusement. "'Intensive training.' A very practical approach."

Now Toreth grinned. "Yeah. I've been spending too much time on training courses at work. The jargon creeps up on you and the next thing you know you sound like some management tosser. God, did I tell you about the course last week? Nothing you don't want to hear about. It was 'Safety in the office environment.' Don't trip over chairs, don't fall down stairs—which bastards from outside always have to make some crack about, like we haven't heard it a hundred times before—and don't run with scissors. Talk about a bullshit waste of time."

"Unfortunately, they're a legal requirement. The staff at SimTech are no more enthusiastic, I can assure you."

The conversation moved on to other topics, leaving Warrick to wonder briefly if Toreth would ever mention the retraining center again.

Warrick couldn't sleep. There were too many images competing for his attention, crowding each other. Half were memories of Tim and Tamara, all vivid pictures, scents and sounds and remembered feelings. The others were created scenes, purely imaginary.

He had no idea how Toreth had looked as a teenager; Warrick couldn't imagine him as anything other than his tall, well-muscled, physically confident self. And if it was hard to create a picture, it was flatly impossible to place him in the role of victim, to conceive of him being forced into things. Dominated and taken against his will.

Somewhere deep inside, a dark, dirty thread of excitement twisted, looping around his guts and tying almost painful knots. He felt sure that if he could really imagine Toreth being hurt like that, the thrill would vanish. But as it was, shadowy pictures, unreal and strangely compelling...he pushed the feeling away, sickened.

Toreth's voice in the dark startled him. "Are you awake?"

"Yes." Warrick rolled onto his side, facing Toreth although the room was pitch black. "Wide awake."

"Me too. You made me think about it—about the RC. I haven't thought about the place for years." Toreth sounded reminiscent more than anything, certainly not distressed. The kind of tone Warrick associated with old university stories. "The beds were fucking awful. Hard as bricks. The real psychos were in single cells, but the kids they could trust not to strangle anyone in the night were in dormitories. Mind you, there were still cameras and they never really switched the lights out, just turned them down, so they knew what we were up to."

The bed shifted. Judging by the new position of his voice when he spoke, Toreth had rolled over onto his stomach and propped himself up on his elbows.

"Funny how it all comes back. There's other stuff. Like, there were a dozen of the guards who did most of the fucking. With the others it was every now and then, if they had some tension to let off."

"Mm?" Warrick said, trying to make the sound noncommittal, but encouraging if that was how Toreth chose to take it

"Yeah. Someone would turn up in the dormitory, that was the routine. Go along the beds. They'd strip the covers back if they wanted you to go out with them. Kids used to hide under the sheets anyway. Under the beds, sometimes. Not me, though—I used to sit up and wait. There was a rec room they used a lot. Sometimes they'd pull some of the real basket cases out of their cells, just for a bit of extra fun. Oh, God, that was usually—" He snorted quietly, then stopped. "I expect you don't want to hear about it."

Selfishly, he kept quiet, because he didn't want to hear and he had no idea what to say if Toreth went on. It was rare enough for Toreth to mention anything about his childhood, though. Rejecting the offered confidences outright would be cruel.

Toreth shifted, and when he spoke again, his voice was different, almost muffled. Cradling his chin on his hands, perhaps. "Some kids hardly got touched by anyone. And then there were the other kids, the ones they all wanted: the better-looking ones, the ones they could tell what to do and who'd understand in less than fifteen minutes, the ones who weren't so fucked in the head they'd bite their dicks off just because."

Toreth must have fallen into all three categories.

"Some of the kids used to fight every single time. And then the guards would kick the crap out of them every single time until they cooperated. They had bruises every day they were there: black eyes and broken noses and whatever else. No one cared. I never saw the point, though—going along with it hurt a hell of a lot less. It was just fucking, anyway, and I've always liked it."

"Always?"

"Yeah, most of the time. Sometimes, okay, it wasn't fun. Pretty fucking grim, I suppose. But most of the time... I'll tell you what—the real difference was *who* you went along with." He sounded more insistent now, with an edge of defiance. "I did the guards and the couple of teachers, but after the first few months none of the kids touched me unless I let them. *None* of them. And I had to do some real damage to make that stick, but it did. By the time I left, I was one of the ones who could take first pick of the new kids if I wanted them."

It was odd—he knew what Toreth's answer would be, but he had to ask. "Even though it had happened to you?"

"That's how the world works, isn't it? Food chain. If you're not on the top, you're on the bottom."

"Figuratively speaking."

"What? Oh, right, yeah. Anyway, that's more or less it. Just thought you might be interested. That's what I was doing when you were letting Tim suck you off while you thought about his sister's tits."

"Good God," Warrick said without thinking, because that was literally true. It had probably been on some of the same evenings when he'd—

"What?"

Toreth at fourteen, learning lessons about sex and control while Warrick had been exploring the power of imagination and discovering that all it took for people to believe was an illusion that felt good enough.

"What?" Toreth asked again.

"It's... the idea suddenly made it seem a lot more real."

Toreth chuckled. "Yeah? You want real, you should have been there. God, you'd have gone mad with boredom. I nearly did sometimes. But, you know, I think it was still better than being at home."

Sudden silence. Warrick felt so tempted to comment, but there was nothing guaranteed to make Toreth leave faster or in a worse temper than trying to discuss his family. Even—or especially—after he'd brought the topic up.

Another test, perhaps. Warrick breathed quietly, listening to Toreth's breathing in the dark, trying to judge what to say. Considering that they lay in the same bed, the distance between them felt unclosable. He put out his hand and stroked slowly down Toreth's back. A muscle twitched at the base of his spine, and Warrick imagined the panther at the zoo. There was no glass here to save him from making a mistake.

It'd tear your fucking throat out... That'd teach you not to feel sorry for things that don't fucking need it.

Although Toreth certainly didn't need his pity or understanding, and possibly didn't want them, Warrick couldn't help himself. Something had to be said, to break the silence. "I don't..." I don't think of you any differently, knowing about it. True, and maybe even what Toreth wanted to hear, but perhaps not the best phrasing. "It doesn't matter. It was a long time ago and you did what you had to do to survive."

He half expected a furious explosion. That Toreth simply ignored the comment told him he'd guessed right about Toreth's motive for resuming the conversation.

"Let me fuck you," Toreth said suddenly.

The peculiar phrasing caused a near-disastrous hesitation. Warrick covered it by sliding over to Toreth—bringing them together now that sex had made it permissible.

"Of course," Warrick said, his mouth against Toreth's shoulder. "Anything you want."

How truthfully and how broadly he meant that disturbed him, for as long as Toreth allowed him to think about it.

Friends in the Right Places

❖

"Do you want another one?" Ali asked.

She was pressed against him under the duvet, legs entwined, and the naked heat was made all the better by the fact that he was missing an afternoon lecture to be here with her. It felt illicit, like a real affair, although as far as Greg knew she wasn't married. Greg kissed her and then shook his head. "Don't forget what we're doing this evening."

She laughed. "I think we can stick up a few posters even if we're stoned."

"But we have to do it without being caught." Sometimes he worried that Ali didn't take their anti-Administration acts seriously enough. She'd only been involved with the group for a few weeks, and she was only college serving staff, not a student, but it didn't take a Cambridge undergraduate to work out that putting up idealist posters wasn't safe.

She opened the plastic bag and shook it invitingly. The earthy smell of dried mushrooms mixed with the warm smell of sex and some kind of incense she'd brought along. God, he hoped that incense was all it was. The college took a dim view of students fumigating their rooms with illicit substances.

He shook his head again, and she sighed, mock-pouting.

"Two's enough," he said. Actually, two hadn't done anything much for him, but he wanted a clear head for later.

"What shall we do instead, then?" she asked, and her hand slid down between his legs.

He laughed, breathless, letting his eyes close as she touched him, his cock hardening quickly. God, she was good. Not just good in bed, but funny and kind and sometimes he wondered if he'd fallen in love with her, short as the time had been. Pity his parents would never let him make anything more formal out of it. She was too much older than him, too far down the social scale, too—

The door opened and a calm male voice said, "I hope we're not interrupting."

"Greg!" Ali yelped, pulling away from him and wriggling under the covers.

Greg yanked the duvet up over them and rolled over, trying to make out the shapes backlit against the corridor. He didn't recognize the voice and he was sure he'd locked the door. "Who the hell are you?" he demanded.

The main light came on. Two men stood just inside the open doorway—both blond, both tall, one slightly older and broader across the shoulders. Both wore black, and Greg's mouth dried.

"Do you recognize this uniform?" the older man asked.

Greg nodded. "You're—" He cleared his throat. "You're from I&I."

"Yes. My name is Senior Para-investigator Toreth, this is Senior Investigator Barret-Connor." He closed the door. "Get out of bed, please."

"What?"

"Your security file doesn't mention a hearing defect."

Slowly, Greg slid out of bed. He couldn't take the duvet with him without stripping Ali, so he left it. Embarrassingly, he was still half-hard, although that problem was curing itself rapidly as the situation sank in. I&I. Shit, shit, shit. Were they just here for him, or did they know about any of the others? How in God's name had they found out?

Hard as he tried, he couldn't stop the flush that rose as the para-investigator examined him.

"Looks like we *were* interrupting," he said.

Greg looked towards the door, where his dressing gown hung. The para-investigator shook his head. "Leave that for now. Stand there."

Greg moved to the indicated spot.

"Right, now you," the para-investigator said.

"Me?" Ali asked.

"Funny thing about the uniform—it seems to make everyone deaf. Now move!"

Ali cringed back, and with an exasperated sigh the para-investigator started for the bed.

Heedless of the second man, Greg lunged forwards and grabbed the para-investigator's arm. "Leave her—"

Then, somehow, he found himself slammed face-first against the wall, his right arm pinned painfully behind him. He heard Ali gasp.

"Don't be an idiot," the para-investigator said. His tone hadn't changed. "Now, either you behave yourself, or I break your arm and we can start all over again from there, with a charge of impeding an I&I officer thrown in for free. Choose."

He made an abortive attempt to struggle, which ended with his clenched fist pulled a few centimeters further up towards his shoulder blade. He stilled. "I'll behave."

"Good. Are you right-handed? Of course you are—it says so in your file. But do you wank right-handed, too?" Without warning, he twisted Greg's wrist upwards again and he couldn't help a gasp of pain as his tendons stretched. It fucking *hurt.*

"You, in the bed, get out before I put him in a cast and up your workload. No, leave that behind."

Greg heard movement behind him: cloth shifting, then the soft thump of bare feet hitting the floor.

The para-investigator released his hold and stepped away. "She's your type, B-C, you deal with her."

Greg turned his back to the wall, rubbing his wrist. "I'm—"

"I know exactly what you are. Stand there and shut up."

Without another glance at him, the para-investigator crossed to the dresser and started opening drawers. Greg breathed a silent thanks that he hadn't taken charge of the posters this week. Nothing in the room incriminated him.

"ID, please, Ms...?" the investigator said.

"Alison Rice," she whispered. "And I—I don't have it with me."

"You are aware that's a category one offense?" From the investigator's stoic expression, he might have dealt with naked, frightened women every day. Maybe he did. "Then you can give me your address and ID number."

Poor Ali was trying to cover as much as she could with her hands. Greg looked away from them, burning with secondhand humiliation as the investigator took her details.

"Well, well, well. Look what we have here."

The para-investigator was holding up the bag of dried mushrooms. Greg groaned. He'd forgotten all about them in the worry over other things.

"Interesting," the para-investigator said as he returned. "And very helpful of you."

He produced a drug screener from his pocket. "I'm sure you know how it works. Good lungful, hold for five seconds, slow even breath until you hear the beep." He held the unit up. Greg set his mouth, and the para-investigator sighed. "Or we can do a screen back at I&I. I really don't care which; you're coming back anyway and 'failure to cooperate' will do just as well for an initial charge."

Greg breathed in, held, and blew. After the beep, there was a silence in the room as they all waited. Eventually, the para-investigator tapped the screen and smiled. It didn't make him look any friendlier.

"Do you know how many legal recreational pharmaceuticals there are, B-C?" he asked.

The man standing by Ali smiled slightly. "No idea, Para."

"Should hope not—taking drugs is a disgusting habit. But there are a lot. Hundreds. Thousands, probably. Apparently not enough for our little corporate heir, though."

Suddenly, everything felt more real. Not that Greg wanted to use his family to get out of this, but the knowledge that he could had held off the urge to panic. At the back of his mind he'd known that whenever he wanted to he could drop the

Ballester name and watch the arrogant bastards back off like it was a hand grenade, probably apologizing to boot. He'd seen his parents do it often enough. But if the man knew, and didn't care…

The para-investigator changed the mouthpiece on the analyzer. "And you, beautiful."

"I took them, too," Ali whispered.

"I'm very glad to hear it, but now the machine wants to hear it, as well. Nice deep breath—I think we'll all enjoy that."

Greg watched, cursing himself silently. If he couldn't protect himself, what could he do for Ali? Part-time college bar staff probably didn't have any claim on college protection.

The para-investigator checked his watch. "Right, get dressed, both of you."

Greg took the time to find clean clothes, picking out a suit. Looking as grown up and corporate-respectable as possible couldn't hurt.

As he dressed he tried to recall what names the unwelcome visitors had given when they'd arrived. The para-investigator had called the younger man B-C just now—he'd been Barret or Barnet-something. The para-investigator himself he couldn't remember at all. Greg could hear his mother's voice in his mind. *Always take the names of officials, Gregory. Then they know that they can be held responsible for their actions.*

Of course, how far that applied to I&I was a different question.

At least, Greg thought on the way from his room to the gate, they hadn't been handcuffed. Then he realized it might have been better. If someone noticed them, they might be able to warn the others. At the college lodge, a slight, dark-skinned woman in the same black uniform as the investigator stood behind the porters' desk. The three porters on duty, grouped to one side, looked at him unhappily.

"I'm sorry, Mr. Ballester," Mills said.

Greg nodded to him slightly, not wanting to draw the para-investigator's attention to the man any more than was necessary.

"Any trouble, Mistry?" the para-investigator asked.

The woman shook her head. "All quiet. You're just in time, though. Political Crimes will be here any moment. They—"

She stopped speaking as a dozen more I&I officers entered the lodge from the street.

The man leading the group stopped them, spoke quietly to the woman beside him, then came over. He had the same uniform as the para-investigator, with the same logo on his shoulder and the same unfriendly eyes. His hair was only a shade lighter than the uniform, though, combining with his olive skin to give him an all-over look of dark menace. Alison edged closer to Greg.

"Christofi," the para-investigator greeted the newcomer.

"Toreth? What the—what are you doing here?"

"Picking up a suspect."

Toreth. Greg repeated the name to himself, fixing it in his mind.

Christofi looked more closely at Greg and Alison, then his eyes narrowed. He expanded a hand screen and glanced at it. "Gregory Ballester. He's—"

"Part of a General Criminal IIP. He's in my custody."

Christofi took a step closer, so that only the two para-investigators and the prisoners heard his next words. "I don't know what you're trying to pull, but I want him handed over, right now. He's mine."

The para-investigator lowered his voice, too. "I was told to pick him up. I was told exactly what *time* to pick him up. And I'm just doing what I was told. You can call my section head if you don't like it. I'm sure Tillotson will explain."

After a moment, Christofi nodded. "I'll sort it out when I get back."

"You do that. I'll keep him safe for you. Anyone else you want, you're welcome to them." He nodded to the porters gathered in the lodge. "I'm sure the loyal citizens over there wouldn't do anything to impede an investigation, but if I were you I'd leave someone in here while you round the rest up."

Christofi's gaze settled on Ali. "Who's she?"

Greg swallowed, fear twisting its fist in his guts again. If Ali fell under "anyone else," his last hope of protecting her would be gone.

"Alison Rice. The system says she's a casual college worker, although I bet they don't pay her for what she was doing when I found her—she was fucking my suspect."

Beside Greg, Alison was staring at the floor, her cheeks crimson. Bastards, Greg breathed. Talking about her like she wasn't even there. He found her hand with his, and she squeezed back.

"Is she on your list?" Toreth asked.

Christofi consulted the screen. "Nah. You can keep her—I'm after resisters, not whores. She doesn't look that bright, anyway." He turned to his group. "Right. Just forget we saw this, and we'll get on with the pickups. Wyman, stay here."

Once the guard on the porters had been changed, Toreth prodded Greg in the back. "Move."

The black car stood right outside the gates, in a no-waiting zone. B-C and the woman got into the front, then the para-investigator opened the rear door.

"Get in and sit down. Make yourselves comfortable." He climbed in behind them and closed the door. "It's a long drive back to New London."

All the way down the motorways into New London, Greg somehow hadn't believed it could really happen. Then, through the tinted windows, he saw the high gates closing silently behind them and they were inside the Int-Sec complex.

He recognized the fences and the vast white buildings from a citizenship class trip. They'd even been inside I&I itself: there'd been a lecture on the danger to society of irresponsible idealism, and they'd met some of the black-clad protectors of European citizenry.

That had all been long before he'd met anyone who openly talked about anti-Administration feelings. Back then, he remembered distinctly and uncomfortably, he'd rather admired the smart uniforms and the monolithic white buildings. The place had the same air of order and immutable solidity as the corporate headquarters with which he'd been familiar all his life. Now he mostly remembered how few windows there had been, and how many guards.

And he remembered the stories he'd heard more recently about the things that went on in the place. What they didn't show to citizenship classes—what the interrogation part of the I&I name really meant. Unbelievably horrible things, and he wished now that he didn't believe them.

They drove past the towering statue of Blindfold Justice, and then on past the double doors at the front of I&I. Prisoners obviously went in by another route.

Around the side of the building, the car turned in through a second gate in an even more formidable fence, and finally pulled up.

"Here we are," the para-investigator said, and after a few seconds the car door opened.

Surrounded on three sides by the sheer white stone walls, the area they stepped out into was shadowed and cool. The para-investigator led the group into the building, scanning his ID at an unmanned security station. Then they stepped inside and the door closed behind them—no loud, ominous clang, just the disappearance of daylight and a change to fluorescent lights that made Ali look even paler than she had outside.

B-C and the woman from the porters' lodge went one way, escorting Ali with them, leaving him to go another way with the para-investigator. The slightly stale, recycled air had a faint tang that he couldn't identify.

Greg was rather hazy on the details of arrest, still less arrest by I&I, and he wished he'd thought to look them up. He had expected—hoped for—some kind of official processing, maybe even a chance to call his parents or a corporate lawyer. Instead they went down a long corridor, through another two doors, and into a small, pale gray room. The only furnishings were a table and two chairs, and a large screen on one wall.

He sat, uninvited, and the para-investigator sat opposite him, still not speaking.

Greg cleared his throat. "Have I been arrested?" There was a nervous edge to his voice that he didn't like. "I want to contact our lawyers."

"No. You're here informally. Assisting with our inquiries."

It struck Greg forcefully that if there was no official processing, then there would be no evidence that he'd ever been brought here. Surely a corporate heir couldn't simply disappear? The porters had seen them taken away—didn't that mean something?

He sat up straighter in the chair, trying to dismiss the fears. More likely, someone at I&I—maybe this "Tillotson" whom Toreth had mentioned—knew Greg couldn't be arrested but thought a few hours at I&I would be enough to scare him into being a loyal citizen. Well, they were wrong about that.

From his pocket, Toreth produced the bag of mushrooms and dropped them on the table between them. "Why are you messing around with this shit?" He poked the bag. "There are a thousand perfectly legal drugs, if that's what you want."

He took a deep breath. "The legal recreational pharmaceutical trade is an oppressive tool of the Administration, used in collusion with the corporates to drug the population of Europe into passively accepting the illegal secret dictatorship of the departments." Then he sat back, his mouth dry and his heart pounding.

Whatever reaction he'd expected, laughter wasn't it. It took a good minute for the para-investigator to get himself back under control. "I never knew there were idealist drugs." He shook his head, still chuckling. "No wonder the resisters I meet are all so fucking miserable."

Greg had no idea what to say. That kind of thing never failed to get an angry rise out of his parents, his father especially.

"Do you really believe that crap?" Toreth asked.

"Of course."

"And I thought you were supposed to be smart. Or did you parents buy your way into Cambridge?"

He ignored the goad. "They'll get me out of here, you know."

"Or Christofi might get to keep you. Ballester lawyers won't impress PC. If you're classified as a political prisoner, then you won't see anyone until your Justice rep shows up to explain how fucked you really are." Toreth leaned back in his seat. "But you're probably right. It doesn't matter to me—it pays the same either way."

Greg tried to read his expression. As he did so, he realized that he'd never really looked at Toreth before. Since the door to his college room had opened, he'd seen only the uniform; even in the car on the way down, he'd been more worried about what might happen to Ali. Now Greg was trying to find the man, and failing. It was like looking into a well, a cold, empty darkness, showing fractured glimpses of something almost human, a long way beyond his reach.

He shook his head slightly. God, this place really was freaking him out. As if to prove that, a soft chime sounded, making him jump. Nerves, he chided himself.

The noise was the para-investigator's comm. He listened to his earpiece in silence for a while, then finally said, "Yes, sir." He stood. "Come on."

❖❖❖

"Are there so few serious crimes in the city that you have the time spare to spend chasing children for taking a few illegal substances? I wish to know the names of everyone responsible for this outrage. Who carried out the arrest, who ordered it, who gave *them* permission. *Everyone.*"

Greg didn't remember seeing his mother in such a magnificent temper for a long time. His parents must have been out somewhere; his mother was dressed in her favorite long fur. She was beautiful—everyone always said so, although Greg didn't often notice it. Right now she looked like a sleek, angry she-animal—a mink defending her cub—as she faced down the looming para-investigator. Greg's father stood nearby with his usual air of coiled watchfulness.

His parents were like fire and ice, and Greg couldn't believe how glad he was to see them.

The para-investigator listened patiently to her diatribe, his face still unnervingly unreadable. "Ms. Ballester," Toreth said finally, "the Political Crimes section arrested several of your son's associates tonight in connection with an investigation into active recruitment of resisters, premeditated sedition, and the willful dissemination of anti-Administration materials within the university. All serious criminal offenses."

That stopped his mother dead. "Gregory? Is this true?"

"They barged into the college, yes. I don't know who they arrested." Who *had* been picked up? Not everyone, surely?

His father stepped forwards. "Answer the question, Gregory."

He dropped his gaze. "Yes, it's true."

"Did you have anything to do with it? With the political part?"

Greg looked up at his father and squared his shoulders. "Yes."

There was a long silence before his father said, "Para-investigator, might I have a word with you in private?"

The two of them moved to the other end of the room, leaving Greg with his mother.

Now came the exercise of privilege, Greg thought. The word in the right place from the right person which could put people above the law. He'd written freedom declarations denouncing it, but much as Greg hated the whole thing, he had to admit a sneaking relief that he'd be out of here soon.

The low voices continued.

"Are you all right?" his mother asked.

"I'm fine." He thought about telling her about Ali, maybe asking for help for her, but now didn't seem like the right time.

Toreth tapped his comm. Almost at once, a guard opened the door. "Take the prisoner back to the interview room," Toreth said. When the man hesitated, Toreth pointed to Gregory. "No need to cuff him unless he resists."

"You can't do that!" Gregory's mother said.

Something in Toreth's stance hardened. "Ms. Ballester, I can. Your son isn't under formal arrest—not yet. Senior Para-investigator Christofi will speak to you when he returns. Until then, if you have any further questions I'm sure the section head of Political Crimes will be delighted to answer them."

Numb with surprise, Greg accompanied the guard out of the room.

"Sit down and wait," the guard said when they reached the room. Then he went back into the corridor and closed the door.

It looked to be the same room, but there were probably dozens exactly like it. The door was locked. The table and chairs were secured to the floor. The screen had no obvious controls. So Greg sat and waited, wondering what had happened to Ali and how long it would take his parents to get him out.

Your son isn't under formal arrest—not yet.

Not yet.

It couldn't happen. His parents wouldn't let it happen.

His watch said an hour had passed when the door opened again. Toreth entered, alone, and sat opposite him.

"What's happening?" Greg asked.

"Christofi's back and he still wants you transferred." Toreth yawned and checked his watch. "And I should've gone home half an hour ago. Other than that, nothing that concerns you."

"Sorry to keep you here."

That failed to draw a smile. "Want something to watch?" Toreth asked after a moment. He expanded his hand screen. "Looks like we've got to wait until everything calms down, so I might as well entertain you."

The wall screen came to life, divided up into sections. Greg looked between the faces, not for the people that were there, but hoping that there were some who weren't. His stomach twisted up, and he swallowed. Now he knew what "several of your son's associates" meant. Everyone. They had everyone. Even Tam's new girlfriend. He couldn't remember her name—she'd only come along to the last meeting because she and Tam were going somewhere afterwards. She'd spent the time writing an essay. He wondered if telling the para-investigator that would do any good.

Only Ali was missing, and he didn't know if that was good or not. Did they think she wasn't involved, that she was just sleeping with the corporate heir? Or was she somewhere else? Somewhere worse than the interview rooms he was allowed to see?

Toreth touched his hand screen again, and sounds joined in with the pictures.

Feeds from each interrogation, one at a time, moving slowly through the rooms. A minute with one friend, a minute with another. Almost everyone sounded to be talking about what they had done: leaflets posted around campus, meetings, 'net discussion sites, and anonymous mail-outs. He caught his own name mentioned, but not yet Ali's.

After they had cycled through everyone once, Greg put his head in his hands. "Shut up," he whispered. "Shut *up*."

Toreth laughed, short and cold. "Enjoy the show. I'll be back."

This time he was gone for only five minutes, during which Greg tried and failed not to listen to the collapse of the fledging resistance group. He could look away from the screen, but he couldn't ignore the sounds, and putting his hands over his ears would be childish. If the other rooms were on camera, this one could be, too, and he wouldn't give them the satisfaction.

Tam was talking about his girlfriend, trying to excuse her involvement and digging them both in deeper with every word.

Greg had met Tam's parents once, when they'd come up to take Tam out to dinner on his nineteenth birthday. They'd been awed by the college and so proud of their son: that he'd won the scholarship that had got him there at all, that he was doing well academically, that he was fitting in. That he'd made respectable friends. Neither of them was the kind of person Greg was used to mixing with, but they'd been good people. Good citizens. This would kill them.

Greg didn't look up when the door opened and closed, until the smell of coffee made him lift his head.

"I brought you a drink," Toreth said as he sat again. "I doubt it's what you're used to, but it's all there is."

The coffee was revolting, but at least it was hot, and it gave him something to do other than watch his friends betraying each other.

When he'd finished the coffee, the sound feed switched back to Tam's interrogation. He was crying now, looking down, fighting the sobs like a child trying to hide tears he's been told he'll be punished for.

"If you don't stop that noise, I'll give you something to cry about" had been a favorite threat of Greg's great-grandmother, although she'd been far too soft-hearted to ever carry it through.

Suddenly, he couldn't bear it any longer. "Will you—please, would you switch it off?"

The para-investigator smiled faintly. "Of course."

The screens went blank.

"It was just posters, that's all," Greg said. "That's the most we ever did."

"You were breaking the law, though. You were spreading sedition. You knew that, didn't you?" He tilted his head, curiosity surfacing, like a man contemplating a mildly interesting puzzle.

"Yes." Something about the scrutiny compelled him to try to explain. "But we didn't... we didn't mean any harm, not really. It wasn't serious. It was hardly even ideological, just sticking two fingers up at the college—at authority. It was only..."

"Only a game?"

He nodded.

Toreth drained his own coffee and stood up. "Come on. I want to show you something."

They went down three levels in the lift. When it stopped, Toreth pressed the hold button. "Sorry about this, but I have to cuff you. No unsecured prisoners on the interrogation levels."

Greg held out his hands, and he couldn't stop a shiver as the metal closed around his wrists. Toreth smiled slightly.

"Okay." He pressed another button and the door opened.

The first thing that hit Greg as he stepped out was the smell, a harsh, chemical grace note to every breath of air, without even a pretense of perfume to cover it. It brought back vivid memories of his great-grandmother's last days in the hospital. She had been his father's grandmother, and right to the end she'd been too proud to take a cent of his mother's family's money. The Administration-run basic care facility had had this same smell, and he wondered if all Administration buildings used the same disinfectant.

A pair of security guards sat in a glass-enclosed reception booth beside a heavy security door. Toreth showed his ID.

"Transfer, Para?" a guard asked.

"Little tour for a guest," Toreth said. "Anything lively to show him?"

The guard grinned, unpleasantly feral. "Try one-six-seven. They're six hours into a level eight."

"I know, if that's Don Chevril."

The man checked a screen. "That's right, Para."

The door opened, and Greg hesitated.

"Move," Toreth said quietly.

"Where are we going?" Greg asked as they started down the long gray corridor.

"To see the place you'll end up if you keep playing fucking stupid games."

Greg didn't ask. It was very quiet, the gray plastic flooring dulling their footsteps and killing echoes. They'd taken a turn that put the entrance out of sight when a door a little way ahead opened. As they drew level, Greg caught a glimpse of a white room and movement before a woman dressed as a medic stepped through and closed the door. She looked around and saw them, and her face lit up.

"Toreth!"

"Oh—evening, Mandy."

She glanced at Greg. He saw her gaze light on his cuffs, then lift dismissively away. "Do you have a moment, Toreth? If you're not busy."

"Not at all." Toreth's voice had become warmer, more conversational. "What can I do for you?"

"Did I hear that you've been given a second junior para post on your team?"

"Good news travels. There's still some paperwork, but I'm planning to pick out a fresh one in October." He raised an eyebrow. "Any particular reason?"

She smiled. "Yes, of course. Someone I know has a son finishing his training this year. Joel Starr. I was hoping you might be able to give him a chance at a place."

"Send the name to Sara and I'll have a look at his training records." Toreth held his hand up. "No promises, mind."

She nodded. "I understand completely. Thanks. See you around."

She headed off the way they had come. Going home, perhaps, and Greg envied her. As they started walking again, he realized that after the initial scrutiny she hadn't even glanced at him again. It was as if the cuffs had made him invisible.

They met a few other people, including a couple more medics but mostly guards or men in black suits like waterproof overalls. No noises came from the rooms they passed—the security doors probably muffled most sounds. They also passed corridors, both crosses and T-junctions. After half a dozen turns, Greg was thoroughly lost. The doors and corridors were labeled in numbers and letters, but he couldn't catch the pattern. "C" was prominent; he was still trying to work the rest out when Toreth stopped by a door labeled "C167-O."

"Here we are."

He swiped the door, and it opened. Greg recoiled at the choked scream which shattered the silence of the corridor.

An expert push sent him stumbling through the doorway, and he reflexively tried to bring his hands up to cover his ears. The crossbar of the cuffs caught him hard on the mouth, and he tasted blood. The door closed behind him and he turned sideways, against the wall, trying to find a hiding place from the awful noise.

The para-investigator grabbed his upper arm and forced him around. "Look."

It took a few moments for the glass to register. The window filled most of the left-hand wall of the small room. The space they stood in was unlit, but the much larger area beyond the glass was bright white. A woman, strapped into a solid chair, threw her head back and screamed again. Her short hair, matted with sweat, was brunette. Her face, under the bruises and blood, might once have been young and pretty.

The black-uniformed man beside her, his back to the window, stood out shockingly against the harshly lit white. He had something in one hand, something Greg had never seen before, made of black metal and plastic.

"God," Greg whispered.

A second man, short and gray-haired, sat at a table, reading a screen. Greg had to look twice before he could believe it—he was wearing earplugs.

The interrogator by the chair moved, fast and precise, and another scream, hoarse and horrifying, came through the speakers. Greg cringed away again and the fingers digging into his biceps tightened, pulling him away from the wall and up to the glass. When he was only a few centimeters from it, the para-investigator released him and stood behind him, blocking his retreat.

"Can she see us?" Greg asked.

"No."

The relief was as strong as it was ridiculous. The woman didn't look capable of noticing anything, but he couldn't bear the thought of her knowing that she was on display, like an animal in a cage.

It's not for me, he told himself. It's not just a lesson for me. It was happening anyway. The guard said so. Six hours. (God, six *hours.*) She isn't here because of me.

Ali might be, though. Somewhere in the building, Ali might be in a room like this because he'd dragged her into a stupid, pointless show of rebellious bravado without thinking that she didn't have a rich family or the protection of a corporate name.

He heard a movement behind him, then the sounds from the room cut out. The para-investigator's hands landed on Greg's shoulders, and he felt the warmth of a body too close behind him.

"See that?" the para-investigator asked unnecessarily.

Greg nodded, unable to speak.

"Being in that room doesn't depend on what you've done—it depends on what we think you've done. It can take a long, long time to convince us we're wrong. And sometimes even that isn't enough. Sometimes telling us everything you know isn't enough, either. That girl—she's going to die in there. She doesn't know it yet, but that's what will happen."

"Why?"

"Good question." He sounded approving. "She helped embarrass someone. A friend of hers tried to blackmail... well, let's just say someone who wouldn't be too worried about pissing off your parents. She was the one who got the blackmailer the information he needed."

"She won't give you his name?"

"Oh, no." A soft, obscene chuckle in his ear. "She gave up the name. And once Chev's decided she hasn't got anything else left to give, he'll also make sure she can't embarrass anyone ever again with what she knows."

He leaned even closer, body solid against Greg's. Greg fought to keep still. He had nowhere to go but forwards, and the idea of touching the glass made him feel sick. He was sure it would be warm, like skin.

"How much did your suit cost?" Toreth asked.

For a few seconds, surprise distracted him from the scene in front of him. "What?"

"Come on, it's an easy question. Not like the ones she doesn't know the answers to. How much?"

"I don't know. My—" Greg felt himself flush. "My mother and I went shopping, we went into the tailors, they measured me, they made it up. I never asked what it cost."

"Doesn't surprise me: nice fit, pricey material." He rubbed circles over Greg's shoulders with his thumbs. "You've got a cushy life, corporate boy. Your parents protected you this time and they didn't even know they were doing it. The name was enough. They'll do the same thing the next time, maybe even the time after that. Then, one day, when you've done something stupid enough, they'll have to choose between you and their corporate standing. What do you think they'll do?"

Greg fixed his eyes on the thin trail of blood running down the leg of the chair.

He wanted to say, they'll choose me, of course they will. But something that had been a certainty all his life seemed suddenly hollow. Outside—at home—in college—he would have been sure. Not here. Not underground, in this soundproofed room with a nameless woman screaming the last hours of her life away beyond the glass. Had she been someone friendless, like Ali? Had she had protection, like him, which hadn't been enough?

"Well? What will they do? Will they give up everything they have?" The grip on his shoulders tightened. "Will they put themselves in that room with you?"

Hands. He tried not to think about the things those hands had done. "I don't know."

"Is that where you want them? You want to stand here some day and watch your mother trying to answer questions we're asking because of you?"

"No!" Greg tried to look around, but Toreth held him still.

"Then if I were you, I'd think about that when I was back at college, while I was looking for a new set of friends."

The girl in the chair slumped forwards suddenly, head hanging and hands limp. The man at the table looked up and frowned. Greg found himself hoping, horribly, that she had died. Then the interrogator picked up an injector from a selection laid ready to hand, and injected something into the side of her neck. After only a few seconds, she started to stir again.

Greg heard himself whimper in protest.

"Seen enough?" the para-investigator asked.

"Yes." Greg closed his eyes. "Yes, please."

Toreth didn't speak for the whole journey back upstairs, not even in the lift as he unlocked the handcuffs. Greg breathed deeply, concentrating on every breath. As the lift rose it felt like leaving hell behind, the fading stink of disinfectant playing the part of brimstone.

To his unutterable relief, when the interview room door opened Gregory saw his parents waiting for him. The relief was strong enough that he didn't even object when his mother hugged him and kissed him.

When she turned to Toreth, though, she was all arrogance again. "We will take our son home now," she said in her best speaking-to-lackeys voice. "We have spoken to your superiors and cleared up the misunderstanding."

"Ms. Ballester, there was no misunderstanding involved." Toreth spoke respectfully but firmly. "Your son committed a crime—a very serious crime. If he wasn't who he is, or, more to the point, if you weren't who you are, he would be under interrogation right now. As it is, he's being given a second chance."

For a moment, Greg thought it would set her off again. Earlier, it had been funny. Now he couldn't shake the memory of the woman below them. Still there. She would still be there, in that room, if she wasn't dead yet.

Someone who wouldn't be too worried about pissing off your parents.

It could happen. Rarely, even the most important corporates might be arrested if they stepped out of the shelter of corporate privilege and acceptable levels of corporate sabotage, and into out-of-control vendettas or political crimes. And as dead sure as he was that neither of his parents would contemplate such a thing for a nanosecond, Greg wanted to grab his mother and warn her to shut up. Riches or prettiness wouldn't make any impression on the para-investigator if he had her down in that interrogation room.

Don't push him. Don't you know what he *is*?

"I'm sure Gregory has learned his lesson from this," his father said smoothly. "Haven't you?"

Greg glanced at Toreth, who raised one eyebrow slightly. It looked almost like a challenge. "Yes. I won't get mixed up in anything like that again, I promise." It was the sensible thing to say—the only possible thing—so why did it feel so much like cowardice?

"There you are," his father said. "Is that good enough for you?"

"Of course," Toreth said blandly.

His mother cleared her throat. "I apologize for my earlier manner, Para-investigator. I'm grateful for your efforts to keep Gregory's name clear of this unsavory matter."

"We're here to protect respectable citizens, Ms. Ballester. Even from themselves, if we have to."

Toreth accompanied them all the way to the main reception. Greg felt almost giddy with the relief of escaping from the place. It wasn't until they were actually outside, waiting for the car to arrive, that he remembered.

He walked a few meters away, trying to avoid his mother's gaze, and beckoned Toreth over. "What... what will happen to Ali?" he asked in a low voice.

Toreth looked at him blankly.

"The girl in my room."

"Oh. That depends on whether the others implicate her. Will they?"

Greg bit his lip. It meant implicating her himself, but what else could he do? "They might."

Toreth spread his hands. "Then she'll be interrogated. What happens after that depends on how good a rep she can afford."

"Please, can't you . . ." What the hell could he ask, or offer? Nothing for it but to see how much of a Ballester he was. He squared his shoulders and looked Toreth right in the eyes. "She was never really involved, Para-investigator. If you could find a way to get her out of it, I'd be grateful. I might not have a great deal of personal power now, but I will have, and I'll remember this evening."

To his surprise, Toreth seemed to consider the request. At length he said, "Are you going to stay out of trouble?"

"Yes." God, yes.

He smiled, and this time Greg thought he caught a touch of genuine warmth in his eyes. "Then I'll see what I can do for her." He half turned, as if to go, then paused and touched Greg's arm with his forefinger. "Don't fuck it up, corporate boy."

Greg nodded and the para-investigator turned away, back through the I&I doors.

"Gregory," his mother called. "The car is here."

The main door closed behind Toreth, and he sighed. A Friday evening wasted nannying idiot corporate brats when he should have spent it fucking Warrick against a handy vertical surface until they were both too knackered to do anything except eat takeaway and browse through Warrick's weirder porn services on the screen in his bedroom. Some of that stuff raised even Toreth's eyebrows, not to mention occasionally crossing his eyes.

He took the lift up to the fourth floor, wondering idly if Warrick claimed the porn subscriptions back on corporate expenses as sim-fuck research.

As he'd hoped, Toreth found Christofi in his office. The general office outside was empty, the admins long since departed. Good. He wanted to keep things smooth with Political Crimes, but he didn't want an audience for the apology. He knocked on the half-open door and went in.

Christofi looked up. They'd known one another a long time, since Toreth's own brief stint in Political Crimes, but there was still a moment of tension before he waved Toreth over. "Sorry about that," Toreth said as he sat down.

Christofi shrugged. "I know how it goes. Someone gets twitchy over a big name, and they want to cover their arse. I already got a bollocking from Ravi about not pointing out to him that Gregory Ballester was a scion of the Ballester-Hodders-Simone, Inc., dynasty. I wonder if he even reads the bloody IIPs."

Toreth nodded, relieved by Christofi's understanding tone. "Ravi must've had a word with Tillotson. Tillotson told me to pick the lad up and hold him for something—anything—until the rest of them were safely locked up."

"Always the bloody same. Don't touch the big corporates, and then they wonder where the resisters get their money." Christofi sighed. "Is he gone?"

"Yeah. Off in a corporate car with mummy and daddy. They got here before you did, but when I explained why he was here daddy asked me to give him a scare. I took him down to level C."

"Good." Christofi smiled grimly. "Maybe it'll teach the little bastard not to do it again and waste my surveillance budget."

"Want a drink?"

"Sure." Christofi checked his watch. "Give it ten, and Roth will be along. I hear you had a proper eyeful of her."

Toreth grinned. "I had to send B-C up to the pharmacy for tranquilizers when we got back. Too much stimulation for his fragile system. If she's a sample of the undercover agents you send in, I'll start plastering level five with anti-Administration posters myself."

"You'd probably get Wyman—he's next up on the rota."

"Wyman? Could be worse. Roth's not going back into the college, then?"

"Nah." Christofi waved to the screen, where the collection of pictures taken during prisoner processing made a pitiful group. "They're just a bunch of student losers—waste of her time and mine. Half of them will go for re-education, half will get lawyered out of it. We got a couple of names of contacts outside the college which we might chase up. But 'Alison' will send in a resignation tomorrow. I need Roth on real cases."

"Yeah?" Toreth grinned. That should work out beautifully. He could buy Roth a drink, apologize for the "take a deep breath" crack, and ask her to drop an in-character note to Gregory which would win him a nice set of brownie points with the brat. It was always handy to have friends in the right places.

Smoke and Cameras

❖

Toreth examined the map on the car's screen, trying to work out where the hell it was going. The streets outside were unfamiliar—he'd left the heart of New London behind and moved out into one of the industrial zones.

No obvious destination sprang to mind. Toreth shrugged to himself and sat back. Warrick's instructions had said evening wear, which he had on, and he'd been more or less ready when the car arrived so he'd be on time. There was nothing more he could do except wait.

Eventually the car drew up at a sturdily serious-looking gate, which gave access through an equally formidable wall. An armed guard stepped out of a security station, and Toreth had a moment's unease before he spotted the SimTech logo on the man's shoulder.

The guard looked at the car, cross-checked something on a hand screen, then tapped on the window.

"ID, please, sir," he said when Toreth opened it.

Toreth handed it over, fairly confident now of where he was.

The ID was evidently acceptable, because the man nodded. "The car will take you up to reception, sir. Please don't stop the car before then, or try to get out. If the car stops by itself at any point, please wait inside it—some of the security systems are a little overzealous at the moment."

Toreth sat back as the window wound up, wondering what "overzealous" meant and how fatal it was likely to be.

Beyond the fence was a large, rectangular building with a discreet SimTech logo on the side. There was, interestingly, no visible entrance. After ten meters the car turned left, directly towards the building, and the road dipped down into a short tunnel. At the far end a pair of heavy security doors opened, and the car drove into a plain room and stopped. The doors slid silently closed behind him.

Get out here? There was nothing in the room, though, except the doors behind, another pair of doors ahead, and an assortment of electronics on the walls above.

Toreth couldn't remember ever being anywhere with such tight security, not even the high-security section of the detention levels at I&I.

After a minute, the door ahead opened and the car moved off. When it pulled up again, it was beside yet a third set of doors, these ones sized for people rather than vehicles. A sign above them announced them to be the entrance to SimTech Central Production Plant Visitor Reception, so Toreth opened the car door and climbed out. He half expected a pack of slavering Dobermans to materialize. Instead, the doors opened and a SimTech-uniformed security guard stepped through.

"This way, please, sir."

After the ominous approach, the mundane office reception area beyond was both a mild surprise and a disappointment. Toreth had been half expecting a phalanx of armed guards and a full body scan. The place was expensively decorated, though, and obviously new—no routes worn into the SimTech-blue carpet, or impressions on the seats of the gray leather chairs.

A receptionist he recognized from the university campus SimTech building handed him a security badge with his name and picture—a rather flattering one, and Toreth wondered for a moment where Warrick had found it. Of course, it could easily have come from the sim records. He clipped it onto the lapel of his jacket and nodded to the guard.

They passed through two more sets of doors—secure access but no longer so heavily built—then into a lift up to the ground floor. When the lift doors opened, a hum of voices met them.

Toreth stepped into an open space surrounded by half a dozen rooms, partitioned off with glass walls. The expanses of glass would opaque for privacy; all but a couple were currently clear. The suite of rooms had all been decorated for the party, but Toreth guessed that in their real lives they were meeting rooms and places to entertain visitors. A thick gray carpet, with the SimTech logo woven into it, covered the floor, and in the center a disconnected sim couch stood on a matte gray metal pedestal. Deeply upholstered blue sofas and low tables in the same material as the pedestal surrounded it.

Expensive people in expensive clothes occupied the rooms, filling them with a background noise of cultured voices and perfectly pitched laughter. Corporate animals relaxing in the comfort of a herd of their peers. Light glinted from champagne glasses and jewelery. Toreth breathed in—alcohol, food, perfume, aftershave. Money. Funny how it *was* possible to smell it. Even the faint new-building smells of carpeting and paint had a classy touch, a richer edge.

"There you are."

Toreth turned to find Warrick beside him, smiling warmly. "Okay, what's the occasion?" Toreth asked.

"We finished the first production run today. The units are in the warehouse right now—" he gestured to the right-hand wall, "—waiting to be shipped out. Except for that one in the middle—that was the very first one completed."

"Great. Do I get a drink to celebrate?"

Warrick laughed and beckoned over a waiter.

Once Toreth had acquired a glass of champagne, he raised it to Warrick. "Well done. Fucking excellent."

"Yes, it is." Warrick grinned, looking happier than Toreth could remember seeing him in any context that didn't involve sex. "Absolutely fucking excellent in every possible way." Then he looked across the room, and lifted his hand to someone. "One moment. I'll be back directly, I promise."

Toreth nodded, not believing him for a second.

After Warrick had departed, Toreth had another drink and looked more carefully around the crowd, recognizing many of them. Asher Linton and her husband Greg, Lew Marcus, Dillian, a sprinkling of the senior staff—all the usual suspects for a major SimTech event. He spotted familiar faces among the sponsors, too, including Marc and Caprice Teffera. He'd never seen so many corporates looking so happy—even Lew Marcus was smiling. Although that was hardly surprising when there were so many young women with trays and short skirts.

An evening for high-powered sponsors and employees only. And him.

Even after all this time, it occasionally surprised Toreth how much he'd grown used to these events. Forays into the corporate world with nothing to do but enjoy the free food and alcohol and try to amuse himself. There would usually be, somewhere, a group of other peripheral people, the spouses and partners of guests, and Toreth would kill time talking to them. And occasionally a little more than talking, although he did his best to be discreet about it. Nothing put Warrick in a worse mood than catching him swapping numbers with a sponsor's wife. Except, possibly, if it were a sponsor's husband, instead.

In this case, Toreth realized quickly that he'd met the other halves in the crowd before. All had already proved unattractive or unavailable, except for the two women and one man—previous conquests—who determinedly avoided his eye. Still, buoyed up by the infectious atmosphere of excitement and triumph, Toreth didn't mind.

Time passed. Champagne flowed freely, helped down by delicious canapés. Toreth flirted idly with one of the waitresses and watched the guests. Eventually Warrick appeared again, this time holding a glass of what was probably iced water—he'd be staying sober to ensure things went smoothly. There was a brief pause as Toreth conveyed to the waitress that her presence was no longer required, then he turned to Warrick. "Everything going well?" Toreth asked.

"Perfectly, I would say." Warrick checked his watch. "We've got a little time. Come upstairs—I should show you round the place, since you're not likely ever to need to come back out here."

Toreth nodded easily and followed Warrick back to the lifts, acquiring a fresh glass of champagne on the way. He didn't particularly care about a tour of the offices, but upstairs sounded promising.

For a production facility, the lift was certainly plush, with a carpeted floor, and mirrors on the upper half of the walls that gave Toreth some interesting ideas. He watched the floor numbers tick smoothly past—two, three, four. Of course, customers might make it into this part of the building, and SimTech would want to impress anyone who could afford—

The lights went out and the lift dropped sickeningly, then juddered to a halt as the safety systems caught it. Toreth stumbled, keeping his glass miraculously upright, reaching out with his other hand and finding nothing to grab. "What the *fuck?*" he exclaimed.

The lift remained pitch-dark, except for a small green square of light, reflecting back and forth from mirror to mirror, away into infinity. In the blackness, it was oddly hard to judge how far away it really was. Combined with the sudden drop, it left Toreth disoriented. Something bumped his forearm, then a hand closed around it.

"Don't worry," Warrick said. "We've been having problems with the power all week. The emergency system will cut in soon."

They waited.

"Or not," Warrick added. "Be careful if you move—I spilled some of my water, and probably the ice. I'll put the glass down by the wall." He released Toreth's arm, and the green square disappeared, reflections and original, obscured by Warrick's body.

"The lifts are comms shielded," Warrick said. "In fact, everywhere in the building is. But there's a link to security somewhere over…here. Hello?" A pause, then Warrick said, "Yes. This is Dr. Warrick. I'm stuck in one of the lifts. Can you—" A much longer pause. "I see. Very well. No, no, concentrate on the guests first, naturally. Thank you."

The emergency panel closed with a metallic click, and the green square reappeared.

"Well?" Toreth asked.

"We've lost power to the office end of the building. They have no idea why, as yet, but for some reason part of the emergency system has shut down, too. The drawbacks of highly automated systems. It will take at least twenty minutes to bring the generators online manually, assuming whatever's wrong with the system will allow them to do it."

"And if it doesn't?"

"They'll need to find the fault and fix it. No telling how long that could take. Damn."

Toreth moved over carefully towards the light. Now that his eyes had adjusted, it was bright enough to reveal Warrick as a dim shape. "Well, as long as it isn't anything serious," he said.

"But it is. Everyone else, including the sponsors, are as much in the dark as we are." Warrick sighed sharply. "So much for a celebration."

"Oh, they'll love it." Toreth reached out and found Warrick. Judging by his voice, it must be his front. He slid his hand up Warrick's arm, then moved around to stand close behind him. "Bit of excitement, people will remember it. Give them more of a reason to talk about it tomorrow."

"Mm. I suppose so."

Toreth drank some champagne, and offered the glass to Warrick.

"Security will find torches or something, and it doesn't take electricity to open bottles. Pity we didn't bring more to drink." Toreth lowered his head, and his voice. "We'll just have to think of something else to pass the time."

Warrick sipped the champagne. "If I didn't know it was impossible, I'd think you'd arranged this." He pulled away, but not very far, and added, "There are cameras in all the lifts."

"They don't have any power. Not for twenty minutes."

"Unless the systems power up by themselves. There's always a chance they could come back on any moment."

Toreth slid his hands down, pulling Warrick's wrists behind him and pinning them. Warrick still held the glass by the stem, twisting his fingers around to keep it upright. "And what, exactly, are you going to do to stop me? Run? Nowhere to go. Scream? Who the fuck will hear you? Fight? I'd like that."

Warrick drew his breath in, then let it out on a long, slow sigh.

Toreth released his hands and took the glass from him. "Strip."

Warrick turned, his face lit faintly from the side. "No."

"If you don't, I'll tear your clothes off. How will that look when the power comes back?"

"Toreth, *no.*" Then, as Toreth took a step forwards, Warrick held up his hands. "Yes. All right."

Toreth took the items one by one and folded them. A requirement for fast dressing wasn't unlikely. He glanced up towards the blinded camera and the familiar thrill of danger, of the risk of discovery, of being seen with Warrick, shivered down his spine.

Naked, Warrick's body showed far more clearly in the lift, shadowing dimly in the surrounding mirrors. The darkness still hid Toreth himself, and he savored the thought as he set the clothes down in the corner. "Put your hands behind your back. Close your eyes."

The pale gleam of the whites of Warrick's eyes vanished. Toreth dipped his finger in the champagne, bubbles tickling, and then rubbed the tip over Warrick's nipple, feeling it harden. He repeated the wet caress on the other side, then bent down and licked. Warrick hissed, flinching minutely before pressing back against Toreth's mouth.

"Keep still." He moved to the other side of Warrick's chest, savoring the dry tang of champagne on his tongue and a faint hint of sweat, probably from the shock of the lift dropping.

Toreth straightened and put the glass to Warrick's lips. "Drink. Finish it."

Warrick tilted his head back, and Toreth heard him swallow. When the last champagne had gone, Toreth stroked the glass over Warrick's cheek, then down his chest, over his stomach, barely brushing the cool glass over his skin. Up again, skimming over his ribs, to finish by drawing a line down his other cheek.

Quick, quiet breaths sounded loud in the silence of the lift. How rare, Toreth realized, to be somewhere both indoors and completely free of electrically generated noises. "Kneel."

A hesitation, and he thought Warrick might protest again, but instead he knelt and bowed his head. Probably wanting to get this over with quickly. Toreth checked his watch and smiled.

"Better." He set the champagne glass down beside Warrick's glass of water, then stood in front of him. Dark changed to pale as Warrick looked up. Toreth pictured the scene, how they would look on a monitor somewhere as the lights came on. No doubt there'd be guards anxiously watching to see what kind of a mood the director was in.

The position reminded him of something they'd done a long time ago, during the early days, only a few months after Tanit's death. When they'd been exploring and pushing boundaries, something they didn't do enough of anymore. It had been light then, because he'd wanted to watch Warrick's face as they talked. Now he knew him well enough that he didn't need to see it clearly.

"Are you hard?" Toreth asked.

"Yes."

He knelt in front of Warrick, as close as he could be without touching him. In the darkness, he caught a hint of movement from Warrick's eyelashes, but before he could say anything, they stilled.

"Tell me why," Toreth said.

"The way you held my wrists. The threat. When you touched me with the glass, I imagined it was broken. Your voice." Warrick's own voice was tight, strained. "Being naked when you're dressed makes me feel vulnerable and that's very arousing. Uncertainty, because we haven't done anything exactly like this and I don't know what you're planning to—to do to me. What you want from me."

"I want you to tell me why all that makes you hard."

Warrick's head bowed.

"No," Toreth said. He twisted his left hand into Warrick's hair, forcing his head up, then releasing his hold. "Let me see your face. Now, tell me why."

"I don't know," Warrick said after a moment. "If there's an explanation, it's biological, or it's so far back I can't find it. It frightened me for a while. A long while, even though I didn't allow myself to think about it. Now I know it's part of me. There is no why. Toreth—" His voice cracked, and he cleared his throat. "Touch me again. Please."

He laid his hands lightly on Warrick's shoulders, feeling him twitch, then spread his fingers, running his thumbs up and down Warrick's throat. Warrick's lips parted, barely visible. This was where they'd stopped the conversation before, all that time ago. Even now the temptation to kiss Warrick, or to stand up and fuck his mouth—to take him, to possess him unequivocally—almost overwhelmed him.

He stroked gently along Warrick's collarbones, and Warrick shivered.

"There are drugs that give men erections no matter what," Toreth said. "We use them at work, for prisoners with the right psych profile. Mix it with something else, so they don't know we gave it to them. Scares the hell out of some prisoners to get that kind of response to being hurt. They'll talk to stop that as much as to stop the pain."

Warrick tensed under his hands. "You know I don't want to hear about I&I."

Normally, that would have closed the conversation, but in the darkness, Toreth felt oddly confident that he could press on. "You're right, I do know. You hate I&I, you fuck me. So how does that work?"

"I fuck you, not your job," Warrick said, cool and precise.

"So you say. You don't, though, do you?"

"Meaning what?"

"Meaning that it matters." He paused. "Touch yourself."

The muscles under his right hand shifted and after a moment Toreth heard the soft, slick whisper of skin on skin.

"It matters that it's me," he continued. "It matters that I know how to restrain prisoners. How to hurt them. How to read it. How to tune it. If people at work could see this, Christ, they'd take the piss. Do you know what an interrogator junkie is?"

"I think I can guess." Warrick's voice had turned to ice, but his shoulder still flexed beneath Toreth's hand.

"So guess."

A hesitation, then Warrick said, "Someone who's sexually excited by the idea of interrogators or interrogation?"

"Spot on."

"I'm not. Not in the least."

"I know. Which is why I asked. So, how does it work?"

"I haven't the faintest idea about that, either." A hint of warmth crept back into his voice, or at least his tone changed to the more measured delivery of Warrick pursuing an interesting observation. "I suppose I can't deny there's a significant thrill from the knowledge that I *cannot* stop you, if you choose not to stop. So, from that point of view, the fact that you're an interrogator isn't important per se. Any kind of training which meant you could overpower me would be equally as effective." He shivered, back arching slightly. "It all—it all feeds back into the fundamental desire to be possessed: your physical superiority, the chains, the cabinet, being hurt."

What the hell was that? Toreth lifted his hands and rocked back on his heels. Looking around, he saw nothing new. But something, some minute warning sign, had grabbed at his senses.

"You forcing me to do damn stupid things like strip naked and masturbate in a lift in the middle of—"

"Warrick, stop." Hard to see in the dim light whether he had obeyed, but the soft sounds vanished. Toreth sniffed, hoping he was wrong. "I think I can smell smoke."

Warrick's eyes opened. "What?"

"Smoke." Toreth stood up. "Something burning. Can't you smell it?"

A pause, then Warrick said, "Yes, I'm afraid I can."

"Fuck." Not good. Not at all good.

Warrick stood, too. "And it's getting stronger. Where are my clothes?"

"In the corner. Hang on a minute." Toreth opened the panel by the green light. Inside, a row of buttons glowed. He pressed the manual override on the emergency lights and the interior of the lift lit up, seeming bright after the darkness. Reflections sprang up, distracting Toreth with a multitude of naked Warricks.

Blinking at the light, Warrick smiled, then bent to pick up his underwear. "I wondered if you'd seen the panel."

"No, I just guessed. Not my most brilliant deduction. All lifts have battery—" He stopped dead. Smoke curled into the lift through the air vents, writhing in front of the strip of emergency lighting. "Bollocks."

Warrick looked up from pulling on his trousers. "What... ah."

Toreth wrenched the panel open again and hit the fire alarm button. Nothing.

"I imagine the detectors would've set the alarm off, if the system were functioning," Warrick said. "Try the comm again."

Toreth took his earpiece out of his jacket pocket and fitted it. He pressed the link into the building's secure comms half a dozen times before he admitted failure. "Dead, too. Fuck."

Warrick slipped on his shoes. "Stay or try to get out?"

Toreth reached up to snap the air vents closed. "I don't know. What's above us?"

"One more floor and the roof." Warrick paused, thinking. "If I remember the plans correctly, there is a ladder running the height of the lift shafts, with exits to the floors. And there should be an entry to a fire refuge room on the floor above us."

"All mod cons."

"If they are working," Warrick said as he shrugged into his shirt and jacket, not bothering to button them. "If we had a better idea of where the fire was, we'd know which way to try first. There's a sprinkler system, of course, but if the alarms are out it may be safer to assume that's nonfunctional also. I think we have to go."

Toreth reached up and released the catch for the hatch in the lift roof. As soon as he lifted the corner, smoke flowed through the crack, making him cough.

"Close it," Warrick said.

"Look, we need to—" Toreth stopped, watching as Warrick opened a second panel. It revealed a fire extinguisher and beside it a thin fire blanket, which Warrick took and spread out on the floor.

Warrick produced his gadget-crammed penknife and cut the fireproof fabric in half diagonally, then stopped. "Oh, *hell.*"

"What?"

"I didn't think. What are we going to do if the fire spreads to the manufacturing sections?" Warrick frowned, the dismay almost comical. "In the clean rooms even smoke would be a disaster. It would set everything back months."

Toreth nearly laughed, but a sharply indrawn breath set him coughing, and the amusement vanished. "Warrick, there are more pressing problems than SimTech's fucking production schedule."

"Of course." Warrick shook himself and folded one half of the blanket, damped it with the remains of the water in his glass, and tied it over his mouth, then offered the second half to Toreth.

Not a bad idea.

This time, when Toreth opened the ceiling hatch, the smoke stung his eyes but he could breathe. Warrick boosted him through the opening, and then he reached down to pull Warrick up behind him.

"Close the hatch." Warrick's voice was muffled by the cloth. "If we have to go back, there's no point letting it fill with smoke."

When the hatch snicked into place, darkness wrapped around them. Dull gleams of light marked emergency exits, but the light they cast was too feeble to make it into the body of the shaft. Toreth tightened his grip on the lift roof.

"Hang on," Warrick said and Toreth was embarrassed how much of a relief he found Warrick's steady voice. "There we go."

A thin beam lit up the smoke, reaching through it to pick out the far wall. It made the smoke seem thinner, and Toreth's breathing eased. Purely psychological, but still welcome.

The light came from Warrick's penknife. "It really does do everything, doesn't it?" Toreth said.

"Everything except cook and fuck." Warrick stood up. "There's the ladder."

Toreth followed the light. The gap to the recessed ladder wasn't wide—only a single step—but... he glanced over the edge. Cables led down and far below he caught a glimpse of the roof of the second lift through the smoke. He couldn't judge the distance, but it was certainly far enough for a fatal fall. Light dipped down past him, then away again. When he looked around, Warrick was shining the penknife upwards.

"I think the smoke is thicker up there," Warrick said. "Shall we go down?" Without waiting for an answer, Warrick crossed the lift and stepped over the gap. "Let's not hang about."

Toreth adjusted the mask to cover his nose more tightly, and followed. He'd never been bothered by heights, and while the prospect of burning or choking to death didn't appeal, there didn't seem to be an immediate danger of either. Nothing to panic about just yet.

He pulled on the ladder—firm and secure, as something in a newly constructed building ought to be, with a safety cage around the back, leaving a gap at the sides for access. Warrick was already climbing, the torch shining upwards to light the ladder for Toreth. Without looking down, Toreth stepped over and followed him.

It wasn't far before they reached a door beneath a muted emergency exit sign. Toreth waited on the ladder, eyes watering from the smoke, as Warrick stepped onto the narrow ledge. After a moment, rattling echoed in the shaft.

"Get a fucking move on," Toreth said.

"The door won't open." Warrick tried the handle again, then said, "Wait while I try to find a card slot."

"There won't be a locked access on a fire escape."

"There might. Parts of the building have a dispensation from the relevant safety regulations. Commercial sensitivity. Ah—got it."

Silence. Was the smoke thickening?

"Well?" Toreth asked.

"It won't open. The system must be out, along with the rest." After a brief pause, Warrick said, "We'll have to go up."

"What fucking good will that do?"

"The fire refuge won't be locked; the security there stops you leaving the room, not entering it. Even if the door out into the rest of the building won't open, we can wait in there until they bring everything back on line."

Toreth climbed slowly, wondering for the first time about the source of the fire. An accident, or possibly corporate sabotage? In the latter case it might be no coincidence that it had started when they were in the lift. With deliberate arson there was no telling how much of the building might be involved.

"How secure is the refuge?" he asked, keeping his breathing shallow.

"Theoretically the rest of the place can be gutted and it will remain safe and survivable as long as the building doesn't collapse. Even then, the refuges are all on a reinforced structural core which should hold up to anything less than quite a lot of high explosive. They're hellishly expensive; most of them were put in for data storage and critical computer systems. You should be there now."

Toreth reached out and found empty air, then a floor. He climbed up onto it, and Warrick's shoulder brushed against Toreth's calf as he came further up the ladder.

"Pass me the torch," Toreth said, bending down towards him.

Under most circumstances, it wouldn't have mattered. Warrick released the penknife a fraction before Toreth took it, and it slipped from both their hands. Toreth let it go, but Warrick grabbed once, twice, then lost his balance.

"Toreth!"

The tumbling knife swept fading stripes through the smoke; reaching blindly in the darkness, Toreth caught one of Warrick's flailing hands in his. The safety cage rattled as Warrick bounced against it, then he slipped sideways and down.

Toreth went down on his knees, barely feeling the hard contact, managing to hook an arm around the ladder before he took Warrick's weight. Even so, the jolt jerked him downwards, wrenching his shoulder and jamming his knuckles against the rough wall. He couldn't stop the yelp of pain as Warrick's fingers tightened. Toreth hung on, listening to the scrabbling of feet on metal echoing dully in the lift shaft, until the tension on his arm relented.

One deep breath, and even through the makeshift mask the smoke choked him, sending him into a fit of coughing.

"Toreth?" Warrick's grip tightened again.

"I'm—" He swallowed, fighting down the spasms. "It's just the smoke."

Warrick released his hand. "On my way up."

Toreth knelt by the ladder, ridiculously anxious, until Warrick squeezed onto the narrow platform beside him and leaned against the door. He coughed, too, then swore softly.

"Are you okay?" Toreth asked as he stood.

"More or less. My chest. I caught something sticking out of the ladder when I slipped."

Toreth reached out, finding warm stickiness, and Warrick flinched away.

"Sorry," Toreth said. "I can't see a fucking thing."

"I think there may be a torch in a niche by the door."

Toreth searched. "Not on this side."

"Wait, then, I—here it is."

The light clicked on—rather larger than the light on the penknife—and Warrick shone the beam onto his chest. A long, shallow cut ran down the left side, blood welling in places through the dark hair.

"Nothing serious," Toreth said, "but I expect it hurts like hell."

"Mm." Warrick straightened. "Actually, it's not that bad. The adrenaline is winning for now. Are you all right?"

"Banged my knuckles, nothing else."

"Good. Now let's get the hell out of here."

Toreth had forgotten the door. He found the handle, praying this one would open. The smoke hadn't grown noticeably thicker, but he was thoroughly fucking sick of the lift shaft.

"Thank fucking God," he said as the handle turned and the door gave, and Warrick laughed breathlessly.

The room beyond was dark, but mercifully free of smoke. They closed the door quickly, trying to keep it that way. Toreth pulled off the mask and dropped it, and the torch beam jerked as Warrick did the same.

Toreth sucked his scraped knuckles—blood, but not too much of it. He took deep breaths of deliciously fresh air, enjoying the relief even if it was still pitch black, until the thought of the fire intruded. The danger hadn't gone away, safe refuge or not.

Toreth spotted a familiar green square a few meters away. "I'll see if the comms are working. Shine the torch over here. Keep it steady."

The light danced over the panel and away, and when Toreth turned he found Warrick leaning against the wall by the door, his hands at least shaking violently.

"Are you okay?"

"Fine." He took a deep breath. "I don't actually like heights all that much."

He'd never mentioned that before, and Toreth suspected it translated to "I just scared the shit out of myself."

"Jesus. Now you tell me."

"I didn't want to worry you. Take the light before I drop it."

Toreth took the light, found the switch and clicked it off, then put it in his pocket. Rescue could wait for a moment—if the lights were still out, odds were the comms wouldn't work, anyway.

When Toreth took hold of Warrick's shoulder, he felt Warrick make an effort to stop the trembling. Moving closer, pressing against him, Toreth kissed him. He tasted of smoke and, faintly, champagne. He rubbed against Warrick's hip, surprised by how arousing the contact was, and how quickly. Adrenaline and, for novelty value, not generated by an argument.

Toreth lifted his head a fraction, meaning to ask again if Warrick was okay, but before he could speak, Warrick pulled his head back impatiently, kissing him again.

Take that as a yes, then.

"... me," Warrick muttered.

Toreth missed the first word, took a guess, and ran his hand lightly down Warrick's stomach—shirt still unbuttoned—and unfastened his trousers. Warrick sighed, shifting against him, suggesting the guess had either been correct or a perfectly adequate alternative.

One hand still cradling Toreth's neck, Warrick slid the other down his spine, pressing them together. With his free hand, Toreth reached back, finding Warrick's hand in the small of his back. He laced their fingers together, imagining the desperate grip on the ladder—holding Warrick, stopping the fall. Warrick broke the kiss briefly, panting, then returned, his mouth aggressive and demanding.

A change in the room made Toreth open his eyes, and he almost spoke. Then he closed his eyes again, deciding it could wait. Unlike other things. Everything felt sharper and somehow more real than the game in the lift—the hard cock in Toreth's fist, Warrick thrusting back against him, pushing his hip against Toreth's cock. It was too intense to last, for either of them. Warrick moaned into Toreth's mouth, hand tightening on his. Toreth turned his head away and gasped, "Not yet."

"I can't—"

"Please, not yet." His voice sounded hoarse. "Not yet. Not yet. Not yet. Not—ah, fuck, *Warrick*."

The adrenaline charge from the near disaster heightened the orgasm as it burned through him. Perfect, coming perfectly together, with Warrick quiet for once, almost choking, twisting against Toreth as he pulled him close. Toreth panted for breath as the waves receded, leaving him aware of the stink of smoke in Warrick's hair against his open mouth.

I could've lost him, Toreth thought, the idea shockingly sudden. He could've fallen and fucking died, and then . . . oh, Christ, what the fuck would I have done then? Unbearable. Toreth leaned his head against the wall and breathed deeply until the idea resumed its proper proportion. Something that hadn't happened, and didn't need to be thought about. Forgotten.

When Toreth opened his eyes, the first thing he saw was one of Warrick's lazier, more satisfied smiles. Enough to drive any lingering unpleasant thoughts away. With his face smudged with smoke, his hair messy and his eyes closed, Warrick looked wonderfully dirty and used. There was a scratch along his cheekbone, a smear of blood drying on his skin.

Without opening his eyes, Warrick said, "What was that about? You're not usually so fussy about timing."

"I can see you," Toreth murmured.

Warrick's smiled widened. "Mm?"

"Because the light's on again."

Warrick's eyes flew open. "Hell!" He looked around the room, then turned away from the camera, buttoning frantically.

"And I thought if you came first you might open your eyes," Toreth continued. "And then where would I have been?"

"You *knew*?" Warrick looked up, tucking in his shirt, glaring. Then he laughed, the sound harshened by smoke. "Sometimes I could kill you."

Toreth gave him the finger, only then noticing the state of his sleeve. He picked up a discarded face-mask and wiped his hand and arm. Not one of their tidier fucks. Still, with the mess they were in, Toreth doubted anyone would notice another stain. Smoke blackened his shirt, grease from the lift smeared his sleeves and trousers. Warrick—when restored to semirespectability—had suffered even more badly, probably during his slide down the ladder. As well as the smoke and grease, and a ragged flap of cloth hanging down on his left thigh, spots of blood had begun to soak through his shirt.

"How's your chest?" Toreth asked.

"Fine. I'll get someone to have a look at it when we get out of here." Warrick straightened his ruined jacket ruefully, then fingered a tear in the front. "I'm in a lot better shape than my suit, anyway. I'll try the door."

Toreth caught his arm. "No. What if there's a fire right outside?"

Warrick stopped dead, his expression halfway between horror and embarrassment. "Top of the list in the fire drill, yes. Never use a door unless you have to. Comm first."

Toreth watched as Warrick opened the emergency panel and activated the comm. "Hello? Yes, this is Dr. Warrick. No, I know I'm not—I'm in fire refuge, ah, one-four-c. Yes, I'm fine; the smoke in the lift was rather thick, that's all. Now, tell me—ah."

He listened for a while, nodding. Judging by his expression it was good news.

"Everything's under control," Warrick said when he closed the connection. "Although we caused something of a stir when the comms came back up and we didn't answer from the lift."

"What happened?"

"A small fire, right outside the base of the lift shaft, unfortunately for us. The cause isn't entirely clear, but they suspect that the contractors left something flammable behind. Sheer bad luck that it took out part of the power system, and then, presumably, some of the safety systems. They're sending someone up to manually override the door lock and let us out."

Toreth glanced up at the camera. "They didn't know we were in here?"

Warrick smiled. "No. The cameras are still out—luckily for you."

Much later, Toreth sat in the reception area drinking a large and welcome glass of brandy and waiting for Warrick. Toreth had had enough of corporate entertaining for the evening; when they had finally made it downstairs, he'd slipped away and left Warrick to face the fuss of security guards, senior SimTech staff, and anxious well-wishers. Warrick had promised to follow as soon as he could; like most corporate event promises, Toreth hadn't set much store by it.

When someone opened the door, he thought for a moment it was Warrick. In fact it was Dillian.

"Hello," he said. "Having a good party?"

To his surprise, she sat beside him. "How are you?"

"Wheezy and slightly battered." He held out his grazed hand. "Kiss it better?"

Surprise became astonishment as she took his hand and complied, a gentle touch of lips on each knuckle in turn.

"Er, thanks," he said when she lifted her head.

She smiled—Warrick's familiar smile on her lips. "No, thank you."

Then he realized what was going on. "No problem. Any time." Nice to be a hero, especially Dillian's.

"He told us after the medic checked him over. Me and Asher and Greg, and a few of the others."

I could've lost him. He could've fucking fallen and—"Reflexes, that's all. Lucky grab."

Dillian shook her head. "We all had to evacuate outside. I was sick with worry when they said he was still in there and they'd lost the comms. And the strangest thing was that I was actually relieved that you were in there with him. Not that he isn't perfectly capable of taking care of himself, but it was nice to know he wasn't alone. And a good thing, as it turned out."

Talk about a backhanded compliment. Toreth grinned. "See? I can make myself useful out of bed, too."

Before she could reply, Toreth heard a hoarse cough from across the reception area. Dillian looked down and released Toreth's hand abruptly, as though she'd forgotten she was holding it.

"There you both are," Warrick said as he walked over. "Asher and Lew said they'll finish up here, so I've been excused for the rest of the evening. Toreth—"

As her brother stopped beside them, Dillian jumped up and embraced him tightly, with the unselfconscious ease that always left Toreth inexplicably uncomfortable.

"Hey!" Warrick stroked her hair. "Careful—you'll make a mess of your dress."

"You idiot." Her voice sounded almost as smoke-damaged as Warrick's. "You frightened me to death."

"I'm sorry." He held her for a moment, then eased away. "And there's something I forgot to tell you earlier—I lost the penknife you gave me. Or rather, I know exactly where it is. It's at the bottom of the lift shaft, but I expect it's broken."

She sniffed, then laughed, and Toreth wished he could see her face. "I'll buy you another one," she said. "If you promise to take better care of it."

"Of course. Now..." Warrick disentangled himself and took her hands. "Can I give you a lift back to the city?"

Toreth was willing her to say no when Dillian glanced sideways at him. He obviously didn't hide his expression quickly enough, because she smiled slyly. "No, I don't think so. I'll keep Asher and Greg company and go back with them. I'll come round and see you tomorrow, though. You aren't going in to work, are you?"

Warrick hesitated, then shrugged. "I doubt it."

"Good. I'll—well, I'll see you then, then."

She stayed where she was, though, hovering. Tempting to stretch it out, but for once Toreth couldn't be bothered to do it simply to irritate Dillian. He stood up. "I'll ask reception to fetch the car, shall I?"

As he waited by the desk, he watched the pair of them talking. About him? Probably, or something else Dillian didn't trust him enough to talk about in front of him. He could ask Warrick, but he wouldn't give her the satisfaction of knowing he cared what she said, even if she wouldn't know he'd asked.

He was still trying to find the logic in that when he realized Dillian had gone. Warrick stood alone, staring back into the building after her.

Toreth went over to him. "Ready to go?"

"What?" Warrick looked around. "Oh, yes."

Curiosity overcame reluctance. "What did she want?"

"To tell me she's going to Mars." Warrick shook his head, looking perplexed. "She mentioned before that she'd been offered the contract, but I thought she'd decided to turn it down; I had wondered about it, because she loves off-world work. But apparently she's changed her mind and she's going."

"Women, huh?" Toreth put his hand in the small of Warrick's back—just a gentle guide towards the door—and started walking. "Thanks for the invitation tonight, by the way."

Warrick looked at him sharply, and Toreth smiled.

"No, really. I've had a great time. Like I said in the lift—it's been an evening to remember."

Sunday Game

❖

"Ah, fuck," Toreth breathed into his ear. "*Fuck.*"

He'd been repeating the phrase about every thirty seconds for the last ten minutes. Warrick wasn't sure if it was an observation (in which case it was undoubtedly true), information (in which case it was entirely redundant, because Warrick had noticed), or a request (in which case Toreth would have to do more than ask). Right now, Warrick had no intention of doing or saying anything which might cause Toreth to stop.

He lay still beneath Toreth, paralyzed with exquisite, lazy pleasure as Toreth rocked slowly into him again and again. Heaven was very probably something like this. He'd changed the sheets earlier, when Toreth had gone to make coffee, and the crisp, clean, cool cotton beneath him was an added delight. From time to time Warrick lifted his head, rubbing his cheek back against Toreth's, and Toreth would moan and sigh, and probably say it again.

"Fuck. Ah, *fuck.*"

Only a dozen centimeters from Warrick's nose, a crumb spoiled the pristine expanse of sheet. He blew at it for a few seconds before he had to admit defeat and drag his hand over to flick the crumb away. Maybe it would be more sensible to wait to change the sheets until after they'd finished eating in bed, but that wasn't possible. Not on Sunday.

Sunday breakfast was one of the highlights of his week, and not because of the chance of a leisurely, well-rested hour or two in bed with Toreth afterwards. It was because the start of this particular game required breakfast in bed, so they could only play at the weekend.

The rules of the breakfast game were complicated, and Warrick didn't know them all. That was a part of the game.

It had started some indefinite time ago, when he'd brought Toreth breakfast in bed and, while he was eating, Toreth had picked up a strap that had been left in the bed from the night before. He'd trapped one end under his foot and started running the other through his hand as he ate. Not really paying attention, simply playing with the leather. It had been unexpectedly and deeply arousing.

Warrick was never sure if that had been the start of it then, an accidental discovery, or if even that had been planned in advance. Toreth must spend a lot of time planning things for them, but he was also quick to exploit an opportunity, so either was possible.

At first the rule had been single and simple—Warrick could sit and watch and talk, but he couldn't touch (Toreth or himself) and he couldn't ask to be touched. Then, week by week, more rules had been added to the game.

Warrick had to sit on the left-hand side of the bed.

Then, a week later, it could be no closer than a meter from the end of the bed.

Then he couldn't use Toreth's name.

Then his own.

Then he had to kneel by the bed.

With his hands behind him.

The rules became more complicated, and changed without notice. Warrick found out they'd changed when a word or a movement or something else that had been acceptable the week before was greeted with a calm "You can't do that." Or sometimes he forgot a prohibition, only to discover that it has become permitted again.

Sometimes it was nearly impossible to work out what action or omission had triggered the admonishment. And then he'd make the same mistake over and over again, until he finally found the connection and fitted the new rule into the pattern in his head.

He'd never written the rules down, although he had no idea why. Toreth certainly hadn't told him not to. In fact, he refused to even admit the existence of the game. Questions about the rules, or anything else to do with it, were deflected with blank incomprehension. He did wonder whether Toreth had everything written down somewhere, whether he sat and revised and rewrote them, or whether he too kept it all in his head.

In the end, if he performed satisfactorily, to whatever standards Toreth had set that day, Toreth would eventually set his tray on the floor and sit for a while, watching him. Then he would stand up and tell him where to go, what to do. "Lie down," or "Kneel there," or "Against the wall," signaling that the game was over. Warrick had won, and they would move on to a new game.

The number of mistakes he was allowed to make changed from week to week as well, without any logic he'd ever been able to determine, beyond Toreth's whims. Sometimes, after more than a dozen mistakes or as few as one, Toreth would drop whatever he was playing with onto the floor and shake his head. "Christ, you're pathetic. How simple do I have to make things for you?"

And then there would be a silence, until finally Toreth would sigh and say,

"Come here, then," or "Kiss me," or "If you can't do that right, do you think you could manage to fuck me?" Game abandoned, they would fuck without any rules at all and afterwards they would usually fall asleep again, still entwined, wonderfully warm and intimate.

Somehow, Warrick supposed, this must constitute losing.

From time to time he'd tried to lose deliberately, making mistakes on purpose, doing new things in the hope they would turn out to be forbidden, or simply not trying his hardest to remember the rules. But however subtle he made it Toreth would always spot his intent.

"If you aren't even going to *try*, then there's no fucking point, is there?" Then Toreth would get up, get dressed, and more often than not go home.

So he'd given that up and accepted Toreth's rules. There was no alternative—other than refusing to play at all—and it was an enjoyable intellectual exercise, not to mention its other attractions. Besides, by accident or design, they usually ended up doing what he would have chosen to do in any case.

This week, this Sunday, Warrick had lost.

"Ah, *fuck*."

Warrick nodded, not really meaning anything, just making a contribution when for once he couldn't come up with any words. At least not any that Toreth would want to hear.

Who needed words anyway, when they had this?

Paws for Thought

❖

Fran had offered him a room, an empty office upstairs. Tom preferred to sleep downstairs in the Shop, in one of half a dozen places he'd found and turned into little nests. As a concession, he'd accepted the use of a wardrobe, tucked away in a corner, for clothes and shoes. The rest of the time he could be found on top of a storage cupboard, or under a table, or napping on a leather examination couch, the buckled straps tucked neatly to the side.

He was curled up dozing on a pile of clean sheets for the play rooms when a loud sneeze followed by violent coughing disturbed the afternoon quiet of the Shop.

Tom lifted his head at once, ears pricking. The sound hadn't come from the foot of the stairs, so the customer must've been here, unnoticed, for some time. Tom uncurled and hopped down, stretching before he padded softly away.

Familiarity with the confusing echoes of the Shop led him in the right direction, and another cough pinned down the location exactly. A corporate type stood in a little-visited corner, brushing dust from his expensive suit. The sober, dark fabric made him difficult to see, because the moving lights of the Shop didn't go into the particular alcove.

The lights didn't follow Tom at all, unless he beckoned them over. He liked to think it was because he was a secretive creature of the night, and the lights recognized that instinctively. In reality, he suspected Shel had programmed them to stay away from him.

With a last swipe of his sleeve, and a soft, annoyed exclamation, the customer abandoned the alcove. Tom shrank back, watching him pass from behind a rack of leather harnesses. The man seemed familiar, his high, straight nose giving him a distinctive profile. Tom thought he'd seen him in the Shop more than once before, but never alone. That was different, and different was always interesting to a cat.

Tom followed, taking delicate steps, sticking to the shadows.

The man wandered aimlessly, opening drawers and inspecting merchandise hung on the walls. He passed through the book rooms without pausing, and spent a good five minutes inspecting chains. A smudge of dust still clung to his dark hair, until finally he ran his hand distractedly through it and sighed. Whatever the reason he had come to the Shop, he looked disappointed.

Doubling back, Tom went through half a dozen brick arches and so, strolling casually like he had no interest in the situation at all, he came across the man.

"Oh, hello!" he said. He stepped back, rubbed his paw over his nose, and added, "Can I help you?"

Instead of answering the question, the man examined him carefully. "You were at the party here, weren't you?"

"Yes, probably. I've been to a few. But I work here, now. Were you looking for something in particular? I know where everything is."

"A present. And, no, nothing in particular. I was hoping for inspiration, but I don't seem to be finding it."

"For your friend? The blond man?"

"Yes."

"Mrowr." Tom flicked his tail from side to side automatically while he thought it over. From the times he'd seen the couple in the Shop since then, he knew his guess at the party had been correct—the blond man he'd licked off wasn't someone at home in a collar. This one didn't seem to be either, at least not now. Sometimes humans were hard to understand for a solitary animal. "Does he like surprises?"

"Hm. Now you mention it, not really, no."

The man seemed to be fascinated by the motion of the tail. Tom twirled, showing off, twitching the end.

"It's bionic. My mum bought it for me. I'm saving for a real graft, but I've had some money problems and so I had to postpone."

The man's eyebrows lifted. "A graft?"

"Yes. B-mods." Tom held out his hand and flexed the tendons, sliding the claws free of their sheaths. "Like that, or my eyes."

The man examined the claws with careful attention, then looked into Tom's eyes. "Fascinating. I thought they were lenses."

"No, full eye grafts. I had to do it like that to get the new iris shape. And the—" Tom blinked his nictitating membrane across, and grinned at the customer's surprise. "Plus the retinal modifications so I can see in low light and my eyes reflect properly, which is awesomely cool. I do still have human color vision, but the eyes cost a *fortune* and my mum paid, and part of the deal was that I didn't lose anything. So technically I can see too much red."

"I see. Couldn't you filter it out?"

Tom sidestepped a little with surprise. The practical question wasn't the usual human response. "I suppose. It's not a huge deal, just a bit frustrating that they aren't quite perfect. But it was so great of her to do it for me at all, I don't really mind."

"Very generous," the man agreed. "So do you plan to have more of these—what did you call them?"

"B-mods—body modifications. Yes. Like I said, I'm saving for a tail."

The man tilted his head, looking Tom over assessingly. "The one you have is very realistic."

"To look at, but not to feel." Often Tom didn't like being stared at, but this man had an open, honest curiosity in his gaze which made him want to preen, not hiss. "It was supposed to happen a while back, but... well, I had an owner for a while, and he promised to pay, but that didn't work out so well in the end. I mean, he was great, really, but he didn't see things going the way I did. He wanted, like, a human partner who played at being a cat."

"And this is more than a game to you?"

Tom grinned. "Exactly! I'm already a cat, like, inside, and it's just taking me a while to get there physically. Probably it was for the best. I used to wear a collar for him, but now I'm not such a house cat, which is neat because I am a bit feral." He waved his paw at the space around them. "Fran and Shel are letting me stay here, so I'm being a shop cat for a while. I fetch things for people, watch the Shop—catch mice and rats too, sometimes. The leather attracts them. Did you know cats were originally domesticated to keep down vermin?"

Reflexively, he licked his lips. Then he wondered if the man might ask what he did with the mice, but from his expression Tom thought he'd probably guessed. Still, the flicker of disgust—no, distaste—only lasted a moment.

"Anyway, you were shopping for something," Tom said quickly. "Can I help you find it? I'm good at finding things."

"Perhaps later. If you don't mind... could I possibly ask you a few more things about these body modifications? I don't want to pry, but it's fascinating."

"Prrt! No, that's great! I mean, lots of people don't want to hear about it, so it's cool. Come on, we can sit down over here."

Tom led the way beneath the arches, wondering if the stranger was transspecies, too. He didn't strike Tom as the type, but sometimes people didn't. Sometimes people's true selves were so deeply buried that they could hardly get out at all. They were the best people to help, really.

A door on one of the long side walls opened into a room with low upholstered couches. The man sat on a couch, and Tom curled up beside him.

"My name's Tom Cattermole, by the way. Really. Lots of people don't believe that, but it's true. Tom Cat."

The man hesitated, then held out his hand. "I'm Dr. Keir Warrick."

Tom rubbed his head on his fingers, then licked them carefully. He smelled nice, Tom thought. "Great to meet you. So, what did you want to know?"

"Well, anything, really. I know nothing at all about it. Perhaps—perhaps you could tell me more about the mods themselves. How you go about having them done, how you adjust to them."

"Getting them's easy. It's not illegal or anything, and a lot of the surgeons come out of cosmetic surgery. If you think about it, b-modding is just a subset of that, anyway."

"I suppose so." Dr. Warrick looked away, considering the idea for a moment. "I suppose it's all a question of perceived imperfection. Or restoration of something lacking."

"Exactly!" Tom purred a little, because it could take forever for people to get that. "Some people just want to be taller, or thinner, or fatter, or whatever. Some people want more. There are only a few places that really specialize in the extrahuman mods, though, and they're the best ones to go to although they're usually pretty expensive. Like, it's really niche to grow hybrid cat-human eyes, because it needs the cat developmental control genes, so good clinics have people in the labs who have a veterinary background, or are specialist developmental biology scientists. But actually, a lot of the basic tech is pretty old, like gene targeting and tissue grafting."

Dr. Warrick nodded. "I knew someone at university who lost an arm in an accident. We'd just had time to get used to him walking around with the protected stump—only a few weeks—before they'd grown a new one."

"Right, there you are. A tail is just like limb replacement, except there wasn't a limb there before. Of course, even for people wanting the extrahuman mods, it isn't always extreme. Some of them are pretty trivial cosmetic work, like eye or skin color."

"Selective genetic changes." Dr. Warrick looked at him assessingly, and Tom twitched an ear. "What else are you planning to have modified?"

Tom flexed his wrist, claws sliding out.

"Back claws, sometime. Maybe some of the nonvisible stuff, like gut and metabolism adjustments, so I can do a total diet switch. I did some research into it, but genetic mods like that are stupidly expensive, because it's so niche. For physical mods, um—" He looked sideways at Warrick, but there was something about the man, the lack of any judgmental tone in his voice, which made him trust him. "Some private bits, like spines on my cock. Fur, probably, before too long... although I know how much it would upset my mum. So I'd probably do the back claws and a lot of other little bits before that. Maybe even get my color vision fixed, and just not tell mum I did."

He stopped. Dr. Warrick was staring, and Tom could tell that he was listening maybe fifty percent. Not that he was surprised—pretty much the only people who really wanted to know detail were other mod freaks.

"Sorry. Am I being boring?"

Dr. Warrick blinked. "Not at all. You were talking about getting rid of the last imperfection in your eyes. Which I quite understand. You might say that my job is largely about finding and removing imperfections. At least, the favorite parts are."

Tom was about to ask, "imperfections in what," when Warrick waved his hand, then curved it over.

"To tell the truth, I was watching your tail. It's quite distracting. You 'talk' with it, to emphasize points."

"Yeah. I don't even have to think about it now. Mind you, I still really want the proper grafted one, which would be so great, I can't say. But they'd have to grow the whole thing from my cells, with some genetic-level reprogramming, and then graft it onto my spine."

"And what about learning to control it?"

"That's supposed to be the hard part, because there's nothing in the brain to relate to the new nerves and new muscles." Tom shrugged. "But it's going to be fine. I can nearly feel it already—I've always had a tail in my head—and I cracked the bionic tail really quickly."

"I see." Dr. Warrick reached out, pausing for Tom to give permission, then ran Tom's tail through his hand. "So how far do you want to take it, in the end?"

Tom couldn't remember the last time he's met someone who seemed so totally strait-laced and corporate, and yet so interested and—more weirdly—so undisturbed.

"I—" Tom only hesitated a moment. "All the way. Seriously. Or as far as I can. I want to have my ears done, which is really hard because it means moving all the inner ear and auditory nerves. That one's a bit scary, actually. And—I'm thinking about getting my face reshaped eventually. But the biggest problem would be going from being bipedal, and I'm not sure I can ever afford it. And it's maybe not even technically possible, at least not yet, because it means reshaping the spine and pelvis and shoulders and everything. Complete weight redistribution." Tom stretched his arms and legs out in front of him, frowning at the ugly shapes. "I mean, you just have to look at the difference in a human's arm and leg length, and try to map that onto a cat to see it's a big problem."

"A very big problem," Dr. Warrick said. He was frowning too now, but not like most people did at that idea, like they were freaked out or disgusted. More like it was a problem he'd never even considered the existence of before, and he was giving it his full attention.

Tom nodded. "It's, like, a *huge* thing to try to do, but I've got my whole life."

"And what if you later regret something? Or you find you can't adjust to it after all?"

Tom sniffed. "I won't. Although, I mean, I could get most of the stuff I've had so far reversed pretty easily, if I could afford it. You can even get a clause in the contract for a reversal if it's within so long of having it done. But I don't usually bother with that, because it costs more. I'd only think about getting a reversal-inclusive contract if I wasn't sure about the mod to start with, and I usually am. I wasn't with the teeth, partly because I already had a great set that I could wear except for eating with, and partly because it might have ended up with me sounding really weird, which they couldn't completely predict. But in the end they were fine and so I'd wasted the money, which was annoying because they were the first things I paid for totally by myself."

Dr. Warrick was still looking at him thoughtfully. "It must be quite an art, making the mods. I imagine there must be a lot of predictive modeling involved, individual to each patient."

"Oh, yes. If something isn't totally right, then there's no point having it done at all. And they have to *understand,* you know? Or they don't ever get why it's important that everything is real. Actually, a lot of the people who work in the clinics—not always the surgeons, but the other staff—are into mods too and have stuff done. That's great, because it means when I go in they don't treat me like a freak."

"And one would need to have trust..." Dr. Warrick nodded. "Now, I have something to ask, or rather, to offer. How would you like to really be a cat?"

"Oh, that's what I'm going to be." Tom pulled his claws through his whiskers. "Some day."

"And how about next week?"

Tom blinked at him, wondering if the man was tripping. Or possibly really a lot weirder than he looked.

"I can give you a cat body—a virtual reality one," he continued. "You'd be inside it, you'd feel everything it feels. With a little research and some time to prepare, we can probably simulate cat sensory input to a high degree of realism, although I can't guarantee that you'll be able to process it perfectly."

"Sensory input?" Tom looked at him skeptically. He'd tried headsets and biofeedback suits, running around in pretend forests, and it had been okay but not *real.* "You mean, I'd actually feel what a cat feels?"

"As far as your brain can interpret it, yes. You would look down and see a cat body. You would run on all fours, and your muscles would be cat muscles, not human ones. It would be as though your human body entirely ceased to exist in your perceptions."

The idea made Tom shiver, and his suit fluffed in response, the fur echoing his mood. Imagine actually feeling the follicles lift...with a flick of his tail, Tom jumped off the couch and prowled a small circle, then turned to face Dr. Warrick.

"Will it be expensive?" Whatever the man was talking about, it must be top of the range, way beyond anything he had heard of before. "Only, I'm saving for my tail, and I can't waste money."

"It will be entirely free, on a volunteer basis."

His fur lifted again, with suspicion. "How come?"

"Because I think it would provide us with incredibly valuable and unique data for the sim—that's the virtual reality system we're developing."

"Oh." Tom prowled one more circuit, then stopped. "Really, truly, I'd be a cat?"

"Hopefully." Dr. Warrick leaned forwards, his voice becoming more formal, as if Tom had turned into a whole audience. "I have to be honest about this. It might not work for you. Accurate modeling of the real world is central to the sim, but perhaps equally as important is the freedom from the constraints of the possible, both with the world model and the user's avatar. But most people experience problems, physiological and psychological, trying to interface through a radically different body. First of all I want to know if, as I suspect, you won't experience those problems. And then, if that proves true, I would want to make a detailed analysis of your brain to find out how you process your discordant self-images, and how that maps to motor controls and so on."

Tom frowned. "You're not going to try to fix me, are you?"

"Good Lord, no!" Dr. Warrick looked affronted. "This would be purely scanning, no active neural manipulation. Some interviews, too, or at least we'd need you to answer some questions. Nothing more than talking, like we have been—you articulate experiences very clearly."

The suspicion still niggled, despite Dr. Warrick's shocked tone. "Only, that self-image thing, that sounds a lot like the stuff the psychologists my dad sent me to said about me."

"Ah, I see." His mouth curved into something cool, not quite a smile. "I understand. People wanting to fix one gets tiresome very quickly. I promise, you'll have fully detailed consent forms, which will set out exactly what we're trying to achieve, and how we will do it. We can provide a technical interpreter, too, if you need one, and if you feel uncomfortable at any point you can withdraw from a protocol. And of course, if after the initial session we did want to perform an extended study, then obviously we would offer compensation for your time."

Tom's ears twitched. "Compensation?"

"For such an unusual opportunity, I can promise a generous scale. And if the data ultimately yielded useful sim algorithms, there would be further payments. That's our standard deal."

Tom grinned wide, feeling teeth prick his lip. "I'll do it!"

Tom felt a little disappointed that Dr. Warrick wasn't there to meet him when he arrived at SimTech. Even for humans, it was only polite to be there when welcoming a stranger into your territory. But instead a tall, pale-skinned man with slightly receding hair, a long fine nose, and sympathetic brown eyes was waiting in reception, reading from a hand screen.

He stood at once when Tom entered. "My name is Hendrik De Nijs. I'm the senior psychologist at SimTech."

He offered his hand, and Tom shook it carefully. He'd pared himself down to the minimum today, just ears, gloves, and the tail tucked away up the back of his black jacket.

"Dr. Warrick sends his apologies," De Nijs said as they walked to the lift. "He asked me to be here to greet you. He seemed to think he had quite a find for the testing program."

Tom smiled, trying not to show too much of his teeth. "I hope I can help. The sim sounds amazing."

"It's . . . a unique experience," De Nijs said. The lift doors closed, and he touched the control panel. "It raises a lot of questions, I always find."

"Dr. Warrick said he wanted to know how I can be a cat inside."

De Nijs gave a thin, precise smile. "He has a great eye for an opportunity. Now, the plan for today is that we'll run through the basic consent forms, and then while you're being scanned for the sim I'd like to conduct a more detailed interview."

Tom had liked Dr. Warrick, but he didn't think that extended to automatically trusting any random psychologist. "What for?"

"Part of my job here is to make sure that trial volunteers aren't placed at any psychological risk. I need to be sure you understand everything about the trials you're volunteering for, and that you aren't vulnerable to harm from the experience."

"Oh. You mean, you want to make sure I'm not loopy to start with?"

De Nijs laughed. "That's one way of putting it. And the other part of my job is to make a thorough evaluation of you prior to your first sim experience. A psychological baseline, if you like. I'll explain more about it when you read the consent forms."

Tom hesitated for a moment, but nothing sounded too bad, so far. Dr. Warrick had said he could withdraw at any time, after all. "Okay, sure."

"I've had scans before," Tom said as the technician showed him around the impressive scanning suite. "Plenty of them."

The technician nodded. "I'm afraid the scanning today will take a little longer than it usually does, because we're running some more detailed neural scans than normal."

"That's okay. I'm good at keeping still."

Tom stripped off his clothes without hesitation, including his gloves, and unhooked his ears and tail from the bionic sensors. Then he hopped up onto the scanner table and lay down. The technician draped a thin white sheet over him, and told him the fabric was specially designed not to interfere with the scanning equipment. Tom settled himself in carefully. The padded scanner table molded itself to his shape, but he knew from experience that what seemed like a comfortable position at first would feel quite different in an hour's time.

"We can interview at the same time," De Nijs said. "At least for some of the scans, if you can keep still while you talk."

"Of course."

The scanner started at his head, enclosing him from the shoulders up in a way which was both claustrophobic and horribly exposing. When De Nijs spoke his voice sounded slightly muffled.

"Have you always felt you were a cat?"

"Oh, yes. I completely adored cats, for as far back as I can remember. When I was a kid, people used to buy me cat things and it was like a joke because of my name—like, a Tom Cat—but it was always more than that to me. Cats are so beautiful and perfect and sensual and they just are themselves, totally. They're the most self-contained things in the world. And they feel *amazing*. I can just touch cats for hours. Um. Not in a creepy way."

De Nijs laughed. "Don't worry. I never thought it for a moment."

"Some people do it, though. That's not right. At least..." Tom hesitated, but the man was supposed to be a professional, and not out to try to fix him. Maybe this would help him work out how true both or either of those were. "I mean, if a big cat, a queen, ever wanted me to mate her because she knew I was one of her kind, that would be just the greatest thing in the world. But it's such a long way to go."

"Of course." The words were slow and drawn out, and Tom had the feeling he was making notes. "It would be a sign of acceptance, I see that. Anyway, do carry on. You mentioned getting presents as a child—tell me some more about that."

"Sure. I had a ton of pictures and stuffed toys and a lot of other great stuff. Ears and tails and a whole lot of cat playsuits that I kept growing out of, but I kept them anyway. I learned to do different kinds of cat makeup from a really old stagecraft book my granny gave me. There's full face, and then there's more subtle things which I could wear outside back then and *I* knew I was a cat, but people didn't stare so much. I don't have the book now—my dad got rid of pretty much everything when we started having rows."

Tom stared up at the blank curve of the scanner above. He wanted to twitch his ears, or his tail, but with them stripped away he was naked in a way which had nothing to do with skin. He felt diminished.

The scanner moved down, and suddenly he could see De Nijs again, sitting in a chair, closer than Tom had imagined.

"Did your family keep pets?" De Nijs asked.

Tom cleared his throat. "Yes. We had a cat, who was just the most beautiful thing in the world. Also called Tom, although that was a bit of a mistake because she was a queen. We used to pretend it was short for Thomasina but really there was just a mix-up at the place they got her. When my parents split up, Tom went with my mum, and I really, really missed both of them."

"That's a shame," De Nijs said. "Losing a parent is always hard, even if they're not dead."

"Yeah. And especially when you kind of aren't wanted, or not how you are." Tom licked his lips. "My dad honestly just thought I'd grow out of it all at some point. And when I didn't, he didn't really try to understand it. He's pretty rich, and things usually work out how he wants them to. He thought I was acting out something to do with mum leaving, which is ridiculous. He made me go to lots of therapy and boring, stupid stuff. It's not like there's anything *wrong* with me, not mentally. When I hit thirteen, he wanted me to go to some kind of re-education thing where they were supposed to be able to really 'fix' me. So I ran away and found my mum again."

"Your father didn't try to have you returned?"

"There was some back and forth and legal custody stuff, but in the end they let me stay with her. My dad got to keep my boring brother, who's incredibly straight in every sense of the word and who doesn't talk to me at all. Which is great, because he's a prick."

This time De Nijs didn't laugh, but his mouth twitched.

"Do you have a brother?" Tom asked.

"No. I'm an only child. But I do know that many only children I've met have wished for siblings, and many with siblings wish to be singletons."

Tom laughed. "No one's happy with what they have. I guess it's the story of my whole life."

"As you say, of many people's. Do you still live with your mother?"

"No. See, at first mum was pretty cool about everything, because she'd got me back, and she let me wear all my stuff in the house unless we had visitors who didn't know about it. But..."

"You don't have to tell me," De Nijs said after a pause. "As it said on the forms you signed, disclosure of anything beyond basic questions required for sim safety is completely optional. It won't affect my fitness assessment, I promise."

"No, it's okay. I just don't want to sound like I'm saying anything bad about her, because she's been great, really. But when I started wanting the mods, she said no. After I hit fifteen, I didn't need her consent any more, so I used to talk a lot about getting things done anyway, cheaply, or maybe even going back to dad to try to get the money, and in the end she'd pay so I could go somewhere safe. She bought my eyes, and gave me most of the money for the claws. I don't feel so good about that, looking back, but it was just my feline nature."

"It doesn't even need to be that," De Nijs said. "Every fifteen-year-old does selfish things."

"Some statements are very hard to argue against, even from a psychologist," said a new voice—Dr. Warrick.

Tom tried to flick his ears with surprise, then remembered again he wasn't wearing them. "Hello," he said. "Have you been there long?"

"I just came in to see how the scanning was going, and to make sure De Nijs wasn't scaring you off. I'm sorry I couldn't be here when you arrived."

That didn't, Tom noticed, answer the question. "I'm fine. I've been telling him about my mum."

For some reason, Dr. Warrick seemed to find that incredibly funny. He was such a serious-looking man it was rather disconcerting to see him laugh out loud.

"Did you get on with your mum when you were fifteen?" Tom asked. He wondered if Dr. Warrick remembered, as he was rather old.

"Yes, I did. She was a very—she always made sure we felt loved," Dr. Warrick said. The statement had an odd formality.

"Well, I moved out when I was sixteen, that's what I was going to say. But it was only because I was kind of freaking her out with the permanent mods, and that wasn't nice. So now I go see her, and I dress like a human and we're okay. She bought me the bionic tail for my seventeenth birthday."

"She sounds remarkable," Dr. Warrick said. "And a model of parental acceptance."

Tom smiled, relieved. "Prrt. Yes."

"If you'd excuse us?" De Nijs said over his shoulder.

"Of course. Please, if you'd call me when Tom's ready?" Dr. Warrick turned to Tom. "I want to go into the sim with you."

De Nijs shook his head slightly as Dr. Warrick closed the door.

"What?" Tom asked.

"Sometimes he—some people have an ability to make unfounded assumptions which are even more annoying because they're so often right."

Before Tom could ask anything more, De Nijs lifted his screen again. "If I might ask—do you have many friends?"

Tom almost shrugged, then remembered the scanner moving slowly down over his chest. "Some. Most humans don't get it, and after a while it gets so boring explaining it over and over again, especially when they don't really even want to try."

"But sometimes even humans do understand?"

"Oh, yes. A few, anyway. Dr. Warrick got it really quickly. There's Shel and Fran at the Shop. They're totally cool about the transspecies thing. Shel supports self-determination and self-actualization." He managed to get both words out without lisping. "Fran says she's just happy there's someone to take care of the mice, but she doesn't mean it in a bad way."

"So you'd consider them friends?"

"Oh, yes! And there are a few humans who really like cats, and don't mind the mods. Some of them mostly want sex, of course, but I like sex, so that's great, too."

De Nijs's expression didn't flicker. He simply made another note, then said, "How about other transspecies people? Do you have friends there?"

"Yes. It's much easier with them. There are clubs and things, places we meet up without having to worry about outsiders not understanding. And I've met some great people at the clinics."

Another note. Tom wondered if he were passing the loopiness test or not. "Would you mind telling me about one or two of them?" De Nijs asked.

"Um." Tom tried to think who wouldn't mind being mentioned to a psychologist. Maybe it would be okay if he didn't give any names. "There's a girl who's totally into cats, too. We hang out a lot, and sometimes when she feels she's in season I'll mate her." Tom smiled happily. "She's so beautiful when she's a cat—she's a silver tabby, which is just great. I wouldn't mind being tabby, but in my head I've always been black with a white chest. Dr. Warrick took some pictures of me at the Shop."

"Yes, I saw them. Does your friend have mods, too?"

"No. She worries too much about what her family will think, and about people saying stuff to her in the street, which, yes, is definitely horrible because humans can be really nasty. But I'm trying to show her it's fine if she goes further."

"Because of your own experiences with modification?" De Nijs asked, and Tom nodded. "You find the process enjoyable?"

Tom considered. "Well, it can be a real pain, you know? Not just in the literal way—all the tests, having to take time out from doing things to have the procedures. I like the results."

"And if something happened to stop you having more surgery?"

Tom shifted, trying to send a twitch to his nonexistent tail, and the technician made a warning sound.

"Sorry," Tom said. "I'll keep still."

De Nijs leaned forwards a little. "Having to forgo surgery would distress you?"

"Of course. I need to keep doing things, you know? Or I get really down and moody—it's like I'm not making progress. But if I've got a mod worked out and I'm saving up or waiting for space at the right clinic, then I know I'm going in the right direction and I don't mind waiting. It's such a great high, waking up after getting something done. And, okay, I know a lot of people don't approve, but it's better to be happy in the body you want to have, right? That's what I tell—" He caught himself just in time. "My tabby friend. Don't you think it's true?"

"To be perfectly truthful, I would say that it depends on the circumstances," De Nijs said. "If a change results in a lasting improvement in mental state, then maybe so. But sometimes wanting physical change is a symptom of psychological problems, and the underlying problems don't go away with any amount of surgery. In those cases, it would be far better to address the problem itself."

"Oh." Tom tried not to scowl, but he wished very hard he hadn't said so much.

He should've known better than to trust any psychologist. "Is that what you think about me?"

"I think..." De Nijs ran his thumb over his lips. "I think that there's no fundamental reason I should stop you taking part in the initial trials."

"Really?" It took all Tom's strength not to jump with joy. "Thank you!"

"But I do want to raise one additional point with you before I countersign the consent forms."

"Oh, right. What?"

"Suppose that the sim provides the best possible experience for you, and you fully integrate with the cat avatar. How do you imagine you will feel when you have to leave the sim?"

The scanner moved again, and Tom used the excuse to hold very still and not answer. What was the right thing to say?

"I think it will be very hard," Tom said. "But it'll be worth it, because the harder it is, the more I'll know I'm right. I mean, I know now. But I'll have proof that I'm working towards the right result. I'll remember it and I'll always have something to strive for."

"Mm. And what about the other way round? What if you can't handle the cat body?"

That one was easy. "Then there's something wrong with the sim. Because I am a cat."

"I see." De Nijs nodded. "Then thank you for your time, Tom. I'll let Warrick know you're passed fit to take part."

"Now open your eyes," Dr. Warrick said.

Tom slitted opened his eyelids cautiously, because that was the safe way to check out dangers, then his eyes flew open wide. Only a minute earlier, a different technician from the one who had taken the scan had strapped him into a couch, and lowered a close-fitting visor over his face. Now the lablike room had vanished, and he lay on a reclined chair with a canvas seat, surrounded by a sweeping expanse of grass. Somewhere nearby, water rippled past. He drew in a deep breath, the scent of flowers tickling his nose, and he sat up.

"Wow."

Dr. Warrick, standing up from his own chair, laughed.

"I can't believe it! I—" Tom looked down, disappointment washing over him. "But this is still my body!"

"Yes, sorry. I ought to have warned you. I'll need a period of calibration. Plus, there's a small chance that you might react badly to the sim per se—I think someone will have explained sim sickness to you?"

Tom nodded.

"Well, I need to be sure, if you become disoriented or sick, that it's because of the cat body and not simply the sim itself."

"Oh, okay. I see. But, like, soon?" Tom asked hopefully.

Dr. Warrick smiled. "Soon, I promise. Sim sickness is becoming much rarer, and we're getting much better at detecting the early signs. In the meantime, what do you think of this?"

Something about his posture suggested that he was concentrating. In the air in front of him, a control panel appeared from nothing and hung there. Tom was so occupied in staring at it that he almost missed the movement in the trees at the top of the long, grassy bank. Then, utterly incongruous in the placid countryside setting, a black panther prowled into view. Tom jumped off the chair.

"Oh, my God!"

Dr. Warrick smiled. "Do you like her? I spent quite some time on the modeling. Partly a personal project, partly something to impress the sponsors."

Tom eyed the panther a little nervously as it sniffed a tall thistle, then padded down the slope towards them. Only a computer program, he told himself, but the sleek power of the muscles and the casual, vaguely curious glance the panther threw their way still made him want to back away.

"Don't worry, she's quite tame," Dr. Warrick said.

"Is she?" The fear changed abruptly to disappointment. Of course she would be—everything here was made to specification. "Oh."

"You can even call her." Dr. Warrick crouched down. "Here, kitty!"

The panther's head swung around, and her ear flicked before she turned and flowed through the grass like sculpted nighttime let loose under the sun. She halted in front of them, surely far too solid to be mere programming, and stooped to rub her head against Warrick's knee.

Tom crouched down too, running his hands through her fur. It felt coarser than he'd imagined it might.

"Could I—" He looked up. "Could I be inside one of these, later?"

Dr. Warrick nodded. "In fact, ultimately, I'd like you to try a range of bodies—even a few nonfeline animals if you don't mind, for comparison purposes. But we have a number of different cats of various sizes and breeds. Which reminds me, I have something to show you."

Dr. Warrick touched the control panel again, and Tom wondered if it were really necessary to work the sim, or if he just did it for show. Then the air around the chair Tom had arrived in shimmered, and a new shape faded into view. Curled up on the recliner, as though asleep, was a black and white cat.

"What do you think of this?" Dr. Warrick asked.

Tom knelt down and inspected the cat closely.

"It's . . . he looks like me. Just like me. Exactly the same markings, and everything! He's even the same size."

"Really? Excellent! We modeled it on the pictures I brought back from the Shop last week, of you in full, ah, full—" Dr. Warrick waved his hands at the cat, and Tom wondered what word he was avoiding. "Costume," probably.

"I call it my second skin. Why didn't you tell me? I could've said anything!"

"I wanted your honest reaction. Politeness can be a terrible problem when one is trying to conduct research."

"It's amazing," Tom said.

"The only real question I had was of scale." Dr. Warrick frowned at the cat, as though blaming it for the missing knowledge. "Obviously, enlarging a house cat-sized creature to the size of, say, a lion, is more complex than simple scaling—forces and stresses need to be take into account, and questions of lifestyle, and so on. I did the best modeling I could with limited time."

On the chair, the cat seemed to be breathing gently in his sleep, the light catching dust motes in the near-black fur on his flanks. Tom scrutinized it carefully, mentally fluffing his own fur at the unexpected questions raised.

"Is something wrong?" Dr. Warrick asked.

"I don't know. I mean, I guess I always knew it would be impossible to be that much smaller, however many b-mods I had. So I've never really thought about size, not like that."

"Well, we can leave it, then," Dr. Warrick said briskly. "Often with the sim the most effective technique is to follow your instincts, at least once you've mastered the basics."

Tom nodded. "So, can you show me the basics now, please?"

"You're sure?"

"Yes!" Tom forced himself to keep still. "Yes, I'm sure."

Dr. Warrick smiled. "Of course. Kneel down, like this." He dropped down onto all fours, remarkably smoothly for someone who was so old, and Tom mirrored him. "Now, you have to imagine yourself inside the cat's form."

"Is that all? That's easy."

Tom screwed his eyelids shut. After a couple of breaths he was quite sure he'd done it, but he kept his eyes closed for a while longer, just so it seemed like he was following the instructions. Then, unable to wait any longer, he opened them.

The grass was much closer than it had been before. Not as close as if he were a house cat, but the difference was large enough that he wasn't at all worried when he looked down and saw his paws. He heard a happy noise of feline surprise, and realized he was the one who'd made it. His *real* voice. He looked over first one shoulder and then the other, admiring himself. The white tip on the end of his tail twitched, and he spun around, trying to grab hold of it. He twirled madly, then rolled, grabbing for his tail until he finally caught it. Giving it an admonitory lick, he pinned the end firmly under one paw for safekeeping, and looked up.

Dr. Warrick was still there, watching him. Tom made a questioning chirrup.

"You have a real gift," Dr. Warrick said. "An extraordinary one. Some people take a whole session simply to be able to stand up on four feet."

No one had ever called it a gift before. Tom licked his tail again, then stood up. He looked around, enjoying the satisfaction of proper perspective, and wondered what little creatures might be lurking in the long, rippling grass. Or the river—were there fish in it? He hadn't eaten a live, wriggly fish since his brother's goldfish. Without thinking, he took a couple of steps, then stopped. Probably Dr. Warrick would want to do all kinds of tests.

"You can run," Dr. Warrick said, as though reading his mind, and for a moment Tom wondered if that were possible in here. "Please, explore—go as far as you like."

Tom turned, then paused, wondering whether running too far away would spoil the test. He tried to direct the thought to Dr. Warrick.

Warrick smiled. "Everywhere inside the sim is just as close to the sensors as where we are right now. There is no physical distance involved."

And that made it feel, for a moment, just a little bit less fun. Nothing here meant anything, and however good it felt to him, his flesh-and-blood body lay on its couch, and he was still trapped inside.

Then Tom turned and bounded across the meadow.

Tom had been to a beach a few times as a child, but the beach in the sim was much better. Quiet, for one thing, not crowded with other holiday makers, only himself and Dr. Warrick to leave footprints and pawprints in the sand. Cleaner, too, with not a speck of man-made debris to spoil the heaps of drying seaweed and driftwood and no stinky algal bloom in the water.

It made a good place to try out new shapes, with hard sand for easy running, and soft sand for something more challenging, and water for when Tom got really ambitious.

"And how about this one?" Dr. Warrick asked, as a new body appeared on the sand. Pale yellow fur matched the sand, and a friendly face looked at Tom, eyes bright and tongue lolling.

Tom arched his back and hissed. "A *dog*?" he thought.

"Well, not if it would be unpleasant for you, but I thought it would be interesting to see how you coped with a body which was similarly sized, but very definitely not 'yours,' as it were."

"Okay," Tom thought dubiously.

They'd already run through several cats, a monkey which had felt very strange indeed, and a dolphin. The latter he'd struggled with for twenty minutes while Dr. Warrick's dolphin bobbed easily in the water beside him to demonstrate the proper tail movements. Finally, after Tom had inhaled and swallowed so much virtual seawater he'd begun to feel virtually sick, they'd given up. Dr. Warrick had given him the cat body back, and he'd chased up and down the sand, startling seagulls and trying to catch fish in a rock pool which had ended with an unfortunate encounter with a crab hidden in some seaweed.

Now Tom lay down, copying the pose of the dog, and concentrated on the new shape. After a couple of minutes' concentration, he looked down at his paws, still stubbornly black against the sand.

"I'll keep trying," he thought. "It's much harder, though."

Even getting into the dolphin shape had been easier. Tom was still concentrating hard, struggling to shift even the shape of one paw, when the dog stood up suddenly and took a couple of steps towards him. Without meaning to, Tom jumped up and arched his back again, spitting angrily.

"Sorry. I didn't mean to scare you." Dr. Warrick's form appeared abruptly beside the dog, which lay down placidly on the sand again. "I thought it might help to have a movement model."

"You just startled me when it moved all sudden-like, that's all." Tom sat down and curled his tail over his front paws. "I wasn't scared."

"No, of course not. It can be very disconcerting when something you thought was inanimate suddenly comes to life."

Tom would bet a lot of money that nothing in the sim ever startled Dr. Warrick. Probably not much outside it, either. "I can try again, if you like."

"No, it's all right. Just the attempt produced some interesting preliminary data."

"Really?" Tom looked around. "Can you see it in here?"

"Oh, yes. As I said, it's fascinating."

A screen appeared, hanging in the air. When Tom craned his neck, it floated down towards the sand. The numbers and graphs full of overlapping lines meant nothing to Tom, but he stretched and kicked his legs, and watched the lines move. He was all numbers, now, he supposed. Nothing but a lot of ones and zeros floating around and changing in obedience to his thoughts. If only his real body worked the same way.

"And I'm sure there'll be a lot of interest from the user adaptation team once they see the data," Dr. Warrick added. "Now the first production units are shipping, everyone is eager to get back into basic development and find ways to keep pushing the technology. This is exactly the kind of thing we need."

"And so I can come back, another time?" Tom couldn't help the hopeful eagerness he was sure Dr. Warrick must be able to detect in his thoughts.

Sure enough, Dr. Warrick laughed, but not unkindly. "There's certainly great potential for further investigation, and for myself, I'd love the chance to take the study further. But it will depend on various factors."

"Like that psychologist?" Tom thought crossly.

"Amongst other things, Dr. De Nijs's opinion will count, yes. But also, the data will have to be analyzed properly. Now, we don't have much time left, so perhaps you'd like to choose what to do with the last few minutes of the session?"

Tom considered briefly. "Can we go back to the meadow, please?"

"Well?" Dr. Warrick said.

The challenge in his voice made Tom's ears prick up. Properly, as he'd just finished refitting his bionic links, with hands that felt ugly and clumsy after his beautiful paws.

De Nijs nodded. "You were right. It's extraordinary. The tail and the ears, yes, I concurred there. There's real neurological interfacing already in place. But the rest...I've never seen anything like it in a sim scan."

"Like what?" Tom demanded from his seat on the other side of the sim room. They had to be talking about him, and that was *rude.*

De Nijs turned to him at once. "I'm sorry. Warrick made a prediction, and I didn't believe him. But then, I'm not the expert in the sim. Somehow, in your brain you have an almost complete set of processes for living inside a feline body."

Tom frowned at him, puzzled. "Well, yes. That's what I told you."

"You'd be surprised at how often people don't understand what's going on in their own heads."

De Nijs had been waiting for them when they came out of the sim. To Tom's eyes, the unequivocal success of the sim experiment hadn't pleased him anything like as much as it had Dr. Warrick. And the longer they looked at the screen together, the more Dr. Warrick smiled, and the thinner the psychologist's mouth drew.

"So, how many cosmetic surgery centers do you think will want to buy a sim suite or two?" Dr. Warrick asked the psychologist.

That question seemed to mollify the psychologist's mood a little. "Given the value of outcome satisfaction? All of them, I should think." De Nijs shook his head. "Actually, I can't believe that the marketing department never considered this before."

"The sim is new, so the markets are new. Sometimes it just takes a lucky coincidence, or a conversation with the right person." He smiled over at Tom. "And then fresh vistas open. Cosmetic surgery planning is only the beginning, though. If we can find a way to artificially induce the same parallel state in the general population of sim users, that could open up even more potential applications."

"Do a lot of people want to be cats?" Tom asked doubtfully.

Warrick shook his head. "The specific alternative body isn't the issue. The question is, can we generalize the process of having two simultaneous functional self-concepts? If we can find out how to temporarily duplicate the parallel state, rather than require each user to develop skills from scratch, it could dramatically cut adaptation times."

"No," De Nijs said. "The real question is, would that be wise? Is it safe?"

"Once we have the studies planned, the ethics committee will address any pertinent issues of volunteer safety."

De Nijs snorted. "The ethics committee will agree with whatever makes the most money for SimTech, as they always do."

"Then as this is a highly preliminary investigation with no certainty of success and no guarantee of a marketable outcome even if it is successful, they shouldn't have too many euro signs in front of their eyes to blind them and stop them doing their jobs."

"Sarcasm isn't helpful, Warrick. You know quite well what I mean. Like anyone, they can be swayed by how a case is presented and you give an excellent presentation."

"And of course, you're welcome to make whatever submission you feel is necessary to the committee, if you feel mine is inadequate."

Tom looked between them, fascinated. It was like watching two lions at the zoo, squaring up to one another in a small cage.

"You're willing to dismiss my concerns just like that?" De Nijs asked.

"No. But as you yourself admitted just now, you don't have as much experience with the technicalities of the sim. My experience suggests that this will be no more harmful than other tested and proven protocols."

"And I would argue we don't fully understand the long-term effects of all of those."

"This would be just another temporary processing shift," Warrick said. "Which you have to admit is one of the longest-established and best understood techniques. In essence, it would be no different to sense-memory patching."

De Nijs actually laughed. "Warrick, please. The comparison is absurd. Giving someone the memory of smelling a particular strain of rose isn't even close to inducing an entirely aberrant mental state in a healthy individual."

Even though he wanted to hiss and scratch, Tom settled for drawing himself up and giving the man the iciest stare he could. "I beg your pardon?"

From his expression, Tom was pretty sure the psychologist had forgotten he was in the room. "Aberrant in the sense of... not typical of human consciousness."

"I know what it means. I'm young, I'm not stupid."

"I apologize," De Nijs said. "I misspoke. I shouldn't have used that word. Warrick, perhaps we should continue this conversation somewhere else?"

"I was rather hoping to let young Tom know whether or not we'd require his assistance in a full research program."

"You'll have my report on the proposal when it's ready," De Nijs said stiffly.

"And I assure you it will be read seriously, as they always are."

The promise didn't seem to appease the psychologist. "It will be ignored if it's inconvenient, as they always are. And I'm afraid I'm starting to think that I don't have what it takes to get you to listen. And, frankly, given the historical precedent here, I don't want to have."

Warrick went very still, like a cat hearing a noise he didn't expect, and Tom wondered if it was a threatening noise or the kind of noise which meant prey.

"What do you mean by that?"

"That you listen to my advice as much as you listened to my predecessor's, and if it takes what happened to Dr. Tanit to happen to me before my opinions are taken seriously, I don't have that level of dedication to my job. Do you know there are *still* more safety trials based on her old reports than on any concerns I've raised since I've worked here?"

Now it was Dr. Warrick's turn to glance at Tom, but having set the precedent of talking in front of him, he didn't seem to feel he could back down.

"If that's the perception you have, I apologize."

"Warrick, it isn't a *perception.* I can count—I have counted."

"Then it's something I hadn't noted, and we need to take a closer look at it. Please, if you would, I'd like you to put together a list of safety areas where you feel we need to take a closer look, and you can put it to a directors' meeting. We'll go through it item by item, and set up additional safety trials as necessary."

De Nijs looked honestly taken aback. "Really?"

"Absolutely. Talk to Gerry and set a date, at your convenience, for as much time as you think it requires. Tell him to make sure that Asher and Lew and I are all there, and the safety team leads."

Whatever their disagreements, once Dr. Warrick had made the offer, De Nijs didn't seem to doubt that he meant it. "Thank you. I have notes already—I'll get to work on a presentation right away. I warn you, it isn't a short list."

Dr. Warrick smiled. "I'll make sure that Gerry arranges refreshments for the meeting."

De Nijs held out his hand to Tom. "Thank you for coming in. It was a pleasure, and very interesting to meet you. And I apologize again for that unfortunate remark."

If it hadn't been for the apology, Tom wouldn't have shaken, but just to be polite—and thinking about the report De Nijs would write—he took the man's hand, still on some level surprised to find his sim-paws had gone. "It's okay. It was nice to meet you, too."

Tom watched De Nijs go, striding off rather positively. He wondered what had happened to this Dr. Tanit that just her name could make Dr. Warrick change his mind like that. Probably, it was some big corporate secret, and they were mostly really boring, at least in Tom's experience. Maybe the sim had better corporate secrets than his dad ever had, though.

But—a sudden thought made Tom flick his ears.

If De Nijs's safety worries were being taken seriously, now, what about his thoughts on what was "aberrant"? Was that the end of Tom's chance in the sim? One day—it wasn't fair. Just to taste that, even knowing it wasn't real, and then having to come back to *this* without any prospect of relief…

A growing hollowness inside made him squirm on the chair. Tom scratched at his chest, as though he could rub through the T-shirt and find the fur which ought to be underneath. He needed his suit; he should have brought it with him. He opened his mouth to ask, then closed it again. Better not to know for sure for another minute.

Dr. Warrick wasn't the lingering type, though. He turned briskly to Tom. "Thank you very much for all your help. I apologize for the corporate squabbles—we like to encourage healthy debate, but things can get a little heated."

Tom's tail drooped. "I guess I'm not coming back, then? At least not for a while."

For a moment, Tom was absolutely certain that Dr. Warrick was going to say no. Then he gave Tom a small smile.

"I'm sure that we can find some slots free. You're already approved for the investigative tests, and whether we use the data in the way I envisaged or not, it will still be very useful to have it."

"Thank you!" Tom beamed at him, and wondered if he'd take offense if he rubbed his head on Dr. Warrick's shoulder. "Thank you so much. I'll do everything I can to help, I promise."

And when the trials were done… well, he'd worry about that then. Maybe he'd be able to use some of the compensation Dr. Warrick had mentioned to buy his real ears and tail.

www.ingramcontent.com/pod-product-compliance
Lightning Source LLC
LaVergne TN
LVHW091045080826
845145LV00002B/629

9781934081129